W9-CCM-671

Lucky Strike

ALSO BY NANCY ZAFRIS

The People I Know (short stories)
The Metal Shredders (novel)

Lucky Strike

NANCY ZAFRIS

UNBRIDLED BOOKS

2005

Lyrics from "Once I Had a Secret Love" by Sammy Fain © 1954 (renewed) Warner Bros. Inc. (ASCAP) used by permission

Unbridled Books
Denver, Colorado

Library of Congress Cataloging-in-Publication Data
Zafris, Nancy.
Lucky Strike / Nancy Zafris.
p. cm.
ISBN 1-932961-04-6 (alk. paper)
1. Uranium mines and mining—Fiction. 2. Single mothers—Fiction.
3. Uranium miners—Fiction. 4. Prospecting—Fiction.
5. Widows—Fiction. 6. Utah—Fiction. I. Title.

PS3576.A285L83 2005
813'.54—dc22

2005000113

1   3   5   7   9   10   8   6   4   2

Book Design by SH • CV

First Printing

For Sam and Jim, and Marjorie Kinnear Sydor

To borrow a word from this novel's title, I am lucky indeed to have such an amazing editor in Greg Michalson. The devotion and vision that Greg, along with Fred Ramey and Caitlin Hamilton Summie, brings to Unbridled Books is a dream come true for a writer. Some of the research for this book was carried out at the University of Utah library in the Oral Histories section.

In the 1940s and 50s, the U.S. demand for uranium ore to supply the nuclear arms build-up instigated a rush of fortune hunters: interested readers should check out Raye C. Ringholz's book, *Uranium Frenzy*, which offers a fascinating history of this postwar phenomenon. I would like to thank Gail Hochman for all her hard work, Linda Hengst of the Ohioana Library Association for sharing their wonderful Lois Lenski collection with me, Susanne Jaffe, Dan Kobil, Lynn Larsen, Kit Irwin, Gretchen McBeath, David Lynn, Ellen Sheffield, Julian Anderson, and Bob Harrist always. In particular, I am grateful to Joe Freda for his invaluable aid; Erin McGraw for her wise and witty counsel; Brad Kessler for supplying a crucial bit of research; Tara Ison, ever the passionate teacher, for the instructive conversation at Noah's Bagels; and Jim Zafris.

PREFACE

One of the things Harry liked to do was make up songs. He was a cheerful traveling salesman dressed in a seersucker suit, and he often visited us in camp. At first his singing was something we ignored, like a few raindrops, like Harry himself as he pitched his tent. Then came the downpour, the original words and music of Harry L. Lindstrom heard twice as they echoed off the canyon walls. At length it became up to us to close him down. No one could accomplish this with the effectiveness of my mother, who was fond of shooting off her pistol.

It was 1954. My brother, Charlie, was twelve and I was ten. We were camping out with my mother in the red rock of Utah, prospecting for uranium. An adventure was what we were after. We were alone and words like *claim jumping* painted exciting action images coated with violence. When one of the old prospectors offered my mother a pistol, she accepted. She discovered a desire to shoot off guns, and became first-class at it, a regular Annie Oakley. During the long silence that hung heavy after one of her blasts, you could hear breathing form a circle around you; you could feel the jumping of a heart that hardly belonged to you. Pretty soon without knowing it you were humming a secret tune of your own. I was always right on the verge of catching this song in full when *bang* would go another of her pistol shots and there they went, all the notes scattering like a flock of birds, until finally most of them returned and settled into this. It's a bit different and some pieces are missing, but it's enough to provide a pretty good idea.

Beth Waterman, Uranium Girl

Desert

ONE

The two children were up there on top of the rocks. Harry caught a glimpse of them but then had to turn away. The sun had decided without warning to knife a wayward beam right into his face. He almost ran off the road, if a road was what you wanted to call it.

He was driving an International Harvester truck loaded down with wares: detection instruments, portable compressors, bits, jackhammers, shovels, picks, a couple of wheelbarrows. He was constantly talking or singing to himself. Arriving at a mining camp after journeying hours alone, he never even had to clear his throat. He was always in midsentence, heading toward that motherlode noun and its precious adjectives. When he reentered a town, civilization as he liked to call it, he had to remind himself to clamp his jaw shut so he wouldn't seem crazy. Probably too late. He had a feeling he had already built a reputation.

It was a boy and a girl up there. This much he could tell despite the sunlight bouncing off at crazy angles to blind him. Well okay, so that was it, they were using hand mirrors. He wondered if the children were doing it intentionally to bedevil him. He didn't really care in a way. He wondered if his easily hushed temperament was there by nature or forged by his religious upbringing, and was it a good or bad thing? Maybe it had more to do with loneliness. Here were some people—children, of all things.

He was pushing through the road in first gear. Lord amighty, first gear, whoo, top speed. He put an imaginary wife in an imaginary house and there she was in the doorway wagging her finger at him—don't you bring me any more of your speeding tickets! His foot came off the clutch and he stalled out. He couldn't tell you the last time that had happened. The Harvester jerked to a halt. He'd been meaning to stop anyway to check on those children.

He was thinking he also had in the truck a few bargain Geiger counters. The children's mom and dad might be interested. Another family out for the afternoon to strike it rich, although they were way too far from town to be making a picnic of it. May was already ending and the heat was perilous. These Sunday dogstakers got themselves into dangerous pickles and couldn't get out. This was not a department store with a down escalator you could take when the prices got too high. Actual risks were involved. Learning this lesson midway marked a lesson learned too late. Well, here he was, Harry Lindstrom. Here was Harry Lindstrom, here to save the day. He realized he was singing. Better stop.

The oddest thing happened. He got out of his truck and was standing there and the tire he was staring at decided to deflate on him. Just like the heck with this or some such thing that the tire was saying to him. The leak was not slow but it wasn't fast either. The rubber coughed out its air with enough leisure to torment him.

He kept the jack and the tire iron behind the passenger seat. The spare tire (two spare tires) was in the back of the truck, loaded up last so it could be retrieved first. He undid his belt and took off his still clean pants and folded them. He found his straw boater on the driver's-side floor. It had fallen against the brake pedal and looked to be hanging on a rack. He patted the boater atop his head. The sun was beating down.

He twirled off the bolts with the tire iron and tossed them in the hubcap's dish. The bolts came off readily, relaxing into their true purpose. Their true purpose obviously was to get screwed off at regular, ever shorter intervals. Their true purpose was to make Harry Lindstrom's life miserable. He was feeling sick at how good the ruined tire was. He could sink his finger full into the curvy treads. And now here were two children watching him. He'd forgotten all about there being children. The boy was older but the girl looked stronger. All this he could tell without turning his head. He was still seeing them out of the corner of his eye.

"Did you see the nice treads this tire's still got on it?" He addressed the children without turning around. No use getting them scared.

"I saw a big hole in it," the boy said.

"There's no hole in this tire. It's just the curse, that's what it is."

"What's the curse?"

"You like reading the Greek myths?" Harry asked him.

"That's her line of work," the boy said, pointing toward the girl.

"Okay." Whatever he was going to say about Greek myths was gone anyway. "I'm not too happy right now," he said. "I hate to have you exposed to a bad influence with my temper showing."

Now he could confirm that the two children were brother and sister because they did one of those sibling glances—quick, furtive, genetically synchronized. He saw that, too, even though he hadn't yet turned his head. That kind of glance had often passed between him and his real brother (but not the other ones). He'd have to tell the children about his x-ray, back-of-the-head vision. They might not think he was joking, though. Might get scared. Save for later.

The girl had stepped forward and was checking out the dusty windshield of his International Harvester. A long crack looped across the windshield, magically forking in half right where the driver needed to look out. The crack forked north and the crack forked south, leaving the driver's equator undisturbed. The windshield had become the map of Utah to Harry, and sometimes his old toy soldiers from childhood went marching across the towns of his youth, shortening his ride by an hour or two as he got lost in their battles.

Harry picked up the tire iron and pointed out the windshield's splintered trail. "That here is also the curse." His finger traced the crack to its lucky detour and drew a circle on the unblemished glass at the driver's line of vision. "And this here's clean living."

The children weren't responding. Well, who would really. Would he respond to himself if he were acting this way? He moved to the back of the truck and pulled out one of his brand-new spares. He rummaged for an old Prospectometer. New, $149.50. He was selling it for $69. Good deal. They might be interested. He ran across a rope instead. "Here's a rope," he said.

"We could use that," the boy said.

"Fifty feet of fine hemp." He found another Geiger counter, a used Babbel-200. This was better than the Prospectometer, made more sense for a family. He pulled it out and held the mike attachment toward the boy's head. "Ticktickticktick." He was trying to kid, but the boy didn't react. "Maybe your dad could use this. Got a revolving shield. See that? Helps protect it. See. Three ranges of sensitivity." He held it out. "You want to hold it?"

"If you want me to."

Harry placed it in his hands. "It's heavy, isn't it?"

"Yes, it is heavy," the boy said, and Harry was briefly enchanted by the melody of a complete sentence. He liked this boy.

"A fallout comes by, you gotta get it covered. Can you believe that? The thing it's looking for'll ruin it. With fallout it'll read every hogback as radioactive. That flat tire, for instance. It'll tick like it's got uranium retreads."

The boy nodded. His hands were shaking a little bit, holding it, and that made Harry like him more.

"Think your dad could use it?"

The boy shook his head.

"Already got one?" Harry asked him.

"It's just my mom."

"Just your mom and you?"

"And Beth."

"Who's Beth?"

The boy pointed toward his sister.

"Of course. I meant you in the plural. You plural and your mom singular."

Your mom singular. That had a nice ring to it.

The boy just looked at him.

"Where are you from? I'm from Scipio. My name's Harry, by the way. Harry Lindstrom." He reached out but he couldn't shake the boy's hands because the boy was holding the Geiger counter. He pantomimed a handshake and the boy gave him a half smile. From this little fellow, maybe that was enough. Maybe a half smile was a whole victory.

"I'm Charlie."

"Pleased to meet you, Charlie. Where you coming in from?"

"Dayton."

"Dayton?" Harry repeated the word, mentally scanning the map of Utah, searching for a little spot named Dayton. Couldn't find it, no matter how hard he looked. He knew the towns of Utah pretty well, was raised in one after the other in fact. Brothers and sisters scattered in seven different towns, all in Utah.

"Ohio," the boy said. He waited for Harry to click back in. "Dayton, Ohio."

"What?" The word *what* was echoing inside Harry's head, which meant he must have screamed it. He had a sentence looping around and bothering him: I am Harry Lindstrom and I am in midsentence screaming what.

Now he saw that the children's mother was standing on the road, if it could be called a road and not a bed of blown-up boulders bulldozed by the Atomic Energy Commission in secret government collusion with his wheel bolts, holding her daughter's hand. Another tire gone, and him Mr. Sisyphus of the road crawling along in first gear and still the tire blows out, probably not fixable either but maybe it was, and no boots on the mother's feet. Boots were like a good set of tires out here. The mother had on a party dress of all things, wilted in the heat and hanging on her like Tarzan's loincloth, but a dress all the same, in other words something useless. No boots. That he couldn't believe. She was dressed like she was poolside at the Stagecoach Oasis Motel. He had perhaps never seen anyone so remarkably reckless and naive and he was tempted to say stupid, though she looked nice, actually very nice, a singular mom. He didn't want to say pretty because it might show on his face and she'd step back in caution, thinking he was a predator. He didn't want her getting scared and then scaring her children. He was glad he hadn't told them about his x-ray vision. Too much too soon. He couldn't believe no boots.

"Look at this," he said, pointing to his flat tire. "Dayton Tire and Rubber."

"What about it?"

Well, he meant, see, kind of—funny . . . something. He shrugged. Did he just shrug helplessly? The mother was looking at him like he had. Bewildered man. Poor, wayfaring, bewildered stranger. Another song.

"Do you always do that?"

He was doing several things at the moment. Which one did she probably mean?

"Sing." One of the children had helped him out—the boy. Charlie.

"Got to keep myself company." He decided that this was about the best answer he could have given. He had thus presented himself to this mother in the manner of an amiable gentleman who could enjoy a laugh on himself. He hoped she understood the gentleman part. A 100 percent absolute gentleman. That was not probably included in the answer. He would have to think of something else to say to let her know that. Men were rough out here. She might be worrying she was in harm's way.

"You don't have to fear me," he said. "I'm a gentleman."

Charlie's sister started to snicker and he could see the brother turn with a foot prod to shush her. The girl hung her head and looked down at the dirt, silent, but with trembling shoulders. He was directing his remarks to the mother anyway, which he barely, just barely, prevented himself from telling the girl. Arguing with a little girl was not a good way to present yourself as the gentleman you claimed to be. The mother was looking at him without expression. But he was a salesman, a traveling salesman, who in his travels met all kinds of people, and he knew that lack of expression was in fact a very expressive expression.

"Maybe you would like something to drink," the mother said.

"I don't drink."

Her shoulders drooped. "I mean water."

"Flavor Aid," Charlie said.

"Something. I think you need some water."

"Okay," Harry said. "Okay, that sounds good. Okay!" He was following the mother and when she turned to aim that no-expression look at him, he stopped with the okays. He was glad at least his last okay had sounded so friendly and enthusiastic. Okay! Come on, kids, let's all go get some water! Translation: Don't be scared, kids, it's just me, Harry Lindstrom. He hoped they weren't afraid of him. He wondered if they needed a Geiger counter. The Babbel-200 sold for $400 brand new but he was selling this one for half that and maybe for them he'd take it all the way down to $180.

"Put your pants on, please," the mother said.

"Good heavens," Harry muttered. He went back to the truck and found the pants folded nicely on the front seat. He was glad the tails of his shirt were so long, almost to his knees. He noticed his knees as he pulled on the pants. He saw two perfect blushes of red dirt. The tails of his shirt were starched stiff as pogo sticks and they were seamed in maroon. He was one of his toy soldiers, wounded, marching across the windshield. If he tucked in his shirt the maroon might seep through his pants, which were still very clean. Was it rude not to tuck in his shirt? He couldn't tuck in a shirt in front of children. They were getting scared, he could see it. He wished he were a Navajo right now, he could just raise his hand and say, *How*. *How* was the universal language. He lifted up his hand and found a surprise. "My sleeves have been rolled up," he said.

"Let's get you in the shade," the mother said.

Two

Harry's face was painted with sunlight and shade as he lay in the sand under a piñon tree. Beth continued to watch him while her mom rummaged inside the Rambler to find something to eat. The piñon tree, gray and stunted, was no bigger than a climbing limb of their back-yard maple (meaning their backyard back there, a million miles away), and its branches shielded Harry's face about as well as the fingers of a hand. Before falling backward into a sound sleep he had accepted two cups of water but had not downed them with any kind of urgent thirst. He kept pausing to talk, the cup held by his mouth. Eventually her mom had pushed the cup to his lips practically forcing the water upon him. He waved away a third cup as if it were medicine. He said, "That's an inter-esting piece of equipment, isn't it?" to Charlie, who sat in the dirt wor-shiping the Geiger counter before him, and then Harry's head lolled back and he was gone before Charlie's question about what's this part for? could reach him.

Beth thought of him already as Harry and not Mr. Lindstrom or him or that man. Maybe because Harry was someone who forgot to put his pants on, who had to be taught to drink, who had an excitable way of talking that most men didn't, and who could fall asleep so contentedly he did not register the light baking his eyes. The way that Charlie's hands hovered around the Geiger counter instead of diving in and exploring like he so clearly wanted to do meant that Harry was still Mr. Lindstrom to him. Giving Charlie permission wasn't up to her, but if she'd been interested in Geiger counters she'd already have been experimenting with it by now.

The sun on Harry's face was painful to witness. Beth had experienced for herself what the sun could do. She and Charlie almost first thing had unpacked the magnifying glass and set a strip of paper on fire. It took maybe ten seconds. As much as possible she stayed in the shade. She was nervous now about her skin, which she viewed as a sheet of paper that might go up in flames, and she thought of her grandma and her white nearly transparent skin. A corner spot by the canyon wall managed to stay protected no matter where the sun moved. That was where she tended to stay when she wasn't working for Charlie, doing the slave labor for his experiments. She leaned against the cool flat rock. She dropped one of Charlie's marbles on top of the other. She did that over and over until her brain began to play tricks on her. Her mind was jumping in the hot bronze emptiness of the desert's palm, it was jumping like a jumping bean from nothing to nothing, and the only thing keeping her occupied was writing book reports on the complete works of Lois Lenski: *Strawberry Girl, Coal Camp Girl, Houseboat Girl.* She was already way ahead of schedule and almost to the end of her supply and pretty soon she'd have to write reports on make-believe books or write the books herself and then report on them.

Charlie couldn't be bothered with books. He had his compass and his chemistry set and he was working on a topographical map, and of course, most importantly, he had his own sister to use for all his calculations of heights and distances, shamefully exploiting her so his map could be as precise as possible. He may have been the inventor of the bethometer measuring system, one bethometer equaling one of her strides, her height equaling two bethometers, but she was the guinea pig who enacted his theory in all its dangerous glory, thereby proving its worthiness. Her legs were tied off for complete accuracy. In case she thought the bethometer system silly, Charlie reminded her about twelve inches being the foot of the king of England. He sent her tied up over the rocks, twice, and up the outcroppings, twice, while she counted off her hobbled strides. Three times if the counts didn't match. Beth Waterman, Human Surveying Tool. This would probably be the first book she wrote after her Lois Lenski supply ran out, and in it she would detail the many desert adventures she'd been having, starting with her death-defying climbs in the name of science and ending with —at the moment, ending with a man taking a nap.

She couldn't stand it any longer. She found the straw boater, crawled over, and dropped it over Harry's face.

Her mom called and Charlie went over and they started discussing the upcoming meal as if it could be something out of a restaurant, as if it could come with dessert, which was what she wanted more than anything. Up until now she hadn't asked a lot of questions. She knew the main answer, Charlie's Adventure, to the main unasked question, but she didn't know any of the smaller answers to the smaller questions, for example, what exactly are we doing? What are we doing tomorrow? Maybe that had been a mistake, not asking questions. Her mom was starting to remind her of someone on a trampoline who wouldn't get off.

In the brown silence Beth was always hearing voices. A whisper between Charlie and her mother echoed back to her in a near scream. The air blocked nothing; everything traveled through it undiminished. And the rock walls sent the words back amplified. It was not such a big deal after all that Indians had such great hearing. If she lived out here, she'd have great hearing, too. She could guess, for example, that the engine she found herself listening to was miles away though it sounded directly upon them. She could guess big truck coming, many cylinders. The motor churned to a pitch, then rewound itself and wrenched and churned again.

When the truck doors opened and slammed shut, it became real. Her mother had already turned from the cooking and was standing alertly. Her hair was tied back but the strands that always escaped were hanging down her face. Before she could push them back, two men walked into the camp, hands on their hats as if to remove them. "Hello," one of them said. "Sorry for the interruption." They bowed their heads, fingers dipped into the felt creases, but the hats stayed on. "Hello there. Good afternoon."

"Hello," her mother said plainly. A big metal spoon in her hand was hanging by her side but her grip was tight and the spoon arched upward. The men were probably amused, thinking, This lady figures she's holding a weapon.

"Saw Harry's truck out there, supplies on the road. Everything okay? That is Harry's truck."

Her mother nodded toward Harry, still lying asleep under the piñon tree with the straw boater over his face. The two men chuckled through their noses and gave each other a raised eyebrow.

"Don't want to interrupt his nap, but his truck's blocking our way," the one man said.

Her mother didn't say anything, just stood there with her spoon.

"So how do you know Harry?" the man asked.

"I don't," her mother said. "I just met him." Her hands started toward her hair but stopped, and Beth knew the strands hanging in her mother's face were driving her crazy. "He introduced himself to me," her mother said pointedly.

"And went directly to his naptime. Sounds like Harry, doesn't it?" The men's clothes were nice but dirty. They were precisely donned. The pants were pushed into high work boots. The shirts were tucked in and the belts looked buckled too tight, above their belly buttons. The underarms of the shirts revealed lapping salt patterns like the white dustings around the waterhole she and Charlie had found (the unappetizing waterhole that was waiting for them when their own supply ran out. Soon). And the men wore unzipped khaki vests with lots of pockets. One of the men dug into his vest pocket as he went over to Harry. He lifted the boater, felt Harry's cheeks with his fingers, and shook his head.

"Dry and crepey. Right, oh right, sorry, ma'am, I'm slow to catch on."
Whatever was in his vest pocket he put in his mouth as he stood up.
"Didn't mean to be rude. I'm Paul Morrison, and this is my partner,
Ralph Graver. We run the mining camp down the road. Well, six miles
down the road—if you take the road. A whole afternoon's outing, in
other words."

The man who was Ralph Graver laughed.

"What's so funny?" her mother said.

"It's that thing out there they call a road. I see it did Harry in again.
I call it Bataan's Missing Link." Paul Morrison's hand sliced like a swimming fish toward the desert. "Or three miles if you shoot through there."

"You mean walk."

"Burros. Walk. Yes, ma'am."

"I don't think she gets your jokes," Ralph Graver said.

"Probably not," Paul Morrison said. The belts above their navels
made their abdomens swell a little, almost as if they were women. "I
shouldn't joke about Bataan. Lost a friend there."

"You did not."

"I did. Ralph, I did." The man who was Paul Morrison walked over
and gave his partner some of the gummy stuff from his vest pocket and
when they moved apart, a third man was standing there, right behind
them, as if he were the finale of their magic curtain trick. Beth realized
right away the magically appearing man was an Indian.

Well, things were looking up. An Indian. She loved Indians.

"Looks like Harry's gone and given himself heatstroke," Ralph
Graver told the Indian.

"My God, he did that before," Paul Morrison said.

"Last year just about this time, wasn't it, Joe?"

Joe the Indian nodded. Beth watched as the Indian's eyes somehow
focused on her mother though his line of vision was pointed elsewhere.
The two men were also taking her in. They tried glancing elsewhere to
disguise their stare, but a stare was what it was. Her mother's hand

started toward her hair again but stopped. She probably didn't want the men to think she was trying to look nice for them.

"Check Harry's front seat. Bet his canteen is full. He filled up at our camp. Bet he didn't take a single swig. Thinks he's a camel."

"Harry and his seasonal heatstroke."

"Lots of polygs do. Ever since Hole in the Rock they think they're camels." Paul Morrison shook his head again, then spat out a black thread.

"Or Navajos. Harry might be trying to out-Navajo you, Joe. Look out."

By way of acknowledgment, Joe's eyes closed and opened slowly. Suddenly Ralph Graver scratched hard at his eyebrows as if he were a cat.

"And I'm sorry, I didn't catch your name," Paul Morrison said to her mother.

"Jean Waterman."

"How do you do."

"How do you do."

"And that would be Mrs. Jean Waterman."

"Yes."

"And would Mr. Waterman be around?"

"Mr. Waterman is deceased."

"I'm sorry. Truly sorry, ma'am—Mrs. Waterman."

"Thank you, but it's been many years."

"But you're so young, forgive me for intruding."

"Well, sometimes fate doesn't take that into account."

"I don't imagine." Paul Morrison checked behind him, nodded toward Joe, who had not moved a hair, then put his hands on his hips. His glance caught Beth a fraction before she had removed her stare from the Indian. She was hoping he hadn't caught her, but she knew he had.

All her attention had been on Joe. She couldn't help it. After all her books, he was the first Indian she'd seen in person, except for the ones posing by their resplendent colorful tepees next to trading-post luncheonettes and filling stations. He was a Navajo, too. She liked Navajos. She looked at Joe and believed he was standing there listening to the things the white man couldn't hear.

"Little girl, did you know *Ohio* is Indian for *Good morning?*" Paul Morrison asked her. "Joe knows all right. He knows you came in from Ohio."

Her mother's eyebrows rose.

Paul Morrison nodded toward the Rambler. "The license plates. You're pretty far from home."

Beth still couldn't pry her eyes off Joe. She knew he was keeping track of her even though his gaze was off to the side. Despite the heat, he wore a long-sleeved shirt—a red shirt, although the actual colors varied from orange to clay to something almost yellowish. In the end everything red had been sunned out of it, yet it remained a red shirt. Why was it still red? Exactly. Read her next book report to find out. She'd been wanting more than anything to add some philosophy to her reports.

"So you're here alone. You have children. Two of them." Paul Morrison filled in the bits of information as her mother failed to. "A boy and a girl." He took a preparatory breath. Instead of speaking, his face went through a variety of expressions. He winced, then nodded with his eyes opening wide. "Okay," he said. "I've seen this, too."

Her mother stood calmly. They had probably guessed already she was stubborn.

"That mother and her three boys, last year? Ralph, remember? You were the one found them."

"Jonas," his partner corrected.

"Jonas found them? How come you're the one with all the nightmares?" They both chuckled. "They were a little farther up here." His hand flagged toward a direction.

Her mother didn't respond.

"We warned them just like we're doing you. Didn't listen to us. They died."

"Gotta correct you, Paul. The oldest boy lived, I believe."

"You're right. Thank you, Ralph. Of course what good is his life now, his whole family gone, an orphan in one of those orphanages."

"Well, at least you warned them," her mother said. "You can't blame yourself."

"Okay. Well, you've caught on to me pretty quick." He turned to his partner for acknowledgment.

"I guess she does get you," Ralph Graver agreed. "But it's a little lie that illustrates a bigger truth."

"That's well put, Ralph."

"Thank you."

"But I have seen all kinda things happen, ma'am. Maybe this particular thing didn't happen quite this way—"

"Or not at all," her mother said.

"—Or not at all. Maybe not at all, but the idea see is true. It could happen, especially the way things are going and getting out of control. Which I'm sure you have noticed. It's dangerous see in all kinda ways and that part's true." Paul Morrison turned serious. "And people do get into trouble. There's been a murder or two."

"That's true," Ralph Graver said. "That's the God's truth."

"Yes, it's true," Paul Morrison said.

Her mother shrugged. It was settled.

"But it's mainly the elements that will get you. You're not the type to be out here. I hate to speak so boldly but there it is. You're a lovely lady, you're refined and high class, and I don't mean to ridicule you when I say that you're a faucet turner. And I mean, those high heels look nice—well, they do look nice, don't they, Ralph?"

Even Beth knew that her mother was supposed to ask what a faucet turner was, but she didn't.

"Very nice," Ralph said.

"Now where's your water, may I ask? Can't live without water. You learn that stuff pretty quick. Don't know where Harry's been taking his lessons."

"We found a waterhole," her mother said.

Paul Morrison grimaced. "That'll do you in an emergency, but you don't want all that alkaline on a daily basis."

Beth looked at Charlie. He had taken note. Alkaline.

"We'll get it from town and tote it in," her mother said.

"Believe me, with that plan you will die. I'm being serious now. The board springs aren't looking too good on your Rambler. Can't believe you made it this far without a truck. Well, it took its toll. I'd say you have one trip left in that wagon and I would use it for a fast exit. What would you say, Ralph?"

"I'd say the same thing."

"Eventually," her mother said.

"Eventually what?"

"Eventually we'll make a fast exit. But not right away."

Paul Morrison glanced back at his partner. Though a slight shake of the head was all he displayed, Beth could read all kinds of topsy-turvy activity going on inside him. He turned back to her mother with an I-give-up shake of the head. "We'll set you up with a little water buffalo— a little tank, see, we'll fill it with water for you. Can't promise about no murder. Men might kill themselves fighting over you."

"Thank you for the water."

The men went back to the road. Beth followed Charlie out there and they watched Paul Morrison clamber into Harry's truck and gun it off the road. They picked up the supplies Harry had strewn about and loaded them back into Harry's truck. Paul Morrison asked Joe to find a paper bag and tape it over the Rambler's carburetor. "Dust," he explained to Charlie. "How old are you, young man?"

"Twelve."

"Twelve. You sure? You don't look twelve."

"I'm twelve," Charlie said.

"Did your mom tell you to say twelve?"

"No. I told myself."

"You told yourself to say twelve which means you told yourself to say this number instead of the correct number, which means how old are you really?"

"He was born in 1942, that's why he's twelve," Beth said.

"And how old are you?" the man asked.

"Ten," Beth said.

"Well, okay, you could pass for ten. Your mom making you do this?"

"No."

"This is what you want to do?"

"Yes."

"What about school?"

"We have permission," Charlie said.

"Permission from what?"

"Permission from the school."

Paul Morrison let out an exasperated sigh. He went back to the campsite and knelt down by Harry and shook him. "Come on, Harry, you need to wake up." He shook again until Harry roused. Then he held out the canteen and told him to drink.

"It's hot as tea!" Harry's eyes were wild.

"How would you know what tea tastes like?" Paul Morrison said.

"I know what hot tastes like."

"That's because it's been sitting in your truck in the sun. Take better care, Harry. What the heck are you doing, anyway?"

"It's nothing," Harry said. "Just my way of telling myself summer's coming on." To Paul Morrison's harsh gaze, he said, "I'll drink more."

"You need the doctor? We're heading into town."

"What's Randolph going to do except give me a blanket?" Harry said.

"You need a blanket?"

"Yeah, that would be all right."

Paul Morrison glanced at Joe, who left the campsite and came back with a blanket. "Heatstroke," Paul Morrison muttered. "You of all people.

We're all sitting here sweating, Harry, I want you to know that. We're sweating and you're shivering."

"I'll be all right."

"You going to be more careful?"

"Thank you. Yes, I will."

"And look who you're imposing upon." Paul Morrison turned to her mother. "I'll take him into town if you want, ma'am."

"He'll be fine. We can handle him."

"I'd say you're lucky, Harry. You're imposing mightily on a young mother and her two children."

"I'll give them a good deal on a Geiger counter."

"Oh criminy, Harry." Paul Morrison stood up and tugged his belt even higher. "Let's go."

Her mother didn't say anything as they left. The men weren't talking either or Beth would have easily overheard. The truck engine started up and painfully bucked into gear.

"Charlie, that was an Indian," Beth said.

"I know."

"Was his name really Joe?"

"I think that was another one of their jokes," her mother said.

"What's so funny about Joe?"

Her mother shrugged. "I don't know," she said.

THREE

Harry woke to the smell of baked beans and canned meat. He stood up and hurried away. The moon hadn't arrived; he touched the canyon wall to guide him through the dark. He was rounding the rock when he couldn't hold back. The campsite was a perfect amphitheater and as he vomited, the embarrassing detonations of his sickness—his stupidity—were perfectly reported back. He kept moving farther out. He left the rocks and dashed across the sand, but there was no privacy sound-wise to be had. Soon a flashlight was upon his back and he was handed a towel. That someone of the gentle sex had to witness this was to his discredit, but when she took his hand, he was taken aback by the strength of her grip. She helped him up. He wasn't dizzy exactly, but he had long passed the deadline for watering his vital organs. His experiments never worked; he would just have to keep drinking as much and as often as everyone else. The lady's grip had coiled around his upper arm, as if to keep him from staggering. He wasn't staggering. He was Harry Lindstrom. He did not stagger. He remembered his mother, his real mother. He had never admitted to anyone how much he disliked the other one.

"I have to tell you something," he said.

Her grip on his arm, helpful and distrustful, locked in.

"I've already been warned about you."

"I'm not a threat. Did they tell you I was a threat?" Inside his head was a mute dried-up scream. Better shut up now but he knew he wouldn't. The lady's grip tightened so he wouldn't fall. When he turned he saw the two black shapes watching him. She wasn't meaning to help him. No, she was keeping him away from her children.

He wanted to prove that he was a gentleman but so far if he listed back the things he had just said they either made no sense or were frightening. The children's mother had turned off the flashlight and his eyes as they adjusted brought her features to him, and she was assuredly scared of him. Somehow he needed to make her see the same picture he was seeing: a photograph of himself as father, his hand on the son's shoulder while he leaned over with a smile and explained it to the boy, now stick this Geiger's probe under a rock, keep an eye on the meter. . . . What boy wouldn't want a dad like that?

"Go back to the camp," the lady told her children. "Go back to bed."

Harry found himself the last in line, pulled along, his hand secured in the mother's. He plopped down by the piñon—his old spot. He liked the sound of that.

The mother stood over him. He could see from her wilted dress it had been a long hard day. He liked the way the flimsy scraps hung on her. Behind her the moon was now up, bright as a desk lamp, and it shone through the material. The body inside the dress made itself discernible as a black skeleton, not bone of course, or even bone thin, but flesh, nice flesh with a nice shape. The black outline swelled and shrank as he heard a sigh. "Do you have a tent? Do you need—?" She cut herself off. "You can take care of yourself. Do I need to worry?"

"I'm from around here," Harry told her.

"So you've said." The mother's hands planted themselves on her hips. "So you're okay."

"Oh yes."

Her black outline twitched, her hands dropped, and she turned away. She paused and her head angled back. "Why do you do this to yourself?" she asked.

"There was a man who ate nothing but air for thirteen years." It came pouring out of him, this confidence. This man had frightened him for much longer than thirteen years. This man was strong as a horse but had eaten only air; the very idea kept him up all night when all his own training failed. Terrorized by this man, he had been training himself since childhood and it had all failed.

"Is that why you won't eat?" the mother asked him.

"Oh, I eat. I'm trying not to drink so much."

"I thought your religion didn't let you drink."

"So you know about that already. Water, I mean," Harry said. "I'm training myself not to drink water."

The mother squatted low, but her bottom did not touch the ground. The dress spread across the lap her knees had made. She rested her elbows on her thighs and brought her hands together. Her chin rested on her hands and she stared at Harry. Her eyes shone. Harry had never seen anything so wonderful as this elegant figure so awkwardly postured, so perfectly balanced. "Why?" she asked.

"Which why to what?"

"Why are you training yourself?"

"Because then I'm trained."

"And then?"

"And then nothing bad will happen."

He couldn't see the expression on her face with the bright moon behind her, but her head shook no. "Something bad will happen. I trained myself to live without my husband and I succeeded. But other bad things will happen." She stood up and the moon caught her. Her black outline walked away.

This was why Harry loved the desert and loved it at night. He could be lifted out of himself and sometimes he was floating toward a tragedy that never showed up. Sometimes he was floating toward a love that never showed up. At night in the desert people might say something to you they would otherwise save till their deathbed. Just like that he and the mother had each shared a secret. Her divorce. His monster. He was floating. Tonight it had showed up.

Vaguely he heard something that sounded like the delayed echo of his own vomiting. It was coming from inside the tent. He located it there where the mother and the two children were. He knew only that the choking and hacking and sounds of smacking couldn't be anything bad. He trusted the mother and was fairly certain he was already in love with her.

FOUR

Jean and the children accepted his invitation to drive to the town. Harry dropped the stack of reading material from the passenger seat onto the floor. Jean propped her feet on the magazines and old newspapers; when she looked down her heels had cut into a *Life* magazine. She picked up a piece of the cover photo: a pair of intense eyes, darkened almost into a Zorro mask. She fit the ripped edges to another piece and Greta Garbo stared up at her.

Harry and his International Harvester reminded Jean of something she had read concerning the ease of finding uranium:

> *"I'd been driving along the same road to and from work for years. One day I stopped to change a flat tire and became one of the richest men in the state," said a former plumber's helper and one of the state's newest uraniumaires.*

When Harry showed up with his flat tire, it was exactly like one of these testimonials in her many instructional booklets (except for the getting-rich uranium part). She was loaded with these booklets—in addition to the articles from *National Geographic* and *Look* and *Arizona Quarterly*. She had photographs as well, tons of those. To her own mother in

Springfield, Ohio, she showed only the photographs that depicted hazards and close calls, adopting a flabbergasted air at her mother's panic.

Most of the photographs arrived from the government, however, and the government pretended that searching for uranium was an enjoyable social outing that involved pulling a Geiger counter from a picnic basket. Enticing. Why don't you join us?

For example, a smiling man and a smiling lady out on a uranium date. For example, a family of five out for a day of picnicking and uranium hunting. The government pamphlet explained that it was this simple. The uranium sat up grayish yellow in the carnotite rock. You could spot it with field glasses or opt for the simplicity and ease of a Geiger counter. After you found the uranium, the Atomic Energy Commission would help you bulldoze roads so you could mine it out. The AEC would do all it could to help with expenses. Some people like Vernon Pick became millionaires overnight.

Jean didn't believe any of it, or at least not all of it. Her own plan was vague but specific and aimed mostly at Charlie and his scientific nature. Charlie, whom she couldn't stop thinking about. Charlie her son, Beth her daughter, she was the mother who was everything to them, who put them before all else, who wanted to grab them and keep life at bay. Nevertheless, a part of her left over from childhood urged her to be the errant daughter, to shock, displease, and unleash in her own mother hysterical permission-denied fiats that could no longer be enforced. Another part of her haughtily dismissed the maternal interference she kept inviting. The one thing she didn't want was a truce. As long as she could go on fighting with her mother like the old days, the pre-Charlie days, the world was normal.

She was quiet as she sat in Harry's truck. She had arrived once again at the image of her own mother weeping and still begging no at the Greyhound bus station. No, don't go—her mother so proud all the time, so careful of her appearance, so careful to step lightly like a dancer—

reduced to this. Everyone at the bus station looking at this weeping, youthful grandmother. And now as the errant daughter, was she happy as she drove away in the Rambler station wagon? Was she happy now with the tent she had bought from a lady whose husband had died in Yellowstone Park, with the pickax she had been given, with the hammer, with the knapsacks, with the Tupperware, with the pamphlets and the shovel and the cans of chili con carne, with the golf club for beating off danger, with the clothespins and antique washboard, with the flimsy notion that she was ready for this?

She stroked Beth's perspiring forehead as Beth slept deeply, mouth open, flopped against her. Harry and Charlie were busy talking to one another. Secretly she was glad Harry had talked her into this ride.

After two hours the boulder trail they were driving on settled into a bumpy dirt road trenched by heavy machinery and rainstorms. Harry downshifted once, then turned to Charlie and said, "Go ahead, take her down another gear." The mother saw how Charlie's face was carefully expressionless to hide his pleasure and again she wanted to grab him, to hold him tight against the world.

"We're getting close to town," Harry said. "Looky there."

Ahead in the road, parked in a draw, was a broken-down jalopy with an old man sitting at the wheel. The Jeep didn't look like it had ever run. The old man looked like petrified wood.

"Is he alive?" Charlie asked.

"'Course he's alive. That's Ace King. He's what happens to all you fortune hunters."

A sign propped on the jalopy read, *Ace King, the Uranium Prince. Genuine Uranium Claims, $25 and Up.*

Harry gave a toot as they passed.

"He *is* dead," Charlie said. Harry let out a big laugh.

"Preparation is nine-tenths of prospecting," Harry said. "Before you even think of doing it, you've got to get maps, study them, read geological reports, talk to the field office people. You need to check out the aerial photos, too, and see if you can get ahold of some anomaly maps."

In the middle of Harry's remarks Jean realized he was speaking to her.

"What preparations have you done? Out there in Ohio, I mean. How'd you get yourself ready?"

She didn't answer. One of the pamphlets she had read said, *Pick up a rock. If it ticks, you're rich.*

"Then maybe do a reconnaissance on horseback or mule," Harry said. "Before you start in earnest. You're not answering me."

"What is your question?"

"I have a feeling you didn't do any preparations."

"You sound like my mother."

"Do you have a detection instrument of choice?"

"I think you already know the answer to that, Harry."

"Then you'll need a promoter," Harry said. "Unless you're thinking being Mrs. Ace King is the way to go. In that case I could help you make a sign nice as his. We could get a cardboard box and some markers."

"Why do I need a cardboard box?" she asked.

"A promoter promotes, gets the rumors spreading and the frenzy going. Drives the prices up. I've never seen it go different."

"Is that how Vernon Pick did it?"

"You know about Vernon Pick, huh?" When she didn't answer, Harry said, "Everyone thinks they're going to come out here and be Vernon Pick. Everyone thinks it. Happens to nobody. I've never seen it go different."

She said nothing. She had been planning to leave when the bottles of water ran out, wondering if the busted springs of the station wagon would get her back as far as the town where she could make repairs before heading home. Nice of course of that Paul Morrison fellow offering to set up a water buffalo, but she didn't really need it. She was just waiting for the look in her children's eyes that said they'd had enough. Even kids at a swimming pool eventually got that look, and then it was time to go home.

FIVE

Beth and her family were lucky. The springs of their station wagon had given out beside a natural shelter, a horseshoe of overhanging rock. A sandy crescent was perfect for a tent. The sand roughened with bristles as it spread toward blackbrush, sprouts of silvery winterfrost, and tough cheat grass. A tiny piñon tree sprang out of nowhere, as if from one of her play sets. Beth liked sleeping on the sand as long as a beach blanket was under her. She and Charlie had searched for waterholes and found only the drying, white-rimmed pond that they now called *emergency alkaline* thanks to Paul Morrison. She imagined them out there day after day searching for water, tricked by mirages, until they were crawling on their knees half dead, and when they finally fainted their bodies would roll down a dune into a waterhole. Saved at the last minute.

Her mother thought the water they had bought in town would see them through. Beth had never seen water sold before. The water was probably why the Rambler's springs had given out. In case she thought otherwise, Charlie told her that a cubic foot of water weighed sixty-four pounds.

She woke up confused in Harry's truck, her brain lost in the heat.

"Who's that groggy little girl over there?" Harry asked.

"Almost there, sweetie." A smack as her mother's wet arm separated from hers. They were high enough so that they could see the town below them, the whole town, all of it, how it wasn't round, circling out from a dense center, but went off like a Hershey bar between two ranges and then just stopped, one end of the town bitten off and irregular, the other end smooth. The road they were on was still a dirt road, but now there were ragged signs of life. Shacks and half-buried cars and squatter camps. Not a single person.

Closer to town the road was paved. Fences had been erected and the fields within were beaten with housing trailers. *Monthly Rates,* read one sign. Two children stood by the road, arms hanging dead, and stared at them as they drove by. The town had a big church, a bank, a post office, a bus station that was part of a restaurant. A banner strewn across the downtown street advertised a $14.99 bus ride to an A-bomb test site, *barbecue included!*

Harry turned down a side street and then into the empty parking lot. The motel's sign, *Stagecoach Oasis,* was turned off. Beth could see a swimming pool. The door to the motel office was thrown open and held by a brick. Through the screen door Beth heard radio music. "Once I Had a Secret Love." A sad song but leaping with happy static. Her grandmother loved that song and always said turn it up at the exact moment that her mother said turn it down.

"Hello there!" Harry called.

"Hello, Harry," mumbled the lady in the motel office. She didn't look up. She was bent over her desk with a bottle of glue. A red pipe cleaner, clenched like a rose between her teeth, explained her muzzled voice. She wore bib overalls and a pink sleeveless shirt with an upturned collar. Her naked arms were thickly freckled and were on that border between looking strong and looking heavy. The fan in her office was turned off. The thing she was working on was laid out on a cooking sheet, tiny white shells and colored mostly turquoise fishbowl stones and colored mostly fuchsia strings, all of which she was arranging Hawaii-like inside a picture frame.

"Got a couple of uraniumaires for you," Harry said.

"Do you now." The lady looked up and Beth could see the surprise on her face to be locking eyes with a little girl—a little girl of her talent and good looks, she might add, which would further the surprise. Right away Beth guessed this lady was the kind of person who liked protecting her deeper feelings. The lady suddenly aimed a big smile directly at Beth as if she had read Beth's thoughts and was protecting her reaction with amusement. She plucked the pipe cleaner from her mouth and put it on the cooking sheet with the rest of the stuff and told Harry to turn on the fan. She let the fan rotate around the room, dodging with the cooking sheet the fan's shifting aim until she found a spot where the wind wouldn't disturb the pattern of colored stones and shells. "Are these your friends?" she asked. Her hair was long and extra thick and she grabbed it up in a ponytail to let the fan's air hit her bared neck.

"They're staying up near Swing Line Wash."

"Good Lord," the lady started to say before lifting her hand to alert them. That sad but happy song on the radio was nearing its end and it leaped into full static and the lady leaped with it: "Now I shouted from the highest hills! Even told the golden daffodils." The radio's crunching took over and she switched it off. She sighed with disgust. "If that radio was a Geiger counter, I'd be rich. And I'd have a better radio." She looked at Beth's mother. "You going to stay the night, honey?"

"Yes, Mom," Beth said.

"I guess so," her mother said. "You didn't tell me this part," she added to Harry.

"I'll pay," Harry said.

"No. It's not the money. It's the work we have to do."

"Oh," Harry said.

"What work is that?" the lady asked.

"All the preparations Harry was so kind to explain to me."

"That's Harry," the lady said. "Honey, I do have weekly rates. You're just as likely to find uranium under one of my beds as in those hills. And it's a good ways more pleasant."

"Exactly what I was trying to explain. You're more succinct," Harry said.

"Of course I am, Harry."

"I think one night will do fine." Her mother shifted and her foot landed on the tail of a tabby cat. Both her mom and the cat jumped.

"Out, skedaddle," the lady ordered. "Don't mind him. He's been run over twice."

"Is he your kitty?" Beth asked.

"That one? No, darling. Wild as they come. Except the two cars have knocked it out of him a bit."

"How does he eat?"

"I have some guests who take care of that."

"And these folks are all the way from Ohio," Harry said.

"Lordy," the lady said, shivering her body.

"Can we go swimming?" Beth asked.

"Absolutely," the lady said. "That's the first thing I meant to say."

Beth saw her mother hesitate.

"I have bathing suits they can borrow," the lady said. "I keep a pile going. Some are pretty nice. Got one that would fit you, too."

"That's very kind of you."

"I like kids." She stopped for a moment and then she gave Charlie a big smile, probably because he had been silent and ignored all this time. She seemed like someone who wanted to make sure everyone was having a good time. "Mine are seventeen and eighteen." She snapped her fingers, said, "Like that," and shook her head. "And I can wash their clothes while they're swimming."

"I'll be happy to do the washing if you show me where."

"Your choice," the lady said. But in the end she took all their clothes and gave them a good wash in her own personal machine. Beth put on the borrowed swimwear and jumped in the pool. Charlie quickly joined her. He was not one to give up the water. He did a racing dive in the deep end and stayed under and didn't come up until he was in the shallow end, where three old ladies sat around a table in seashell metal chairs painted yellow, green, and blue. They had set aside a card game and were having their drinks. Snatches of their conversation came to Beth, *Died of a stroke at what age? Here it's Saturday and I thought it was Thursday.* The tabby had returned and was hanging around the old ladies' feet. Beth looked over at her mom, lounging nearby in a borrowed bathrobe, and she looked pretty content. *Oh that reminds me of Betty. Someone should let him know.*

The lady manager in the bib overalls came out with a net attached to a long pole and fished out the dead insects from the pool. "There," she said with satisfaction. "So you kids can get a proper swim." She returned with a tall drink for Beth's mom, and popsicles for Beth and Charlie.

Beth stayed in the water until Harry came back from stocking up his truck with supplies. He asked if they wanted to go out to eat supper in a restaurant. "Let's go out," he said. "Do you want to go out?"

"Have you eaten at all today, Harry?" her mother asked. Her voice took on a concerned warning, but Beth knew she was avoiding an answer. Out here with no one she knew and no one to contradict her, her mother was building this new life and pretending to live it. Harry insisted about the dinner and her mother finally said they were all too tired, which Beth knew meant Charlie, but of course she wasn't going to correct her and say, But I'm full of energy! Her mother had told her these things were private.

Harry said he would get something and bring it back. He got in an old DeSoto, brown with a cream-colored top. The lady manager was driving; she stuck her head out the window and yelled, "Last call for stragglers!" and Beth said, "Please Mom, can I?" and her mom said, "Go ahead." Beth jumped in and waved from the backseat. They went to the Atomic Café, and Harry and the lady talked a lot to the man who owned the place. His name was Dewey Durnford. Beth still didn't know what the lady's name was. Dewey Durnford complained about not getting reception for the TV. He talked about missing the Rocky Marciano fight. He talked about one of the guys who'd gotten uranium rich going up above the clouds in his private plane so he could get the fight's reception on his TV. Dewey Durnford said, "I've given that guy so many free meals in his sourdough days he could have invited me along to see it." Beth ate french fries. No one seemed to care she wore a sweater over a bathing suit. Dewey had dewy hair, that kind that chicks had, and his small teeth razored inward, the opposite of buck. Toward the end of her french fries (and she hoping someone would suggest more), Beth heard Dewey call the lady manager Miss Dazzle. Miss Dazzle said she didn't like fights, heavyweight championship or not, and she reached out and squeezed Dewey's hand and said, "But I'm sorry for you." She sipped on a Coke and Dewey said, "You want that I should add something to that," and she said, "Why, absolutely." Dewey took out a bottle with a missing label, as if that was going to fool someone, and let the last of its contents drip into Miss Dazzle's Coke. He slapped the bottle as if it were ketchup to get a final drop. Miss Dazzle's body sagged peacefully. Another plate of french fries appeared before Beth and she just couldn't hold back a smile and everyone laughed. She felt happy, boundlessly happy; she wanted to throw her french fries in the air. Then Dewey Durnford reached down below the counter and brought up a record album and presented it to a stunned Miss Dazzle. "The new one?" Miss Dazzle stuttered. "Does it have it on there?" Miss Dazzle's voice was anxious as she scanned the cover photo—a picture of Calamity Jane with a Civil War scout cap perked over her blond curls. Beth's grandmother had the very same album with that song she listened to six times in a row. "Oh, you're a sweetheart!" Miss Dazzle cried. "Oh Lord! You're a sweetheart!" She stood up and grabbed the sides of Dewey's face and planted a big kiss on the bridge of his nose. Harry said he agreed about not liking fights. Dewey fixed up milk shakes and hamburgers and more french fries and they took them back to the motel. On the ride back to the motel Miss Dazzle talked about her boys being seventeen and eighteen—she snapped her fingers again—and how they were hitchhiking to California for the summer. They had a cousin who lived there and thought they had a used car coming to them simply because they were old enough to drive and cars just happened to appear out of nowhere once you were old enough to drive, right, Harry? Look at *her* car why don't you. She was sure she could afford another one for their summer outing, like heck. But why complain? She touched the record album. Right now she was about as happy as a person could be.

Harry and Miss Dazzle ate with them in their motel room. The skin on Charlie's face had that shiny blushed look so Beth knew her mother had pounded him and he had hacked out the visitor for another night, which was how they referred to Charlie's situation. Miss Dazzle thought Charlie had taken a nap because he looked "refreshed." They all went to bed late. From time to time Miss Dazzle would look around at all of them and a big grin would spread across her face. Harry finally stood up and said good-night. Miss Dazzle had no choice but to follow him out though it seemed to Beth she was just getting started. She was a people person, Miss Dazzle was, sort of the opposite of her mother. Harry went to his truck. "Harry, just take a room for free," Miss Dazzle told him. Beth overheard them. She went to the window above the bed and watched as they stood together in the parking lot. "I couldn't do that," Harry said. "Besides I need to guard my wares." He disappeared into his truck and Beth saw the shadow of Miss Dazzle shaking its head.

"What's going on now?" her mother asked. Her mother was sitting at the tiny desk in the motel room while Beth did the spying. "He needs to guard his wares," Beth told her. Her mother shook her head just as Miss Dazzle had done. They heard the engine churn over. Beth looked out again. "I guess he's leaving." The red brake lights of Harry's truck lit up Miss Dazzle's face. "For goodness' sake," Miss Dazzle was saying, "don't be silly, park here overnight, Harry." She was aflame from the red brake lights shining on her. Magicians' scarves appeared to fly out of her hands. Her sweeping gestures left a neon trail of red in the sky. "You can help guard the motel," Miss Dazzle told him. The engine switched off. "Is this place dangerous?" Beth asked her mother. Her mother laughed. "Why does Harry need to guard us?" Charlie said, "She's just trying to make him feel good." Her mother laughed again. Beth turned back to the window and saw Miss Dazzle disappear into the office. She heard the screen door bounce shut. The phonograph came on. The music was turned low but it was that song again and Beth heard a big whoop that belonged to Miss Dazzle's voice. "Why do you hate that song?" Beth asked her mother. "What song?" her mother said. "I don't hate any song." Beth jumped down on her soft mattress. It felt so unusual to sleep in a bed again, as if her adventure had lasted months rather than a few days. She wondered where the wild tabby went during the night.

Six

Jean lay in bed, holding her daughter. Through the screened window she heard the strains of Miss Dazzle's phonograph. She recognized Doris Day's voice. Miss Dazzle's loud enthusiastic harmony almost drowned her out. Beth was mostly asleep but still humming along.

Miss Dazzle was that friendly, ebullient type, the kind someone like Jean might like to have along to fill out her own personality: those dark holes where the bright colors of congeniality had somehow been dug out. She could come up with justifications for it: the mothers in the hospital who panted sweetly and obediently for the staff got adored by the head-patting nurses but got nowhere as far as procuring real services for their child. But she knew, really, this was an excuse. Something of her true nature had been released, not changed, by Charlie's illness.

She remembered visiting the house of the widow who had sold her their tent. She would have sent her mother on the errand had her mother not been so opposed to this adventure, since it required the fluid charms of someone who loved etiquette. The widow, Jean could tell over the phone, was another etiquette-lover.

The widow's house was strangely designed. As soon as Jean walked through the front door she was on the staircase. It was as if the house itself were an aggressive salesman—Up or Down! it immediately demanded. On the coffee table where the widow put their cups of tea were photographs framed in velvet. The people in the pictures were too dated: none could have been the husband who had died of a heart attack in Yellowstone Park. She smelled that the widow's oven was on. Its heat had loosed other smells. When they went upstairs to the husband's closet to retrieve the tent, there drifted in the empty air a seasoned perfume, and Jean instinctively knew this was not the widow's perfume. Even though the closet had been vacated of suits and ties and shoes, the perfume had remained, finally to have its say, one traitor turning upon another.

The tent was made by the Camel Company. The pickax a hunter had given her was a U.S. Forest Service brand, such a tempting item although nothing she was ever likely to use. As she lay in bed, she began to list the names of Geiger counters, the ones she could remember, the 1-Eleven Scintillator, the Price Ranger. She had researched the different types of detection instruments but had never considered purchasing one. The Lucky Strike was the cheapest Geiger counter by far and the name she liked best. The others vied for dullest: the Babbel Counter, the Gordon, the Winford-Bunce, all descendants of the Geiger-Mueller tube. It must have been a type of infidelity that she could remember pieces of equipment better than she could her own husband, for the Geiger counters were named after men she was sure.

In the morning they enjoyed breakfast by the pool. Eggs and bacon and raisin toast with icing for them; pastries for the three elderly ladies. Miss Dazzle served coffee on a tray, then sat down with Jean. Miss Dazzle was a talker who didn't always need to talk. There was some comfort in that. There was a lot of comfort in that. Jean leaned back and breathed in the early morning. The air was still sleepy and unbroken, yet the sun sharp as midafternoon. No clouds. Never a cloud. On the chair between them was a stack of clean, folded clothes that Miss Dazzle had put there. Catching their aroma gave Jean a physical pleasure that traveled through her body.

Miss Dazzle refilled the silver pot of coffee for the three ladies and then took Jean and the children to the post office, where Jean collected the mail that had arrived for her. A lot of mail had arrived, but every single bit of it was from the children's grandmother. Jean tried to view her mother this way—the children's grandmother—to neutralize the pain, but it didn't work. Upon seeing the handwriting she felt herself a daughter again. She was paralyzed. But of course her mother had anticipated this very reaction. Foreseeing that any sealed envelopes would never be opened, her mother had sent only postcards. At least a dozen of them. Brief messages popped out like ad campaigns, one after the other, until a letter's full contents were equaled.

High school graduations caused such a traffic jam some of the graduates didn't graduate, they were stuck in traffic. Ha!

Strawberries will come in early because of the heat and rain.

The Millers called. Surprised you left town.

Lucky you, your driveway's been blacktopped—wonder who???

Bing Crosby NOT coming to Vets Memorial after all. Boo!

All normal stuff about everyday life—but it caused in Jean an intense ache. Everyday life was a feeble joke, but her mother insisted upon living it, and sharing it.

The kids bought stamps. Back at the pool Beth wrote a letter with alarming untrue facts, principal among them that they would be going broke soon because water was not free here you had to buy it and the stores overcharged and pretty soon they'd have to live like the two dusty children they had passed living in a field, *but don't worry Grandma we're having lots of fun.* The stamp affixed to this proclamation of looming poverty said *ATOMS FOR PEACE*, which was, Jean thought, just as hysterically misleading as Beth's letter.

Charlie didn't wait for Beth to finish her letter. He pulled on his borrowed swim trunks and jumped in the pool. His skinny stomach looked hard as a rock. Harry would be here any minute and they would be leaving, but in the desert air the swim trunks would dry in ten minutes. On the chair next to her still sat the stack of clothes Miss Dazzle had washed for them. The clothes folded thick, thicker, thickest, a cozy cottage of clothes, deep in an enchanted forest.

Seven

At the filling station Beth and Charlie pulled out cold soda pops from the vending racks. Harry told them to save the bottles to use as claim notices. Beth didn't miss the glance Harry gave her mother when he said this. Harry was very tall and because he was so skinny he seemed floppy, and his personality seemed floppy, too. But in his glance Beth could see his strong inkling that they had staked not a single claim. It wasn't up to her to tell him he was right or wrong.

Harry pulled out an orange soda for himself. "I'll add it to your collection," he said. "What have you been putting your claim notices in before this?"

"Cans of chili con carne," her mother said. She gave Harry a glance of her own.

Harry needed to pick up his laundry. They drove over to Mel's Cleaners. Harry piled the stack of fresh shirts on the front seat. They were folded up and wrapped like presents. Harry said it always made him feel good to pick up a bunch of shirts. Right there he went through every shirt, pulling out the cardboard that kept the shirts folded and stiff. He presented the cardboard pieces to Charlie for his ever-expanding map of the campsite and environs.

They went next to the hardware store. Harry picked up tape for Charlie's map and then a supply of different-colored inks. Beth went over to look at paper she might need for her book reports. She wasn't running out yet but she liked thinking about running out. Harry came over. He must have thought she was feeling left out because he bought her paper and a fountain pen and then ink cartridges in her choice of color (peacock blue). Then he went off for his own stuff.

The hardware store had an excited buzz to it, like people shoving in line to catch a glimpse of a movie star. Most of the customers were prospectors and they were holding rocks in their hands and all of them were pushing into the same aisle, where the Geiger counters were lined up on shelves like coffee percolators. What sounded like Miss Dazzle's radio static emitted from them. The static added an angry discharge to the bumping and muttering of the prospectors as they ran their rocks over the sensors.

In the middle of the turmoil Beth kept thinking how lucky they were to have found Harry.

Beth studied the prospectors. They were too occupied to notice her stares. She had read her mother's pamphlets. She had seen the photographs of a clean showered smiling lady and the clean showered smiling man holding their rocks up like delicious milk shakes, but all she was seeing here were men, dirty men, looking dried up and not very nice, and not a single one of them with combed hair or a shaved face.

An old prospector stood off to the side, drinking from a dainty teacup. Amber-colored cracks branched through the porcelain. Beth saw that he was using the teacup to hide his face, to hide the fact that he was scrutinizing her mother. She realized all the men under normal conditions, these kinds of men that is, would be leering at her mother since every once in a while Beth remembered how pretty she was. She pointed out the old man to Charlie, who kept watch while she went off to find Harry. Harry was using his salesman's discount to buy the claim stakes and powder charges her mother said she needed. He followed Beth to the other side of the store and they looked around until Charlie waved them over. They found her mother with the old man. They were picking out bullets together for the gun he was giving to her. He was giving it to her for free. Harry said, "Oh no. No. Thank you but no." The old man said it was just a .22, he had more where that came from, and he said, "This one's not like the others"—meaning her mother not the gun, Beth got clear on that after he nodded toward the jostling, filthy men some of whom flung their rocks to the linoleum floor before stomping out.

"Yeah, get the gun, Mom," Charlie said.

Her mother's hair had worked loose again and the strands were hanging down. She hooked the strands behind her ear, the old man enraptured by her every gesture. As they were leaving, the old man said he wouldn't mind a peck on the cheek but perhaps he'd clean himself up a little first. She said that would be fine, she'd look forward to the occasion. She shook his hand.

Before going back to the campsite they went to the grocery store for some fresh fruits and more emergency alkaline at sixty-four pounds per cubic foot, and then to the Grand Vu Theater. They had planned on a movie and ice cream and then, her mother said, time to get back. Set up inside the movie theater was a Magic Uranium Booth. The man in the booth hammered a penny with uranium to make it radioactive then ran it over a Geiger counter with the silken sweep of a magician. The needles started clicking. "I'll get you each a lucky penny to put in your pocket," Harry said, but her mother said, "Thank you, Harry, but we're going to pass on that one." Next to the Magic Uranium Booth was a hot-dog stand that Harry said was run by the owner's wife. He said the hot-dog stand used to be a kissing booth but her kisses were like poison. The wieners of her hot-dog stand were displayed inside a small glass oven and they were dry and hard as the desert, as if she had poisoned them, too. Still, Beth wouldn't have minded eating one. They didn't get ice cream. The ice cream was ruined because the freezer couldn't get cold enough.

Twenty minutes into *Captain Horatio Hornblower* the brownouts started. Harry said the single generator couldn't keep up with all the newcomers pouring into town. The moviegoers milled outside. Beth had seen enough of the picture to figure that since the movie took place on a ship there wasn't going to be a searching-for-water-in-the-desert scene, so she wasn't too disappointed when her mother suggested they try another time. They got more soda pop for the claim notices, and Harry treated himself to a large paper cup of iced tea and said he didn't care who knew it. "And I'm sure the whole world is watching," her mother said. In the truck they ate peaches which dripped all over them and Harry hurried to beat the darkness, which arrived like a yanked curtain just as they reached the campsite. The sun flared red as it dropped. Although still above the horizon when they got home, it was setting directly behind the horse-shoe. The overhanging rock eclipsed it and suddenly the sky grew dim. Harry parked in the road. It got darker with each step toward their shelter. It seemed darker, too, because of the suddenness of it. Beth almost didn't realize there were other people there at her campsite until something big and silver loomed ahead of her. She was tempted to call it a spaceship.

Eight

Harry knew an instant before the others that someone was there. He pulled on Charlie's collar and drew him back. The mother and daughter were too far ahead. The first thing he thought of was the pistol, which was one reason he hated guns, because they became the first thing you turned to when things went wrong. Nevertheless, he was about to step back to the truck and retrieve it when he noticed the silver Airstream trailer. He relaxed. Just more dogstakers.

A kerosene stove the size of a small piano was already set up. A woman was peeling potatoes. A man was sitting on a portable chair. A young man, roughly aged. He was hunched over, staring between his knees, somehow rough-looking in just the way he hunched. The man knew they were there, but he took his time looking up. Harry knew his type right away. Just as they knew his type, probably. "How ya doin'!" the man finally called over. It was supposed to be a friendly greeting, but it came out bully-loud.

Harry knew he had to answer quickly or the man would have a reason to take offense. The man was looking for that reason already. Harry had to think of something to say before the children's mother jumped in, which he knew she would, and that wouldn't be good. She didn't have a feel for this part of the country. She dressed for uranium hunting like it was the PTA. Of course he really didn't want it any different, not if she were going to be his wife.

"This is a surprise," Harry said. "We thought we were alone."

"You're not no more."

"What are you doing here?" The mother.

Well, she had jumped in.

"I'm *doing*..." The man spat out the word. "I'm doing what everyone else is doing." Harry thought of Dewey Durnford and his love of boxing. This man had put on the gloves. Already. No call for anger—look at them, a mother and two kids, and here's a man who sees that as cause to fight. But that was how it worked out here. A man itching to square off for no reason meets another man itching to square off for no reason. That was why, in a town that had swelled to three times its original size in five years, new trouble was brewing all the time. Miss Dazzle was smart to set her rates as high as it took to keep out the prospectors. He'd seen her rates double on the spot when some undesirable meandered in.

"This is our campground. You'll have to leave." The mother again. Harry wished the mother hadn't said anything. She had though. It was war now. That was quick.

"Oh. Oh." The man laughed cruelly. "Oh."

There were so many people to dislike out here. This one was a winner. Harry could tell he'd been here for a while. Moving around from one dry hogback to another. Broker than when he'd arrived. Getting desperate. Starting to blame his troubles on the wife.

Of course they had that nice Airstream and the red pickup that pulled it. That took something from the pocketbook. Harry hadn't figured out that part yet.

"The road was so bad. It just stopped." The wife spoke. She had a sweet voice and she was trying to apologize. A higher-caliber human being than her husband, that was clear. Harry immediately wondered what the story was. Well, when it came to that, he knew. He'd seen it all the time in his own life. And actually he wasn't such a good judge of character though he kept thinking he was. He was prepared to look upon this lady in the morning, prepared to discover she wasn't a lady at all, wasn't so young as she looked, wasn't so sweet as she seemed. Because those were the kinds of surprises he'd been coming upon his whole life.

The man stared hard at his wife as she spoke. He didn't say anything.

"I'm Josephine," she said. "Really, Jo. Just Jo. Jo Dawson." Her husband fumed silently. Harry moved to light their lanterns, something to distract everyone. Okay, no more ladies saying a thing, everyone quiet, let's just get through the night.

"This is my husband, Leonard," the wife unwisely continued. "I mean of course Dawson, too, Leonard Dawson." She sounded breathless.

"We're not here to be their neighbors," the man growled.

Harry was right. The man had anger wanting out. He wasn't glad he was right, but he was right. Everyone should have listened to Harry. Don't say another word. He'd seen it happen.

"But we are their neighbors," Josephine persisted.

"I said we're not here to be their neighbors."

Unfortunately the mother decided to speak again. "I'm Jean. These are my two children. We won't be neighbors after you leave in the morning."

The man continued with his mocking oh-ohs.

"It's best if we leave them alone." Harry drew close and whispered this, hoping she could read his warning. The mother's blue eyes had a shade of green in them. Somehow he could see all their colors in a way he couldn't during the day. In the sunlight her eyes were always on the verge of iridescence and Harry was struck by them yet blocked from really discerning the color. The desert had already begun to dry her skin and she would be surprised upon going home to discover there were now wrinkles creasing her forehead. Ladies didn't like that sort of thing, but to Harry the new lines in her face made her more beautiful. She wasn't unreachable. Something had reached her, even if it was the desert and the sun.

The mother didn't acknowledge his warning. But she did stop talking.

The red pickup had been detached from the trailer. So maybe this Dawson fellow was planning to drive off in the morning. His type tended to be gone for days, weeks at a time, long enough for people to wonder, dead? dying? struck crazy? Then they showed up in town and went straight to the bootleggers for their drink, took the Lucky Strike at its unreliable word when they ran their rocks over it in the hardware store, and celebrated away all their money until the assessor's final verdict denied them their million bucks. Then came the beat-up wives and no hospital to take care of them, just one little office and Dr. Randolph who was a quack. Harry preferred to take his injuries to Miss Dazzle, who was as good as a nurse, having worked for Randolph until she got fed up with his passes. She'd been his secretary, but in between trying to collect bills from people they couldn't track down, Randolph had her giving shots and stitching up. Why give 'em a real doctor till they started paying for it—that was Randolph's attitude.

"Don't worry," Harry told the mother. " I'll stay here with you and the children." He saw right away this was the wrong thing to say. Harry Lindstrom, Protector. No, she didn't want to hear that. She set her jaw.

"I have to take care of Charlie."

"That's what I mean. I'll help you."

Her set jaw was protruding now. She looked around for a way out. She walked back to the truck. Harry and the kids followed. "Take me back down the road a bit," she said.

"We were here first. We can stay. It's ours." Charlie was speaking now.

"It's time, Charlie," she said. "We'll come back when it's over." She turned to Harry. "You don't need to say anything, but I'd appreciate it if you'd take us down the road. Out of hearing distance. You don't need to say anything. I don't need a comment or a question."

Harry took them down the road and stopped the truck. Never said a word, nothing. A song or two popped into his head, but he kept quiet. "Is this okay?" he asked.

"It's fine." She made no move to get out. Charlie looked ashamed. His head hung down.

Beth jumped out. The mother stayed put, excruciatingly so. She looked elsewhere, avoiding Harry's eyes. Harry opened the door and got out. He stood in the road. He pretended he needed to check his tires. Just stooping down to check here. Looking pretty good. A cry left his throat and he fell back. The smack that he heard was terrible, and more smacks followed. He fled backward, staring at the truck in horror, the awful thumps and hacking. Beth didn't seem to be bothered. She followed him as he stumbled backward down the black road. He coughed out something about her book reports. In the darkness she couldn't see the expression on his face. He hoped she couldn't hear the shaking in his voice. He asked her to recite one of her reports for him. Somehow he wasn't surprised that she could. He grasped at the words and held on tight, *Strawberry Girl by Lois Lenski. A book I like is Strawberry Girl by Lois Lenski. Strawberry Girl by Lois Lenski is the story of a girl who picks strawberries for a living. She lives with her mom and dad who pick strawberries for a living, too.* He held on. The hacks rose higher, like screams. *The colors of red strawberries can change from orange to clay to yellowish. Sometimes there isn't anything red about a red strawberry but it's still a red strawberry.* He knew the child wasn't showing off, she was helping him get through this. He concentrated on the words, *I like Strawberry Girl by Lois Lenski because it tells you a lot about strawberries,* but his grip was giving way. He couldn't hold on any longer, but the noises stopped, he caught his breath, and they went back to camp.

Nine

Jean found a place outside the tent and lay down. Each time she turned her head she had a surreal moment when the big silver bullet came into view. The light from the moon bounced off it. The man and woman were inside. It was quiet. She could almost pretend they weren't there. She wondered if she owed Harry an explanation of some kind about Charlie's lung disorder. The name of it had stayed back in Dayton and everyone, even Charlie, felt better for it. Charlie looked healthier and stronger, and he was certainly happier.

She went inside the tent and stretched beside her children. It was a big tent with sturdy framing. It had taken up a big part of the widow's walk-in closet. She could use Harry's help breaking it down. She remembered how the widow had almost balked after going to the trouble to advertise it. The widow had acted as if she were putting the tent up for adoption. Her eyes narrowed at Jean after each question and Jean had felt herself grow nervous, as if there were right and wrong answers about one's intentions concerning a tent.

The canvas sucked in, then flared out. A wind had kicked up, and with it blew in the sudden hint of perfume. The same perfume she had smelled in the widow's house, in the dead husband's closet. So now she saw it. The other woman had been here in the tent with the husband. She had always thought it odd the way the widow had sat her down and interviewed her. How strangely covetous of the tent the widow had been. Perhaps she was reluctant to let go of the symbol of her widowhood. Perhaps she liked kicking the tent, booting the other woman each night before she went to bed. Perhaps, growing older and ignored, she was reluctant to let go of this minor power she had over another's desire. "What *exactly* are you going to do with it?" the widow asked Jean suspiciously. What *exactly*, as if there were so many wicked things one could do with a tent.

The wind outside reminded her of Ohio. She heard a train in the distance and waited for its whistle. The train bore down and she jolted up and scrambled outside. For a second she twirled helplessly in a circle. "Get up, get up!" she whispered frantically to her children, dropping to her knees and pulling them from the tent until their limp arms sprang to life. They ran to the Rambler and she shoved them in. She tripped toward the road and found Harry there and she was shaking. "It's all right," he told her. "We're up high, we're not in a pour-in. Do you think I'd let you stay in a spot that would flood?" For a moment she was sorry she didn't treat him better. The rain twisted through and they sat in the Rambler and watched it. Water poured out in two spouts from the back of the red pickup. The rain beat against the aluminum trailer, its smooth silver like wet skin in the moonlight. She thought of the widow's husband and the other woman, in the rain somewhere, in their tent, far away, their skins wet. They would have been safe in the rain. They would have been far away. No one would ever know.

TEN

In the morning she and the man, this Leonard Dawson, had a talk.

"All my claims are staked and registered," Jean said. "I don't need to tell you that claim jumping is a crime." Jean said this, but all the while her mind was going through pictures of breaking down the tent, folding it up, and tying it to the Rambler's roof. Charlie's fifth grade teacher had helped her tie it securely to the roof, the perfect excuse for him to be there when she left. She could get Harry to help her with it for the ride back. She was imagining her mother's face when she saw them again.

Leonard Dawson laughed.

"I don't know what's so funny," Jean said.

"I'm going up high anyway," the man said. "I seen a plane been circling that rimrock." He tapped his forehead. Smart.

She remembered a photograph she had showed her mother and the screech of hysteria it had caused. A biplane was circling low into the canyons, its wings inches away from scraping the rock. The caption said, *Rimflyers are the daredevils of the uranium business, flying their planes low into canyons and scouting ledges for uranium beds. Dangerous business, but it can pay off.*

Leonard Dawson threw a pack into the bed of his pickup. "Wouldn't be circling if there wasn't something there." A blackened forefinger congratulated his noggin again. His wife, Josephine Dawson—Jo, she insisted—appeared in the trailer's doorway with a satchel of groceries. She was wearing a yellow party frock whose skirt she was pushing down like Marilyn Monroe in that famous photograph. She hopped down from the trailer with a girlishness Jean instantly noticed and considered fraudulent. Josephine smiled at her, brightly but timidly. Jean decided to ignore it.

In the distance came some blasts, not too loud, just little pops. She heard their minor key with some relief.

"What's that?" the man asked.

It was Harry out there building a toilet, but she didn't think she owed the man any kind of explanation.

"Is there a name for that rimrock?" the man asked.

"You'd have to ask Charlie," Jean said.

"Who's Charlie?"

Charlie and Beth had gone off with Harry. They had shovels and planks of wood, and the powder charges Harry had bought at the hardware store. All the while Jean pictured packing up the tent.

Leonard Dawson had climbed into his pickup and started it up. The truck lurched dramatically. He was giving it too much gas, afraid to stall out in front of her. She smirked, in case he was checking her in his rearview mirror. The pickup heaved down the escarpment and was gone.

The two women were left alone. Josephine Dawson stood, obediently lost, as if mislaid at her end of the campsite. The Marilyn Monroe imitation was over, but this new lost-little-lamb act irked Jean just as much. If Josephine Dawson expected help in the form of concrete orders that she could obey (Why don't you help me with this tent? Why don't we make sandwiches for the kids? Why don't you quit smiling at me?), she was sadly mistaken.

"So what do we do now?" Josephine Dawson said. Half a joke, but half not.

Jean shrugged. She threw a couple of canteens in a backpack, put on the Mexican field hat she had bought at a trading-post filling station in Colorado (Beth had begged to stop at every single one), and set off toward the place where a new toilet should be waiting. She hoped the children had stayed at a safe distance while Harry lit his charges. She was sure Harry had good intentions but they might not go together with competence. Josephine Dawson was sitting on the trailer step, looking defeated. She rolled the ends of her hair around a brush curler. She could wield a brush curler with an Oscar-winning deflation. Jean was sure this lost soul had hoped for a friend. She couldn't blame her for that.

She found the kids and made them drink more water even though they claimed they had just had some, but she didn't trust Harry on that score. Beth had learned a new word, *detonation*, and seemed anxious to use it in every possible sentence. They were completing the toilet, laying down the planks of wood. At least it would be there for someone else.

"While we're out here, we might as well stake a few more claims," Harry said.

"I've already staked as many as I want to," she said.

Beth said, "Yes, Mom, we should at least stake one before we leave."

"Did you bring any empty cans of chili con carne?" Harry asked. She noted his irony and his inability to take it any further and capitalize on his exposure of her. It was the reason she liked him and the reason she would never like him more. She walked back to the camp to gather up the empty pop bottles. She roped together some stakes as well. They were there, Harry had bought them; she might as well use them. She rummaged through food in the back of the station wagon. She grabbed cans of fruit cocktail and spaghetti. The fruit cocktail would be too hot, the spaghetti too cold. Josephine Dawson sat watching on the trailer step. This time she was removing the brush curler from her hair. She was still trying to smile. Jean was about to go to Harry's truck and retrieve the pistol when Josephine Dawson spoke: "Looks like fun."

The girlishness irked Jean, but she also heard the tremor in Josephine

Dawson's voice. It had taken some effort to try again. Jean decided at this point it would constitute meanness not to invite her along, and meanness would put her on the same side of the fence as that husband.

"Do you want to join us?" she asked.

Jo leaped up. Didn't shrug and say, "I suppose so." "If you insist." Didn't look around as if checking on something important before she could decide. Didn't say, "Yes, thank you," with a tepid tea-party enthusiasm. She leaped from the stairs like a hungry doe, dispensing with language altogether. She never said a word as she scrambled to join an already departing Jean. Jean quickened her pace to keep a little ahead because she could sense this pressure, this ballooning inside Josephine Dawson, she could just feel it, almost touch it. Josephine Dawson was bursting with things to say, and Jean was afraid the first sentence would go something like "I know what you must think of my husband," and then that would start it, the story of the marriage and either all its problems or all its justifications, or both, and it would never stop gushing out. Jean was unable to ditch her, however. Somehow the yellow frock and heeled sandals and the stakes she had flung over her shoulder didn't prevent her from maintaining a quick step. They walked side by side, but Josephine Dawson offered not a single comment, or single word, or even a single attention-getting throat clearing, all of which Jean appreciated.

The sand gave way to hardpack flayed open by dryness and heat. The crust of the hardpack was papery and curled up. Like a sunburn peel, she thought. Even the nonliving was tortured out here. The rain the previous night had skittered off the top. Nothing had soaked in.

The children sounded close by, but they were a ways off. She could hear a conversation. They laughed at something Harry said. "Where'd you go?" she called out. Then Beth appeared on an outcropping and waved them over. Jean checked out her son, leaning back against the rock. Sometimes Charlie grew tired and wouldn't admit it. The initial stage was hidden to others because it looked so much like an increase in thoughtfulness. Charlie caught her looking at him and glared.

Josephine Dawson spoke. "So, hello," she said with a friendly but nervous smile. "Officially, I mean. I hope we can all be friends." She fell hopefully silent after this.

Jean pulled at the bundle of stakes. "Do I just put one in?"

"Hi. Me, too," Beth said, waving to Josephine Dawson.

"You're going to stake a claim here?" Harry asked. He pulled off his boater and wiped his forehead.

"Why not?"

"It's just dirt, Mom," Charlie said.

Harry suggested they keep walking until they got to some slickrock, and not just sandstone, something with some colors in it. "What color do you like?" Jean asked. "I like black," Harry said. They marched across the scrabble, heads down. They climbed over a mound of slickrock until they came to some interesting pockets and mushroom domes. Charlie suggested his own bethometer system to measure out the claim, which Jean knew from her pamphlet studies was six hundred by fifteen hundred feet. She didn't want to disappoint him but she didn't want Beth trudging along elevated rock with rope tied around her ankles. Instead, they followed Harry as he stepped off the measurements.

"This doesn't seem right to me," she said. "Are you sure this is the right way to do it?"

"Oh yeah," Harry told her, "anyone who's been here for a while knows what to do."

"I don't think Lenny knows what to do," came a surprising voice. Josephine Dawson had been careful all this time to position herself at the tail end. So she wouldn't be interfering, Jean guessed. She never breathed heavily, so Jean had stopped noticing her. Jean didn't see how Harry had any sense of the distance with the steep faces and elevation changes, but who was she to pass out instructions?

"This just doesn't seem right to me," she said.

At each corner of the claim they pounded in a stake. After stepping off all four corners, Harry announced it was time for the soda-pop bottle. Should they do grape, orange, or RC? On a piece of paper Harry wrote out their first claim notice: *June 2, 1954*. "And what's the name of this claim?"

"Something with love in it," Josephine Dawson suggested.

"H_2O," Charlie said.

"H_2O sounds good," Jean said.

"Love of water," Josephine Dawson agreed. "Perfect!"

Charlie did the honors. He wrote down H_2O, then rolled up the paper and tapped it into the neck of the pop bottle. They stuck the bottle into the sand around a scrub root and secured it further with a flat rock. Harry recorded the information in his notebook in case they wanted to register it officially at the assessor's office. "You'll have to do a hundred dollars' worth of assessment work each year to keep this claim," he warned, popping shut the notebook.

"Oh fine, Harry, fine," Jean said.

In the middle of their claimed territory the children found a shallow cave. All of them sat inside for a while and cooled off. Jean brought out the cans of spaghetti and fruit cocktail, and Josephine Dawson told them she'd be glad to cook supper for everyone, she'd fried extra potatoes last night. They lay back groggy in the cave and perhaps each of them at different times drifted away for a few minutes or more.

There was a coziness as they all awakened. Harry stretched and left the cave for a break. The subject of the children's father was bound to come up. Josephine Dawson asked why the children called their father Harry. "He's not our father," Charlie said. Jean wished this woman had saved such a conversation for later. "Their father is deceased," she said, meaning that's it, end of discussion.

"I'm sorry."

A mistake to continue, but Jean found herself adding this: "It was a long time ago."

"How did he die?"

"Suddenly. An aneurysm."

"He was old?"

"He was young. He had a defect no one knew about until it killed him."

"I wasn't even born yet," Beth said.

"I was pregnant." She kicked herself for giving in to Josephine Dawson's unspoken curiosity.

"Harry's their stepfather?" Josephine Dawson asked. "Uncle?" Her face grew not quite scandalized: intrigued.

"He's a salesman," Beth said.

Jean smiled. It occurred to her that Harry could have saved them all a lot of trouble by borrowing one of the Geiger counters from his truck. They could have found uranium that way. They'd spent all afternoon on this one claim that probably held as much uranium as her gravel driveway back home, now blacktopped if her mother's postcard was true. Charlie's fifth grade teacher had wanted to blacktop it for her, another of his offers.

She remembered the staged photograph from one of her information pamphlets: the happy family with their Lucky Strike. So now she'd been sucked in, too. Of course there was no uranium. Harry's Geiger counter would have proved that. Over and over. Claim after claim. She looked at her son's happy face. It had been at the tip of her tongue to berate Harry for not making it easy on them with a Geiger counter when all along he'd done the right thing. But it was hot out. So hot and getting hotter, even in this cave. The sun did things to one's brain. By the time they got back to camp she was wilted and struggling not to show it. She could still do what needed to be done, but she was too tired to take Charlie far enough away that Josephine Dawson couldn't see or hear. A boulder in the camp fitted Charlie perfectly and he walked over to it and hugged it. He was too exhausted himself to hide it. She set into her hard thumping with her palm. Directly in their line of sight, Josephine Dawson set up her stove. She caught the look on Josephine Dawson when the face peered up from cooking, the stirring spoon paused in midstir. Jean had expected pouty-mouthed mugs of sympathy, but the expression on Josephine Dawson's face was neutral and observant.

At the grocery store in town she had bought cheap housedresses, the coolness of the flimsy material a blessing. She sponged Charlie off and he didn't protest, and she handed him the sleeveless housedress, which he put on. Josephine Dawson dragged over lawn chairs and there was a housedress for her as well since Jean had about ten of the cheap things, clearance items mixed in a bin, and they all sat in housedresses except Harry. They ate the macaroni and cheese and fried potatoes Josephine Dawson had prepared and Jean had to admit it was one of the best meals she'd ever eaten. They heard blasts way in the distance, from Paul Morrison's mining camp. It was like Fourth of July for the blind, and her daughter got to begin and end her day on a new word: *detonation*.

ELEVEN

While the grownups napped in the cave, Charlie showed Beth what he had found. Carved on the stone wall was a stick figure in a big cowboy hat. One stick arm was extra long in order to reach the reins of his horse. The horse had a friendly smile scraped back from its bit. Underneath was the deep scratch of a name: *Rawhide Joe 1881*. They didn't tell the others. Beth thought of Rawhide Joe as her secret weapon. In the morning, whether Jo's husband would be there or not, it didn't matter. She had this avenging ghost.

But Jo's husband didn't come back and in the morning when Harry said he had to make a delivery and would they like to accompany him, Jo hopped in, too. Some squeezing was now involved with an extra person, but there was room for bodies behind the front seat. Beth sat on the tire jack. Every time she put her hands down she touched another paper bag full of screws or tiny springs. Her feet kept slipping on the torn covers of magazines. Harry was in a good mood with two grown women on board. He kept apologizing for wearing underwear as his shirt.

They were on the road to town, their only byway. After an hour of hard driving, Harry veered off. A narrow trail strayed across the sand between the scrub bushes. The trail got softer not harder and the truck thumped and lurched. Harry stopped the truck and cached some of his heaviest equipment at a little oasis. The few junipers and froggish cacti would have qualified as a dead spot in the lush area around their home in Dayton, but here in the desert the brief dull swatch of green seemed like a prospering forest. Jo helped Harry unload. She seemed anxious to help at all times. It didn't matter that her dress was getting dirty. Beth found something exciting in the sight of Jo's princess dress marred by red clay. She looked like a movie heroine shot in the stomach. *Her name is Jo,* she sat down and wrote in her latest letter. *Last night she made us macaroni-n-cheese. This morning she fried potatoes. We went detonating yesterday with Harry. We detonated a big hole for a toilet and then put wood around it. Her husband is a stinker Grandma like you call people but as long as he's not around we're having fun. There's something wrong with Harry's truck and we're stuck out in the desert so I'm sitting down in the shade and I have time to write.*

Harry called Charlie over and said, "Looky here." He bent down and released some air from the tires. "Makes her ride better in the sand. A little trick." He smiled up at Charlie. They climbed back aboard Harry's truck and plodded through the sand on the flabbier tires, and then they were on rock again and starting to climb. It took Harry another hour to go not very far, engine gunning, one jerk at a time. Her mother and Jo elected to walk it. The jolting and the drop-offs were making them ill. Beth watched them to see if they were talking to each other, but her mother's head was down and she marched on alone.

In the distance Beth saw yellow bulldozers, drill rigs, and scurrying figures whose heads glinted in the sun. Though high up, the mining operation was sunk in a volcano-like mouth. At the edge of the camp Harry stopped the truck and stepped outside to fix himself. He washed his face and neck with a hand cloth, cleaning them but also bestowing on his cheek a streak of red dirt that hadn't been there before. He bent over, whisked his hair forward as if beating flames from it, then combed it all back and smoothed it with his palm. He opened up one of his shirt packets from Mel's Cleaners and buttoned it over the undershirt he had apologized for wearing. He swept his arms through the seersucker jacket that

Jo was kind enough to hold out for him, found the bow tie in the pocket, and clipped it on. Jo must have seen the smudge on his cheek because of the way she smiled at him, but she didn't say anything. Beth was glad to see her mother hand him a canteen. Harry considered it for a few moments, then took a swig.

The mining camp looked like a lost city flipped on its head. Exposed were its roots, the tangle of rock spires and pinnacles and the clumps of meaty red buttes. It seemed that all the machinery was in futile service to right it properly.

Hardly anyone in the camp looked up as the International Harvester trundled in. Shuttle cars rode tracks deep into the earth. Above the tunnel was a sign: *Beware Bigfoot's Radon Daughters Loose in This Mine.* Harry was here to deliver a new belt for the ventilation fan down in the mine but he said it was a trivial thing. The ventilation fan was just government regulations about radon. In truth the Navajo lung could handle anything. The Navajos made money on their lungs, side wagers on whose breath would push the needle of the Geiger counter the farthest and register the highest radioactivity.

Jo turned to everyone with a smile. "Lenny said the Indians have a lot bigger lungs than normal people."

"All the more reason why they shouldn't be breathing in radioactivity," her mother said.

"They don't have bigger lungs," Charlie said. "The Quechua Indians have bigger lungs."

"Who are they, Charlie?" Jo asked.

"They live up high in the Andes."

"The Andes Mountains?"

"That's right," her mother said.

"Navajos can go up high," Jo said. "That's why they use them on skyscrapers."

"That's the Mohawks. The Navajos go down low."

"You're just saying that," Jo said.

"Harry, what are you up to now?" came a voice, and Harry bowed his head so he could murmur, "Owner," undetected.

A man came climbing up to them, pushing through the sand with huge leisurely strides. He was dark and handsome and everything about him was big. He was dressed for an African safari. Harry jumped away and ran zigzagging toward the back of his truck. Harry's leaping off like a chased animal was sudden and bizarre, and it made Beth's mother and Jo laugh. The man smiled and ducked his head in greeting before veering toward Harry. They were on top of a hill with nothing around for shade. Beth was starting to feel like a shiny nickel in the sun, shinier and shinier and more beat up. She watched Harry tear things from his truck. She wondered what was going on with him.

The man took off his African safari hat and wiped away his sweat with a bandana. He wiped his eyes, which emerged wide open yet wearied. He scoured each of his fingers, twisting them through the bandana, and when Harry still hadn't finished, he walked over to Beth's mother and Jo and offered them his scrubbed-clean hand. "My name's Jimmy Splendid," he said. "How do you do?"

"You're the man in charge," her mother said.

"I'm the man in charge." His voice reminded Beth of the voice you would use to a sick baby. He said *how do you do* as if the words were *there there now*. The tone didn't seem at all to fit what he was saying yet it did make Beth, languishing in the heat, feel a little better. Maybe the man was just tired and this was his tired voice.

"Here it is!" Harry cried out.

Jimmy Splendid signaled to a group of men, and they came over to get the fan belt. They were Navajos, dressed all in mismatched white men's clothes.

"I've got two of them," Harry said.

"We'll take both," Jimmy Splendid said.

Harry began talking fast and excitedly about the stuff unloaded on the ground. The rush of his words wasn't like salesman patter, more like someone trying to beat the buzzer. The buzzer was probably someone always saying *shut up* to him. Beth wondered who in his life this buzzer had been. Maybe his grandfather? She liked Harry. She didn't have to think of him as an adult at all.

Harry was rushing to say that he had several of these portable compressors by dad and would be delighted to unburden himself of them. He'd come a long way by dad to deliver just a fan belt. Jimmy Splendid interrupted him here and said, "Not just any fan belt, Harry. *My* fan belt." Well, yes, Harry knew that of course, that's what he meant. And two fan belts at that, Jimmy Splendid added, and no he didn't need any compressor bits. "Not the bit," Harry began. "Don't need 'em," Jimmy Splendid interrupted. A blush reddened Harry's face, and the dirt streak on his cheek brightened into war paint. Jimmy Splendid looked up from a gold cigarette lighter he had taken out to study and said, "All right, have the boys go through their tool sets with you. We're short on stoop labor supplies."

"You can always use a shovel," Harry said.

"We can always use a shovel," Jimmy Splendid agreed.

"People don't . . ." Harry paused. "In the midst of all the . . . Shovels are important," he finally said. He scurried off with the Navajos. Beth saw Charlie take a step toward Harry and the group of Navajos, but Harry was so nervous and excited he forgot about Charlie and about how maybe he'd like to tag along. She could guess how bad Harry would feel if he figured it out later.

Jimmy Splendid lingered behind. Under the strong sun the gold cigarette lighter blazed in his hand. He began working on it with a key-chain screw. He said something like, "Think I'll catch my breath for a minute," and her mother answered something like, "Might as well." His head stayed down, aimed at the cigarette lighter, but his eyes were watching them. Beth knew that trick; everyone in her class at school knew it.

After a good spell, he lifted his head. "Well, I find myself not quite understanding this situation," he said.

Nobody answered him. Beth might have liked to answer him, but she had no idea what he was talking about.

"How about you?" he suddenly asked Beth, and she felt her face about to burst into flames. Everything about Jimmy Splendid had a frightening authority. Even his handsomeness was authoritative. His face laid down the official rules of handsomeness and all these other faces were breaking the rules.

Jo came over and put a hand on each of her shoulders. "Young man," Jimmy Splendid said, turning to face Charlie. He walked over and held out his hand. Charlie looked at it, and then slowly reached out to shake it. "There you go." Charlie began to pull out of the handshake, but Jimmy Splendid wasn't done. He held on to Charlie's hand. "And are you taking care of these women?"

"I guess," Charlie said. He watched his hand, waiting for Jimmy Splendid to let go. He sneaked a helpless glance at Beth.

"Quiet," Jimmy Splendid said. "Right? Quiet and observant."

"He doesn't miss a thing," her mother said.

"So you're the man to ask," Jimmy Splendid said. "And what's the name of this man to ask?"

"Charlie," her mother said.

"Charlie. And you're Charlie's mom."

"Yes I am."

"Charlie's got good hands," Jimmy Splendid said, finally letting go. "You know what I do, Charlie—"

"No," Charlie said.

Jimmy Splendid chuckled. "Before I hire a man, I shake his hand and I take a study of that hand in the palm of my own, and I find out what I need to know. Charlie, whenever you want, you've got a job with me."

What Beth liked about her mom was that she didn't step in when Charlie declined to respond to this.

"I guess what I'd really like to know, Charlie: Would I have a job with you?"

Charlie didn't answer for a few moments. "We'll see," he said.

Jimmy Splendid laughed heartily and flipped the cigarette lighter in his hand. He probably didn't have much chance to enjoy himself if some exchange like this, which made absolutely no sense to Beth, was giving him so much delight. He reached in his shirt pocket and still chuckling pulled out a metal case and snapped it open for Jo who said no thank you and her mom who quickly plucked a cigarette. Her mother avoided cigarettes. Meat and cigarettes. She avoided meat because there were too many things that could go wrong, even a little thing: Suppose the cow had the flu? Vegetables didn't get the flu or get herniated or cough up blood. Her reason for avoiding cigarettes was that they clogged up the lungs. Who runs *into* a house filled with smoke?

Avoiding meant avoiding, however, not refusing altogether. When hamburgers were on the grill and the line couldn't be avoided, she picked up a paper plate with the rest of them. If someone passed her a cigarette, she lifted her chin for a light.

Jimmy Splendid acted like a simple handshake with Charlie constituted magic. He acted like he knew everything now about everybody.

Harry was back at his truck. He pulled out a grocery box marked *Good & Plenty* and handed it to a Navajo. Now Beth could see that although Jimmy Splendid was tall, he was no taller than Harry. In fact, Harry was taller, but Jimmy Splendid was very strong-looking and big around the chest, and of course handsome in that policeman or soldier way, not wobbly you-can-laugh-at-me handsome like Harry. People were talking about her. She could hear her mother saying something about Beth collecting information for book reports because they left school a bit prematurely this year.

"What else do you know about Charlie?" To her own surprise Beth added her own voice to the voices she was hearing.

Jimmy Splendid fixed a scrutinizing gaze on her and it was so unnerving she thought she might faint, which would be all right, everyone would just blame the heat and she'd have an excuse for her audacity. "I think that's a good question," Jimmy Splendid said, slowly unwrapping a lazy, contagious smile that convinced everyone else to smile at her. She thought she might burst into tears.

He took Charlie's hand and displayed it next to his big muscular one. His point wasn't clear. Beth was beginning to get uneasy. "Look there," he said. "Our hands have the same symmetry. You play the piano, Charlie?"

"No," Charlie mumbled.

"You could," he said.

"Charlie's good with his hands," her mother said. Charlie pulled away and returned his hands to his pockets. The sleeves of his T-shirt flagged loosely around his thin arms. Jimmy Splendid acknowledged that Charlie was not the most sizable fellow around, but his hands were wide and the fingers graceful. Charlie allowed his hands to be pulled from his pockets and put on exhibit again as Jimmy Splendid explained what he meant. His voice was the one thing about Jimmy Splendid that didn't scare Beth, and as he spoke about things boding well for Charlie his words wove a blanket of comfort and when he asked everyone to stay for lunch, Beth cried yes before the invitation was completed. "Don't get too excited," Jimmy Splendid laughed. "It's just hot dogs and baked beans." But Beth had been wanting a hot dog ever since seeing those shriveled-up ones in the Grand Vu Theater. The Navajos kept on their hard hats and carbide lamps while they ate. They sat on the ground and leaned back against heavy-looking canvas sacks that nonetheless looked soft enough to massage their backs. Jimmy Splendid asked Beth if she knew what was in the sacks. Flour? Beth guessed. Uranium ore, all crushed into powder. Something for one of her book reports.

Harry and a worker were checking off the supplies Harry had unloaded. Jo went over to him with a plate of food but Harry said he had to get air in the tires first and he drove over to a huddle of vehicles.

"You probably didn't believe me when I said hot dogs for lunch," Beth heard Jimmy Splendid say to her mother. "Sorry it couldn't be more."

"It's very nice," her mother said.

"I'll have to make it up to you. In fact I could do that this evening."
Jimmy Splendid added that he was off to town. He said they should all
ride to town with him. Her mother thanked him for the offer but said
they didn't live in town, they lived at a campsite. Jimmy Splendid's head
cocked and he waited for her to continue but she didn't. Finally he said,
"Not that polyg camp up the road from town?"

Her mother paused for a few moments. "No," she said.

Harry had returned just as Jimmy Splendid was saying how it
amazed him what kind of squalid conditions passed as a nice place to settle down to polygs, no offense Harry. It sounded like a football play, the
no offense Harry. Jimmy Splendid said women shouldn't be out there
wherever they were and where the heck were they Harry? Another football play, the where the heck Harry.

Beth took out her letter in case she got brave enough to ask Jimmy
Splendid to mail it for her when he went to town. The envelope was already addressed and affixed with an *ATOMS FOR PEACE* stamp. She
just had to finish it. The Navajos had gone back to work and she picked
one of their spots and leaned against a canvas sack. *Guess what Grandma?*
I'm sitting against a sack of uranium ore. It's radioactive. Bye. I have to go now.

Jimmy Splendid's new idea was that Harry could break down their
camp and pack it up and the rest of them could go into town. Jo's eyes
flitted back and forth, trying to figure what side she should be on. As
they stood up and brushed themselves off, Jimmy Splendid mentioned
that he was also the sheriff in town. Her mother laughed outright at this,
and Jimmy said no really, but Beth thought he was looking like he'd
rather not convince her, he'd rather go on hearing her laugh. Her mother
said they had to get back, she didn't want to miss work. "What work?"
Harry asked. Her mother didn't like that and gave Harry a look and said
they'd better get going. Jimmy Splendid walked them to the truck. He
tried to drop behind but her mother didn't drop back with him so he

moved up and touched her arm and when she turned around he seemed at a loss. "Well I've got these for everyone," he said.

He gave one to Jo and one to Beth. Beth looked down at a thin white painter's hat in her hands. *R&R Mining* was written on it. It wasn't as nice as the turquoise cowboy hat she had begged for at one of the trading posts, but it was still nice. "Charlie, take care of these ladies," Jimmy Splendid said, passing him a hat. Beth's letter to her grandmother was in her hands, there for Jimmy Splendid to see, but he was not good at reading her mind and she couldn't get up the nerve to ask him. Her mother was looking at the new hat in her hands. "I'll see you," Jimmy Splendid said to her mother, waving his hand casually here and there as though the slickrock seats and the chairback sacks of uranium powder were part of a Parisian café both of them were likely to be frequenting, "around."

TWELVE

Several weeks earlier a stone had kicked up and cracked the windshield of the International Harvester. Within a couple of days the crack had lengthened and grown a curve. It hadn't taken too much inventiveness to detect the shape of Utah there on the glass. As soon as Harry was able to imagine that, his old toy soldiers came to life, marching their leaden way back and forth across the windshield through the towns he had grown up in. He was happy to have his old friends returned to him, the buglers and the flag bearers, the Johnny Rebs. But in keeping him company they also stripped him down to loneliness. He was about at the end. Then there came the mother and these two children. And now there was Jo. Harry wondered how he had ever made it these past six years, traveling alone. The crack all of a sudden was starting to bother him.

On their way back from Jimmy Splendid's he stopped the truck at the cache point and refueled from one of the large canisters he had stored. Jo helped him lift the canister. "I guess you two can handle it?" the mother said. The gasoline gurgled in. He and Jo were frozen in awkward positions, straining to angle the canister into the gas tank. They watched the mother and Charlie trudge away.

"They're off again," Jo whispered.

Harry nodded.

"You don't know what it is?"

Harry shook his head again. He took this exchange of confidences as an opportunity to lean closer. "Has she talked to you?"

"She's hardly said more than hello to me. She hates me."

"She likes you. That's just the way she is."

"How long have you known her?"

"Three days."

Jo smiled.

"Three or four. You get a sense of her pretty quick."

The mother and Charlie were still visible as bobbing heads over the scrub pine.

"That'll do," Harry said, easing the canister down. He looked around for Beth, but she was off somewhere. He started loading up the equipment. He had done pretty well at Splendid's camp. He fantasized about selling it all, all at one stop, every single compressor, that would be something, wouldn't it, then going back for another full load, selling all of that, and all the detection instruments and jackhammers, and give us every single shovel and pick you got, too, Harry. He could start thinking like that and it could be like some game he was addicted to. That must have been what had kept him going all this time. Just one time, selling every single thing in his truck at one place. The game seemed pretty stupid in light of all the bad things in the world. Of course he could tell himself that, but the game was still important to him and he kept on playing it. Just like selling that whole box of Good & Plenty back at Splendid's—his heart had spun with the thrill of it. He had figured out this thing, that Navajos like licorice, and taken a chance on it and boom, just like that, a bushel of it sold! Tomorrow he was going to a new mining camp to try out his luck. Maybe Jo would go with him. Something was wrong with Charlie yet he was thinking of Jo and he was thinking of the two of them traveling in his truck together and he was thinking how beautiful she was and how he was waiting for her to tell him about her terrible, unhappy marriage. And how he kept expecting her words to come out in a Southern drawl. She had that look. And how he was still a little caught out each

time she spoke and there was a clip instead of a softening. Yet he was also
convinced that he was in love with the mother. He could go back and
forth, shocked at how easy it was, worried that he had polygamy in the
blood. Traits were passed down in families, he knew that. Believing that
polygamy qualified as a trait was foolish—he knew that, too—yet he often felt foolish enough to believe anything. He resembled his mother in
almost every way, physically, emotionally. She had hated in secret the
whole idea of celestial marriage. Harry had always wondered what he and
his father had in common, what little thing. Harry couldn't even throw a
ball the regular way; he was the only man he knew who couldn't cock it
like a guy. He always thought fate was trying to make it perfectly clear to
him that he should stay away from his father's habits.

"I'm surprised to find someone like you out here," he finally said to Jo.

"Why's that, Harry?" she asked, her voice still a surprise to him.

"I don't know. You seem . . ."

"I seem?" The way she helped him along. She'd gotten a lot of this.
Attention, that is. She probably got attention wherever she went.

"Oh, a party girl."

"A party girl? I'm not a party girl."

That was the only way he could explain it to himself about Jo and the
man she had chosen to marry: a party (Georgian mansion, white columns,
martinis floating in buoyant rings across a swimming pool), having too
much fun, out of her head fun, and a revolting creature named Leonard
Dawson suddenly on the scene, resembling something acceptably good at
a moment when everything else seemed exceedingly wonderful.

"How did you meet him?"

Jo made a face. She peeked around the corner of the truck. "Where's
Beth?" she asked.

He shrugged. "She likes the shade."

"I was a farm girl, Harry. He got me off the farm. How many times
have you heard that story?"

"It doesn't have to be a permanent situation."

"I don't know about that, but it's the situation I'm in. It's not great. It's not even good. But it got me off the farm. All we did was work. I barely knew my dad was my dad. We were just his hired hands."

"You're stronger than you look. I guess that explains it."

"Not hired actually. He got us for free. I can tell you one thing: he was sorry to walk me down the aisle."

The Geiger counters and scintillators were last to go in. He always kept a few at the ready, just in case he met some hope-addled dogstakers along the road. He still couldn't believe himself back at the camp, how he had packed the fan belt way in the rear of the truck. He was always so careful—except whenever he had an opportunity to shoot himself in the foot. He couldn't remember a time when he hadn't made half a fool of himself in front of Jimmy Splendid—and now in front of the ladies, too. Everyone thought he just sold compressor bits, but he sold the whole compressor, too, and all the parts for the Chicago Pneumatic and Jagger. How many times had he tried to make that clear to Jimmy and Jimmy didn't listen? And now Jimmy had cut him off once again and Harry was reduced to selling him shovels—shovels!—all in front of the ladies. Maybe polygamy wasn't a trait, but by God ridiculous shovel-selling must be.

"Lot of stuff in this truck," Jo said.

"I have a new mining camp to go to tomorrow," Harry said. "Guess I'll try them out."

"I wish I'd been a man ten years older so I could have gone off to war. England or France or Germany. I would have stayed. I never would have come home. Do you believe that?"

"I believe you," Harry said.

"That's what I wish."

"I'm leaving this evening," Harry said.

"You're not staying the night?"

"Got to get a head start."

"I hope it pays off."

"I do, too."

"When will you be back?"

"I have a tent." Harry chanced a glance into her eyes. "You could go with me if you'd like."

"What, and leave my husband?"

"I'm a gentleman," Harry said. He'd always been quite sure of that whenever he'd said it before.

Jo fixed the pleats of her dress, removed a sandal, and shook out a stone. "Then I'd have to leave you, Harry. And then the next person and the next, all the way to England." She kept her head down, concentrating on the pleats.

THIRTEEN

At first the sessions with Charlie were like fights with a loved one: what followed was an aftermath of passionate craving. She and her husband had fought only once, a real fight, that is, beyond a disagreement. She could no longer remember what little thing had precipitated it, but she knew now that the true cause had been longing. When the fight ended, they had tumbled violently into each other. It devoured them for two days. She felt like one of the saints who fasted, continually near death from not letting any of the stuff of real life enter. She knew from that moment they were headed for either the fervent eager repeats of divorce threats or a fireless graceful marriage, for reasons absolutely contrary to anything she had been told. She had stumbled into the huge lie of romance and betrothal. None of her friends talked about it. If they were waiting for her to bring it up, time ran out and she was a widow with two babies.

At a younger age her children had wept often. They had clung to her so tightly as to reenter her and find the womb's safety. She wondered at these moments what passion she would have had left to give to her husband, had he still been alive. She was afraid, none. This new thing that had overtaken her, so carelessly coined as maternal love, it superseded everything, even recklessness, even pleasure, even the two of them combined.

Now when she and Charlie had their sessions they were no longer like lovers. They were parent and child at the dinner table, the child forced to finish his vegetables. There was stoicism but also rebellion. At the cache point Charlie followed her silently, stiffly, embarrassed and blaming her. She knew he wanted to help reload the truck with Harry and Jo. She took him to a draw of cottonwoods. Lavender tamarisk tangled between the trunks. By the end of the pounding she was sweating through her blouse and out of breath. Her own gasps were louder than Charlie's. This time she held him on her lap and hugged him until it must have hurt and when his arms reached tight around her and his head unburdened itself on her shoulder, she fell backward from the weight and they continued lying there embraced. The ground beneath her was damp, and it felt good out here in the desert. She remembered what had happened after the fight with her husband, how they had lain there on the third day embarrassed not about the fight but about this other thing that had exposed them. Neither one of them could bring it up. Neither one of them did. It was destined never to be repeated. Their inability to address it had mattered terribly at the time. She would spend the afternoons practicing conversations and the evenings failing to begin them. Now he was gone of course and had been for a long time and nothing that had happened with him seemed real anymore, the only reality was Charlie and besides when was it? almost eleven years ago that he had died not knowing about Charlie?—quite literally another lifetime ago and it was over and done with and—well. It still bothered her, this fact that she had never begun the conversation. It still mattered—at least as much as anything else mattered. It mattered. Everything mattered. She and Charlie were still lying there together and her back was soaked. It shouldn't have been a surprise that the ground was drenched and hiding it; she had learned that cottonwoods meant water. The last adhesive of ground crust gave way and she was sinking into spongy pulp. She described it to herself as it was happening. She was always using up her thoughts on other things. And she knew she needed to talk to Charlie. And she knew she wouldn't. She knew she never would.

FOURTEEN

It was now an official tradition: coming back to camp to a nasty surprise called Leonard Dawson. He who expects nothing is never disappointed, her mother often said. Beth never remembered this warning beforehand. Time and again she strode blindly into her disappointments, although disappointment wasn't the right word to use where Leonard Dawson was concerned. Maybe nausea.

Harry parked the truck on the road. Beth was glad to get her rear end off the tire jack even though the trip had been fun. Evening was getting on, but the sun was extra bright, the sky tightening its hold right before sunset. Jo looked a mess but in a good way. "I've got to get supper going," she said. Beth appreciated having this part of their lives taken care of since it was, after all, a pretty big part and nobody on their side had been doing much about it and she felt hungry and unsatisfied most of the time, so much so that her memory of the french fries at the Atomic Café had become the primary memory of her life, a three-day-old experience usurping several scrapbooks and years of fun.

The tent would be in the shade by now. She had a book to finish; it would feel good to lie down in the coolness and read. And when she looked up, there would be a nice dinner.

"Where have you been?" Leonard Dawson said.

Beth's heart jumped. *He who expects nothing . . .*

The way Leonard Dawson glared up from his lawn chair replicated exactly the first moment she had seen him. He went back to hunching over, staring between his legs, replicating the other movement he had performed that evening. Looking up, looking down, the only two things he could do. She would have to work something about a wind-up villain into one of her book reports. Much as she liked Lois Lenski, she was starting to feel stymied by just staying on the topic. She felt like the reports needed something more to fire them up.

At Leonard Dawson's feet were bottles of beer. No alcohol in Utah, none at all, yet everyone seemed to have loads of it. Because liquor was like the opposite of God here. If you could believe that God existed despite nothing in the way of proof, you could just as easily go in the other direction and believe that liquor did not exist despite the proof of bottles staring you in the face.

"I suppose you'd better go," Jo said to Harry.

"Yeah, I suppose you'd better go," Leonard Dawson said.

Harry picked up one of the fisted-up pieces of paper scattered over the campsite like snowballs.

"Get out of here, you stupid polyg. Stay away from my wife." The threat was delivered more to the ground than to Harry. Leonard Dawson's filthy head swayed back and forth in his filthy hands. Everything in the campsite shrank before his bad mood—even the campsite itself, in the way nothing moved, not a branch of the spineless piñon tree or the skittering dust on top of the dirt. The air, too, was heavy with a cowardly silence.

Her mother made some kind of motion with her bobbing head like stay away now, you kids. Harry left quietly. Beth and Charlie followed him and waved good-bye. Beth asked, "When will you be back?" and Harry put his finger to his lips. He held up two fingers, then three. The sun's setting beam narrowed and sharpened the way it did angling off their signaling mirrors and it came to Beth like that. As soon as Harry pulled away, Beth and Charlie ran to get their mirrors. The sun was almost ready to drop and when it got started it went down in a quick swallow. Charlie took his mirror and hid behind the camp. Beth started to climb. She knew her mother didn't want her up there. She and Charlie had measured the overhang at forty-five bethometers high, but with her ankles untied Beth had no problem scrambling it. She signaled with her mirror from the top. Charlie's signal came from behind the camp. They had practiced their own brand of Morse code: *Indians attacking! SOS!* That was all they had worked on, but it could fit almost every occasion, even this one. She angled the mirror, taking final advantage of the sun, and shot a beam of light onto the back of Leonard Dawson's neck.

Leonard Dawson slapped at it like a mosquito, jerked around, and looked up. She ducked her head. He sat back in the lawn chair and said to Jo, "I got an offer for a partnership."

"What does that mean, Lenny?"

"It means I found a man who's willing to grubstake me."

"That's wonderful if it's true."

"It's true."

The words bounced against the rock and came to Beth louder than if she were on the ground next to them. She could lie up here and observe him. The top of his head was not very round. She saw how his hair grew forward in greasy black filaments. His shoulders muscled up like a buffalo hump. His eyes, his hair, the forward set of his shoulders—everything about him was ready to pounce.

The sun had started to go. She angled another shot at the back of his neck.

"I'll tan your hide, little girl," he yelled, jumping up from the chair again.

She watched her mother stride to their unstated boundary line and stand there in front of him.

"Keep your brats under control."

"Lenny," Jo said.

"I mean it. I'll tan her hide."

"He doesn't mean it," Jo said. Her mother walked away, throwing a glance behind her. She went to the Rambler and scrounged inside. It was cans for supper again.

"The hell I don't," Leonard Dawson said.

Her mother kept her head inside the Rambler as long as Leonard Dawson's voice was raised for her benefit. As soon as he decided to shut up, she stood up from the Rambler with her cans and shut the door and went theatrically about the business of cooking dinner. She wove an upward gaze into her dinner-making movements, spotted Beth immediately, and said in an even less than normally loud voice, "Getting dark in a minute." Beth scooted back from the edge and started down. She heard Jo clear her throat.

"Lenny, tell me more about his offer."

"He's a bigwig in town. Owns his own plane and helicopter."

"That's nice. So he's an important person."

"That's what I've been trying to tell you."

"Why is he . . ." Jo's voice stopped.

"Why what?"

"Why . . ."

"Go ahead, say it. I know what you're trying to say."

"What am I trying to say, Lenny? You know more about how this works than me."

"Why is he interested in me? Is that it? Why is somebody so important stooping so low?"

"That's not what I meant."

"Someone like me. Imagine!"

"If he's already rich . . . And we're not. That's all I meant."

"Rich people spend their money and then they need more money to stay rich. Turns out his last claim was salted and he'd already bet on it. So now he's got me."

Silence. Presently: "What do you mean he's got you, Lenny?"

"Not like that, like he's trapped me. Quit putting words in my mouth. Do you think I can't look out for myself?"

"Why is he making you a partner, Lenny? Why doesn't he just hire you and pay you for your services?"

"My services! We're partners!"

Silence again.

"He gets rich, I get rich."

"He's already rich. Why does he need you?"

"And I told you. The rich need to get richer. So he needs a partner."

"You don't have enough to be a partner."

"I'm one of several partners."

"Oh, Lenny."

"No, no. No let's not do the *Oh Lenny* routine."

"What's the catch, Lenny?"

"*What's the catch, Lenny?* Okay, now we're doing that routine."

"What's the catch?" Jo demanded.

"There's no catch."

"You're not using any of our money?"

"You got to put in to be a partner. I know what you're thinking, but you got to put in to be a partner."

"What have you put in, Lenny?."

"This is a big opportunity. I can't let it slip by."

"What have you put in, Lenny?"

Beth was down on the ground, standing there watching. Her mother waved her over.

"I haven't put in any of *our* money yet. But I will. Do you remember where that money came from? I don't think she was your mother, but you sure don't mind taking it. He wants me to square it with you before he'll take it. That's the type of guy he is. So now I've squared it with you."

"No you haven't, and I'll tell him so."

"No you won't."

"I will, Lenny. That's our money and he just wants to take it for himself. You'll never see it again."

"I'll see that much and more. You can't be a partner without doing your part."

"That's something he told you. A little rhyme to make you believe him. He's brainwashed you."

"Nobody brainwashes me."

"Somebody has. How much money then? Answer me if it's nothing to be ashamed of."

"Two thousand."

"Two thousand! That's everything we have! It's all we have left in the world. That's it from your mother, Lenny. She's not going to die again and leave you more."

Beth realized that she and her mother and Charlie had arranged themselves into a funny-looking audience. They were standing in a line, same postures, same chins up, looking like roll call for gym class. When Leonard Dawson sprang up and waved his fists, all three of them scurried.

"You shut up now," he shouted. "You've said enough. I'm not taking your grief. Why do you always want to bring me down? You want me to fail. You want me down. Down."

"You can't spend this. It's all we have. I won't let you."

"You shut up or I'll make you shut up."

"You can't, Lenny."

"I don't care if kids are here or not, you shut up or I'll make you shut up." He blasted his fists one-two-three-four against the trailer. The detonations carried across the desert.

"You're horrible," she said.

"I'm horribly rich." He kicked the trailer, shoulder-butted the door, and went inside.

FIFTEEN

Late at night, with the children asleep, Jean still kept an eye on the trailer. It would explain something to her if Jo were to go inside to be with him. She was curious how it worked with other people. It wasn't so mysterious that Jo had married someone like Leonard Dawson—it didn't flabbergast her the way it did Harry, who was beside himself trying to figure it out. If Jo went inside to be with him in the trailer, that was all the figuring out Jean needed. She wouldn't blame her. In its own way it was something hard to resist.

But Jo stayed outside and sat on the trailer step, staring out. Now and then she turned and stared at Jean. She stared as if she had the freedom to, as if she couldn't be spotted in the dark. Yet they could see each other's faces pretty clearly. The moon was up and their eyes had adjusted. Jean thought Jo looked like some creature. She had stopped being a woman, a human. And in the way you watch any creature, Jean was waiting for it to make its move.

The creature looked right at her, then stood up and matter-of-factly moved away. In a few minutes it made its reappearance, stooping to pick up the wads of paper strewn over the campsite, returning them to a pile near the stove. It proceeded across the boundary line, melted into the darkness, and then reemerged, standing before Jean, an offering. Jean could smell it, that perfume that lifted off the tent. The tent was eight feet by eleven. It would be hell to pack up in the morning. "If you want, you can sleep in there," she said.

Jo played with the pleats of her dress. "I would really like something else to wear." With a flashlight Jean directed her to a corner of the tent piled with clothes she could choose from. When Jo reappeared, she was wearing a man's undershirt. "Does that feel better?" Jean asked. Jo put a blanket around her shoulders and sat outside with her. Jean wondered if she would remember this moment, this silence, this sky of stars. She wanted to. She didn't have faith that she would.

Sixteen

In the morning Beth woke up to Jo sleeping beside her, dressed in an old shirt. Jo had thrown the blankets off herself and her legs were bare. Beth was glad Charlie wasn't here to see, but who knew how long she had been sprawled like that.

The sun beat on the tent. The brown canvas was yellowish in some spots but black and opaque in others. It was already very hot and Beth could feel drops of sweat on her neck, yet when she touched her face the skin was dry. She wiped her face anyway and licked her fingers. She'd had a sweat test in the hospital and everything came out fine, but now she worried about giving off too much salt. Too much salt meant the visitor was coming. It sounded like a scary movie—the visitor is coming, the visitor is coming. Her mother was crazy to think her motherly way of putting it turned it into harmless fun.

She looked at her hand, glowing from the sun's presence inside the tent, and it was shaking. She tested her skin one more time to make sure. A wet spot splatted her forehead and she looked up at the tent's ceiling and the opaque black designs streaked over it. Then a drop fell on Jo.

Outside her mother was pulling stuff from the Rambler. She was taking everything out and arranging the items small to big on the flat rocks. "Good morning," she said to Beth. "All this dust. It gets in everything." Over the tent was laid a variety of wet underwear, her mother's dress, a towel. Her mother looked clean and fresh, and her hair was damp and hanging loose, and she was in a chipper mood.

"Good morning," Beth said. She blocked her eyes and stared at the ground until she got used to the light.

"Is she still asleep? You'd better wake her before he gets up." She nodded toward the silver trailer.

"Where's Charlie?"

"He's taking a walk."

"What?"

Her mother shrugged.

"Why is he taking a walk?"

"He's . . . That's what he wants to do."

Her mother was giving nonanswers again, which meant there was a secret involved. Beth hurried out of the campsite to the road, preparing herself to be outraged for missing out on something, but there was nothing there and no Charlie. She rubbed her eyes, then went back and sat on the rocks.

"Would you wake her up, please?" her mother asked.

"Okay," she said, still sitting.

The trailer door slammed open—*detonating the silence*—and the specter of Leonard Dawson filled the doorway. His shoulders were bunched up. Twigs and leaves seemed to be growing from his head, but it was just his muddy hair standing on end.

Her mother didn't turn around at the sound of the slammed door although her shoulders sagged and Beth heard her sigh. She continued pulling stuff from the Rambler.

"Where's my wife?"

Her mother kept on working, but next time she got yelled at she yanked around with a pickax in her hand. "I don't keep track of her," she told Leonard Dawson.

"I asked you a simple question. No reason to go off."

"And I answered you."

"Where is she then?"

"You know, sometimes women have hygienic issues they would like to keep private."

"I knew that excuse was coming up."

"Maybe she went to the movies then."

"That's very funny," he told her. He stomped off and disappeared behind the overhang.

"He doesn't mess with you," Beth said proudly.

"Oh no, he doesn't mess with me," her mother scoffed, flapping open the tent just as Jo's head peeked out.

"Quick!"

Jo emerged fully dressed and ran barefoot to the trailer. She stood there. Her arms flew out helplessly. "He'll never believe me!" she whispered.

Her mother pulled off the damp towel from the tent. "Use this for evidence."

Jo dashed back, tiptoeing over some prickles, and took the towel. Then, seeing Beth's mother's wet hair, she grabbed one of the bottles of water, leaned over, and poured it over her head.

"You're using up all my good water," Beth's mother said.

"You used it."

"It's my water."

"I'm sorry. It's an emergency."

"Calm down," Beth's mother said. "You're heaving like you're up on a trapeze."

Beth pushed sandals into Jo's hands, and Jo hopped into them as she staggered toward the trailer, too afraid to stop. She was stretching the clothesline when Leonard Dawson walked back into camp. "There you are," Jo said cheerily in one of the worst examples of acting Beth had ever witnessed. "I wondered where you went." She flamboyantly toweled at her hair before throwing the towel over the line. ". . . let this towel dry off," she mumbled helpfully. "Thanks for the shampoo!" she shouted over.

Her mother didn't react, which was actually the best acting so far.

Leonard Dawson said, "Where'd you get the water?" and Beth expected the worse.

Jo said, "Sometimes if you're nice to people, Lenny..." and she sounded pretty convincing, like all of a sudden she'd gotten into her role.

"So you had a good shower."

"I can't write home about it, Lenny."

"Someday you'll be able to. I'll get you everything you want. I'm going to make it big. That's a promise." Then again, Leonard Dawson was so bad at his own performances it was no surprise he couldn't detect a tin delivery in others. Though his anger the night before had been real, it had sounded exaggerated and false, and now this, his morning smooth talk, was just as bad. He strutted about his props, his truck and his trailer and his big heavy tools, like an actor auditioning to play his own life.

Sometimes Beth's teachers were like that. Now and then duty called upon them to impersonate people of wisdom and give lectures about life and the detonations of behaving badly, and it was so obvious they were acting. The one exception was Mr. Jackson. Beth hadn't had him yet, but Charlie said his lectures about life and the dangerous ripples of cheating always involved his own experiences and sometimes took place in fighter planes where cheaters nearly cost people their lives, and they were good stories, every single one. Mr. Jackson was the fifth grade teacher, and he had continued to look out for Charlie through sixth grade. Whenever Mr. Jackson played basketball with the seventh and eighth grade boys, he made sure to install Charlie as the scorekeeper. Beth ate her lunch in the gym so she could watch. Mr. Jackson liked to take long shots from so far away no one would think to guard him. None of the boys could even throw the ball that far, much less get it in the basket. Right before sending up a set shot, one of Mr. Jackson's hands would break free and push up his eyeglasses and then he would finish aiming and shoot. By then everyone was already yelling, *Shoot! Shoot!* When the balls went in, which they did almost half the time, there came wild cheers and stomping on the bleachers.

Though his name was Mr. Jackson, one day when he phoned their house he identified himself as Kenny, as if he were a boy, and that was when Beth understood. The only problem with Mr. Jackson was that Beth thought he was a little old for her mother. Somebody said he was thirty-eight. Somebody else said he was forty.

Leonard Dawson announced for all to hear that he was packed up and ready to go off and guarantee their future. Jo didn't say anything and only limply complied with his kiss and the dramatic sweep of his hug. He bad-acted getting into the pickup and he bad-acted starting it up. The pickup bumped through the campsite with more bad-acting roars, and when two men appeared out of nowhere carrying a large keg, Leonard Dawson didn't stop. The pickup barreled through faster, the engine revving. The men tried to dodge and were thrown off balance, enough that the keg dropped from their hands and rolled in front of the pickup. The pickup kept going. The keg was knocked down the small rise to the road and out of sight.

Beth ran with the two men to the road. The keg had rolled beyond the road and over the rocky drop-off. It rolled slowly, jolted from one boulder to another, almost stopping until another jolt got it going again. Finally the wedge between two boulders caught it. The two men were already right behind it, lightly scampering down the rocks. They checked out the keg, pushed it from the wedge, then heaved it up. They climbed half a step before setting it down with a shake of their heads. Beth looked beside her and there was Navajo Joe, his unseen arrival another magic-curtain trick. Beside him stood Charlie. And now Jo and her mother arrived and looked down.

"Is everyone all right? Are you all right, Charlie?" her mother asked.

"There goes our water," Charlie said.

"That was our water?" Beth asked. "Now what are we going to do?"

Navajo Joe went to his truck and unloaded two sawhorses. He was wearing Beth's favorite shirt, his red shirt that wasn't red. The two men climbed back to the road. Each went to Joe and received a sawhorse. Beth saw that they were Navajos, too, and they wore mismatched white men's clothes just like the ones at Jimmy Splendid's camp. The men walked the sawhorses into camp.

"Where do you want these?" Navajo Joe asked.

"Where do I want what?" her mother asked.

Navajo Joe didn't answer.

"What are they?" her mother asked.

"For your water buffalo." He nodded toward the keg down below.

"It's down there," her mother said.

"I'll be back with another one," he said. He climbed into his truck.

"No, no, that's too much," her mother said. "Let's forget about it."

"Just down the road," Navajo Joe said. "A short trip." He backed into the clearing and got his truck turned around. The two men returned and jumped in, and Joe started off. The truck moved slowly enough that Beth's mother could walk beside it.

"Wait," she said. "Just wait a minute. I don't need it."

"The little girl wants it," Navajo Joe said.

Beth watched her mother and the truck moving together at the same speed. It formed a nice picture with a John Henry feel to it, the human being just as good as the machine. Gradually the picture broke apart and her mother was more at the front of the picture with the truck in the background. And then her mother got bigger as she returned to them and the truck dwindled away.

The little girl wants it. So, Beth thought, Navajo Joe liked her. At least that much was clear.

SEVENTEEN

Jo grilled toast and fried some eggs and called them over. Jean pretended she and the kids had completely forgotten about breakfast, but in reality she had been counting on Jo and wondered if it was as obvious as it felt. She suffered a little guilt for wanting to take the food to an outcropping so they could have a private family picnic. That was just another way of saying *eating without Jo*. She suffered a little more guilt for expecting Jo to cook for them in the first place, preserving Jo in a role she might be trying to escape, especially with a little encouragement. Who knew what Jo was planning, or thinking? Jean didn't, but neither had she bothered to ask. Of course Jean had other issues in her life, more important issues than social interaction, but that didn't mean (as her mother so often liked to tell her) that she had to abandon good manners altogether. But she had, she knew she had. And usually she didn't care. Usually it gave her a perverse pleasure.

It didn't matter now. In a few hours Jo would become someone else they wouldn't see again.

She was about to tell Jo that she needed a little private time with the kids and hoped she didn't mind—good manners, in case anyone was looking—but Jo was preoccupied by her hair, which had dried before she could set it with curlers. Jean slipped away. At the outcropping she sat the kids down and from her canteen poured them some grape Flavor Aid she had stirred up.

"You know where we are, don't you?" Charlie said.

"Utah."

"Mom, you get lost a lot."

"Don't worry. I left breadcrumbs."

"We're eating breakfast at a toilet," Beth said.

"Oh," Jean said. "Oh, that's right."

"You didn't know?"

"Mom, where do you go?"

"It's a really big desert out there. Has anyone noticed? Speaking of which," Jean said, "today is moving day. We're going to pack up and . . . head out."

"Leave?"

The panic in Beth's voice made Jean happy and sad, nostalgic actually. "We'll stay at the motel for a few days," she told her daughter.

"We're leaving?"

"I don't want to leave," Charlie said.

"I know, honey. We'll stay at the motel while the car's being checked out."

"It's not the same."

"Not now," Beth said. "We're this close."

"This close to what, honey?"

"Finding uranium."

"It's because of me, isn't it?" Charlie asked angrily.

"Calm down, Charlie. No, it's not because of you. It's too many other things. What if something happens?"

"Like what?" Charlie asked.

"Yeah," Beth said. "We're getting running water."

"Not running water, just water. Speaking of water, everyone . . . the swimming pool, remember? Wouldn't you rather be in a swimming pool?"

"What about Harry?" Charlie asked.

"What about Jo?"

"They know where to find us," Jean told them.

"Harry doesn't."

"Harry will figure it out."

"What if he can't figure it out?"

"He can ask Jo, and Jo will tell him."

"How will Jo figure it out?"

"Because I'm going to tell her." That seemed to Jean to cover all the bases. She could see them starting to make the mental shift. They were good kids. They might resist, but they would never think of resisting beyond a certain point. *Adventure* was a grand idea, but *swimming pool* felt better on a hot day. "Eat, Charlie."

Beth said, "Charlie, we have to go to the cave before we leave."

"I know," Charlie said in a stern whisper.

"We'll bring him some Flavor Aid," Beth said, oblivious to the looks Charlie was shooting her. "I bet he's never had grape."

"Who's this we're talking about?" Jean asked.

"Nobody," Charlie said.

"Rawhide Joe," Beth said.

"Who's Rawhide Joe?"

"Never mind," Charlie said.

"He's our secret friend," Beth said. "He protects me from Leonard Dawson. And I'm going to give him my fountain pen, too."

"Stop," Charlie said.

"He does protect us, Charlie. At least me."

"You're ruining it!" Charlie cried. "Stop talking about it!"

"Okay, don't get upset about it, Charlie."

"Then tell her to be quiet about it."

"Mom," Beth started.

Jean raised her finger and her daughter's mouth obediently shut and she hung her head. Jean stood up and said, "Beth, come over here." They went to the other side of the outcropping. Tears were already falling from Beth's face. Jean hugged her. The tears seeped through Jean's blouse and she felt the moisture against her stomach. Even after she was through being upset, Beth would keep hugging forever, and then it became a way to stall and avoid. Jean let her hug a little longer. "All right," she whispered. "Who's this man?"

Beth mumbled an answer into her stomach and when Jean said she didn't understand Beth mumbled it again. This was another tactic.

"I can't understand you, Beth."

Beth mumbled it again.

"My stomach can't read lips. Speak clearly."

"Rawhide Joe."

"Who is Rawhide Joe?" Jean lifted Beth's face and stepped out of the hug. "You mean Navajo Joe?"

"He's not real. He's a drawing on a cave wall."

"Oh," Jean said. "Oh. I see. All right."

"He's a cowboy and he drew himself and his horse, and the date underneath says 1881."

"Really?" Jean said. "So he's very special. All right, well let's not talk any more about it because it upsets Charlie." She gave Beth another hug and they walked back. Charlie was huddled in a ball, arms wrapped around knees. His shoulders were shaking. There were big mistakes you made in parenting and small mistakes. The big mistakes you made allowed you to continue smugly about your business, for they would wait a good while before springing their repercussions on you. The small mistakes immediately stabbed you in the heart. Charlie's shaking body nearly killed her.

"It was supposed to be a secret," Beth said.

"It's my fault," Jean told her daughter.

"Shut up!"

"Charlie, I'm sorry. I'm sorry." She went over and rubbed his back. "Mommy didn't mean to ruin your secret."

"Don't talk like that," Charlie said. "Stop it."

"I know he's your special secret."

"Stop!"

"I mean special friend." Another mistake. She knew it even as she said it, yet she plowed ahead, sure a sentence existed out there that could fix it. "Why don't you explain it to me. He's your friend on a cave wall?"

"Stop talking about it!" Charlie drew up tighter, trying to keep his weeping silent.

Jean's impulse was of course to hold him as tightly as she could, but that would officially acknowledge in Beth's presence that he was crying and that would embarrass Charlie further. She tried to ignore it. For a second she ignored it. She couldn't ignore it. She began to wrap her arms around him, but Charlie would have none of it. He was pushing her off of him and she was falling back in the sand when Jo came upon them.

"Hello," Jo said, looking down at them. "I thought I'd join you. Or is it a private picnic?" Her face fell and she dropped to her knees by Charlie and covered him with her arms. "Charlie, what's wrong?" The demonstration hit Jean unawares and she felt stung. Her eyes filled; a wave hit her chest. To her surprise, Charlie didn't resist. Jo stroked his head and shoulders as he spoke. "She ruins everything," Charlie wept into his knees.

Jean motioned to Beth to follow her back to the campsite.

"Charlie's not supposed to cry," Beth whispered to her.

"I know."

"Will he be okay?"

"He'll be okay."

"He's crying though."

"I'll take care of it, honey. It'll be all right."

"He's not supposed to cry. That has detonations."

"Repercussions," Jean said.

"Yes, it has repercussions."

At the campsite Jean lifted the hood of the Rambler, removed the paper bag tied around the carburetor, then got behind the wheel and turned the key. Nothing. She stuck a twig in the flap of the carburetor and tried again. Nothing again. She got a knife and scraped the battery connectors. They looked obligingly encrusted. By now Beth had gotten into the car to offer moral support. She was in her usual spot, backseat, passenger side, and when Jean turned around in the driver's seat Beth smiled at her. It was the exact replica of every moment Jean had started the car and reversed it out of the driveway, twisting to see out the rear window, and her daughter there giving her a little smile.

"Here goes," she said, turning the key.

Nothing.

She got out and kicked a tire. She leaned over the open hood and offered a pathetic stare at the battery, as if it had the power to be nice to her, to give in to her flirtation or tears.

Perhaps trying to start the car should have been the very first thing she did this morning. Perhaps then she could have simply asked that Indian fellow to bring back jumper cables from Mr. Morrison's camp.

Jo and Charlie walked back into camp, and Charlie trudged silently into her arms. She looked for the fatigue lines in his face, but his skin was clear. He didn't seem clogged up from crying, but it was probably time.

"I did it," Jo said.

Jean narrowed her eyes at Jo.

"I pounded him," Jo said. Jean remembered how Jo had looked the night before, some kind of creature. It was either this aspect of Jo's personality or her eagerness to be the family slave that had pushed her to take such a step. "Charlie helped me. I think I did it right," Jo said.

"She did it okay," Charlie said with a shrug.

By rights she could have been angry at such an intrusion. She'd seen the mothers in the hospital get like that, patrolling for signs of encroachment. She finished filling a canteen, slung a rucksack over her shoulder, and put on her trading-post hat.

"Was that okay?" Jo asked.

"That was fine," Jean said. "If you want to, you can pack up the tent. I need to go intercept that Mr. Joe fellow. I'll be back in thirty minutes."

Eighteen

After leaving the campsite, Harry had driven as far as the veer-off to the R&R Mining camp. Driving in the dark had been a stupid thing to do—brought about because he had so quickly and so stupidly obeyed Leonard Dawson and left.

Once he got as far as the veer-off, he turned and bucked up the sandy trail to set up camp at the little oasis where Jo had earlier helped him cache those pieces of equipment he had no hope of selling to Jimmy. That meant all the Geiger counters the lone-wolf prospectors used—though, hindsight being better than twenty-twenty, he should have thrown in a couple of used Lucky Strikes for the Navajos. He was selling them for $50 but would have come down to $40. A Geiger counter for $40 was a good deal even if it was a total piece of junk. It would serve its purpose for their radiation-breath games. Shoot, they could win back their forty bucks in one round of betting. Should have thought of it. Next time.

He parked the truck and leaned back. He didn't want to move. He was tired enough to consider sleeping sitting up in his truck. In his hand was the paper he'd found crumpled at the campsite. He unfolded it to find a letter from the Metallurgical Division, U.S. Bureau of Mines, Salt Lake City, Utah. Under the truck's dome light he read,

*Radioactive Sample Report: Radiometric analysis gave .087% U_3O_8
equivalent. Sample is an impure sandstone containing quartz, feldspar,
clay, and calcite. Copper and manganese are present in the sample but
no mercury or rare earths could be detected.*

The sample had been examined by R. G. Andersen, petrographer,
and signed off by George F. Gibbs, metallurgist.

Strike three for Leonard Dawson. Harry imagined Dawson battering
the paper and pitching it to the ground. Leonard Dawson had blown all
his hopes and Harry rejoiced. He was a little less tired all of a sudden. He
got out of his car. He opened up the back and poked around for his tent.
Harry hoped Leonard Dawson would lose the rest of his money (flowing
in from somewhere with that nice Airstream), all of it, every last dollar.
If the bottom fell out, Jo might fall with it, released. He was standing
where they had stood together, Jo and he. At the spot where she had
leaned close to him, where her voice had softened to convey a confidence.
Why couldn't all of his life be like these past few days? It was not too
much to ask.

He plopped down. Sans blanket, sans tent, sans eyes, sans everything.
Here he was reciting Shakespeare in the desert. His schooling came back
to him in strange ways. He usually slept without a tent anyway.

He couldn't sleep. Not at all.

In the morning he took his time. He went over by the cottonwoods
and searched for the water that must be there. The streambed had dried
up except for a small pool soupy with algae. He used the algae as soap
and washed himself. Then he retrieved his Bunsen burner from the truck
and imagined Jo watching him. He was going to cook himself some actual
breakfast and eat it. She would be glad of that. His movements setting up
were careful and proud, in case she was hiding nearby. For someone who
claimed he didn't believe in Joseph Smith, he often found himself imagining that other forces were watching him.

Harry wondered about people who had made the wrong turn in faith, who had accepted a religion that believed in Buddha, for example, instead of God. What happened to these people when they found out at the end? Even if they were saved, what could be said of their lives?

His second mother had been the one to tell Harry about the man who ate nothing but air for thirteen years. In the thirteenth year he had died. "Do you know why he died?" his second mother had asked.

"Because he ate nothing but air?" Harry answered.

"Because he got run over by a car," she informed him.

Harry hadn't known what to say, but he was nine years old and frightened.

"He was running across the street to go to a restaurant. To a restaurant to break his vow. That's what happens when you're bad." She tried out the same story on Harry's real brother, but he was much older and laughed uproariously at her and mockingly repeated the story in a rowdy wicked-witch's voice.

He heard the truck coming from miles away. He removed the frying pan from the Bunsen burner and set it in the sand, then tramped down the sandy trail until he could see the road. He ducked when he saw the red pickup. The odor of the meat he was frying was strong. Harry would have easily smelled it from the road. He often found dogstakers that way, sniffing their cooking, then hiking in to their campsite and selling them a Lucky Strike or a Price Ranger. When they got through with Geiger counters, he moved them up to scintillators. When they got through with scintillators, he moved them up to a V-44 Mineralight. When black light failed to illuminate their dreams, they finally drifted away—as Leonard Dawson was bound to do within the next few months. Dawson had no idea what he was doing. As he drove past in his red pickup, he never turned his head toward any smell, and although Harry was ridiculously unhidden by the feathery sage he ducked behind, Dawson hadn't spotted him. If he had turned his head, he would have. That was Leonard Dawson for you, blind to all the obvious things.

Harry walked back to his truck and was startled by a mongrel dog, forcing its snout into the can of Spam. He jerked to a halt in midstride. Carefully he set his foot down. He managed not to make a sound. The dogs were mean out here. It hadn't been a problem until the prospectors brought them in, then beat and deserted them when times turned rough. Harry sneaked toward the truck in long slow-motion steps like the villain in a silent movie. The dog lifted its head at the crank of an opening door. It pawed gingerly at the frying pan but drew back from the heat and re-turned to the can of Spam. Harry felt on the floor for the pistol the old prospector had given Jean. He pulled the first-aid kit out of the glove compartment and rummaged through all the papers and screwdrivers and tire gauges. How he had collected a half-dozen tire gauges was be-yond him. He checked for the pistol behind the seat, in the crook of the tire jack. He settled for laying on the truck horn, but the mongrel barely flinched. A mean one, maybe even rabid. Harry took the rock he kept on the dashboard for a paperweight, rolled down the window, and threw it at the Bunsen burner. He didn't care about the dog, well, he did care about the dog, only there was nothing he could do about it without the pistol, but the one thing he couldn't do no matter what was leave a fire burning. The rock missed the burner—more paperweights where that one came from—and he used a screwdriver to try again. With its worn-down Phillips tip the screwdriver was useless as far as screwing went, and it was no great loss when it missed and got lost in the sand. He moved on to the tire gauges. He flung the first one like a knife. He missed, but he had found the range. The second tire gauge hit its mark and the little stove toppled and spilled its fuel. The fire ate the fuel in a flaring puddle but the flames soon sputtered out in the sand. Harry started the truck and backed up. The dog lifted its head and watched.

When he arrived at the veer-off he paused to consider what direc-tion he should turn. He gave this new mining camp the courtesy of a proper regard and refusal. His thoroughly professional assessment of the situation resulted in a new plan: back to the women's campsite. The fast beating of his heart claimed its anxiety for what the dog might do, be-cause the dog might be rabid and was certainly wild. It could easily roam to their campsite. He would have to go back there. The dog could be dangerous. The dog *was* dangerous. He had no choice, really, this was the thing he had to do. He had to go back to the campsite. He was rushing headlong toward something he had denied himself for years. What could be said of his life if he didn't?

Nineteen

Jo spread out a tablecloth by the forsaken keg of water and laid out her supplies: scissors, petroleum jelly, rattail comb, egg timer, dishwashing gloves, a drinking cup, a biscuit tin filled with clips and metal rods. Beth didn't want a home permanent, but she liked all the names of the stuff. It was exciting to watch Jo act like a surgeon, calling out the names of things during a life-saving operation—neutralizer, waving lotion, pink-paper end wraps.

"So this will be a nice surprise," Jo said.

Home permanents took a long time. Maybe Jo was thinking along this line, too. Anything to stall her mother's flight plan.

"It's been twenty minutes," Charlie called down.

"And look at all the water we have." Jo worked out the plug, held the cooking pan underneath the gush, then poured the panful of water over Beth's hair. The water couldn't have been cold, but it felt freezing against her scalp. Beth lifted her head to let some of the water tingle refreshingly down her neck.

"I love giving permanents," Jo said. "I used to give them all the time, back when I had friends."

"You don't have friends?"

"I used to," Jo said.

Charlie called again from the road, and his interruption irritated Beth. They were just getting to the good part in their conversation. "Somebody shot a pistol," he said.

"That was the mining camp," Jo said. With the rattail end of her comb, she began knifing through Beth's hair and clipping off sections.

"Why don't you have friends anymore?" Beth asked.

"Hmm," Jo said, picking up her scissors and snipping, "a little bit of split ends." She took one of the metal rods and yanked hard on Beth's hair as she rolled. "Does that hurt?"

"Yes," Beth said.

"Has to be tight," Jo said. "And we're going to need that water, too. Why don't I have friends? When I was your age I had a lot of friends. Do you have a lot of friends?"

"Yes," Beth said.

"I did, too. Sometimes you can have friends some of the time but not all your friends all of the time. So you get older and when you get married that's what happens. You see?"

"There it goes again," Charlie called. "Did you hear it?"

"I heard something," Beth said.

Charlie said, "That's Mom. That's her signal."

"What's it a signal of?" Beth asked.

"I'm going to go get her."

"Hold on." Jo stood up and peered up at Charlie. "What do you mean you're going to go get her? I'm not sure I liked the sound of that."

"I'm going to go get her," Charlie said and disappeared.

"Hold on a second, Charlie." Jo scampered up the hill to the road.

Beth saw that Charlie meant business. She climbed back to the campsite and found him packing up a rucksack. He fitted it over his back, cleaned his compass against his pants, and selected one of Harry's shirt panels sketched in with more map business. Beth could see this piece of the map was new: it hadn't been colored yet with Charlie's topographical inks. Beth said that she was going with him. Jo said that neither of them was going anywhere.

Beth put on the hat Jimmy Splendid had given her and marched behind Charlie. Jo blocked their way. She was planted like an angry soldier. Charlie just walked around her.

"Are you coming?" Beth asked her.

"Get back here!" Jo yelled.

Charlie didn't bother with the road. He was taking a different route. Beth followed him right past the toilet toward the path that led to Rawhide Joe. He said this was a shortcut and in case she had any doubts he reminded her about a hypotenuse. Besides, he'd drawn the map this morning and Navajo Joe had gone over it with him so he knew this was correct.

"Freshly made this morning," Beth said. "Right, Charlie?"

Charlie said this was easily half the distance their mother was traveling, that if she had any sense at all, she would have taken this route. But of course she didn't have any sense, which was why they had to go on this mission and she would have gotten lost anyway because she couldn't even follow a road so just think what a hypotenuse would have done to her.

"Get back here!" They heard Jo screaming again.

"Don't you like Jo?" Beth asked.

"Yeah, I guess so," Charlie said.

"I do. I'm glad she's here. How did you know Navajo Joe was coming this morning?"

"I didn't."

"How did you find him then?"

"I was checking out the road."

"And then what?"

"And then that's how I know the road stops looking like a road. She's lost, I know it."

"Did Navajo Joe just drive by?"

"Yeah," Charlie said.

"I wish I'd been there," Beth said.

"He walked up with me to the top and pointed out everything for my map."

"That's not fair," Beth said.

The sand gave way to hardpack just as Beth was losing her energy from the sink-down, pull-out effort walking in the sand required. The hardpack was much easier. It was dried out and cracked and it stretched before them like a sea. A black spider web looked to be laid across it. She liked how a curled thinness peeled off the top and the way it crunched under her feet. She didn't like looking up because everything seemed so far away. They passed their H_2O claim. Within its bounds was the cave where Rawhide Joe awaited.

"Do we legally own Rawhide Joe?" she asked, but Charlie didn't answer. She didn't mind; she was getting out of breath. She tried to concentrate on her next book report. She had a new tactic she was going to try out: topic sentence put second instead of first. *The detonations and repercussions of her capture were heard throughout the land. This is the story of Mary Jemison and you will find her story in* Indian Captive: The Story of Mary Jemison, *by Lois Lenski. I like* Indian Captive: The Story of Mary Jemison *because of the exciting, repercussion-filled detonations that . . .*

. . . that what? That happened? That followed? That filled up the air? That fired up the troops?

"Charlie, do you have a pencil?"

"Hold on," he said. He stopped, unslung the rucksack and opened it. He was breathing hard. "Where's my pen?" He looked up at Beth. "I was sure I brought it. You have a curler in your hair." He studied his scribbles on the shirt panel.

"Do you know where we are?"

"Of course I know where we are."

"I don't."

"Like mother, like daughter," Charlie said. "I was sure I had it. Where's your fountain pen?"

"Don't tell Harry but it leaks a lot."

"Oh, that's why you're giving it to Rawhide Joe." Charlie handed her one of the canteens and she drank as much as she could. "This way," he said. He cut across a rise of slickrock, another one of his hypotenuses, she figured. She wanted to tell Charlie that by the way she already knew about hypotenuses but she changed her mind. As she grew more tired, however, she almost blurted it just to be contrary. The slickrock had appeared level before they started across it, but she was feeling thick in her body as if something were pushing her back. They were climbing, she realized. How was that possible when it appeared so level? She was becoming very disturbed by her legs, two things she hardly ever noticed during a regular walking day. Now they were all she could think of, push off with one, push off with another, use a hand against the thigh to power through, use a hand against the other thigh. She was having a hard time catching her breath. Maybe they were so high the air was leaving. She wondered about her friends at school. She was always in the middle row in the school photographs, two or three in from the teacher. "Charlie, where's the air?" she gasped, but he didn't answer.

Beth heard it coming up behind her. For a magical moment Rawhide Joe's horse trotted behind her. She was getting a ride.

"There you are," Jo said.

"Oh thank you!" Beth said to the horse.

"I made us some sandwiches for lunch," Jo said.

As if sandwiches were just what a dying girl needed. Sometimes Jo had no sense. Her legs were falling off and Jo was offering her sandwiches.

"Everyone okay?" Jo asked. She had changed clothes again. She was wearing capris and a light-blue blouse and light-blue sneakers. She had tied a chiffon scarf around her neck. She looked as if she had just dropped from a department store in the sky, without effort, without having been dragged through a slog like they had. All Jo was missing were little wings on her feet. In the middle of fourth grade Beth had gone through all the mythology books. Fleet-footed Mercury had been her favorite.

"I've got sandwiches for our break," Jo said. "We can all take a break and have sandwiches. Right, Charlie?"

"Let's find some shade first," Charlie said. His voice was irritated but also shaky.

"All right, Charlie. That's what I meant. I didn't mean eat the sandwiches right now this very second."

"Did you bring a pencil?" Beth asked.

"Maybe," Jo said. "I'll look when we stop. I see a place to stop up ahead, Charlie."

"I see it," Charlie snapped. "How could I not see it? It's right in front of us."

"So let's stop there, all right?"

"All right!" Charlie yelled.

There were no bushes or scrub pines to offer shade but a sheltered pocket in the slickrock worked just as well, actually better, for there was sand to sit on and cool sandstone to lean against. Jo felt around in the bottom of her rucksack and brought up a pencil.

"Thank you," Beth said. The sandwich Jo handed her looked scrumptiously lumpy until she picked up a cut half and saw its dissected and wormy insides. "What kind of sandwich is this?" she asked, throwing it down.

"Not a very good one," Charlie said.

"Just try it. It's a spaghetti sandwich."

"That pencil doesn't work without paper," Charlie said.

"I have paper in my pocket," Beth said. But she felt too weak to write.

"I hope the lead doesn't break."

"Charlie, you're being mean," Jo said. She picked up the sandwich and put it back into Beth's hand.

"Spaghetti isn't yellow. What's the yellow stuff in here?" Beth asked.

"Leftover egg from this morning. It's good. Try it."

Beth took a few deep breaths to gather her courage. No need for bravery she found out one bite later. Jo was an excellent cook, probably one of the best cooks in the world. The sandwich was one of the best sandwiches Beth had ever eaten. Almost immediately a new rush of energy hit her.

"I think it's time to go back, Charlie," Jo said softly, reaching out her hand to fluff back his hair.

Charlie's cheekbones showed in his face. They were dipped in bright scarlet. Despite this, his skin had gone chalky. Beth got up and pretended she hadn't noticed. She pretended to be intent on exploring. She climbed up to a very shallow overhang and followed it around. She found a gash in the rock about a doorway wide. She slipped inside. "I'm exploring and I've found something interesting!" she yelled.

The gash immediately narrowed but she could squeeze through sideways. She pressed on until it widened and she spilled into a shaft. Though sealed off from the outside, she could see perfectly well. She looked up. High above, the shaft opened up to the sky. The shaft wasn't very long and a few steps later it ended. Just those few steps had taken her to a much colder spot. The rock walls wept moisture. She stepped up the boulders at the end of the shaft and found she could squeeze behind a hoove of rock. Beyond that was another opening. She pushed into a cavern—no, not a cavern; an inner courtyard. She was standing in a garden. Vines crept down the rocks. Pink tamarisk jumped all over. The place was lit by the sky. Best of all was a large pool of water. Beth took off her clothes and jumped in. The freezing cold was a shock and in a reflex gulp she swallowed water. She floated on her back. The sky was wide and blue. She had all this energy she didn't know what to do with. She was shivering when she put on her clothes. As she climbed out of the garden, squeezing down from the hoove, she put her hand on a ledge for leverage. The ledge pulled loose against her tug and she went flying. She scraped all of her leg against the rock and fell forward with a twist. Her ankle was caught between the wall and the hoove. Her heart was already racing by the time she hit the ground. Her ankle had jammed low in the crack and was stuck there.

The ledge she had tugged loose was still in her hand. It was actually a petrified log. She fitted it under her calf to wedge her ankle higher. The crack widened as her ankle rose—just an inch was all she needed and she pulled free.

Somewhere someone whispered: *Get out of here.*

She stumbled out of the shaft, afraid to look behind: it was chasing her. Her heart was beating so fast she couldn't breathe or feel pain. The energy lighting through her surged into something stronger and frightening. She was shaking as she squeezed through the entrance gash; the walls respiring against her seemed to be rock lungs. She could feel them moving. She jumped outside and collapsed on all fours. She made herself breathe deep slow breaths until the torrent inside her died down. Then she had no energy at all. She could barely make herself stand up.

Charlie was sitting where she'd left him, adding notes to his map. His flushed cheekbones jutted with a more natural color. From the way he busied himself with the map so he wouldn't have to look at her, she knew he had been clapped. The second time that day. She shouldn't keep count but she did. "Jo's looking for you," he said. He glimpsed the piece of petrified wood in her hand and reached out for it. He finally noticed her wet clothes and hair and scraped leg. "What happened?"

"I went swimming," Beth said.

TWENTY

More than once Harry did the calculations. A dog could not have beaten him to the campsite, attacked four people, and dragged them out to the desert where they would never be found. But the campsite was empty, and no amount of calling got a response. He kept imagining the dog dragging them out, its jaws clamped on and twisting. The morbid way his mind worked—he blamed that on her, the second one. His real mother was a tonic for the interloper, but people intent upon doing damage were cannons, and goodness shot mere pellets against them. The second one, she was a cannon camouflaged in flowers. Acted very sweet almost all the time and then told those bedtime stories with a horrible twist. She'd be the first one to encourage the dog scenario.

The Rambler's hood was braced open, a twig propped in the carburetor. The keys were thrown on the front seat. Harry got in and tried the engine. Dead battery. He started up the International Harvester and gunned it over the little ridge into the campsite, lined it up next to the Rambler, and took out his cables and jumped it. The Rambler started right up. Nice car actually. He saw himself driving in it to a root-beer stand, kids in the back. He let it idle for twenty minutes, turned it off, then made sure it could start again on its own.

He should leave. He was losing money and going broke.

He ducked inside the tent. Here was where the mother and two kids

slept. Their pads were laid out. Plenty of room for all of them. He could
smell something. Clothes were folded and stacked in a corner. A cardboard box held Beth's papers and books. Another box held Charlie's
things, the bottles from his chemistry set, panels of his map, a compass,
a magnifying glass, rocks he had collected, some marbles. The other box
must be the mother's. He moved toward it, then stopped himself. He
could smell Charlie in here. Having not known it before, he still recognized it. The tent had captured it.

He lay down on one of the pads. He knew it belonged to the mother.
Could tell by its distance and calculated nearness. He turned his head
and spied a corner of Beth's box soaked with ink. He could smell the ink
if he tried. Once he got used to Charlie's smell, there were others to be
discovered.

The sun shone on the tent, burning the insides amber. He reached
up to touch the canvas, as if to cause a slow leak, the rays of sun striping
through in the whorls of his fingerprint. In the dark yellow flames of the
tent he slept.

He opened his eyes. In his sleep something else had come to him, a
curl of perfume. His hand moved where it shouldn't. He pictured himself, foolish and skinny, foolishly on his knees, scrambling to cover his
foolish spilled self with sand, watching it push to the surface after each
burial, an obscene pee spot that wouldn't stay down. The kids would have
to sleep on it. He jerked up and hurried outside. He looked down. His
pants were zipped. He was Harry Lindstrom, a gentleman. Harry Lindstrom, who believed in the Bible. He was having a confused dream.

He stood there, his hand reassured by the closed zipper, his eyes
squinting against the sunlight that beat off the Airstream. The silver bullet had moved to within arm's reach of him. His hand could stretch out
and knock on the door and he did, and he opened it. The door opened,
clicked like it wanted him there. He stepped inside. A bed, a sink that
was dry, a counter. The inside was devoted to items that would keep it

clean, detergents, a system of buckets with hand towels folded over the edges. It was like walking into a house and seeing only the things that kept it propped up, the piles of sheetrock and exposed studs. The mirror over the sink reflected her dresser with its five flimsy drawers. All he had ever seen in the way of delicates were great white girdling sheets that skipped over youth and romance and went straight to a nursing home. Jo's would not be like that. Sometimes imagining was worse. Sometimes it did the person a greater injustice. Better just to open the top drawer and take a look and get it over with. He was Harry Lindstrom, a gentleman. He did not spy. He did not imagine. He believed in the Bible. He held himself against the sink. He could not stop imagining. He shook with a cry and looked down at what he had done. Foolish and skinny and frantic, he yanked out his shirttail and pressed it into service. Down on his knees, a loathsome maid, wiping himself off the varnished plywood. A shirt button snapped off. He was on all fours searching for it when he heard the engine. Foolish and skinny and frantic and down on his knees. He ran out of the trailer, hid behind the Rambler and tucked in his shirt and zipped his pants. The red pickup gunned into the campsite.

"What are you doing?" Leonard Dawson growled.

Harry cleared his throat. "Jumping their car." It rescued him to be at the Rambler's side. He tapped its roof.

Leonard Dawson glanced at the open hood. His arms were swinging like those of a British soldier taking over India. His arms were happy, energized, his legs angry and stomping and conquering the world. "Is she leaving? Good."

Harry felt soaked down there. Was it showing? He heard angry thumping from inside the trailer. His hands trembled. He checked his pants. Leonard Dawson stepped out with a box of groceries. The trailer door banged behind him. His jaw was set. He didn't glance Harry's way as he passed. He came back and slammed inside the trailer again. After several minutes he kicked open the door and stood with another loaded-up box. "There you are!" he shouted. Harry jumped; the Rambler's hood unlatched and thundered down. The crashing hood would have taken off his fingers. "Where have you been!"

Harry backed against the Rambler. He didn't know how he should answer.

"Stop it, Lenny. I've got two kids who are hurting."

How had Harry not seen or heard Jo? A few more minutes . . . he would have been caught. Harry's heart took a plunge. The shirt button, the obscene spot he still needed to clean. Jo's arm was around Beth and she was steering the little girl toward the trailer. "Hello, Harry."

"The kids are not your problem." Leonard Dawson held his box and blocked the trailer door.

"Behave yourself." Jo grasped the box and used it to pull Leonard Dawson down the steps.

"I said they're not your problem."

"You're taking everything!" Jo said.

"I need everything."

"Where are you going?" In Jo's face Harry saw a change. He hoped it was true that Leonard Dawson had taken everything, all their money, all their food, everything. He couldn't help himself. He wasn't a gentleman; he didn't care. She was beautiful. Life had done its part and taken him to this spot. Now it was up to him. Later somehow he would clean up and find the shirt button and hide all the evidence. Later somehow he would release Jo from Leonard Dawson.

"Did you get Mom?" Charlie asked Harry.

"What? I got the car started," Harry said.

"Where is she?"

Harry shook his head.

"Fix him up," Jo ordered. Harry squinted at her. "Fix him up. Charlie," she ordered again. She went inside with Beth. Charlie was a haze to him. He was in a dream. What? he wanted to ask. What am I supposed to do? Charlie was ill. Harry could identify that smell now. Charlie was sitting cross-legged in the sand. He went over to the Rambler and opened up the back. He took one of the bottles of water, poured it over a rag, and took it to Charlie. "Not here," Charlie said though he remained sitting. Harry helped him up and they went behind an outcropping where Leonard Dawson couldn't see them. "Don't you feel well, Charlie?" Harry asked. Charlie didn't say anything. Harry pulled off Charlie's shirt and sponged him down. "You can tell me," Harry said. Charlie buried his face in the wet cloth. Harry kept a rag at the back of his neck. "Did I ever tell you I had two mothers?" Harry asked. "You sort of mentioned it," Charlie mumbled into the rag. "Well, I did. My dad thought it was okay. That was his religion. That's not any way to grow up, Charlie. I had a lot of questions when I finally figured it out. Sometimes dads aren't all the deal they're cracked up to be."

Charlie rested his face in the rag.

"Should I do something else?" Harry asked.

Charlie lifted his head and looked at him.

"You can tell me," Harry said. "I'll do it."

Charlie shook his head.

"Are you sure?"

"Jo did it."

"You want to sit here for a while?"

Charlie was completely asleep and Harry was starting to doze off when she found them. An engine and the heavy sound of a truck door tracked through something that may or may not have been a dream. Harry opened his eyes. Charlie was lying down, using his rolled-up T-shirt as a pillow. Harry's hand with the washrag had fallen from Charlie's shoulder. "Is everything okay?" Jean asked. Harry shook his head awake. "I got here later than I thought," she said. Her face was dusty and sweaty and the eyes burned with a frightening brilliant shine. Her eyes were turquoise from one angle, aquamarine from another. He had never seen such a shine. "And Charlie?" she began. Now she would have to say it. In a way he wanted to make her. Say it, say one straight thing to Harry Lindstrom.

Someone tell him the truth for a change. She readied herself to speak. "Jo did it," he interjected. "Do you have a first-aid kit, I've got to take care of Beth," was all the response she gave him. "In the glove compartment," he told her. She nodded like that's good, that's as it should be, not like thank you, Harry, thank you so much. She jutted her chin businesslike and turned. "I started your car," he called after her. "Wish I'd known you were coming back," she said as she walked away.

Harry reached out and stroked Charlie's head. He wondered if it had hit Charlie yet. He was Charlie's age when it had hit him, and he'd had no one to go to. The brother he liked, his one real brother, was already married and had defected to the other side of adulthood. He could tell Charlie, You can come to me. Charlie, you can always come to me. He felt at his pants, at the dampness grown thick down there, the shirttail stiff with his secret. There were so many secrets in this world. But what could he tell Charlie? What did he really know?

There was a pop that Harry knew for the pop of a gun. It sounded extra loud in the desert air but Harry knew it for a weak caliber. Just a pop, a .22. He stood up. It wasn't really what it was. He felt himself to be at the end of a rope, dragged slowly back to the campsite where he didn't need to go, where he saw them standing there, every single one of them silent and standing, throwing their tall shadows over Jean, on the rucksack in her hand, on the ground where she lay.

Town

ONE

The Mormon Church was on fire. From the mountains that rimmed the town, you could look down upon the valley and see it, a radiance flaming in the darkness. Scurrying toward it were the townspeople, their figures bleeding into the night. From the mountains they were invisible, but Harry clearly saw the burning light. He could guess the rest.

In his rearview mirror, the darkness behind him was complete. He stopped the Harvester and shifted into neutral and he and the kids looked down upon the sight. He kept an eye on the rearview mirror. "Where's Navajo Joe?" Beth asked. She was twisted around. Harry could feel her panic growing. The darkness behind slightly paled and now Harry could tell her with assurance: "He's coming, don't worry." The paleness brightened into actual light, the light narrowed into beams, and then the Navajo's headlights were upon him. Harry shifted and let the truck rip down the hill.

All the switches had been thrown in the church's basement. The precious drain on the town's single generator could mean only one thing. The signal had been sent out. A dead body was big news. The flock was assembling as if for a sacrament meeting with their contributions of ice. An ice tray here, an ice tray there; if everyone donated, it was enough to keep the body cold. The town had no freezer to accommodate a body. They'd have to keep it like this until the coroner from Grand Junction

came and took it away. It would get laid out on the banquet table. Everyone tried to act sorrowful but tragedy was exciting, after all, and if the
victim was someone people barely knew, then all the better.

Dr. Randolph was not in his house. Harry went over to Joe Istaqa's
pickup. Istaqa poked his head out the window. "Not there," Harry said.
"Probably at the church." It wasn't worth explaining. Either the Navajos
knew about the custom or didn't.

"What now?" Jo called. She was in the back of Istaqa's pickup, sitting
next to Jean. She was shaking.

"How is she?"

"She keeps wanting to sit up."

That wasn't necessarily a good sign, Harry thought. What exactly in
this situation would be a good sign? He got back into the Harvester and
led the way to the Stagecoach Oasis. He tried to explain to the kids who
gave him no response except silence that Miss Dazzle used to be the doctor's nurse. Loose definition of *nurse,* however. Then again, Dr. Randolph
was a loose definition of *doctor.* Could be worse though, right? Having the
Stagecoach Oasis as their personal hospital, right, not so bad? Kids didn't
answer. Harry didn't know actually how it could be any worse.

Miss Dazzle was standing in the parking lot under the unlit sign with
her regulars. Harry caught them in his headlights. He recognized the
three card-playing old ladies. The rudeness of his high beams turned them
stark and ugly. They weren't in reality ugly; they were handsome women.
Dressed nice, and the one styled her hair in an upsweep. "Harry!" Miss
Dazzle said. She walked over and leaned her elbows on the driver's door.
Her head swam in close; in the darkness it seemed something from the
ocean, the head not necessarily connected to anything else.

"We've got a big problem," Harry said.

"I know. We were just about to drive over there."

"No. Not that."

Her head swam in farther. Harry had to lean way back in his seat.
Was she going to kiss him at a time like this? Miss Dazzle gave the kids

her beaming, reassuring smile. Her face withdrew, sobered. Her darting eyes took in an Indian man, then a white woman sitting in the back of the Indian's pickup. Harry got out of the truck and watched Miss Dazzle peer over the sides of the pickup. She was met with the sight of Jean, laid out on the pickup bed. Miss Dazzle quickly blinked back a spark of panic, but it didn't escape Harry's notice.

"What happened here?" she asked.

"She got shot," Jo said.

Miss Dazzle narrowed her gaze at Jo.

"I didn't get shot," Jean said, her eyes still closed. "Is that you?"

"Hello, Jean. It's me, darling." In a moment Miss Dazzle was her lackadaisical self. She relaxed into a sardonic appraisal of Jo.

"She did get shot," Jo insisted.

"Yeah, she did," Harry confirmed.

"Well, I don't see anything," Miss Dazzle said.

"Keep your voice down," Harry whispered, jerking his thumb toward the International Harvester. "The kids have ears."

"Right here," Jo said. She pointed down to Jean's head.

Miss Dazzle reached into the long breast pocket of her bib overalls and pulled out a small flashlight. "That?" she asked.

"It's nothing," Jean said.

"It's certainly not in your brain, if that's what you mean," Miss Dazzle said. She turned Jean's head to the side. "No opening, see?" Tears had started to run down Jo's cheeks. Miss Dazzle grabbed Jo's forearm and yanked. "See? It's just a scrape," she said, but Jo was shaking her head no, no, you're wrong, and again Miss Dazzle yanked her forearm. "Stop," she ordered, but it had all been too much for Jo. Harry wanted to take her in his arms. Miss Dazzle sighed loudly with frustration. She patted Jean's shoulder. "How do you feel, honey?"

"I'm all right," Jean said.

"Head doesn't hurt?"

"I wouldn't go that far," Jean said.

"Sleepy?"

"Sleepy, yes."

"Well, don't go to sleep just yet." Miss Dazzle reached again into her bib overalls and pulled out a thermometer. Why she had a thermometer in her bib overalls Harry had no idea, but it seemed to convince Jo they were in good hands. With her by now filthy hands Jo carefully pushed away the tears, spreading mud across her cheeks. Harry saw Miss Dazzle shoot an appraising glance at her while taking Jean's temperature. On the other side of the pickup Harry became aware of three pairs of peering eyes, three pairs of perched hands, three white hairdos, one of them in an upsweep.

"Well, let's get you in a room. Same one as before? Who is it, do you know?" Miss Dazzle asked. She raised her chin in the general direction of the church.

"Don't know," Harry said.

The three old ladies jostled around the pickup bed and surrounded Harry. "Who is it?" "We need to bring them ice." One after the other spoke. "They'll be expecting us." "They know we have ice here." "Who is it?"

"I don't know," Harry said.

The ladies drew back, disappointed and half angry at Harry. Jo helped Jean sit up. They slid her off the pickup. Joe Istaqa suddenly materialized to catch her in his arms. Everyone followed him into the motel room in obedient schoolhouse file, the three old ladies shortest to tallest, white to whitest, included. "Harry," whispered Miss Dazzle, dropping back and pulling Harry aside. "Guess who came by here since you've been gone? Charlton Heston. Looked right into my eyes. Another time and place, Harry."

When Jean had been stretched out on the bed, Miss Dazzle came over and arranged Jean's hands over her stomach and patted them. "I'll get you a Pepsi," Miss Dazzle said. "The carbonation will be good for you. Don't let her fall asleep now," she warned Jo. She came back with a tray of glasses, Pepsis for the adults and orange sodas for Beth and Charlie, who sat mutely on the other bed. Beth opened her hand and discovered a bottle of iodine and Miss Dazzle took it and said she could use it. From the way Miss Dazzle sat down, Harry knew she would keep watch. She poured a finger's worth from an unmarked bottle into her Pepsi. "Somebody want to tell me what happened?" When no one answered, she reached back and swept her loose thick hair into a ponytail, brushed the back of her neck, then let the ponytail drop loose. Her hands flew straight up and stretched. She poured another finger into her Pepsi. The whiskey smell was already filling up the room.

"You can't smoke," Jo said.

"I wasn't going to, honey," was Miss Dazzle's short reply.

Harry and Istaqa left them. "Mr. Morrison wants me," Istaqa said.

"Don't know how we would have done it without you," Harry said. "We wouldn't have, that's how."

"She'll be all right now," Istaqa said.

"Tell your boss I said hi and I'll be dropping by," Harry called as he left.

Harry could do nothing more now except pace. He was relieved actually when Miss Dazzle asked him to take the three old ladies to the church before they burst. All three sat in the back of Miss Dazzle's De-Soto so that he appeared to be their limo driver. A pitcher of ice sat on the middle one's lap, somewhat ceremoniously. Harry couldn't help but think of a burial urn. He passed the filling station, where he spied Istaqa's pickup and the Navajo standing alone, gazing about. His shoulders were big and cushiony with a soft slope to them; even his silhouette looked relaxed. It was the legs spread apart that gave away his frustration. Joshua Backson who ran the filling station had probably taken off for the church, too. The ladies got into a huff when Harry stopped to help out. Oh, but he has time to stop at a gas station, they said. Missing their drinks hadn't helped their moods. If he went back far enough he probably knew them from somewhere. He got the key taped to the back of the dumpster and unlocked the gas pump. Good thing, too: the pickup had been running on fumes. Istaqa gave him an IOU in Paul Morrison's name. Harry automatically said you're welcome. Istaqa wasn't rude but nothing like a verbal thank-you was forthcoming. Harry waved but Istaqa took no notice as he drove away. A thank-you wasn't just some kind of useless courtesy invented by white men. But Istaqa was a loner, even among the other Navajos. Harry knew Istaqa was a Hopi name; maybe that accounted for some extra difference in his personality.

The old ladies were talking about Harry and saw no reason to stop simply because he had returned. He got back behind the wheel. He'd left the motor running, he saw. They should have just driven off and left him. He wouldn't have cared. "You're a bad boy," one of the old ladies said petulantly, the one with the least white hair. She'd been a blond in her youth and couldn't give it up, that and the red lipstick. The words snapped something in him. In the midst of death and the threat of death, love, the realization of love, even saying it to himself this word: *love*, his willingness to take it on, his willingness no matter what, he was beset by an anger trivial and overwhelming. This was perhaps the most important day of his life, when love had argued him past all the howevers, and here he was ending the evening wanting to pound his hands on the steering wheel and scream at three old ladies. He clenched his jaw shut. If he said but a single word it might all burst and he would run them into the ground with his insults.

Outside the church people had spread blankets and were having midnight picnics. Cronies called to the three old ladies, and one group offered them fried drumsticks. Harry could see they were tempted, but they stayed the course. They were headstrong in their determination to see the body. Harry moved ahead and lost them to the crowd.

In the basement he caught sight of the banquet table, the ice piled up but no body to put it on. He supposed the old ladies would blame this empty bier on him as well. He spied Joshua Backson talking to Dewey Durnford and went over to give him Istaqa's IOU. Dewey's baby skin was flushed and his stranded forelock wet with perspiration. Dewey couldn't stay, he said he had to get back, the Atomic Café was making good money on this. Harry caught sight of a bleeding man slouched on a stool in the far corner of the basement. The blackish blood, looking dirty as the man himself, was seeping down the side of his face, onto his neck and chest. Harry guessed that it looked worse than it was. "Is this what all the fuss is about?" he asked Joshua. If this was all it took, he was glad no one knew about a woman coming from Ohio with kids and no husband trying to go it alone out in the desert and the tragedy that had predictably befallen her. What a time he'd had getting her back to town, leading the way on the perilous road incompletely bulldozed by the AEC. For three hours he'd had time to ponder it, what had happened back there—Beth inside the trailer with her scraped leg and Leonard Dawson stomping back and forth with his loads—and he knew what had happened had somehow come down to him. His saw his shirt button lying on the trailer floor, it was now a medallion emitting a feverish glow, find me find me! And that other thing, especially that other thing.

Joshua Backson was saying, "No, he's not the one. It's Vernon Rutledge. That there's the man who found him."

"What?" Harry asked. He looked around for a place to sit down.

"Harry, you all right? Didn't know you and Vernon were friends."

"Oh," Harry said. "What? It's Vernon Rutledge, you say? You mean the rimflyer?"

"And that's how he went down," Joshua said. "He should be here within a few hours."

"You mean he survived?"

"Oh no, Harry, no. I'm sorry. Your friend didn't make it."

"What good is this ice?" Harry asked. "It'll melt before he gets here." He got up and was shoved into a blind loudness. Joshua whisked him past colliding torsos, careering him toward the bleeding man who had found Vernon Rutledge. The surging crowd was high spirited. If this hadn't been the Mormon church, Harry would have sworn the punch was spiked. Already, steering through the pack of jostling shoulders, he was hearing the banter: *He was looking for uranium, he found it head-on.* Everyone had to add a ha-ha to tragedy to make it go down. They talked about death the same way they talked about women, attracted to it but afraid. Harry had been a little bit acquainted with Vernon Rutledge, and that man would have been the first to add his black comedy to the pot, but Harry didn't think any of it was funny and he never would. If he started joking about death he knew he'd be on the verge of dying; if he started joking about women he knew he'd be forevermore alone.

Joshua shouted above the noise to the filthy, bleeding man, "I'd like to introduce a friend to you!" Thus, Harry found himself formally presented to Timothy Carle. Harry's dejected state spiraled into a character flaw; he found he couldn't muster a polite hello or offer his hand, not that this Timothy Carle, grinning like a simpleton, seemed to notice.

Joshua spotted someone many heads away and raised his hand. With a comforting squeeze of Harry's arm, he scurried off.

Timothy Carle smelled bad and his boots were torn in half and held together by rope. Not twine, either: rope, too fat to be lashed tight enough; an extra sole of sand had packed in between the gaping uppers and lowers. One of his ears was ripped and still leaking blood. It dripped down his grizzled chin. He had a weak chin that shot straight into his neck. He could have been a comic-book character. All forms of politeness choked inside Harry and he wanted to run away. But the man he had hoped to see was here. Dr. Randolph was working on Timothy, stitching up his ear. The doctor was probably hoping Miss Dazzle would arrive so he could put her to work. She'd done all his stitching for him. A cruel thought but probably true.

Timothy told Harry he'd been down at the Colorado River when Vernon Rutledge had dipped low and winged him hello. Timothy thought it would be a good time to take his lunch break. He sat down on a rock, pulled out a sandwich and a drink, and prepared to enjoy the show. Vernon Rutledge's rimflying was so entertaining that Timothy got off his rock and lay down on the sand and pillowed his hands behind his head and stared up at the daredevil plane in the sky that became more and more like a childhood daydream when, right in the middle of this daydream, a downdraft caught the plane and it flew into the rocks at Heel Fork. Timothy nearly crashed the Jeep rushing to get out of there and that was how he hurt himself and he was hours late getting to the doctor for help. Too late anyway, the doctor commented with a shrug. Timothy raised his soup bowl and spat into it. He had chewing tobacco in his mouth and, here in the Mormon church, was trying his best to hide it. Harry noticed how white the walls of the basement were. Cinder block, painted white. He could smell soil down here, not just dried-up dirt. The smell was of something that had never touched the sun. Harry told the doctor he had an emergency, a woman who'd been shot. The doctor was briefly interested until Harry said well maybe the bullet missed. A mistake on his part. He said Miss Dazzle was looking after her. Another mistake. "Did you hear me?" Harry asked.

"Yeah, I heard you, Harry."

"We need you over there. Maybe we have to take her out of here to the hospital."

"Is she pretty?" the doctor asked, ready to get interested again. Timothy tried to rein in his fit of hilarity. His chest jerked and some of his tobacco plug coughed down his mouth and unshaven neck and he looked turtleish. Harry told himself the harsh day had worked all the sensible emotions out of Timothy, who now was trying to add some kind of fresh remark of his own but he snickered too hard and his hand reached up to protect his ear. His blood and the tobacco juice were almost the same color. Harry was hit again with that same burst of anger that had almost overtaken him earlier with the three old ladies. He spun away and ignored whatever the doctor was calling after him and he imagined himself deserting the three old ladies and driving away without them, finally finding a decent road, he might take himself for a long drive just to feel something peaceful and powerful, but he went to look for the three old ladies anyway. Sixty seconds he told himself and then he was leaving. Of course there they were the first place he tried, outside at one of the picnic setups, having fried drumsticks with their cronies. Angry at him for getting them there late, the three ladies were now angry at him for whisking them away early. But the choice was not theirs. They didn't get to choose. Harry dropped them off at the motel. The mother and children's room was dark but the door was thrown open. So many people in there it must be hot. Then he went for a drive.

Two

Scraped leg and all, Beth had kept herself from crying until she saw her mother. She sat alone in the trailer, on Jo's bed, staring across at the sink. Her ankle hadn't swelled at all. Now that she was safe in the trailer, she wished for more visual proof of her trauma. A bunch of scrapes were, after all, just a bunch of scrapes; a swollen, bruised, possibly broken ankle would have been better.

The trailer rocked, the door snapped open. Leonard Dawson walked in. He managed to fill a box without ever looking at it or the things he picked up to put in. Instead he stared the whole time at Beth. Even though she looked down at the floor, it didn't matter. She didn't need her eyes to register his stare. "What's wrong?" he asked in a friendly voice. He knelt down before her. He reached out and smoothed her hair and then did something and his hand came away with the curling rod she had forgotten all about. "You got one curl in your hair," he said. "Maybe tomorrow you'll get two. Go for broke, little girl." He looked down at her leg and put his hand behind her knee. "Did you skin your little self?" He lifted the leg close to his mouth. She jerked away but he held firm. "What, you ain't gonna give me no sugar today?"

When the door opened and her mother stepped in calling her name, Beth burst into tears. Leonard Dawson backed away. Her mother knelt before her and swept her up. She saw over her mother's shoulder how

Leonard Dawson had backed away but backed away only a step because of how the trailer was so narrow; she saw how his arms went up in innocent surrender, how he said, "I was just going to make it feel better" and how, when her kneeling mother turned from hugging her, she froze at something level with her eyes. Her mother stared at the sink until her face contorted. Without warning she jumped on Leonard Dawson. Her flying weight knocked him to the back of the trailer and the whole thing rocked and nearly tipped on its side. He pushed her fists off him and scrambled on his stomach to the door. Her mother whipped off her rucksack. Following his scrambling form, she began beating his back with it. It was heavy enough to hurt him. Leonard Dawson was being hurt, Beth could tell from the deep kettle-drum thuds, yet both of them were silent, eerily silent, and it started not to seem real. Just this deep rhythm of the drums that grew hypnotic, with the almost ceremonial way her mother for each blow brought the rucksack full over her head. So Beth just sat there.

Jo rushed in. The first-aid kit in her hands flew through the air as she tripped over the bodies. Her mother pushed Jo aside and leaped again upon Leonard Dawson, swinging at his back. The first-aid kit scattered, the scissors and tape and a flock of Band-Aids. A bottle of iodine landed on the bed. One of the Band-Aids fluttered onto Beth's injured knee. Leonard Dawson's arms were up protecting his head. He spoke his first words. He said in a quiet voice for Jo to get her off of him. It wasn't a plea, it wasn't a harsh command. It was probably the first normally voiced sentence Beth had heard him speak. But Jo couldn't get anywhere near them, their legs and arms were united as eight flailing limbs. The two bodies bumped open the door and bounced down the two steps, and the unreal fight continued outside. They were quiet, neither of them screaming or bothering to shout their hatred. Quiet except for gasps and the hard knocks of something leaden against flesh, the weird draft of air their eight limbs made, the wind-whipping sound of their clothes scraping through the dirt. Beth sat rigid on the bed. In her hand she grasped the bottle of iodine. The Band-Aid was still balanced on her knee, a perfect white wing. "Mom?" she asked the air of the trailer. "Mom?" Her arms could still feel her mother. The muscles and shoulder sockets still throbbed from being jerked, that was how fast her mother had twisted away. Outside came a pop. She knew what it might be. It might be her mother's shoulder, pulled out of joint.

When she stepped from the trailer and down the steps, she saw Navajo Joe. He was standing there, Indian-like, not moving, his face without expression. He was wearing that same red shirt that wasn't red. She wondered why he was here. Why was he here? Why was he here?

THREE

Charlie's fifth grade teacher strapped and belted the tent onto the roof of the Rambler. Jean, across from him on a stepladder, helped to tighten from her side. Charlie stood on the hood and gave progress reports. Beth crawled inside the station wagon to feed the straps through.

The grandmother's sighs provided the heartbeat to all this activity; in its stubborn rhythm it became the loudest sound.

At some point amid the packing Mr. Jackson had taken off his eyeglasses and now he couldn't find them. Charlie climbed from the hood to the roof and patted about the strapped-down tent. Mr. Jackson checked the pockets of the jacket he had laid on the grass; they went inside and checked the kitchen counter and the bathroom counter, the bookshelves, the sofa, between the throw pillows. "I know!" said Mr. Jackson, checking the trash can under the sink. "I know!" said Beth, opening the refrigerator. Fifteen minutes later they surrendered to defeat. It was time to leave and the kids' grandmother had a Greyhound to catch. Mr. Jackson tried to reassure them that he had probably left the glasses at home. Did he have his glasses on when he arrived? Nobody could remember for sure.

Charlie shook hands with his teacher, who then shook hands with everyone one more time and then lingered by the driver's side with his arm stretched across the roof. Jean gave him a quick awkward smile, what Beth called a banking smile, the kind of smile Jean offered bank tellers in between a deposit here, a withdrawal there, and started the car. Still his arm didn't move. Jean was sorry about his eyeglasses but they were in a hurry. His arm stayed solid across the roof, his hand fiddling blindly with the tent. The white cotton of his undershirt came into view under the short-sleeved dress shirt he always seemed to wear.

Ha! There they were, on the dashboard behind the steering wheel. "Here are your glasses, Mr. Jackson," Jean said.

A "Yay!" from Beth in the back.

"I wish you'd call me Kenny," Mr. Jackson said.

Jean shifted into reverse. "Be nice," her mother murmured in warning.

"Maybe when I get back," she said.

"When *will* you get back?" he asked.

Jean's mother sat with perfect posture, the lavender vanity case propped on her lap. She snapped it open and under a top tray of cosmetics pulled out a tiny calendar and a miniature gold pen. "Let's mark the date," she said.

"Very good, Mother," Jean said. She shifted the Rambler into reverse, swung her arm around the passenger seat, and turned to see out the back. There was Beth with her little smile. Jean wondered if that would be the last image to visit her when she died.

"I'm sorry, Mom," Beth said.

"Don't be sorry. Why are you sorry?"

"Did I wake you up?" Beth sat on the edge of the bed and for a minute Jean confused her daughter with her own mother. Beth had inherited the same perfect posture.

Jean scooted over a little in the bed so Beth could snuggle in. The room didn't spin when she moved. That was a good sign. She wasn't feeling dizzy or in any way sharply hurt or aching. She was feeling, she thought, imprecise. She wondered why she wasn't in pain. She knew that pain heeded signals from the brain. Perhaps there were no more signals because there was no more brain. She touched her head. A crust there barbed against her fingertips.

On the next bed slept Charlie. She listened for Charlie's breathing until she caught his distinctive inhale and exhale. His breathing sounded adequately clear. Slumped on a straight-backed chair was Miss Dazzle. Her head had dropped onto the desktop; one arm swayed down like an elephant's trunk. Jean could smell whiskey or bourbon, she thought that was what it was. In a way she wanted a gulp. In another way, she was ill with the thought.

Nothing had come to her, no images of her beautiful children, or of her mother calling to her from the back door, or of a schoolteacher, or of losing her way down a corridor of classrooms. Not even the bare image of a face she could no longer picture, her husband's face. You'd think that would have come in loud and clear, that face particularly, here to lead the way, because for a moment there—there was actually space enough and time enough to contemplate it—she had thought this was it. Then when it happened and she went blank, blankness happened. It was emptiness, followed by further emptiness. But she hadn't died, so her experience wasn't definitive. She wondered when Charlie's last session had been. She had never been away from him long enough to miss a session, but she'd left him, gone to intercept that fellow so they could leave more quickly and they had done that, they'd left in a hurry, or at least she assumed they had.

Jean needed to ask Jo about Charlie's sessions, but she didn't see Jo in the room, not until Jean turned her head and a bulk on the floor came into view. It must be Jo. It was the only place left in the room, unless Jo was sleeping in the bathtub. A lot of people slept in bathtubs actually, especially in the old days. Growing up, her mother had slept in the bathtub. She told funny bathtub stories. But Jo wasn't in the bathtub, Jo was on the floor: Jean was pretty sure the bulk on the floor was Jo, but she wasn't positive. The hair seemed blonder, almost as yellow as that dress she had worn her first day at the campsite, standing in the trailer's doorway like Marilyn Monroe, trying to act girlish. She wondered if this were another trick, if the thing on the floor weren't Jo at all but a mound of covers topped by a wig, the whole thing a slumber-party trick. The body came to life just as she was thinking about it and let out a sigh in a voice Jean recognized. Yes, it was Jo. And Charlie sounded okay. And Miss Dazzle, there on the desktop, her arm tensing in a fleeting jerk. She was okay, too. Beth was still sitting on the bed, tucked into the crook of Jean's hip, posture straight like her grandmother's, twisting the bedcovers into fists, also like her grandmother. They had similarities, those two, both of them characters.

"Is Jo in the bathtub?" she asked Beth.

"No, she's on the floor. Mom?"

"What?"

"They don't have a bathtub here. It's just a shower."

"Okay."

"Did you think there was a bathtub?"

"I was confused for a second."

"Do you have brain damage?"

"I was just dreaming, honey."

"Mom?"

"Yes."

"My leg's all scraped up and I got a splinter in it."

"Does it hurt?"

"A little."

"Is the splinter still in there?"

"It's still in there."

"Why didn't you tell someone?"

"I just recently learned about it myself. I have a flashlight. Do you want to look at it?"

"Let me see it."

Beth pointed the beam to a spot below her knee. Her knees were the dark smudges all children's knees were and Jean couldn't see anything.

"Will you be okay, honey?" she asked. "Should we take it out now or in the morning?"

"In the morning," Beth said.

"Are you sure?"

"Mom, did you know there's a sightseeing bus that takes you to see the atomic bomb?"

"That sounds nice."

"Can I go on it sometime?"

"We'll see, all right? Let Mommy think about it."

"They provide lunch. And that lunch is a delectable barbecue."

"It's a long ride, isn't it? Maybe even overnight."

"It's a late lunch, almost like a dinner," Beth said. "It's in between, I think. There's snacks in the morning. And that late lunch is a delectable barbecue. You have a scab right there. Did you know that?" Beth aimed the flashlight at Jean's head.

"I felt it earlier. How does it look?"

"It looks okay."

"It feels big," Jean said.

"It doesn't look big when you look at it."

"Good. Not in the eyes, honey. That light hurts."

"Do you feel okay?" Beth asked. She clicked off the flashlight.

"I feel fine."

"Mom?"

"Yes."

"It's fifteen dollars."

"It's not the money I'm worried about."

"It is a long ride. Is that what you're worried about?" Beth asked.

"Yes, more or less," she said.

"I'm worried about going by myself on the bus."

"Don't worry, Beth."

"Charlie said he won't go with me. I don't know if I can go all alone on the bus."

"Is it a sure thing that you definitely want to go?"

"I'm still thinking about it."

"It's something that we can talk about then and figure out. Let Mommy think about it later."

"I can't stop thinking about it. It just worries me," Beth said.

"I know, darling."

"Why am I so worried about it?"

"It's natural, honey."

"I'm so worried I can't sleep."

"Don't worry, sweetheart. Come here. Let me hold you. Don't worry, I'm here. Go to sleep. Don't worry about anything. Let Mommy take care of it in the morning."

Jo twisted abruptly in her sleep and her knee hit the foot of the bed. She didn't wake up but she yelped in pain.

"My goodness, everybody's getting hurt," Jean whispered. Her whisper roused Miss Dazzle, who jerked up 100 percent awake and came over to their bed and touched both their foreheads and held their hands.

"How are you feeling?" Miss Dazzle asked.

"I have a splinter in my leg," Beth said.

Four

The three old ladies sat by the shallow end of the pool. They were playing dealer's-choice poker. Jean liked poker and listened to the games they called out: seven-card whores and fours, high-low, baseball, follow the queen. Baseball, oh I like baseball, Jean told them. One of the ladies ran up an outlandish baseball hand, an extra card with a dealt-up 4 and wild cards with a 3 and 9 and another 9 from the 4. Only Jean could follow along and the ladies were delighted to have an appreciative audience over by the deep end. The winner finished with six jacks and bemoaned the fact that only five of them counted. Jean tried not to laugh because it jarred her head. The ladies asked her to be a fourth, but she wasn't up to it, which they understood: Did it hurt much? Not at all, she told them. Jo started to volunteer for the card game but Jean warned her off: poker players don't like to teach. Jo hadn't noticed how the ladies, always so talkative, got silent during the games.

Charlie finished swimming his laps, an activity the old ladies, who found almost everything whisper-worthy (she had heard them whispering earlier, referring to Harry as a lot of nothing), actually engaged in themselves, although usually in the evening. They smiled approvingly at Charlie's undue heaving. Miss Dazzle kicked open the office door and backed out with a tray. She was wearing a stiff new overly blue pair of overalls. A sleeveless shell was barely visible underneath. She had earlier served drinks and now she came out with a lunch of tuna-fish sandwiches. The ladies grabbed at the sandwiches eagerly. Miss Dazzle put sugar in their mayonnaise. Everyone else got their sandwiches without the secret ingredient.

The tabby had finally showed up and Jean saw Beth put down her latest Lois Lenski to twiddle her fingers and call meow. But the cat settled by the ladies' feet and they fed him under the table like he was a dog. Miss Dazzle held up three fingers. "Got hit again while you were gone," she told Beth. "He gets stranger but not any deader." "It must be true about nine lives," Jo commented cheerfully. Miss Dazzle didn't answer. She checked on Beth's leg. Swimming in the pool had helped to dry out the scrapes. Then she came over to check Jean's head. She had already swabbed the spot with iodine. She said well okay, everything was looking pretty dandy and let's just let the sun do its work before we put on a bandage. Jean hadn't realized her scalp was largely numb until she registered the tingling thickness of Miss Dazzle's careless but gentle strokes.

"Charlie, you need to eat your sandwich," Jo said. "Here, let me dry you off."

Miss Dazzle looked a little askance at Jo.

Jean watched her son and wanted to run to him and hold him. He was standing the way all those boys in his winter swim class did after their lessons, dripping, shivering in place, holding their elbows, not a single one of them bothering with the solution of a towel. Jean held up a towel and beckoned to him. Charlie ignored her. With a towel would come a hug, and a hug would be noticeable. She tried never to be noticeably extra nice to Charlie. Extra anything asked the question why. It drew attention—it drew *his* attention—to why his mother treated him so special.

But Miss Dazzle grabbed the terrycloth and went after Charlie with big, bear-hug strokes, holding him against her for one long tussling snuggle. When she released Charlie, the front of her new bib overalls was soaked.

"Probably have a blue bra now," she said, happy to prove entertaining. "Well, the two boys have made it to California," she announced. "They finally got through to me. Lordy, do I have a talker on my party line."

"It's terrible," the old lady with the whitest hair said. "We're up to eight now on our line."

"And I have calls to make," another added.

Miss Dazzle said, "Of course it provides them with a nice excuse not to call their mother and let her know they're not camping in Yellowstone anymore. They can tell me they've been calling and calling but the line was busy—like heck."

"How'd they like Yellowstone?" Jo asked. "Who are they, your sons?"

"Just delicious!" the old lady with a champagne tint called over, holding up a sandwich.

"That means they want more," Miss Dazzle whispered to Jean. She headed to her office, calling back to the ladies, "If I make a few more sandwiches, will you eat them?"

"Don't make them on my account."

"Only if somebody else wants one."

"I'm sure somebody does," Miss Dazzle said.

After lunch Jo said, "Charlie, why don't you show me that piece of petrified wood you brought back?" Miss Dazzle narrowed her eyes at Charlie's and Jo's departing figures. From the motel room came the sound of the radio, turned up too loud. Jean tried to act like it was nothing, but Jo's excuse had been too theatrically casual. She called over to the ladies, "Sounds like another six of a kind over there!" Even though she was a much better actress than Jo, it was no good. Antennae might as well have grown out of Miss Dazzle's head.

"Check or bet," the ladies demanded.

"Check," came the resigned grumble.

The other two cackled at the third one's tone of defeat. "She's got to check every time so we don't fold," they called over gleefully to Jean.

"I win the hand but no chips," the third lady complained. She was the one with the whitest hair, almost a painted white. Jean had been sitting there admiring it.

"Is there something wrong with your son?" Miss Dazzle asked.

"My, you're direct," Jean said. She gave a sharp glance toward Beth. Her eyes swooped toward the old ladies, who, too busy laughing, had missed hearing.

"I have two sons," Miss Dazzle said in a conversational tone.

"I know," Jean said.

"So whatever you're going through I might understand."

Jean again aimed her eyes toward Beth and the ladies.

"Point taken," Miss Dazzle said.

The ladies stalled in their shuffling and tried not to look over. "What did she say?" one of them whispered.

The sky as usual was cloudless, and its vast blueness was almost but not quite the same color as the pool. That little bit of difference made the pool depressing. Against the real sky it could not compete. It had the same lingering dreariness as the Y indoor pool where she had taken Charlie for his lessons. It was against doctor's orders, but she believed the exercise was good for him. Pounding him after swimming, she could always tell that his lungs cleared more easily. And Charlie liked it and he liked the instructor, young and muscular and free, whose crew cut and glasses turned him into an accountant once he was out of the water, and Charlie liked the other boys in the class, too, and the boys all liked him.

A dark-gray truck pulled in and although it wasn't a yellow International Harvester, Harry stepped out of the driver's side. Jean didn't know the smallish man who popped out of the passenger side. He was introduced to her as Dr. Randolph. Harry lingered by the truck, the way a mother might who had a sleeping baby inside. The doctor said something about is this the little lady with the six-shooter, something stupid like that, she didn't catch it all. Miss Dazzle had had her fill of the doctor from what little Jean had learned, but that didn't stop Miss Dazzle from being hospitable. The tray was still mostly full with a second round of sandwiches. The doctor picked up a diagonal half of sandwich and aimed his bite into the center, the way a child would do. Miss Dazzle brought out a cold drink and the doctor said, "You got anything of the stronger variety to put in this drink," and she said, "Already in, Randy." "You know me too well," he said. Jean wondered if the doctor could possibly be named Randy Randolph. She doubted it, but out here anything seemed possible.

The doctor stood over Jean at the pool. He said they didn't have to move to the room for the exam, the light was better out here. The old ladies were so busy craning that the one dealt the cards right off the table. "And of course whatever I say everybody's going to find out anyway," he said. He twisted over his shoulder toward the ladies. "We'll just make it easy for everyone, shall we?" The *shall we* seemed to suit the physique of the doctor, something a little prissy and tiny in its impact. Jean had begun to notice that so many of the men out here in this rough world, suited only for the toughest of men, were physically small.

The doctor dabbed Jean's head with some iodine, clearly not noticing the medicinal yellow already coating it. She smelled the tuna fish anew when he paused and took another bite. He didn't bother with a bandage; he said the air was a better healer.

Miss Dazzle, peering down with him, said, "We have a little girl with a big splinter, too." Her robust flesh and personality towered over him, the thick red hair, teased at the crown this morning, adding another two inches to the two inches she already had on him.

"Let's look at your leg," Dr. Randolph said.

Beth came over and Dr. Randolph glanced down and said something like why that's just a scraped leg. Beth sat on Jean's lap and asked her when they could have the barbecue. The doctor, who stopped being a doctor to Jean at the next moment, said, "Why that's a selfish little girl to put yourself first when your momma's laid up. You should get off her lap and leave her alone."

Jean had already jumped upon one man and pummeled him to no

good effect, so she stayed put. She could only hope he might get close enough to the pool for somebody to knock him in. She held on tighter when Beth tried to get up.

Randolph looked up as Jo and Charlie returned, and Jean saw how his features opened up at the sight of Jo, and she noticed how he took the steps in being a man, drinking, enjoying women, and exaggerated them in opposite proportion to his size. But he made that little mistake, biting into his sandwich like a little boy. Plus she hated him for what he had said to Beth.

She noticed Miss Dazzle studying Charlie. Charlie looked better, his skin flushed and clear. It could easily be from his swim and the sun and the water, but of course Miss Dazzle wasn't going to fall for any of that. Jean glanced over at Randolph's watch: only half past noon. Already Charlie had needed a second session. Miss Dazzle swept up her hair into a hand-bound ponytail. The underarm moons of her sleeveless shell were turning blue. She let her hair drop and fanned out the wet bib of her overalls. The dye of the new overalls was leaking blueness everywhere. When Jean closed her eyes, the smell of chlorine took over. There was something about the smell of chlorine in the summer, especially on your own skin: it turned the everyday into magic.

Randolph said, his smile upon Jo, "If they'd told me there were so many pretty women to take care of, I would have been out here a lot sooner."

"Harry, you didn't tell him that?" Miss Dazzle teased, raising her voice so Harry could hear her down by the truck.

"Did you say we were ugly?" Jo asked.

Harry kicked around uncomfortably by the tires.

"You're not coming up to visit?"

"Gotta get going," Harry said.

"I got some tuna-fish sandwiches all prepared."

"That won't get him up here," Jean said.

"What's wrong with you, Harry?"

"Gotta get going."

The old ladies took note of Harry's strange behavior and added it to their list of whispers. Jean realized (and even with her head injury, saw that she was the only one appearing to realize it) that Harry was waiting for something, that he had some errand, some mission of consequence. She encouraged Randolph, well, don't let us keep you, we know you have important business to take care of. She had never been good at any of the glib social clichés, but now they seemed to spin out of her on their own. They were so much easier to say now that her head had been grazed by a bullet. Her thick skull of self-consciousness had thinned to a porous skin.

Randolph had seated himself in another chaise longue and to her chagrin accepted a second drink from Miss Dazzle. He took a swallow before calling over, "Okay, Harry, you go ahead and take off. You don't really need me. I think I've signed what I need to sign."

Jean thought of things this man's personality reminded her of: a doorknob, a second coat of paint, a plain piece of paper, a penny with an unreadable date, a shirt abandoned to a mud puddle. If only she could talk to a doorknob and get the answers she needed. As a sort of perversity she imagined broaching the subject of Charlie with Dr. Randy Randolph, imagining what he would say. *Some cough syrup should fix him right up.* Even the doorknob would have a better answer: *Turn, then push hard.*

Before leaving, Harry dared to abandon the vehicle long enough to drop three letters on Jean's lap. Not postcards. Letters. Three letters, postmarked from Springfield, Ohio, sealed and crinkled with saliva. Three sealed letters from her mother, thick with hidden words. Perhaps very important words. She would throw them away as soon as she was alone.

"Thank you, Harry," she said.

FIVE

Once she discovered that Harry was headed to Grand Junction, Miss Dazzle came round to the doctor's Mercury truck and pressed a blank personal check into his hand. Through the open window floated another piece of paper: a long list of liquor supplies including jars of maraschino cherries, which were not illegal in their town but were hard to come by and expensive. Seeing him linger mysteriously by the Mercury, scuffing his feet and refusing to come up to the pool, Miss Dazzle had no doubt appraised the situation straight off. She'd done more than her share of covering for the doctor and knew his ways. "What's Randy got you doing this time?" she asked Harry. "As if I couldn't guess."

Harry started up the truck. Both of them turned to glance toward the rear of the truck, where Vernon Rutledge's body lay iced. It was a funny movement perfectly timed and, just as perfectly timed, their heads shot back around. Harry hadn't yet looked at the body and had no intention to. He had no desire to make himself sick. Miss Dazzle's face tightened. Nothing back there she wished to see either. Harry knew the old ladies would have no such reluctance. He could return to their good graces by inviting them down to have a peek at a macabre sight.

Miss Dazzle ducked her head through the driver's window and tapped the list. She said as far as gin went to get anything on sale—she'd pass the savings on to the three ladies. But for whiskey they liked a certain brand.

She didn't know why. With a whiskey sour all you tasted was sugar anyway. Harry could see her face start to relax as she forgot about the torn-up wretchedness in the back and concentrated on liquor brands. Her forearms lay across the window frame as she gave instructions. They were a redhead's forearms, freckled, no hair, the skin crepey, the white skin turned off-white by the sun. Harry thought it was wrong to be noticing a woman's body part so closely. He told himself he was doing it so he wouldn't be thinking of the gruesome errand ahead.

"I better get a move on," he said.

"How'd you land this job?" Miss Dazzle asked.

"Bribe."

Miss Dazzle shook her head.

"Only way I could get him to come and take a look at her."

"He's glad he came now," Miss Dazzle said. "Doubt I can get him to leave. Lot of good he did, too."

Harry had offered to take Vernon Rutledge's body to the coroner in Grand Junction if the doctor would pay a house call to Jean. Randolph was balking because it meant he'd have to file a report since a shooting was involved, and of course he didn't want to do that, he wanted to do whatever caused the least amount of work. Harry had been lingering by the Mercury for several minutes now, the ice melting, the body (probably) floating in a pool, all while he waited to see if the mother needed to be taken to the hospital in Grand Junction. His answer was on the chaise longue playing Hollywood star, poolside with his drinks and women.

"He's happy as a clam," Miss Dazzle said.

Harry said, "I should drop him off on my way out of town. I'm sure you don't want him around. She's got to rest."

"Oh, he'll let her rest. It's that other one he's after."

Harry paused at the way she had referred to Jo, not by her name but as that other one. He wondered if Miss Dazzle had guessed his secret. She seemed to know everything. It would take her only another half step to read his mind, too.

"I'll give him a couple more drinks and drive him home myself," Miss Dazzle said. "I know how to handle him. Don't worry about us, Harry. Have a safe trip. Don't forget—" she picked up the list from his lap and folded it into his shirt pocket. She patted his arm.

"Freezing cold in here," he told her. Miss Dazzle laughed but Harry hadn't meant it as a joke.

As he started to pull out, Miss Dazzle threw up her arms in X's. Harry stopped the truck and backed up. Miss Dazzle ran into her office and returned with a paper bag she tossed through the passenger window. "Now eat these sandwiches," she said. "I made tons. I got a little carried away. But that's me, isn't it? And they're your favorite." Harry smiled, wondering what kind of sandwich his favorite might be. Then Miss Dazzle unhooked the bib of her overalls and tugged back the armhole of her sleeveless shirt to expose her bra. " Look at this, Harry. My bra's turning blue."

"Huh," Harry said. He couldn't help noticing that Miss Dazzle's underarms were hairless in a way that suggested they had never grown hair. Though he hadn't seen Rutledge's body and had no intention of seeing Rutledge's body, he had this picture of death set afloat in melting ice and at the same time this other picture of a blue crescent of breast and un-stippled underarm, and neither one was something he had ever experienced up close, much less up close together.

"If you ever want one of your shirts dyed blue, give it to me and I'll wash it with my jeans," Miss Dazzle said. "And I'm only half joking when I say that. You ever thought about switching to a light-blue dress shirt? It would look good on you, Harry." Harry wondered if this was the half that was joking now or the half that wasn't, so he didn't answer. He wouldn't have known what to say anyway. He wasn't good at joking and anybody who joked with him immediately got the upper hand.

Miss Dazzle didn't seem to mind he wasn't answering. Her face softened and the smile she gave him was tender and almost sad. Her hands hung straight down inside the truck door. Her nails clicked a song on the metal handle. The hands looked sort of fattish almost, with the wedding and engagement rings snug (on Jo's thin finger, the rings were just loose enough for an elegant droop). Miss Dazzle must have noticed his glance; she quit clicking and started playing with the rings. Engagement, marriage, around and around. Everybody knew that guy of hers wasn't coming back, especially Miss Dazzle, but she needed those rings on display to keep the fellows out here in line.

"Say, did you hear me telling the ladies up there?"

"What's that?" Harry asked.

"Boys finally made it to California."

"That so," Harry said. "Well, good. Are they having a fine time, I bet?"

"Of course I don't get to hear much thanks to Ma Bell."

"Tell him I said hi."

"Him, Harry, you said him."

"I meant them."

"You know already? Does the whole town know?"

"What are you talking about?" Harry asked.

"All right then. Never mind." Miss Dazzle withdrew her head. Harry put the truck in gear again, and then she was back. Her head ducked in and she readied herself to speak but didn't. Harry felt his neck flushing. He began staring at the horn on his steering wheel, round like the moon with faces in it if you stared too long. "You're going to make me say it, aren't you?" Miss Dazzle said.

"No, heavens no, you don't have to say anything," Harry answered, with no idea what she was talking about.

"They're with their cousin."

"I know," Harry said, now fearing the worst, a girl who'd been knocked up. The reason for this mysterious overly long trip by two boys still technically teenagers was starting to come clear.

"But he's there, too. Did you know that, Harry?"

"Who?"

"Him. He's there. Him, Harry. That's who. Supposedly moved out there permanently. Well, that's what he said when he married me, sup-posedly permanently."

"You mean your ex-husband?"

"Still officially husband, Harry."

"I'm sorry," Harry said. "I had no idea. I'm really sorry."

"You're lucky you're not married, Harry. And you a Mormon, good Lord, the most eligible guy in town. You got any supposedly permanent girls on a string, Harry?"

Now Harry was taken aback, wondering if Miss Dazzle had orches-trated this whole conversation just to bring it around to Jo. He couldn't believe she thought that man was ever coming back.

"Is that why the boys went out there, to visit their dad?" Harry asked.

"They think they're bringing him back. Oh, the course of true love." Miss Dazzle laughed bitterly.

"Does he have a mind to?"

"If Ma Bell had a mind to let me speak through the hundred other people on my line, I might find out."

"I wish you good luck," Harry said.

"Oh Harry," she said. "You're quite a guy, aren't you." She jutted her chin toward the back. "Poor fellow, huh," she said, tapping his roof good-bye. "I guess some people have it worse." Then she seemed satisfied to let him leave.

A few miles beyond town Harry spotted a white Cadillac heading in the opposite direction and it suddenly occurred to him that this might be the partner Leonard Dawson had been bragging about. Harry knew the man. It was Vincent Flaherty. Despite the Cadillac, the money Flaherty had made on penny stocks had dried up. There had been rumors about his latest mines being salted.

Flaherty gave a toot of his horn as they passed each other. Harry watched him for as long as he could out of his rearview mirror. The road was long and straight and, except for their two cars, deserted. The empti-ness made the heat visible. The tarred road flicked up a black vapor, and the Cadillac appeared to Harry's squinting eyes to be riding on a current of soot. Harry kept blinking to bring the car back into proper focus. He stopped the truck and leaned forward and gripped the mirror. The Cadillac, now a jumping white ember, flared across the road—heading, had to be, toward the Stagecoach Oasis.

Outside, the sun burned the road, but inside the truck it was cold, refrigerator cold, and Harry shivered. He again felt that urge that had daily, no, hourly, begun stabbing at him: protect Jo, protect Jo. He wanted to turn around and head back. Jo would need his help. She didn't know how to deal with Flaherty's type. He checked the rearview mirror but it gave up nothing. He had no choice, he had to get the body delivered. So much time already wasted. The ice was likely melted, the poor body probably floating back there. He stepped on the gas.

He pictured both men after Jo, the doctor and now this other one, Flaherty, each of them crooning so easily the words that in his own throat remained stuck. Each time Harry tried to shove an ingratiating phrase out into the world, each time he tried to visualize the sentence forced into place by these words—just easy simple syllables that combined into easy simple words, just take them one at a time and throw them out there, the sentence will come to life and do the rest of the work for you—the self-coaching never worked, and embarrassing nonsensical sounds replaced his voice. There was something wrong with him, there truly was. Here he was charged with the most grave of missions and was he paying proper respect to a man who had died in his line of work or was he thinking about syllables and a blue crescent that extended into the unseen fullness of a breast and nipple? Unseen until now, that is. He couldn't believe himself. Was he really imagining this? Don't tell him that his polygamous blood was now leading him to include Miss Dazzle as well.

He started to relive the trip back from Jimmy Splendid's camp. He was awash with that afternoon, Jo by his side at the oasis, helping him load up his cached equipment, getting dirty, getting scraped, how they had worked side by side, how over the scrub brush had bobbed the heads of the mother and Charlie, leaving him alone with Jo, who was so much stronger than she looked. Being side by side with Jo was all that had mattered. It was everything. They had stood there together and he had leaned toward her. She had leaned, too, he could see that now.

Harry looked down at the speedometer and saw that he was doing over eighty. He slowed, then pulled the truck over and steadied himself. The road's unswerving black arrow shot far into the horizon. He gripped the steering wheel and leaned his head upon it.

In two days Harry's life had been turned inside out and he had discovered two main lessons in life: love makes you horribly wretchedly happy and love makes you electrically wonderfully miserable. And the thing was, he supposed there were more lessons like these for him to learn, perhaps each more upsetting than the previous one, he should quickly turn his back on this chain reaction the way his religion would insist upon. He didn't want to learn them, he was compelled to learn them. He hated being in love, he loved it. But he was living, you see (by now he was talking out loud as well), really living, living head on and square in the face. He was living without checking in with God every step of the way. Though admittedly this spree had gone on for only two days, he was doing what his religion was most scared of—which was why it gave everyone two wives or maybe three, to trick them into thinking *we're really living now!* Harry was seeing for the first time what living truly involved and it wasn't what necessarily made you content, but it gave you one or two moments of dangerous transcendence. Was it enough to sell your soul for? He could walk away and still be a contented man. A good man, the good man he had never until now doubted he was, a good man who was yet content. It wasn't too late. He could come to his senses and forget about Jo and go back to his regular life and rediscover the contentment there. Which was what he should do.

Which was what he couldn't do.

Six

Beth was already finished with the true incredible story of Mary Jemison the Indian captive and had moved on to *Cotton in My Sack*. She had reached a point where she started imagining the book report she would write even before finishing the first chapter. *A book I like is* Cotton in My Sack. Cotton in My Sack *is good because it tells you a lot about picking cotton. Everyone puts cotton in their sack all day long until their fingers are bleeding and the sack is as heavy as a big bag of Halloween candy but not as nice. The main girl in this book* Cotton in My Sack *has fingers that bleed a lot and she gets splinters, too, ouch!, and she's young and shouldn't even be doing this.*

Now that was a good opening. She ducked her head and put her hand over her mouth so no one would see her self-satisfied smile. Bad thing about the desert and being alone so much: she was starting to act out all her reactions. Nobody noticed. They were all too busy with themselves. She checked her leg, already drying up. She told herself not to pick any scabs, but she knew she'd give in to the temptation.

The tabby had run off again. Beth hoped the cat wouldn't get involved with anything like a car running over him that would cost him another life. Charlie had disappeared, too. He had gone into Miss Dazzle's office. Miss Dazzle had invited him inside, tempting him with the toys she played with when no one was around, the ceramics kit, the wood-burning set, and her own tray of test tubes and the little corked bottles of secret chemicals that got mixed inside them. That was what really tempted Charlie for he'd left his chemistry set at the campsite. Beth remembered how Miss Dazzle had glowed red in the night from the brake lights of Harry's truck, a crimson afterimage mimicking her gestures. It was easy to picture her as a homemade mad scientist holding up a test tube with hot-dog prongs.

She knew it wouldn't be long before Miss Dazzle had Charlie's situation figured out. Miss Dazzle was going through what the teachers in Beth's school would call a process of elimination, which meant applying the principles of dodge ball to taking multiple choice tests. First, Miss Dazzle was getting rid of the easy possibilities, the ones that just stood there and didn't get out of the way. In dodge ball that meant most of the girls, especially anyone named Peggy Anderson. In Charlie's case the easy target was the sun. Miss Dazzle was taking him out of the sun and putting him into her office to see if that helped his situation. Of course the sun wasn't his problem, that was stupid, but no more stupid than Peggy Anderson, who just never got it, like *move* when somebody is throwing the ball at you. On the other hand, you had to get rid of all the Peggy Andersons and clear the area so you could identify your real enemy. And then suddenly, a game that had seemed all too easy became way too hard (meaning, not once had she ever thrown out Tommy Beckwith).

Anyway, guaranteed Miss Dazzle would find out. This Beth knew for certain. Giving up wasn't in Miss Dazzle's nature. It was as if that night in the parking lot the neon-red pantomimes flowing from Miss Dazzle's hands had exposed a part of human nature usually left invisible. Maybe Beth had witnessed Miss Dazzle's soul. More likely it had been her intestinal fortitude.

Charlie and Miss Dazzle were still inside when a dashing white car with fins pulled into the Stagecoach Oasis. Beth leaped up and made a quick panicked survey of the lot. No tabby to get run over. The white car parked. Everyone stopped what they were doing to watch. Several long moments passed before the motor turned off, and several more long moments ticked off before the door finally opened. "Any bets on whether he can get out?" one of the old ladies said. Another one anted up a big mound of chips and they all burst into old-lady versions of belly laughing.

Miss Dazzle came to the doorway of her office. Her arms twisted unhappily in geometric shapes up and down the rose-colored frame. The man used both arms to pull himself from the car. It was quiet, and the way the pool water occasionally lapped into the gutters made it more quiet. When the car door slammed, it broke the air. Everybody jumped, even though they were expecting the sound. Miss Dazzle's limbs twisted out of their unhappy swastika, and she stepped from the rosy doorframe. "Hello, Vince," she said, her voice cheerful. Miss Dazzle always greeted everyone the same, as if they had just arrived for the party she was throwing, even her mother that night she lay sprawled in Navajo Joe's pickup. Her mother might have been shot dead, but that wasn't enough to stop Miss Dazzle from being sociable.

The man named Vince stretched out an arm to the roof of his car and leaned over to catch his breath. He tossed out a salute to Miss Dazzle and dipped his hat. The hat waved over toward the pool in a questioning swirl. Miss Dazzle crossed her arms and shrugged.

The man climbed the three cement steps to the pool. The plumbing-pipe railing wobbled dangerously. "Doctor's in the house in case you keel over, Vince!" Dr. Randolph yelled out. The piping snapped away from the man as he pushed up the final step. Even the old ladies didn't lean upon the railing. The cement at its base was crumbly. The old ladies looked up from the pretend card shuffling they had been doing. Their mouths were swollen shut from the chortles swelling inside. "Is one of you fair ladies the newlywed Josephine Dawson?" the man asked. Only one of the old ladies tittered gratefully, the blondish one, who had reapplied her bright red lipstick as soon as the white car pulled in.

The man then turned to her mother. "Miss Josephine Dawson, I presume." Beth had written enough book reports to guess from the fancy formality that the very next words out of the man's mouth were going to be something like "Allow me to introduce myself." He was acting out some kind of make-believe, bowing as if before a king and queen: as his arm swept out grandly, the businessman's fedora was replaced by a Three Musketeers hat.

Speaking of make-believe, the man was Humpty-Dumpty fat, with a kettle-drum stomach and two stick legs that didn't seem real.

"My name is Vincent Flaherty, and your husband has recently become a partner of mine."

Her mom didn't bother to correct him. Jo had gone back to the room to change into her bathing suit and was missing the whole show put on for her benefit.

"That's Vincent Flaherty," Beth heard the old ladies whispering to each other.

Miss Dazzle appeared at the pool with her tray. The doctor was finishing up his second drink and he took a third one already mixed for him. Vincent Flaherty picked up the bottle and poured his own. His drink was a lot browner than the doctor's drink and he poured only a little. Beth studied the bottle that was on the tray. *Jim Beam* was the name and the very interesting words *80 proof* were on it. It was barely lunchtime, it was more like past-breakfast-time, and everybody was drinking and that was the way this town operated. And yet there was absolutely no alcohol in this town and nobody drank because the law didn't allow it and because they were too religious. Not a single bit of liquor because that was how God wanted it. A guy named Jim Beam, if he could talk, could mention 80 percent proof that there was in fact drinking in this town, but 80 percent was not nearly enough to convince people. Yet these same people took 0.0 percent proof that God existed and treated it like 100. Pretty much the whole town needed to be in her fourth grade math class.

Vincent Flaherty toasted her mother and sat down. He inched forward in the chair until his legs were spread wide apart, furthering the illusion that his thighs and knees had been purchased in the toy department and stuck into his big potato stomach. He was staring at the fedora in his hands, chopping at its crease, when Jo returned to the pool. Vincent Flaherty was so busy living in his make-believe world that he didn't notice Jo until she was at the deep end, untying the robe she wore over her bathing suit.

"Well, okay, that's what we're here for!" the doctor cried.

Jo tried not to look horrified but her face crumpled and she backed away and Beth saw her begin to cave in as she sat down. She drew the robe around her, over her neck and chin.

Beth looked over for her mother's reaction, but her mother had fallen asleep.

"You don't talk to a lady like that," Vincent Flaherty corrected sternly. He pushed himself up to a standing position and that took some effort. Beth didn't understand how legs could be that skinny and a stomach could be that fat.

"You don't give the orders around here, Vince."

"I protect the dignity of fine women and if that means giving an order to the intemperate likes of you, then so be it."

The doctor laughed.

"Hear hear," one of the old ladies said. "You can't come up here and get tight and insult us. We're paying guests."

"No one's insulting you. No one even wants to—"

"That's enough," Miss Dazzle said. Her hand was already around the doctor's arm. "We're going home."

"I don't want to," the doctor said.

"You've got patients waiting," Miss Dazzle said, leading him to her DeSoto. In a moment they had sped away, it happened like that before anyone could see it coming, and Miss Dazzle was seeming to Beth more and more like a magician. She was glad now that Miss Dazzle had taken on Charlie as her project. She was, in fact, filled with relief. For the first time in a long time she felt calm about the whole visitor situation.

"Ladies, I'm sorry you had to experience that," Vincent Flaherty said.

"He's a little man," one of the old ladies said.

"Short," the other two agreed.

"I'm afraid, ladies, that yes there is some truth to the theory of the Napoleonic complex. Young man—" Vincent Flaherty was now addressing Charlie, who had joined them at the pool. "Explain to us for our edification the theory of the Napoleonic complex." Charlie was carrying some test tubes and bottles of chemicals.

"He doesn't need to. Charlie is going to be a tall man," one of the ladies said. Her back sprang erect.

"He'll grow," the other ladies agreed. The ladies liked Charlie. Beth liked the fact that they liked him so much. They were prepared to defend him.

"Charlie, is it?" Vincent Flaherty said.

"I feel sorry for his patients." Jo, who was still grabbing at her robe, stared numbly at the white cement. Vincent Flaherty walked over to her.

"'Allow me to introduce myself,'" Beth whispered to Charlie.

"Allow me to introduce myself," Vincent Flaherty said, bowing before Jo. Beth grinned victoriously at Charlie, who nodded without much interest. Jo hesitated, then timidly offered her hand, which Vincent Flaherty, instead of shaking, kissed.

"How very . . . very." Jo stopped, searching for the word.

"Would that you were Josephine Dawson," Vincent Flaherty said. "You seem much more amenable."

"Well, I am," Jo said.

Vincent Flaherty turned to look at Beth's mother, then at Jo.

"I've been had. Ol' Vince has been put on. Is that it?"

"Oh no," Jo said. "Nothing like that. She's had a head injury."

"Ahh." Vincent Flaherty reared back his head. He paused respectfully. "So she's the one."

"It's too bad," one of the ladies said. "We could use her for our fourth."

"Maybe it's not nice to talk about someone while they're sleeping in front of you," Charlie mumbled.

"What are you doing with those test tubes?" Beth asked him.

"I'm experimenting with my petrified wood."

"Isn't it my petrified wood?"

Charlie didn't answer.

"Miss Dazzle thinks she's curing you," Beth whispered to Charlie.

"I know," Charlie said.

"She's going to figure it out."

"I already told her," Charlie said. "Nothing works on petrified wood. Do you know why?"

"Because it's petrified?"

"Well kind of, yeah."

"Why did you tell her?" Beth asked.

"Because she asked."

"Why didn't you let her figure it out? She would have figured it out. She needs to figure it out on her own."

"Why does she need to figure it out on her own?"

"Because . . ." Beth began. How to explain it?

"Charlie, is it?" The man had walked over to them. He had no qualms about interrupting their private conversation. Beth was sitting on the cement and the upward view of Vincent Flaherty was unsettling.

"Yes," Charlie said.

Vincent Flaherty looked down at Charlie's test tubes. "What are you doing there?"

"I'm mixing calcium nitrate and sodium carbonate."

"And why are you doing that?"

"So it'll explode."

"So it'll explode," Vincent Flaherty repeated. "Boy's doing chemistry." He sent a conspiratorial smile to the old ladies. "What happens after it explodes, Charlie Einstein?"

"It blows up."

"It blows up. That's it?"

"There are other things," Charlie said. "It blows up everything but the petrified wood."

"Ah," Vincent Flaherty said. "And why doesn't the petrified wood blow up?"

"Because it's petrified."

"And that my friends is chemistry!" Vincent Flaherty exclaimed, turning to sweep his imaginary Three Musketeers hat toward the three old ladies. "Charlie, have you ever heard of Albert Einstein?"

Charlie looked at Beth and rolled his eyes.

"No need to be impolite."

"I didn't say anything," Charlie said.

"Charlie, let me tell you something. When elders talk to you, you got to respect what they say. Even if you're one of these straight-A scientist whiz kids, you don't talk back. Okay? We got a deal?"

"I have to ask my mother first," Charlie mumbled into his chest.

"What's that, Charlie Einstein?"

"I have to ask my mother first."

Vincent Flaherty looked at Charlie for a long time, long enough that one of the ladies called over, "Charlie's a good boy, now." The way she said *now* made it into a warning. Since Vincent Flaherty lived in a pretend world where he was a Musketeer who was always chivalrous to the ladies, he had to back down.

"I can see I need to keep my eye on you," he told Charlie.

"Charlie's a good boy."

"A very good boy."

Jo walked over from the deep end and pulled a chair next to Charlie. The chair, green-webbed with shiny aluminum tubing, slid against the cement in a clanging scrape, a sound of summer that gladdened Beth even in the midst of this showdown. Charlie sat cross-legged on the cement with his test tubes. Jo reached out and stroked his hair.

"I can see you like the boy," Vincent Flaherty said. "I will defer to your good taste and give him a second chance."

"Thank you. You'll find out how special he is."

Charlie rolled his eyes again.

Vincent Flaherty raised his arms and shook them at the heavens—and just like that he switched from a Musketeer to Moses. "We are all in a mess out here, aren't we? We are driven by greed and eaten alive by false hope. And do you know who we can thank for that?"

"Who?" Jo asked like a little girl.

"Do you know who predicted a destruction even more terrible than the present destruction of life? A chain reaction great enough to destroy all of this planet?"

"Helen Keller?" Jo asked.

Vincent Flaherty looked to Charlie. "Who?"

Charlie paused. "Albert Einstein," he said.

"Are you guessing or do you know for sure?"

"I'm guessing," Charlie said.

"Not only is he honest but he's an excellent guesser. Charlie, I'm impressed with you. It was the right choice to give this lad a second chance. Charlie, if it weren't for a certain Mr. Albert Einstein and the encouragement of his München mother, we wouldn't be here digging up uranium and getting rich. I like Einstein, I'm a big fan of Einstein's, wouldn't miss him for the world if he stopped by in a parade on his way to a testing site. Left his homeland, saved our behinds for us. But he's created a mess. Albert Einstein, the man who gave us $E = mc^2$ and the big mess that goes along with it."

"Didn't understand word one," said the old lady with the upswept hair.

Vincent Flaherty stared down at Charlie's test tubes. "And what did Einstein have to say about matter?"

"Matter can neither be created nor destroyed," Charlie said.

"Matter can neither be created nor destroyed," Vincent Flaherty continued, not even listening to Charlie.

"Charlie said it first." Beth was happy that the ladies were quick to point this out.

"He's a smart boy."

"Very smart."

"And he's going to be a tall man."

"Let me ask you something, Charlie Einstein. As someone smart and future-tense tall, I bet you saw what happened with your mom."

"Nothing happened. She just fell asleep."

Beth saw her mother stir, as if she knew she was being talked about.

"I mean back there."

Charlie didn't say anything.

"You were a witness?"

Charlie hesitated.

"I just want the truth. I can see you're an honest young man. Right?"

Charlie nodded.

"The unfortunate accident. Fortunately, nobody—"

"It wasn't an accident," Charlie said.

"What's that, Charlie?"

"He tried to kill her," Charlie said. "On purpose. It wasn't an accident."

"Are you sure about that?" Vincent Flaherty turned to his jury of old ladies and smiled in a flabbergasted way. "Mr. Dawson is a man who works for me, a man I trust implicitly."

"He took my mother's gun and shot her," Charlie said.

"What was your mom doing pointing a gun at him?"

"She wasn't pointing a gun at him."

"Then how could he take it away?"

"He knew where she kept it."

"He knew where she kept it," Vincent Flaherty repeated.

"Yes."

"What was she really doing, Charlie?"

"Nothing."

"She was doing nothing and Mr. Dawson went and got her gun and shot her for no reason."

"Yes," Charlie said.

Vincent Flaherty stared down at Charlie and Jo quickly blocked their line of sight with a tray of peanut-butter-and-jelly sandwiches put there earlier by the magical Miss Dazzle. Beth had been observing everything and hadn't seen Miss Dazzle bring out lunch before she left. But here they were, having simply appeared, pb&j sandwiches added to the tuna-fish ones. She felt the thrill of her secret expanding inside her. It was getting stronger, stronger than anything this man Vincent Flaherty could do or say. Miss Dazzle was going to save Charlie. She turned away. She was afraid Charlie would be able to read her mind or read the excitement on her face and she didn't want to give away the secret. Miss Dazzle deserved that much, the joy of telling Charlie herself.

Vincent Flaherty reached for the sandwiches. "And what might these fortifications consist of, my dear?"

"They're just peanut-butter-and-jelly sandwiches," Charlie said in a way meant to discourage him.

"Young man, there's nothing better than peanut butter. You know what peanut butter's got in it? Protein. You know what builds bones? Protein."

"Charlie's bones are fine," one of the ladies warned.

Vincent Flaherty gave Charlie the once-over. "How would you all like to take a ride in a whirlybird?"

Charlie looked up.

"I'm off to do a little reconnaissance flight, and I sure would like some company. What do you say? Ever been in a helicopter, young man?"

Charlie shook his head.

"What's that?"

"No I haven't, sir," Charlie said.

"Well, let's go then."

Jo said, "Thank you, but we couldn't possibly accept your offer."

Charlie stood up.

"You can't go," Jo said.

Charlie narrowed his eyes at her. "Mr. Flaherty asked me to go and I was raised to be polite."

Jo said, "Don't you even think about it."

Charlie moved over to their mother and shook her shoulder. Charlie said, "Mom, I'll be back in a little while, okay?" Beth shook the other shoulder. "Mom, I'm going, too, all right?"

"Neither one of you is going anywhere," Jo said. She reached out both arms and Red Rover–like tried to hold them back. They broke through her arms and headed toward the white car. "Get back here!" Jo yelled. Beth saw that the tabby had reappeared. Six lives and counting.

SEVEN

Three letters, postmarked from Springfield. Three sealed letters from her mother, thick with hidden words. Perhaps very important words. She could see the ink's coiling shadows through the envelopes. She could even make out a word: *evening*. A word not so nerve-racking as *tragic* but not so dismissible as *groceries*. It could be a tragic evening her mother was relating to her. It could be a dismissible evening of groceries and guess what was on sale? How brave and optimistic of her mother to send the letters in a sealed envelope. Certainly she could have guessed that Jean would have no intention of opening them.

The letters' thickness felt thicker than her skull. She was awake and no one was around.

The ramada, overhead shingles painted like palm leaves, had kept her in the shade, all except her feet. She had one shoe on and one shoe off. She almost felt cold. The three old ladies were gone. Their cleared table so empty, a white hole in the air. The muted clacking of poker chips, gone. She'd liked that sound. It had penetrated the blankness she had fallen into, for a few moments anyway, and then it had fallen away, too. Where was everyone? Where were her children? Her heart flared; then she remembered that Jo would be with them. She turned her head one way and smelled chlorine. She turned her head the other way and smelled the sandwiches. To the left she breathed in chemicals of possibility, flight, even happiness. To the right the tuna-fish odors of chores, decay, dereliction.

In her hand the three letters from her mother. Her own head, more papery than the envelopes. The envelopes were stiffened and thick from all the pages of words inside. Their contents, spilling with her mother's verbosity, had strengthened the envelopes into a shield. There was that word, *evening*. What about evening? What had happened to her mother that evening?

Her mother had slept in the bathtub growing up. So far she had told only funny stories about it.

Her head all papery like something was about to jump out.

It was Jimmy Splendid who jumped out. He was suddenly there across the pool. The sun was in her eyes. He was a moving dark statue who blocked the sun, then posed before her. His silhouette: broad shoulders, big legs, a square face oblonged by a crest of thick hair and almost lantern jaw. She couldn't see any of his features or the pockets she knew must be on his khaki vest—too darkened, she was staring into the sun— but it was Jimmy Splendid. Her brain had rushed ahead and identified him. Which made her think, He must be inside my head. I must be dreaming him.

"Are you all right?"

She decided not to answer. Or rather, she got lost in all the possibilities of answers.

With his sitting down came a rapid sunrise. The sun shot up from his head. So that's how it happens, so easily, things jumping out of your head. Now she saw his features and they were mildly squinting at her and his head was tilted inquisitively.

He picked up the letters from the cement and laid them on her lap. His hands were warm and bulky, and as he said, "Do you remember me?" the hands locked around hers. There was something nurse-like in the way he squeezed both sets of fingers. His hands were hot, and she didn't know if he was real.

"What in the world happened out there?" His tending hands had found their resting place on her knees. Her knees, which were close to her thighs. She was looking at him, trying to place his handsome face. He was in the movies. He played the fiancé the leading lady thought she was in love with until she met the far less handsome James Stewart. Was Jimmy Splendid as boring as his handsomeness made him out to be? Her knees, which she had previously thought of as all bone, turned into hot circles of flesh. She could feel her unprotected brain bypassing its usual routes. She was aware of her body in a way she hadn't been for years.

Early in her marriage she had doubted very much that she should have married at all (the doubts lasting, to be honest, until she was suddenly cut off from marriage, widowed). Marriage seemed to attract the enthusiastically boring. Those who weren't boring were unhappy. At any police lineup she could have picked them out: the young happily marrieds from the young unhappily marrieds from the young not married at alls. How completely divergent they all looked, how graded in allure.

She told herself that the twentieth century was different from, for example, 1800s England, her favorite period to hate, with everyone avoiding suicide by taking hours to dress, using up all of the morning so that they had only afternoon and evening to worry about getting through. A husband and wife slept in separate bedrooms and had coitus that produced issue, but blunt erotic need sent the man to someone else who was less boring by definition, who was wild, who might be a servant, and the adventure (for it seemed an adventure after what took place in the wife's bedroom) might be with shocking dirty words on a game-butchering table in the bowels of the scullery.

But then she had children herself and she realized how this whole thing worked. The wife didn't need the game-butchering table. Her need for eros was fulfilled by her children. There was no need for the husband anymore. And it was always a dance to keep the husband away.

That was a long time ago. She hadn't thought about it for years. The strangled romantic needs with her husband had been satisfied by kindred erotic love for her children, and then something else, life and death, had rendered marital passion trivial. But now it was back, and by the end of this hasty route her brain could barely be bothered escorting her through, her thoughts had forged a new conclusion: desire. She was burning with desire for Jimmy Splendid. There was nothing that could hold her back, any more than she could stay his traveling hands.

Fortunately, a car pulled up and honked, and Miss Dazzle stepped out of the DeSoto. The children weren't with her.

EIGHT

The helicopter lifted off like a dragonfly. Beth watched the world she knew resurface in baffling miniature. She watched the color brown turn into a miracle of shades.

"How are you liking it, Charlie Einstein!" Vincent Flaherty had to yell as loud as he could, and it sounded to Beth like someone's desperate last words.

"I like it!" Charlie's voice was high and weak and Beth, pressed next to him, could barely hear it.

"You're my lookout, Charlie Einstein!"

Jo was in the front seat of the helicopter. Her face and neck had abruptly taken on muscles. She was wearing a pink sweater over her summer dress. Her arms had roped around herself, and her hands tugged and kneaded the sleeves.

The mass of canyons below revealed to Beth their taffy stripes of colors. A river wandered through the canyons with a glorious snaky casualness. Beth wondered about God. She was always waiting for Him to send her a sign. But of course, should it be sent, you had to be on the alert for the sign. Otherwise, He'd have to send you two signs, the first sign being the sign that He was about to send you a sign.

So maybe this was the sign, the river snaking below, the rocks rising in twists of pinks and roses and yellows. And now all she had to do was figure out what it meant, which shouldn't be too difficult, she'd put in a lot of practice lately figuring out secret messages.

She felt bad for Jo up there in the front seat. Her mouth had gaped open as if to be sick, but nothing was happening. Beth believed it was better to heave away and get it over with. Jo was just prolonging her suffering. She was frozen in fear, every muscle locked up, too frozen even to vomit. Vincent Flaherty dipped the helicopter and tilted Jo into his waiting arm. He let out a grand squawk, trading in his Three Musketeers hat for a cowboy hat. Charlie wasn't noticing that Vincent Flaherty had turned the helicopter into a bucking bronco. He was pressed so hard to the window he seemed about to burst through and fall.

The snaking river. The bucking bronco. The canyons of many colors, not just brown. The sign had to have something to do with the winding river. The view of the river from above revealed its grand intentions. It wasn't just winding here and winding there. It was going somewhere. It had a plan. A destination. The zigzagging was just to throw people off.

Life is a zigzag.

Ha, that was it! That was God's sign.

Life is not just brown. Life is a zigzag.

Still, she would have liked something a little more personal.

Vincent Flaherty slipped a flask from the inside of his jacket, screwed off the top with his mouth and one hand, and passed it over to Jo. Jo obediently took it and held on to it with two hands. "That's for you, honey!" Vincent Flaherty finally called over.

Charlie turned from the window and shouted something to Beth. "What?" she cried, but her ears were already putting the sounds together into something that almost made sense—*Helen's here!*

The mountains they were approaching layered up into a flat top. She matched its familiar birthday-cake shape to one of the drawings on Charlie's map. *The headlands!*

Vincent Flaherty rummaged in a compartment and brought out a pair of binoculars. He held them up only briefly to his eyes before pass-

ing them over his shoulder. "Charlie Einstein!" he shouted out. "I'm looking for tire tracks!"

Beth watched the way Charlie took the binoculars, without hesitation, without any nervousness that he might not live up to the job. Jo was
still rigid, gripping Vincent Flaherty's silver flask with both hands. Her
hands were shaking. Charlie's hands didn't shake. Already he was stronger.
Already something magical was taking effect. *Life is a zigzag, not just
brown.* That was God's sign—almost God's sign. It was still missing the
Dear Beth part. Right now it was just a declarative sentence on a blackboard meant for the whole class. It wasn't addressed solely to her. Everyone in her class could take that sentence home with them and use it for
their own purposes.

The helicopter had dipped lower. Charlie and the binoculars were
pressed against the window. "Follow the river, Charlie! Look for tracks!"

Dear Beth: follow the river, follow the zigzag. Dear Beth: not just brown
Maybe. Not quite.

Vincent Flaherty pulled the flask out of Jo's hands, then slipped it
back inside his jacket without screwing on the top. Jo clutched her
sweater sleeves again, so hard the knitting was being pulled out. Two pink
floppy doorknobs hung from her arms.

Vincent Flaherty reached down between the seats and fingered a machine. He didn't turn around but his head reared back so his hairstyle
could talk to Charlie. "Know what a scintillation counter is, boy?" He was
yelling to be heard. When he shouted, "boy!" it sounded like one of the
men teachers on the playground doling out a punishment. Vincent Flaherty didn't wait for an answer from Charlie. His finger stabbed at the
meter.

Charlie leaned over to watch the jerking needle. Vincent Flaherty's
hand tightened around Charlie's neck and shook it. "You betcha!" Vincent Flaherty screamed. The fat dwarfish hand on her brother's neck
filled Beth with fear. The ring on the pinkie was big as a platter, with a
diamond as the turkey.

As the helicopter dipped again, Beth felt something knocking against her ankles. A brown bag had burst open and now fresh oranges were rolling on the floor. Not just brown. Of course! Orange fruit, different colors, the rainbow. It was all starting to make sense. Sort of. Charlie turned away from the window triumphantly. "There!" he yelled. When Vincent Flaherty didn't acknowledge, he tapped him on the shoulder. "There!" he cried. Beth craned to look as well. She saw something like two thin ant trails in the sand. She hoped Charlie was right.

"Good man, Charlie Einstein!" Vincent Flaherty tapped Jo's shoulder, then pointed toward the tracks. The helicopter pulled back and rose. The tracks were leading into the mountainous maze of the headlands. Vincent Flaherty leaned close to Jo's ear. "I gave him some dynamite to blow himself a road!" He started laughing.

The helicopter circled around the rocky landscape. Charlie tapped Vincent Flaherty's shoulder again and pointed. The helicopter plunged left. Beth saw a ridge where a red truck was parked. The helicopter started lowering itself in a way that didn't seem possible, as if it were being fed down by a rope that pulled back as much as it paid out. As it landed, a pocket of air seemed to push up against its belly. Jo jerked up from her seat. The helicopter fought against this pushing air and then wobbled onto a capstone of slickrock. "Wait," Vincent Flaherty told them. "I don't want to get anyone's head chopped off." The spinning air current over the helicopter slowed into actual rotor blades. The rotor blades bounced as they slowed, then drooped to a stop. No one moved because Vincent Flaherty didn't move. "Okay," he finally said. "Better to be safe. Right, Charlie Einstein?"

Jo tumbled out of the helicopter and threw up.

"Let's give her some space." Beth and Charlie followed Vincent Flaherty along the ridge toward the red truck. There was no Leonard Dawson at the campsite, but on the dashboard inside his pickup was a note. Vincent Flaherty spread the note on the hood, ironing its edges. "Go ahead and read her out loud, Charlie," he said.

This truck belongs to Leonard H. Dawson and someone thinking oth-
erwise is a dirty theif. It has one hell of a busted water pump not to
mention oil pan so go ahead and test your dam luck. Leonard H.
Dawson has set out on foot heading northeast to the river, some help if
you got it and a ride back. If he don't make it back let the world know
Leonard H. Dawson died braver than any soldier marching the front
line into combat.

Jo walked into the campsite, and Vincent Flaherty said, "Go ahead, read her again, Charlie." Charlie obliged, this time with a little more expression. Vincent Flaherty eyed Charlie intently, then sat down on the bumper of the pickup and pulled out a cigar. He lit a match with a hurrah, the match and matchbox striking together like two tiny cymbals. He studied the flame for so long he had to light another. He puffed on the cigar, gave it a long suck, and spewed out the exhale with a frightening choking noise. He could not lean over much because of his big stomach. A brown string fell from his lips and landed between his unreal stick legs. "We got a soldier out there," Vincent Flaherty declared, and for a moment Beth didn't know what he was talking about, so taken was she with his match lighting and cigar puffing and spittle release. Then she was brought back to Leonard Dawson's letter. "A gallant warrior bravin' Injuns and heat." His body shook in hard bounces, and he puffed again on the cigar.

Jo sighed and buried her face in her hands. Vincent Flaherty looked at her and seemed to remember something. He pulled out the flask and motioned to Charlie to take it over to her. Jo lifted her head when Charlie tapped her. Her face bunched in pain at the sight of the flask and she let out a moan. "Mr. Flaherty," she said, "I don't need that."

"Do you a world of good."

"My husband," she began.

"Yes, the gallant warrior!"

"Oh, Mr. Flaherty, it's not a joke for us. That was all the money we had that he gave you. Every penny."

Using the sharp edge of the bumper, Vincent Flaherty trimmed the embers from his cigar and replaced it in his jacket pocket. He waved Charlie over, said, "Give the old guy a hand, would you, Mr. Einstein," and pushed up from the bumper. Charlie had to use all his strength but tried out of politeness not to show it. Vincent Flaherty was out of breath by the time he was standing. He went over to Jo and placed his fat fingers on her neck. "Better?"

"No."

"No worries, my dear. No money has yet changed hands. In fact, I'm paying him for this little foray. What we in the business like to call a trial run."

Jo looked up, ashen but with brighter eyes. "He hasn't given you our money? Is that the truth?"

"The best version of it I know." He started back toward the helicopter, but paused at something inside the pickup bed. He reached in, opened the tool box, and pulled out a metal case. From the case he pulled out a Geiger counter. He turned it on and circled the campsite with it, interviewing the ground with the probe. The ground said nothing at all. "I'll be damned," Vincent Flaherty said, forgetting to be grandiose. Beth saw that the Geiger counter was the $99 Lucky Strike. Everyone knew to use the Babbel-400 instead. Everyone knew the Lucky Strike was useless. She was only ten years old and even she knew it.

"Whaddaya think, Charlie?" Vincent Flaherty asked.

Charlie shrugged. "Maybe some fallout came by."

Vincent Flaherty moved his mouth like he was chewing gum, trying to get a read on Charlie. Each time he bit down there was a type of smile on his face, although he was sweating so it could have been a grimace. Vincent Flaherty returned the Geiger counter to its case and the case to its tool box. He was still sidelong checking Charlie out as they walked back to the helicopter. "Northeast to the river," Vincent Flaherty mused. "We must have missed him."

"I would have seen him," Charlie said.

"Maybe he doesn't know his directions. Does he know his directions, Miss Josephine?" Vincent Flaherty stopped and waited for Jo. The perspiration drew sideburns on his reddening face.

Jo didn't answer. She looked to be in every kind of pain there was.

"Let's go a little southeast then, see what happens. Yes, Einstein?" Charlie nodded.

"'Cause you're the man in charge," Vincent Flaherty said.

The helicopter lifted off from the headlands and then swooped down low over that part of the river they hadn't covered. Very quickly Charlie spotted a shack, and a figure standing near it. Beth had seen them, too, but kept quiet. Charlie tapped Vincent Flaherty's shoulder and pointed. The helicopter lowered. The river naturally got bigger as they drew closer, but it was a mostly dried-up river with a ghostly outline of what it had once been. It was a streambed now.

The figure was beating his arms in the air. Charlie turned to Beth with a disgusted *oooh* on his mouth. It was Leonard Dawson all right, and he was looking pretty bad, not that Beth had ever seen him look good. As they landed and the glinting spinning air slowed to distinct glinting blades, Beth had plenty of time to check out Leonard Dawson. The helicopter had blown off his hat. The scum caking his face was peaked by a forehead of white. Gnarled neck, buffalo-hump shoulders. Black wiggles for hair, crawling forward over his scalp. Beth hated him. She was pretty sure by now that Jo hated him, too.

Charlie jumped out of the helicopter and locked on to Vincent Flaherty. Jo stayed in her seat. "Look at Charlie," Jo said to her. "I think Mr. Flaherty's found a new assistant." She tried to smile. She closed her eyes and rested her head in her hand.

"Are you okay?" Beth asked.

"I made a terrible mistake," Jo said.

"You mean marrying Leonard Dawson?" Beth said.

"Everything."

"What's everything?"

"Don't do what I did, okay?"

"What did you do?" Beth asked. She said, "You wish he was dead, don't you?"

"Oh no, honey, no. I don't wish that."

"Why not? I would."

Jo turned around to her and her smile deepened and lessened at the same time. Then she got out of the helicopter and walked in the opposite direction, toward what was left of the river. She sat down in the white powder where the river had dried, folded over, and reached out to splash the water to her face.

Beth took a few steps toward Charlie and Vincent Flaherty before stopping short. A bad odor had reeled through, like sewage, and she wondered if it came from Leonard Dawson or the shack. She stayed put. She didn't have to worry about straining her ears to eavesdrop. Leonard Dawson spoke in the overly loud voice of someone who was overly proud. He said he had wandered half dead into the shack, where this Navajo found him. He was pretty proud of the fact that he was still alive.

"Mm-hmm," Vincent Flaherty said.

Turns out it was the Navajo's shack. Turns out this Navajo had found Leonard Dawson and taken him in and fed him, only it turned out he only had Navajo food. Some kind of Navajo mush. And then this Navajo who was supposed to lead him back to a road where some mining trucks might be rumbling through decided to take off somewhere instead, and now Leonard Dawson didn't know where he'd gone to or when he was coming back. But Leonard Dawson was waiting, keeping his end of the promise.

"What promise?"

"The promise to stay here," Leonard Dawson said.

"Mm-hmm," Vincent Flaherty said. "And this all happened in one day, huh?"

"Are you doubting my word?"

"I saw you yesterday, my friend."

"And you're lucky to see me alive today."

"And where is this Navajo fellow now? In one day you almost died from starvation, he saved your life with mush, you made friends, and now he's gone."

"Are you trying to say something? If you are, come out and say it. If I was going to lie about it, I'd have him feeding me something better than mush."

"Mush has Vitamin A in it," Vincent Flaherty said. "I guess you're lucky to be alive."

"You can just go to hell," Leonard Dawson said. His boot toed the ground and he looked ready to charge. He explained in an angry shout how getting as far as the shack required death-defying travails and an iron will. His throat and gullet were lined with corduroy from lack of water. In the white heat of bravery and delirium he slid two hundred feet down a scree slope that sliced his butt and thighs into shreds and burned up his boots. That wasn't all. There was a nest of rattlesnakes, too.

"Mm-hmm," Vincent Flaherty said. He glanced over at Charlie with the barest of smiles.

"Why do you keep looking at that boy?"

"Charlie, run back and get me that flask, would you?"

Beth stood by the helicopter as Charlie ran back and felt around the floor.

"Mom didn't want us to talk about it, Charlie," Beth said to him.

"Ssh."

"She didn't want us to talk about it."

"I'm helping Mr. Flaherty."

"Why did you tell her?"

"Who?"

"Miss Dazzle."

"What are you talking about?"

"Why did you tell her about the visitor?"

"She asked me, that's why."

"Mom doesn't like us to talk about it."

"Miss Dazzle asked me and I just felt like answering. Ssh."

"Mom says it's a secret."

"Quiet. I have more important things to do right now."

"Mom says it's a secret, Charlie."

"Mom's in a coma."

"You found it, Charlie?" Vincent Flaherty shouted over.

"Be quiet, now. You're going to get me in trouble." He ran back to Vincent Flaherty.

"I'm still not understanding the promise you're living up to," Vincent Flaherty was saying.

"I just told you," Leonard Dawson said.

"And what about your promise to me?"

"Did you hear what I just said?" Leonard Dawson was starting to whine, and it gave Beth no small amount of pleasure.

"Let's get back to work."

"What is my wife doing in your helicopter?" Leonard Dawson said.

Vincent Flaherty reared back and thumbed his belt. "Now, you leave her alone. She's plenty airsick and worried to death about you."

"I could take all her worries about me and they wouldn't fit into this." Leonard Dawson held up his little finger.

"Feeling sorry for yourself isn't helping you do your job for me."

"That's all that matters to you," Leonard Dawson sulked.

So Miss Dazzle had simply asked, and Charlie had simply answered. Beth couldn't get over this simple but profound turn of events. Naturally, because God works in strange ways. That was another one of those sayings she had never understood until now. In the strangest of ways the message had turned personal. It all fit now. The declarative sentence on the blackboard meant for anyone and everyone had suddenly turned personal. *Life is a zigzag. Follow the zigzag.* The words were lit up, looped in neon-red tubing. Harry, she had to remember to thank Harry for this. His brake lights had revealed the red afterstreaks zigzagging from Miss Dazzle's hand, *orangeish* red to be precise.

Jo was at the river, down on all fours. The white alkaline traces fanned out and made her part of their pattern. She shook as though vomiting, but Beth could see that nothing was coming out.

"What is my wife doing in your helicopter!"

"I just explained it to you."

Leonard Dawson yelled, "Get over here and say hello to your husband."

Vincent Flaherty reared back again, poking Leonard Dawson with his middle. The stomach was tight as a drum. The poke drove Leonard Dawson backward. "What are you, an animal?" Vincent Flaherty said. "You don't greet your wife when you're dirty and stunk up as a bear. There'll be plenty of time for that kind of stuff. With the profits we're gonna make you can buy a Cadillac. Try saying hello to her in that and then maybe she'll feel you're worth answering."

"You go to hell," Leonard Dawson said.

"I will, but that's down the road." Vincent Flaherty smiled over to Charlie and they turned away.

"Yeah, little boy, you got more than you bargained for. You go to hell, too, and tell your momma the same."

Now Vincent Flaherty swung around and all his playacting was gone. His arm came straight out and the hand gripped Leonard Dawson's throat. The hand, almost deformed by its dwarfishness, seemed possessed of a magical strength. "I'm going to hear an apology," Vincent Flaherty said.

He let go of the throat. Leonard Dawson pawed the ground.

After several moments Vincent Flaherty turned and accepted the flask from Charlie. Leonard Dawson saw it, pawed the ground some more, then said, "Yeah, all right, shouldna said it."

Vincent Flaherty handed the flask to Leonard Dawson, who took two quick swigs. Then Vincent Flaherty took off his jacket and folded it neatly shoulder seam to shoulder seam and slung it over his forearm. The arms that poked through the short sleeves of his white shirt were skinny like his legs.

Leonard Dawson took another swig. "I'll take this off your hands if you'd like," he said, but Vincent Flaherty had already reached out and was pulling back the flask.

"What'd you find up there?" Vincent Flaherty asked.

"Where?"

Vincent Flaherty stared at him until Leonard Dawson looked down and started pawing the sand again. "One more," he said, and Vincent Flaherty handed him the flask. He swallowed long and hard before giving it back. "What am I supposed to do? I busted my water pump."

"What I need you to do is get up in those hills with a pickaxe over your shoulder. That's why I hired you. I don't even see a sunburn on your nose."

"Fine. I'll give you a sunburn and then you can get off my back."

"You have a job to do."

"I can only do so much with no food and no water pump."

"You sure it's your water pump?"

Leonard Dawson shrugged.

"I'm gonna bring you a water pump and a man to help you fix it."

"What man?"

"I'll find a man. There's plenty of men looking for work."

"Just don't send me no Indian."

Vincent Flaherty reached into his pants and took out a pill box and poured out a tablet. "Here. Take one of these. Do you a world of good."

"What is it?"

"Salt tablet."

"How about some water and some food?"

"How about you should have thought of that when you loaded up? You'll get yourself killed acting hell-bent the way you do."

"I'm half dead now."

"If self-pity came attached with a scorpion's tail, you'd be all the way dead."

"What's that supposed to mean?"

"It means you go ahead and spend another night in this shack and someone will be here in the morning." Vincent Flaherty gave him a grudging backward wave as he walked away. Beth jumped in the helicopter. "Come on, Jo!" Beth screamed. Jo was still on her knees by the riverbed, gripping her sweater. Beth was suddenly panicked because Leonard Dawson was eyeing Jo with a simmering gleam, ready to pounce. "Come on, Jo!" she yelled again.

Vincent Flaherty pulled a stiff new bandana from his supply box and unscrewed a water bottle and soaked the bandana. Then he tossed the water bottle on the sand for Leonard Dawson.

"You need to come say hi to me," Leonard Dawson yelled to Jo. Jo ignored him. She stood up weakly and trudged lifelessly to the helicopter. Her arms were hanging by her sides. All her tugging and kneading had ruined the sweater.

Before starting up the helicopter Vincent Flaherty reached over and squeezed Jo's shoulder and put the bandana up to her forehead. She was sweating and shivering at the same time. Jo hid her head in the cloth. Vincent Flaherty turned around in his seat. "Charlie, I'm sorry I ever doubted your version of the shooting."

"He didn't really shoot her," Charlie said.

Vincent Flaherty looked at Charlie a fraction longer than normal; then he picked up an orange and threw it out onto the sand. "I guess that'll hold him till morning," he said.

NINE

Miss Dazzle sprang up the three steps to the pool and gave Jimmy Splendid a big hug. "It looks like everyone's in town today," she said.

"Aren't the kids with you?" Jean asked. She stood up from the chaise longue and immediately lost her balance. Jimmy Splendid caught her and tried to ease her back down, but she wanted to stand up and that was what she did. What a strangely arranged town, she thought. They had passed through it at one end and come to this motel on the other end. It simply began, and then it simply ended. She could see beyond the town to the unreal landscape. The sky in its perfect blueness seemed flat, a piece of construction paper on which were pasted the pieces of a brown mountain range.

"The kids were right here when I left to take Randy home," Miss Dazzle said.

"They must be with Jo. Have you seen Jo?" Jimmy Splendid and Miss Dazzle were staring at her. "I'm fine," she said. Her heart revved up quick and frightened. The way they were looking at her was not right. Their expressions had turned sinister. "Are you sure?"

"Am I sure what, honey?"

Maybe she was a little confused. She decided to sit down. Jimmy Splendid's steadying hand followed her to the lounge chair.

"Do you remember the doctor being here?" Miss Dazzle asked.

"I remember. He thought Beth was selfish going on about her barbecue."

"Oh, Randy's so annoying."

"That little girl?" Jimmy Splendid asked. "I got a kick out of her."

"And it was a private conversation."

"Randy's not, you know, he's not much for kids. But that little girl's a sweetheart, so don't you worry about it, darling."

"The kids aren't with him, are they?" Jean asked.

"No, no."

"Where are they then?"

"They must be with your friend Jo."

"That's right," Jean said.

"It's awful hot out here," Miss Dazzle said. "And you've been out here this whole time?"

"No, it's just that I thought the kids were with you," Jean said. She just said it to buy time, but she was repeating herself and probably to them looking crazy and bewildered. But everyone had invader thoughts, alert unseen butlers to the main topic. Her own adulthood was one big invasion, making it impossible to formulate a free unencumbered conceit. All her previous experiences attended each new experience, familiarizing it before it had barely begun. Yet one had to find a way to live as though life was not one big circular argument, as though it was still possible to forge ahead into original territory.

"You've been out here this whole time?" Miss Dazzle shook her head.

"Even for hot it's hot," Jimmy Splendid said.

Jean looked out over the parking lot. Jimmy Splendid's truck and Miss Dazzle's DeSoto were the only cars on the lot but they were parked side by side, like two lone theatergoers who gravitate close. The motel rooms all gazed out on empty spaces. A line of three mailboxes stood outside the ladies' rentals. The little red flags were up. They were always up. The ladies were always sending notes, sometimes just to each other, using stamps to officially move the note one or two mailboxes down. The mailboxes made everything look lonely, even though the sun was shining brightly.

Jimmy Splendid reached out tentatively and touched Jean's head. "So what'd the doctor say?"

"What he always says," Miss Dazzle answered. "'You look raring to go, two aspirin and don't call me in the morning.' He was on his third drink when I hauled him out of here."

"It's just the sun," Jean said.

"In combination with the head," Miss Dazzle said. "And no water." Miss Dazzle looked around. "Where's your glass of water, Mrs. Waterman? Listen to that. I didn't realize that about your name."

"Waterman," Jimmy Splendid repeated. "That's your name? And what's your first name?"

Jean stood up weakly as she gave her name, losing her balance again. She fell against Jimmy Splendid's hand, still there at her back. The hand didn't stir against her weight. It was like falling against a rock wall. Strong, she thought. "It's my foot," she said quickly, "I'm not dizzy," but their faces didn't look assured. The ramada had shaded everything except her feet, and when she had woken up one shoe was on and one shoe was off. Now she had a sunburned foot, sole and toes included, and it was hurting her. See? She lifted her foot as evidence.

Jimmy Splendid got her to sit again and then he was on his knees, cradling the foot in his hands. It gave Jean a bad feeling; she saw Leonard Dawson bending down to her little girl.

"Are you all right?" Miss Dazzle dropped down to her knees and put her arm over Jean's shoulders. "Let's get her inside."

"Give me a minute." Jimmy Splendid bent his head comically to examine her feet. "Look at this foot. It's got a bad sunburn."

"So the kids are with Jo," Jean said. "Where did they go? Whose car are they in?"

"Maybe they're walking somewhere," Jimmy Splendid said. "What's good for a sunburned foot?"

"Just soak it in some cold water." Miss Dazzle shook her head. "They wouldn't be walking somewhere in midday. My bet is that they're in Vince's vehicle."

"Vince's vehicle?" Jimmy Splendid asked.

"Oh yes. Vince was here. Lot of people in town today," Miss Dazzle said. "That Cadillac of his has air conditioning. That car has everything. I wouldn't be surprised if they took off with him just to cool down. My boys take one ride in that car? Whoo, I'll never hear the end of it. They think they've got a car coming to them just because they're old enough to get a driver's license. They made it to California by the way, Jimmy."

"Your boys? What are they doing out there?"

"Well, they've got a cousin. And you know who else is out there?"

"I see," Jimmy Splendid said.

Miss Dazzle patted Jean's shoulder. "Vince won't let anything happen to them."

"I hope the resolution of this situation doesn't come down to putting faith in Vince."

"That's just you, Jimmy. Now stop."

"Maybe for good reason."

"Maybe for good reason what?" Jean asked.

"Jimmy, you're going to get her upset. I'm talking about trusting Vince to take care of two kids and one adult for one afternoon, meaning bringing them back alive. Not about whether he's going to jump your darn ol' claim or not. They've got a past history, honey, don't pay any attention to him. Now you tell her that the kids are safe with him."

"Of course they're safe with him. I didn't mean that." Jimmy Splendid looked down at Jean. "I'm just curious about what's going on. Question marks follow me around whenever I see you."

"How often have you two met? You don't even know her name, Jimmy. Lord, I guess I need to get out of the house more."

"Harry took us to Mr. Splendid's mining camp," Jean said.

"Oh," Miss Dazzle said, tossing her head back. "Somewhere I've never been invited."

So her children were with Vincent Flaherty. Jean had had a very short conversation with the man, and then, what? she must have fallen asleep. But she remembered him. The Cadillac with those fins that made it look like it should be swimming in Miss Dazzle's pool rather than riding on the street. He looked like he was going to keel over with a heart attack, almost took down the railing on the steps. A curious man with a curious build. The old ladies had something against him though they had something against almost everyone. Jean had rather liked him, the little she had seen of him. The children would enjoy riding around in his air conditioning. In a different situation she imagined an odd duck like Vincent Flaherty could keep her laughing. "Laughter Is the Cure for Everything"—the title of a magazine article her mother had once cut out and sent to her. She still felt it, a physical craving for this handsome man before her who was taking advantage of the situation by stroking her foot, but he would never make her laugh. Physical desire and despair could exist side by side, that was desire's biggest drawback, it didn't cancel out any negatives, but when she laughed her troubles disappeared. But who can laugh all the time? People would think, *Crazy*. They wouldn't be thinking, *100 percent cured*.

"I suppose Jo wanted a ride in that car just as much," Jean said.

"What's that, honey?"

"In that man Mr. Flaherty's car. Cadillac."

"I don't know what exactly they had in mind."

"I'm glad I have Jo around," Jean said. "For the kids."

Miss Dazzle neither shrugged nor rolled her eyes nor sighed, yet somehow by her complete nonreaction she managed to do all three.

Jimmy Splendid was shaking his head. His hand pushed hard against his forehead, as if to blot the sweat that hadn't surfaced yet. "What is Vince up to now? I know he's up to something."

"Jimmy, what are you up to, by the by?"

"Now, Belinda, what's that supposed to mean?" He rested Jean's foot on the cushion and stood up and Miss Dazzle stood up with him, and they were accidentally squared off like boxers, which made both of them laugh.

Jean had never heard anyone call Miss Dazzle by her first name. Instantly it occurred to her that Miss Dazzle and Jimmy Splendid had had a romance. Their names alone. They were both big handsome creatures; she suspected their lust was as oversized as they. Miss Dazzle sported a sly smile as they stood face to face. "Don't kid a kidder," she said.

"Don't forget, I'm still the sheriff," he said, "and I heard there was a shooting."

Miss Dazzle hooted. "Oh Lord, Jimmy!"

"It's my job."

"Oh Lord, Jimmy."

"It's my job. There's been a shooting and it's my job."

"Since when in this town does anybody care about anybody shooting anybody else?"

"This is not exactly a good-riddance situation, Belinda. This is not one worthless mealworm going after another."

"I thought you were here because of the plane crash."

"I heard about it," Jimmy Splendid said.

"So don't you need to do some sheriffing about that?"

"Already interviewed the fellow who witnessed it."

"So you are here about the crash."

"I'm here about a lot of things, Belinda."

Jean had her mother's letters in her hands. The words darkened through the envelope but remained too blurry to read. These two people, handsome and big and most of all overpowering, were talking around and around. It was shadowy as the ink in her letters what they were really meaning to say.

Miss Dazzle patted Jimmy Splendid's chest. "Where's that big shiny badge, Sheriff? Can I fix you a drink or are you on duty?"

Jimmy Splendid shook his head. "Say, Belinda, I might rent out a room for tonight."

"Suit yourself," Miss Dazzle said.

TEN

Harry made a fast escape after signing in with the coroner and delivering Dr. Randolph's papers. "Won't be but a second to unload him," the coroner assured him, "and then you can have your truck back." Harry's expression told everything before he could find the words. He was lingering nowhere nearby for that scene, express unloading or not. The coroner understood, said, "Go watch the parade why don't you. When you come back it'll be like it never happened." Harry didn't shake the coroner's hand and the coroner, thankfully, didn't offer. He didn't know about a parade but he played that he did. He strolled in the direction of the downtown, followed the noise and shouting until he crested a hill. He saw it down below. The bands and the marchers and especially the war veterans were stationed in the street in crisp rectangles. Harry thought the parade more beautiful this way, from this farther reach, with the different groups laid out like the perfect stanzas of a poem.

He thought of his brother, his real brother, who had made it through the war. Said he killed people and didn't have any problem with it and he pooh-poohed all these mental vets drooling in wheelchairs, turned to stone. The VA got volunteers to dance with them, young pretty girls, that was what that was all about. Harry felt too untouched and naive to offer an opinion. He wanted to be able to disagree. The world was too cruel in his brother's version. His brother was older, almost a father figure, and it pained Harry to disagree with him, even in his thoughts.

Here he was thinking of his brother and as he walked down the hill and followed the parade to the bandstand in Lincoln Park, he came upon one of his nieces. She was lined up on the outdoor stage in a bathing suit and he was shocked. The last time he had seen her she was as little girlish as Beth. What was she now? She looked old and young at the same time. He could see the makeup from here. Maybe twenty-three. Maybe only sixteen. He tried not to look. He searched through the crowd for his brother.

A name was called and one of the girls in the bathing suits stepped forward. "Our new Miss Atomic Energy!" The winner of the Miss Atomic Energy contest received ten tons of uranium ore and got an airplane ride over the Colorado Plateau. His niece's name was never called, even as a member of Miss Atomic Energy's sizable court. He went up to the stage afterward and the girls were like the parade itself. Something off-kilter entered the picture up close but resolved itself at a distance—like the blare of trumpets and trombones where you couldn't hear any tune until you stepped back. He found his niece and tried to ask where his brother was, but she was crying and didn't answer. As he escaped into the crowd he glanced back. The garish slashes on the girls' faces had settled back into smiles.

He returned to the coroner's and retrieved the truck. A huge wet spot blemished the ground and although Harry knew it came from the ice he couldn't help thinking in other directions. He had the liquor supplies to pick up for Miss Dazzle, but he first drove to the AEC field office. It was closed. They kept irregular hours. Perhaps they would return after the parade. The fellow who usually worked there was getting on in years and spoke with a heavy German accent. Harry wasn't the only one to be struck funny by this, a German working for the U.S. government to help it find the mineral to make more atomic bombs in order, probably, to defeat the Germans again. But the man was a U.S. citizen born and bred. Just got the accent from his parents was all.

He patted his pocket to make sure Miss Dazzle's check was there. He could try the liquor store first and then come here again, but the store was located out of town on his way home and he would hate doubling back. The dirt lot where he waited offered not a single spot of shade though the truck emptied of its ice retained a lingering coolness that felt good in the heat. Harry picked up the paper bag Miss Dazzle had given him. There were three sandwiches inside—three! He unwrapped one. Peanut butter and jelly. So this was his favorite kind. That was good to know. He took a bite. It tasted pretty good. He took another bite and then looked at the sandwich. The two slices of bread appeared to have been squashed down by bricks and mortared together by an even brown line. The jelly had started to dye the bread purple. It didn't look like it should taste good, but it did.

A bowl of dust followed a jolting truck into the lot, and the old German got out. Harry stepped from his truck. "Hallo," the German greeted, his wave a single mechanical flip from the elbow up. "Come on."

Inside the office were shelves of Geiger counters and scintillation counters, labeled and explained and rated. Ore sample sacks and collecting bags were available for purchase. Maps covered every bit of wall space except for one inexplicable picture: Hermes, in a cheap bamboo frame.

On another set of shelving were ore samples carefully labeled—carnotite, autonite, tyuyamunite, roscoelite, vanadium, even torbernite from the Belgian Congo, different kinds of pitchblende, pitchblende with copper.

Ah, pitchblende with copper. Exactly what he was thinking. And where to find such pitchblende? An old copper mine, of course. No one went chasing such a thing these days because the pitchblende to be had was impure, and its impurity made it harder to detect any uranium. But Harry had the right instruments at his disposal.

"What can I do you for today, Harry?"

Why did the man have to call him Harry? Now Harry searched desperately for the man's name. He was usually so good with names. That was part of his job. Here this guy remembered him. And he was old, too. And he had never made a show of being sociable. And yet he remembered his name and didn't want any congratulations for it. Why did the man have to call him Harry? What was *his* name? No idea. None whatsoever. Total blank. Harry knew what he was going to do now. He was going to cover his embarrassment by acting overly, unduly friendly, to the point where he would probably actually frighten the man. He told himself not to do this. He pointed to the index of publications and asked for *The Mineral Industries of Utah*. He sounded like a twelve-year old, clearing his throat, asking for the prescription his mother had sent him to get, using the change to buy himself a chocolate soda. Looking guilty, staring at the floor. He told himself, Now, stop. Don't say another word. Then he said the man's suit looked nice. Whose suit? John's suit? Jacob's suit? He went through some Bible names, Cain, Abel, Adam, Samson. Hermes' other name, what was that? Mercury.

"I was judging the parade," the man said. He flung his hands along the lines of his suit, top to bottom. He moved to the back room. Harry assumed he was rooting for the publication, but when he came back out, he had changed into khaki work pants. He kept on the suit jacket. "For this parade I have score sheets to fill out. Columns with numbers I have to choose from, and rectangles I have to fill in with comments. If I'm assaying ore, I have an easier job. Big business, parades."

"Did you judge the Miss Atomic Energy contest?"

"No," the man said. He opened a cupboard of maps and publications. "You looking for something in particular, Harry?"

"Old copper mines," Harry said.

"Hmm."

Harry stole away toward a corner so he wouldn't be tempted into friendliness. The German probably interpreted this as secretiveness. Everyone who came to this office had big secret plans. Harry had a secret plan, too: it wasn't exactly *get rich*, it was more *get respectable.* If he could only get hold of a working mine, he'd have something to offer Jo.

Harry wanted to ask for the most recent map of field camps, but he was afraid he'd get too chummy about it and start talking and never stop. He checked over the ratings of the Geiger counters and scintillators to see if they had anything new to say that he could use in his sales pitch. Always his eyes came up against that jarring picture of Hermes with its uneven edges set unmatted in a bamboo frame. It must have been hand-ripped from a magazine like *Look.* It belonged hanging in a restaurant above a booth. Hermes looked like a cover boy. Harry always did a double take, expecting to see Hermes' autograph.

"There you have it," the man said, slapping down the records.

Harry did another double take when the clock chimed. Another thing he had forgotten. A grandfather clock played one-quarter of its tune every quarter hour so that by the time an hour went by you had the whole tune. The trouble was that Harry had never been there for an hour (well, he had been once, but the clock wasn't working; other times nearly an hour but the timing was wrong). The music it would play was tantalizing, and mountingly familiar. And truncated. Harry would be already stepping into the next note when it would stop. The tune was like a cough that wouldn't come out. Harry, the man of songs, could not place this one. He'd inquired before of this man whose name he used to know, but the man just flung out his hand. "Not my clock," he said.

Harry took his publication and map and hurried out. He couldn't get out of there fast enough. He was a spectator to himself falling apart piece by piece in there. Couldn't remember a name, or a song. A harmless mythological figure looked like a mobster restaurateur. Pretty soon he'd start mistaking the Geiger counters for kitchen mixers and he'd be selling them for S&H green stamps. Great idea, copper mine. Fantastic, Harry. Great idea. He started up the truck. Peter! He jumped out, ran back into the office, called, "Peter, I forgot to thank you. Thank you, Peter. Thanks very much, Peter. See you soon, Peter."

ELEVEN

The three old ladies stayed away from Jimmy Splendid. They kept a careful, calculated distance with borders they advanced to but never crossed. Jean had noted this behavior and as she lay in bed, everyone asleep except perhaps Jo, who was likely kept awake by the kind of brooding about marriage Jean herself used to do, she wondered why she was still thinking about it, not about her marriage come and gone, but about him. She wasn't intimidated by him like the old ladies, who in their social dealings were either overly diffident or overly dismissive. He was young and big and successful and he spoke in a deep confident voice. Nearly hidden in his regular features was a whisper of another culture, Indian or Spanish. It was this that was most interesting to Jean. She could think on that whisper and it would grow louder and louder.

The three ladies turned meek and respectful around Jimmy Splendid. They wouldn't think of coming to the pool while he was there. They disappeared into their rooms but kept watch at the windows—front window, bathroom window. Without particularly wanting to, Jean kept effortless track of their bladders. Then the ladies found excuses to come out. They checked their mailbox, went back inside, came back out, put a letter in the mailbox and poked up the red flag.

When Mr. Flaherty returned with the children, further excuses piled up.

The ladies walked to and from each other's rooms, delivering a houseplant, a magazine, some towels. Jean had watched movie scenes like this, maybe the Three Stooges, where chases go in and out of doors and they speed up the film and splice it funny.

As they stood at the pool, Jean became aware of the bad blood between Jimmy Splendid and Mr. Flaherty, but the two of them spilled their grievances in a code she couldn't understand. Miss Dazzle seemed to know the particulars. Probably Harry did, too. One of the old ladies, the one with the hair worn in a lovely upsweep, walked by the pool with a water glass to return to the office. Her gaze was *almost* straight ahead.

Beth and Charlie had been returned to her happy from their helicopter ride. When her daughter was happy, she was happy with abandon, and everyone laughed just to see her. And Charlie, when he was this happy, he looked nervous and wretched. Not as a result of his illness. She understood. She was like Charlie this way and she understood; some kind of wretchedness was involved in the exhilaration of a happiness that put you everywhere at once. She couldn't explain it really, but she knew Charlie was the same. This moment when the somewhere that you are becomes the everywhere you could hope to be.

She didn't get many details about the trip because Jo was quiet and pale and eventually excused herself, and Beth, too happy, left to play in Miss Dazzle's office. Charlie was overdue but she let him stay out until Mr. Flaherty left. In their room Jo stayed in the bathroom, draped over the toilet. She had to clap Charlie by herself, Jo's apologies an echo after every thud shook Jean's head and rattled loose this insomnia and alien headache.

She wondered where Jimmy Splendid was now, if he was with Miss Dazzle—rather, *Belinda,* but no, she couldn't call her that. It was a name that didn't at all fit her. Too single-generation, a recent name without history. Beatrice maybe. Or Bedazzled. Well, *was* he with her?

She could now look back and say she could have done without it, that she had hated almost every moment of being in love with her husband.

Even while swept up in it, a part of her fought the oblivion and hated it. If he wasn't with her every minute, she worked up scenarios that tormented her. In her mind he watched her every move then came upon her unawares as in a book or movie except that of course she was vividly aware and orchestrating her moves because she had planned this very moment and of course he wasn't there because she had simply plotted it in her mind, which meant *where was he then, really?* Each spot she inhabited was the rest of the world she was not inhabiting, which meant he could be in any of those other spots. Love made her too aware of her own limited imprint and the limitlessness it thereby granted others. Eventually a different kind of pain took over, the kind that now wanted him off her little spot on the planet. She wished him elsewhere in the world so she could think pleasantly of him in the abstract.

She might have been thinking aloud, for Jo in the other bed turned over and reached out to pat Beth. She watched them, spooned in each other's arms. Jo's face was peaceful, Beth's in apparent pain, her mouth thrown open in a silent scream. Jean propped up on her elbow to check on Charlie beside her. His face too was scrunched in pain, his mouth opened to yell out. Both her children slept this way and in their pain she could relax. As long as sleep painted suffering on their faces they were happy and well. She stroked Charlie's hair, his temple, his ear. When his face relaxed and turned angelic and peaceful, then she'd panic. But it hadn't happened yet. Until it happened, it hadn't happened. If it hadn't happened yet, it might not ever happen.

She got out of bed and went outside and stood in the doorway. The lot was empty except for the DeSoto. Jimmy's truck was gone. Where was he? Was he staying here or not? Off to one of those private clubs she'd heard about? The ladies' windows were dark. The ladies were each alone in their room. Was that a hard thing for them to do at the end of the day? She could feel her foot, hot from the sunburn.

At night there was no one else. At night she couldn't find other people to blame. Blame didn't travel well at night. She would never look back and say she wished she had never known this pain, for it meant never having known Charlie. But it hadn't happened yet, the pain hadn't happened. It might not ever happen.

The door opened and Jo stepped out and stood with her. "It's lonely without the girls at their windows," Jo said after a few moments.

"Give them a minute," Jean said.

"No one's here."

"Mm-mm."

"Where's Harry?" Jo asked.

"That's a good question."

"It's late, too. Where is he?"

Jean shook her head. "Are you feeling better?"

"Much better. I fell asleep, and now I feel better."

Jean realized a type of bond had formed between them. The casualness about the body that came to mothers who changed diapers had made a second appearance with Charlie. They didn't dwell on such things, but they didn't shy away.

Jean was about to tell her, it's time for us to go now, Charlie's getting worse. She wasn't ready to drive, but she could do it. She wasn't quite ready but it was time. Jean was about to ask her do you want to come along and help drive? (Jo was unhappy enough tonight to leave her husband and Jean figured she should jump at the opportunity Leonard Dawson had inadvertently provided her) when headlights streaked across their bodies and Harry's truck pulled in. The truck door creaked opened heavily; in the dry quiet air the sound was explosive. "The old girls must have heard that," Jean said. "I'm watching their rooms," Jo said. Harry walked toward them and whispered alarmed greetings, what's wrong? why are you up? Ah, here it came. One of the old ladies' lights went on and they doubled over with laughter and Harry looked at them and then looked at himself and they said, "No, it's not you, Harry. You had to be there."

TWELVE

The International Harvester was a bright yellow beauty. Dr. Randolph could have his Mercury truck loaded with shining chrome. Harry loved his Harvester. He loved the crack on the windshield, he loved how every bit of that truck was part of him. Even the tires he loved; just hated seeing them get punctured at such regular intervals. If he was thinking about getting anywhere near an old copper mine he'd better count on more and more ruined tires. He hoped the Harvester would be up to it. He knew it would. That truck was part of him.

It sat right where he had left it in Dr. Randolph's dirt yard among the other cars and Jeeps and pickups that were always parked there—patients and friends and yes, the drinkers, too. That attachment that was supposed to be a clinic? It had its own after-hours going on. Harry wasn't planning to go inside though he had papers signed by the coroner he should deliver in person. That was only proper; that was the right way to do things. But really what he wanted to do was skip the human transaction part, make the exchange of trucks and leave. It had been a nasty business when all was said and done and he wanted washed of it. The sooner he left the better. He could put the papers up on the dash where the doctor would find them in the morning.

He was transferring the boxes of liquor into the Harvester when Jimmy Splendid stuck his head out the door. "Say, Harry."

"Say, Jimmy." At the mining camp it was Mr. Splendid, but here it was Jimmy. Should be; they were probably the same age. Jimmy was suddenly beside him and like the man of the house seeing what his wife bought at the grocery he reached into the box and took out a jar of maraschino cherries, popped a couple into his mouth, and washed them down with some Jim Beam he had pulled out with the other hand.

"You'll have to answer to Miss Dazzle for that," Harry told him.

"I will."

Harry shut the door.

"Cat got your tongue, Harry?"

"No."

"Harry, you're friendly to everyone, that's what I like about you."

Harry didn't answer.

"Those kids are crazy for you."

Harry's head snapped up.

"I was over there earlier checking up on things. Come on in for a minute."

"What things?" Harry handed him the papers. "You mind giving these to the doctor?"

"You're not coming in?"

"No."

"Harry," Jimmy said, "you know a man named Timothy Carle?"

"No."

"Timothy Carle. That Mormon fellow who found Rutledge's plane."

"He's no Mormon."

"You know him then," Jimmy said.

"I was just this moment telling myself how glad I am to be rid of this whole business." Harry thrust the papers at Jimmy until he took them. He bolted up the back, then hopped in on the driver's side of his Harvester. The seat forged through long bumpy rides was now customized to his overly long body. "And finally I am."

"Say, would you take me over to see this fellow?" Jimmy leaned in with his arms draped over Harry's truck like he owned it. On the passenger seat was *The Mineral Industries of Utah* publication bought at the AEC office. Harry quickly threw Miss Dazzle's lunch sack over it.

"Who?" asked Harry. He wasn't thinking for a second. Then he paused. "I told you I'm glad to be rid of it all. Ask the doctor," he added. He shifted the publication to the floor, hoping Jimmy hadn't noticed. Jimmy noticed everything, except on occasions like now, when he was trying to ingratiate himself. That didn't come naturally so it ate up all his concentration.

"Randolph doesn't know where to find him," Jimmy was saying.

"He sewed him up. They seemed pretty chummy, laughing at everyone's expense."

"Harry, you know where to find him. You know everything. I know you know."

"Ask Joshua at the filling station. He knows, too."

"I'm asking you, Harry."

The feel of his truck had settled him down. Harry started to relax. No bodies had been in this car; no bodies ever would. The Mineral Industries of Utah was out of sight on the passenger-side floor. "Well," Harry said, "he's resting up at the Mormon church before he takes off."

Harry went inside the church and brought Timothy Carle out for Jimmy. Jimmy didn't say anything but Harry saw the reaction in his eyes. Yeah, Timothy was a sight all right, just about every kind of mess a man could make—all this mess had taken up lodging in his scrawny body and little turtleish head, both things shriveling fast.

Jimmy didn't try to hide a taken-aback kind of scrutiny. He wasn't playing poker-face. Didn't need to. Timothy wouldn't have noticed one way or the other. He came limping out in his roped-together boots. The doctor's bandage was gone from his ear, replaced by swatches of bloody underwear held in place by a clothespin. Staying in the Mormon church hadn't stopped him from getting drunk as a skunk. Harry didn't know which was the greater sacrilege, stealing Temple undergarments and using them as Band-Aids or indulging in alcohol. Officially speaking, that is. Harry discovered that he himself didn't really care. From wherever he was, Harry hoped Joseph Smith wasn't reading his thoughts.

"Yes, sir," Timothy said to Jimmy.

"Get in so we can talk," Jimmy said.

Harry stayed outside, scuffed himself a circle in the dirt and tight-walked around it. He imagined Jimmy was in the truck introducing himself. In fact he knew he was; he could hear the whole conversation. Then Jimmy called him over and Harry rested an elbow on the big sturdy side mirror of Jimmy's truck.

Jimmy was saying, "So I need to locate where Vernon Rutledge lives."

"That's *lived*, sir," Timothy said.

"Let's not play semantics. Are you playing a game with me?"

"No, sir."

"His death was a tragedy," Jimmy said.

"Yes, sir, it was. He was a good flyer, and he didn't make a mistake."

"Let's give him the respect he deserves with no games. Right, Harry?"

Harry didn't say anything. Reluctantly he nodded.

"Where did Mr. Rutledge live?" Jimmy asked.

"He didn't have a home."

"Everyone has a home."

"I don't," Timothy said.

"This man had a home. You don't fly around in an airplane unless you've got a home somewhere."

"It's not like a car, sir. You can park it any number of places. You don't need a home to park an airplane." Timothy patted his underwear bandage and fingered the clothespin.

Jimmy was silent for a while. He let the silence build. It was unclear whether this tactic was effective since Timothy was drunk and busy turning on the dash light so he could check his fingertips for blood.

"Why do you want to know where he lives?" Timothy asked by way of conversation, not that he seemed to care much, and Harry thought, That's right. That's a darn good reasonable question. You got so caught up in Jimmy's commanding presence you turned yourself into a schoolboy answering charges. Get in the car so we can talk he'd say and you silently obeyed because suddenly you were in the middle of a gangster movie. You got caught up in whatever world Jimmy created for you. But why did Timothy have to answer? He didn't have to answer at all. The things he was in trouble for, drinking and raiding the holy garments, these were things he had to answer for to the church, not to Jimmy Splendid.

Jimmy said, "Vernon Rutledge and I had an agreement. He was drawing up some anomaly maps for me."

"He was rimflying for you?" Timothy twisted his head around at that one and looked straight at Jimmy.

"He was agreeing to share the results of his rimflying."

"He never mentioned it."

"Why would he mention it to you? It was between us."

"Sir, if you want anomaly maps, you can get those from the government. They're posted at the AEC field office in Grand Junction . . ."

"I know all about it, Mr. Carle."

". . . on the 15th of each month . . ."

"The ones I'm—"

". . . at noon," Timothy concluded. His fingers went to the clothespin again. "Fifteenth of each month at noon at the AEC field office. Just trying to be helpful, sir," he said.

"You can help me most by telling me where he lives."

"It's *lived*, sir."

"Lived."

"It won't help you any," Timothy said. "Those maps went down with him."

"Those maps that he was working on, yes. I'm not worried about those maps. They wouldn't have been any good anyway. A fallout coming through this whole week skewed everything."

Timothy burst out laughing in painful coughs; it reminded Harry of that night in the church when he had gotten to laughing for no reason because a woman who was pretty might have been shot.

Jimmy turned to Harry. "Ol' Vince was up in the air over that. You can imagine that, right, Harry? Positively up in the air. Had no idea a tester was riding the wind and chased a reading down a rat hole."

Harry nodded. That explained what Leonard Dawson had been doing up there in the headlands. Harry thought the headlands had been a stupid place to look, fallout or no fallout.

"AEC don't bother to keep you posted on those things," Timothy said.

Jimmy yanked Timothy's hand away from his ear. "He had other maps he was supposed to deliver to me."

"That guy was crazy," Timothy said, shaking his head and laughing. "He was one crazy SOB. I was lying there on the ground watching him fly. He flew in the war and picked up some medals at it. He was a good flyer; he didn't make a mistake. You hear anybody saying that he did, you correct them."

"I'll do that," Harry found himself saying, the only thing he had contributed to the conversation.

"He dipped his wing at me but that's not what did him in. He was crazy but it's a downdraft what did it. He was a good flyer. He flew in the war."

Jimmy waited him out.

"Yeah, I know where he lived," Timothy said.

"So you'll take me there and I'll pay you for your time."

"Right now? Not in the nighttime I can't."

"It's time and a half for night work."

"I can't see it at night, sir. That's an impossibility for me. I been there but once. But I like those rates. I'll take those same rates for morning."

"In the morning then."

"Morning after next, I mean. I been hired for another job," Timothy said. "That man you mentioned. I got to go make a car repair for Mr. Flaherty tomorrow."

"Criminy," Jimmy said. "Can't he fix his own car? All right, day after tomorrow. That sound right, Harry?"

Harry shrugged, having only vaguely listened to these last details. He was already home, pulling into the Stagecoach Oasis, dark and empty and locked up, his headlights bouncing against the surprise of two nightgowned figures in a doorway, when Jimmy Splendid's parting remark to Timothy finally hit home:

"Harry will go with you," Jimmy promised Timothy. "He's got nothing better to do."

Thirteen

Beth was already out by the pool. She was a little girl who liked to sleep late, but here she was up in time to view the sunrise. She drew herself tight under the pink sweater she had borrowed from Jo. In the dark room it was the only thing she could find. Jo wouldn't mind, especially after ruining it during the helicopter ride: the knitting was pulled out where she had clutched herself, and now a round knob hung from each sleeve.

The sunrise brought with it its own mesa of flaming colors, solid enough that the sun seemed to rise behind it. And then it was light enough to read without a flashlight. *Cotton in My Sack* was over. Everyone had sores on their hands and fingers from picking cotton. And in *Strawberry Girl* everyone had sores on their hands and fingers from picking strawberries. Guess what was going to happen to the hands and fingers of the characters in *Beth Waterman, Uranium Girl?* This was called a theme. Lois Lenski had a theme about picking things and what it did to your hands.

Beth's grandmother had beautiful hands and fingernails, and she made sure to manicure them, oiling her cuticles and pressing them back with orange sticks, then filing and buffing the nails, then pressing the tender webs of skin between the fingers to get the blood flowing. She had taught Beth how to give a manicure but Beth didn't want to give any. She didn't mind having one given to her though, especially the hand massage, which felt so good—and was good for you. This was her little-girl claim on the medicinal glass of wine her grandmother set out for each manicure.

Beth had received many such hand treatments whenever the un-wanted capital-V visitor arrived again, each time lingering a little longer in its sightseeing. Charlie would journey to the hospital's mist tent. Beth would stay with her grandmother and when they talked about Charlie it sounded like he was the star of a travel brochure. We should all be so lucky to go on mist-tent voyages, your meals brought to you on a tray thank you very much. The two of them alone would look forward to their night of snuggling. Her grandmother would give her a manicure and lay out the bottles of polish for her to choose from. But sometimes without warning she'd drop Beth's hand and emit a sob, and the spell of elegance would be broken.

Beth peeked over her magazine and caught Harry tiptoeing out of his truck. He headed toward the motel rooms. She went over to the pool fence and leaned over until she caught sight of him again. He continued tiptoeing down the line of rooms, trying every door until one of them opened and he went in. She looked in the opposite direction to see if the office showed any signs of life yet. Miss Dazzle had *True Romance* maga-zines in there and Beth loved them. Now that her work was done with these books, she was going to spend her time reading and rereading the *True Romances*. But the office wasn't open yet. Miss Dazzle was still in bed. Maybe asleep. Maybe lying there enjoying the *True Romances* herself.

For now she had a *Mechanix Illustrated* she'd found in Harry's truck. She went back to her chair. On page 28 began an article that grabbed her attention. Miraculously, it was all about fingers.

People with short fat fingers were usually the life of the party.

People with pointy fingers were not so smart. Some were imbeciles.

The next page of the article showed a photograph of a harpist, a stonecutter, and a chocolate dipper at work. The chocolate dipper, due to his line of work, which was dipping things into chocolate [note from Beth: *dipping things like maybe strawberries!*], got skin eruptions on the fourth and fifth fingers, the fingers that didn't get dipped into the chocolate, which meant that the chocolate had secret healing powers. Which made no sense to her, but that was what the magazine said.

Though she aimed to please, Beth was always looking for a twist in her book reports and here was a perfect opportunity. Her final book report would feature the footnote. She would have to tailor the facts a little, but it didn't matter. *How are cotton pickers different from strawberry pickers? I'm glad you asked that. Strawberry pickers have red thumbs that have secret healing powers from all the strawberries they have picked. If you don't believe me, read* Mechanix Illustrated, *page 30.*

Harry was tiptoeing across the lot again, his shoes held high. He came over and sat on the steps that Vincent Flaherty (the life of the party with his short fat fingers) had nearly fallen dead upon. Harry laced his shoes. His back was to Beth. His wet hair dripped upon the collar of a clean shirt. When he stood up, he kept his back to her and tucked in his shirt. Then he turned around and came over.

"Good morning, Beth."

"Good morning."

"Are you hungry? I have a peanut-butter-and-jelly sandwich I can give you."

"No thank you. I'll wait for Miss Dazzle."

"Do you want anything?"

"No thank you."

"Are you sure?"

"Yes, I'm sure."

"Orange juice?"

"No thank you."

He reached out to her sweater and held one of the round unraveling knobs, a little confused by it. "Would you like a blanket?"

"No thank you."

"I have one in the truck."

"No thank you."

"It's a nice sweater," he said, cupping the soft knob.

"It's Jo's."

Harry's hand jerked back. He cleared his throat. "Pink's her color, isn't it?" he said after a bit.

"Mm-hmm."

"Did I say that right? Is that how you say it with your dolls: this color's her color?"

"Dolls look good in any color."

"I guess you're right. That's why they're dolls. They look good in anything. How would you say that then, in girl talk?"

"'Dolls look good in any color.'"

"That's how you'd say it then, 'good in any color'?"

"Mm-hmm."

"Every specialty has their way of saying things, doesn't it? Like if I said, possibly there's some pitchblende under that low-grade copper, what would you think I was talking about?"

"Uranium," Beth said.

"That's right. That's specialty talk. Not everyone can do it."

"But you're good at it, Harry." When she saw Harry's face light up, she was glad she had said it.

"Thank you. I try to be. Well, I'm off then," Harry said.

"Okay," Beth said.

"I've got to go check out a possible new career."

"Okay."

"It's actually a big secret, Beth. Can you keep a secret?"

"About the pitchblende under the low-grade copper?"

"Can you keep that a secret?"

"Sure," Beth said.

"It's not that I have nothing better to do. Working my own mine is a pretty big career opportunity."

Beth looked up. Adults were mysterious. Sometimes their mysteries were interesting. Sometimes they weren't.

"You let everybody know for me, okay?" Harry said.

"About your new career?"

"No, that's a secret. Don't say anything about that. Let them know I'll be back later, toward evening."

"Okay."

"It's just something that's important for me, so I have to check it out."

"Okay."

"What are you hiding there?" Harry asked. "Something you're good at, I bet. Reading's your specialty, isn't it? Just make sure you're reading the right kinds of stuff." He pushed the magazine down from her chest and peered over the top of the page. There was a photograph of a Harlem Globetrotter palming a basketball in each hand and a subtitle that read, *The size, shape, color, and texture of palms, fingers, and nails are tip-offs to your mental and physical conditions.*

"Why are you reading that?" Harry asked.

"Footnotes," Beth said. She looked up at him with a blank gaze she practiced on adults, her come-on-and-try-to-get-me look cloaked in innocence.

"Goodness. Footnotes," Harry said. "That's great."

"Thank you."

Harry said, "Listen to this." He hummed part of a tune that cut off right before she recognized it. "What is it?" he asked.

"I need to hear the rest," she said.

"Doesn't it drive you crazy?" he called, already moving away. Then he caught himself and quickly brought his finger to his lips and looked here and there, this way and that, at all the people sleeping inside.

FOURTEEN

Charlie was swimming his laps. Without the men there to squelch them the three old ladies had blossomed again, this time in full force, disdaining the rickety piping in their bold march up the steps to the pool. Bedecked in their bathing suits and flipper sandals, they were covered only partially by terrycloth robes short as blouses. They carried with them an old yellow newspaper photo: three girls in old-fashioned bathing suits, holding a trophy.

For the first time Jean realized they were sisters. "We were good swimmers," the quiet one told Jean. If there could be a quietest one in this group of jaybirds, she was it. She was a mix of the other two, white up front, blond in the bun, and a mix of their personalities, too. Sometimes she could pout; sometimes she could take charge. Sisters. It made sense to Jean now. "Is that you three?" she asked, bending close to the clipping preserved in crispy Band-Aids of cellophane tape.

"That's us."

"But those aren't our names underneath."

"We got cheated."

"Three little rich girls got their names in the paper instead."

"Times were different then and it wasn't up to us."

"We got cheated."

"She had no choice. She couldn't go up against that mother."

"You can dress it up any way you like but it still comes out cheated."

They were in it now, all three of them squabbling back and forth, and Jean stepped back and let them go. She imagined jaybirds' heads popping up and down from their nests, a game to go along with their serious hunger. *Because money talks and a lady wanted her daughters' names in the paper. But at least we have the picture. A picture doesn't lie. But we got cheated, and if I ever see them again I intend to give them a piece of my mind. Well, you won't see them again. Mother didn't tell them off. No, Mother didn't say a word. She had her ironing job to keep. She could have found a way. You were the baby and you didn't have any idea what she was going through.*

Jean and Jo and Miss Dazzle looked back and forth during this conversation, their raised eyebrows and puckering mouths carrying on a conversation of their own.

"Are you ready for breakfast?" Miss Dazzle asked the ladies.

"Not yet," they said. Heads tilting sharply to one side, then sharply to the other, they tucked their hair into their bathing caps. The flesh under their arms shook in synchronization. Jean watched their arms shaking and found it beautiful and sad—a new harmony discovered among sisters as they aged. She thought about her own mother—difficult territory, many times explored and nothing discovered. That was what she told herself when she didn't want to confront the fact that she may have fallen short in her duties. The daughter she used to be had almost always managed to be polite to the person who had raised her. She didn't have to wonder when the change had come about. Life was a normal story gone berserk and she had gone berserk along with it. The three old ladies dove in—swimmers' dives; they were set to race.

The bathing caps were brightly colored, emergency flashers in the water. Charlie was churned off to the edge of the pool by their three hurtling lanes. At the far side they gathered, a tumult of waves behind them as if the pool could gauge the weight of years and pride and splash up accordingly. They warmed up with the sidestroke. Clearly it was their favorite stroke. They could keep talking the whole time. *Yes but if I ever do see them again I intend to let them have it, cheating three little innocent girls. But you won't see them again. What did we do to deserve that? It's water over the dam. But if I do run into them I will say something and you can't stop me. They're dead!* Jean could see the spots where the rubber flowers had been pulled off the bathing caps.

"Come on, Charlie, let's race!" they called.

Charlie swam over to them at the deep end of the pool. Beth put down her magazines as Charlie and the three ladies lined up. She was jumping up and down and cheering on the sidelines. "Come on, Charlie!" she screamed. She hopped and twitched and the race hadn't even started. Jean looked over at her daughter, so unrestrainedly happy, so unhampered in her joy. All her experiences were still new and original, still adding up one by one to form the adult she would become. She was a bird singing its unfinished song.

FIFTEEN

Here was something Harry was pretty sure no one else had discovered: a road. The map he'd gotten from the field office showed an abandoned copper mine very near where Harry knew there was a road. Wasn't listed on the map but Harry had driven on it. It took him four hours from the Stagecoach Oasis to get to the spot where an access should branch off, and he had to backtrack and hunt on foot for it, hiking up and down the main road (main road! ha!) opening his mind to new interpretations of *thoroughfare,* meaning, drive up this massive boulder because the flat part of it could be the access way.

And he was right. The boulder was part of the road. Three burro miles later (thinking ahead), he parked, checked his map again, and scrambled up an outcropping. Before setting off with a compass he wanted to scope the area with binoculars. Didn't actually think he could find it that way, things didn't come tied with ribbons out here, but there it sat, a little gift for Harry Lindstrom: an old mine stuck low in a sun-baked, spalling brownness. It looked to be a mountain cave for a troll—a troll fallen on hard times. The small squat entrance was shored with tortured lumber. The weight of the top beam had pushed the entrance base wider and wider. A wheelbarrow was tossed out in front. It was obviously a small-time, mealworm operation—abandoned, Harry guessed, after the copper ore proved too low grade to turn a profit.

Harry returned to the truck and opened up the back. He groaned at the boxes of liquor he had forgotten to give Miss Dazzle. He pushed them aside and pulled out his best detection instruments and considered which ones he should use. He'd been wanting to try out the Halross model so he could provide testament to his customers that this was indeed the finest among portable scintillators.

One thing was certain, he was going to try out black light inside the cave. That was the newest thing on the market, supposedly all the rage, and yet the Mineralight wasn't selling well. Perhaps because not all the uranium-bearing ores fluoresced under black light. Carnotite, for example, didn't fluoresce, and that fact alone was enough to keep most people away. Everyone was chasing carnotite these days—Jimmy was mining a carnotite vein in his operation—but carnotite wasn't what Harry was after. With copper ore involved, especially low grade, he was betting on some pitchblende lurking within. Problem was that only impure pitchblende fluoresced. Pitchblende in its primary state wouldn't. People heard that news and they ran from black light. Did it worry Harry? Let him put it this way: the AEC was offering a $10,000 discovery bonus for primary pitchblende, and so far not a single bonus had been given. So what did that tell you? That told you to go to the Belgian Congo to find your primary pitchblende and not trouble yourself about finding it in Utah because you weren't going to.

Harry carefully packed the Mineralight in his rucksack and started out. He hadn't gone twenty steps when he returned to the truck and exchanged the scintillator for a Geiger counter—think, Harry, think. You're going to be inside a dark cave where flashing lights and ticking sounds might be useful. He picked up the Babbel instead.

Outside the cave he took some background counts. The meter averaged between 3 and 4. The weathered lumber shoring the entrance left him uneasy. But if it had stood this long, it could remain standing another hour or two. He stooped and went inside the mine. The passage didn't go in very far. They must not have made it past their first or second assay.

He imagined someone just like Leonard Dawson as the man behind this. A shoddy operation that showed Dawson's same telltale lack of will. But it predated Leonard Dawson. It had been abandoned years earlier, before the uranium rush. You could see history here, and it told you there would always be generations of gritless men ready to shortchange the world.

At the back wall he set down his pack and brought out the black light. The cave turned into one of those special museum rooms when he turned on the Mineralight. The walls shone with fluorescence. He looked for yellow-green, judged the color as best he could, then chipped out some samples with his pick. He found a thick overburden of rock on the floor and set the Babbel on it. The counter didn't give up anything. He hammered and picked through the rock. His long limbs were cramping from having to squat. When he broke through the overburden he took another reading and the crackling and the lights were steady and stronger, with the meter jumping to 6. He took it down two ranges to the lowest level of sensitivity and still got a reading. He put some samples in his bag, then found another spot and gouged it out, but it offered up nothing. But this had been good. This had been very good. He cased the Mineralight, returned it to the rucksack, and crawled out of the cave.

Miss Dazzle stood alone at the edge of the parking lot. Hands shoved against hips, chin craning down the street. Her wagging finger flew up, and she trotted forward. Harry wondered how long she'd been standing there waiting for him. "Sorry, sorry," he yelled. "I forgot all about them last night." Not bothering to park, he cut the engine, rushed out, and opened up the back of the truck. He started unloading the boxes of liquor.

"Where's the fire, Harry?"

"Thought you were waiting for me."

"Of course I'm waiting for you, Harry. I'm always waiting for you. But I wasn't *waiting* for you."

"What were you waiting for?"

"Nothing."

"You were waiting for something."

"Oh, Harry, we're all waiting for something."

"That sounds mysterious," Harry said. He was in a good mood and he could feel this new ability to joke bubbling up. "Let me get that, now. You just stand here and wait." His shoulder blocked her when she tried to grab a box. "No, really," he said. "Let me carry them in."

"You're such a gentleman."

He turned when he got to the office door. "And you're a lady in waiting." The riposte came too late and by now she was past getting it but that was okay, that was a pretty good joke any way you looked at it.

He brought in the second box and set it on the desk. The screen door slammed behind Miss Dazzle. "I'm sorry I forgot your order," he said. "Had a few errands to do this morning. Left before anyone was up." Harry tried not to sound breathless and proud of himself, but the way Miss Dazzle was glinting at him told him he probably hadn't succeeded. He poked around the liquor boxes; he was smelling fumes. He picked up a few Jim Beams from the box but couldn't find the one with the broken seal. "Saw Jimmy Splendid last night and he helped himself.

Miss Dazzle came over and took a bottle from Harry's hand and gazed at it.

"Jimmy said he was here," Harry told her.

Miss Dazzle nodded. "Was Jimmy here? Oh yes, he was here. What's a month without a little visit from Jimmy? Where did he end up staying last night?"

"I saw him at Dr. Randolph's."

"Hmm. I know Jimmy. He doesn't just show up to make sure everyone other than himself is doing fine. A good enough man, but he comes first. So what's he up to?"

"I don't know," Harry said.

"What's he got you doing for him now, Harry?"

"What do you mean?"

"What little errand did he send you out on?"

"I'm just an errand boy, is that what you're saying?"

"I didn't say that, Harry."

"This was an errand," Harry said, plucking another bottle of Jim Beam from the box. Miss Dazzle came close and squeezed his biceps with both hands. "I think he's sweet on the mother," Harry said. "He kept asking about her."

"Jean?"

"Yes."

"Really?"

"You didn't pick up on it?"

Miss Dazzle shrugged. "And you did?"

"Right away."

"Oh, I forget, Harry, you're versed in the ways of love."

"What's that supposed to mean?" Harry said. "You're in a mood today."

"Jimmy's not going to make a special trip for a woman, believe me."

"Why wouldn't he?"

"Because men don't do that."

"Sure they do," Harry said.

"I'm a woman and you're a man and yet I know more about men than you do."

"Well, I'm a man and my brother's a man and making a special trip doesn't seem like it would take a miracle."

"My husband walking across the room with a box of chocolates for me? That's a miracle."

"That's not a trip."

"It's a trip across a room. My husband—listen, Harry—would drive all the way to Grand Junction to go find some special fishing hook or a piece of beef jerky for one of his buddies, but it would never cross his mind to walk across the living room, not from here to there, for me."

"I don't understand what you're saying," Harry said. "You're not really describing a trip."

"Oh, Harry! If I was sitting there on that sofa bawling out my eyes, which I can tell you happened more than once because of him and his behavior, the guilty party wouldn't even hand me the handkerchief in his hand. What!"

"You're describing a bad marriage, not a special trip."

"Oh, Harry, you're something."

"You should be glad you're rid of him."

"I am, honey, believe me." She unscrewed the Jim Beam and got two glasses. "Come on and have a drink with me. Let's celebrate being rid of him."

"I've had a long day. Out in the field," Harry added with another failed squelch of pride. "One drink and you'll have to wipe me off the floor."

Miss Dazzle eyed him skeptically before bursting into laughter. "Oh, I needed that laugh. Thank you." She poured two glasses and handed one to Harry. "I don't know what my boys see in him. Both of them. Think the sun rises and sets on him. He's got a girlfriend out there, Harry. Ma Bell finally got my boys on the line and they told me."

Harry set the drink on the counter. "You didn't really think he was coming back, did you?"

Miss Dazzle hung her head. She began to sniffle, and Harry hugged her and let her sniffle against his chest. He was dirty and worried about that. He could smell himself, but now he could smell Miss Dazzle. The fumes came to him from their real source, in pulses, with each shuddering exhale.

She pulled back and hunted for her glass. "This one's yours." She handed the glass to him. "He's got a girlfriend; I might as well get a boyfriend. Isn't that how it works, Harry?"

"I don't know."

"You have had a drink before, haven't you, Harry?"

"Sure," Harry said.

"You've had drinks and all that other stuff before, right? I know because of your religion . . ."

"I'm not religious."

"Come on. Everyone's out having some special barbecue. I loaned them the car. Wasn't that nice of me and don't tell my sons. Have one drink with me, Harry, just one."

"I think you've already had one. Maybe even two."

Miss Dazzle laughed loud and long. She clinked Harry's glass, returned to the counter. "You've never had a drink, have you?"

"I have," Harry said.

Miss Dazzle lifted her glass and swallowed. She pushed the other glass at Harry again.

"I'm sorry about your bad news," Harry said. "I thought you didn't want him back." He didn't take the glass.

"I don't want him back. What makes you say that?" She took his hand and like a schoolteacher wrapping a chubby fist around a pencil, she fitted the glass into his palm. She clamped both her hands around his so that there could be no escape. "He's no husband of mine. Harry, I'm free, if that's what you're worried about." Her hands pushed the glass to his mouth. Harry took a nonchalant swallow and leaned away, but the glass continued to follow him upward for more swallows, and it didn't lower until he had swallowed it all. Miss Dazzle was tall but Harry was very tall, and when she moved in to kiss him she couldn't reach his lips and she was too unsteady to remain on tiptoes. But she was almost there and almost there she stayed. She kissed his throat instead. Her hands went to the sides of his waist. Harry was raised to be polite and friendly and now he saw what kind of trouble a polite and friendly girl could get herself into. He froze. It was different with a polite and friendly man of course. Nothing could happen unless a man made it happen, but then Miss Dazzle's hands started to move and he realized that wasn't necessarily so. He caught her hands, but not quite in time to hide his body's betrayal. He took Miss Dazzle's wrists and handcuffed them to his chest.

"Harry," she said.

"We've always been good friends," he said.

"I've always thought you were special."

"We're friends," Harry said. "We've always been good friends."

"You're different. You're the kind who'd make a special trip." Harry began to ease himself away. She pressed closer, against him.

"All your talk about making special trips," she laughed. "What special trips have you made?"

Both turned their heads at the sound of the DeSoto pulling into the lot.

"Jiggers, the cops," Miss Dazzle said. She breathed out a warm vapory chuckle against his throat. As soon as Harry moved to the door Miss Dazzle's freed hands slipped around him from behind. "This is what you're missing, Harry. If you think maybe . . ." Her fingers were quickly inside his belt. ". . . because we don't match . . . our experiences. No, Harry. I would never make fun of you." Her hands moved down farther and, with gasps escaping them both, held him.

"What's got into you!" Harry finally cried out and instantly regretted it. "I'm sorry," he said. "I didn't mean it that way. You're a wonderful person. I value our friendship."

"It's all right," Miss Dazzle said, weeping silently against his back, her wrists once more handcuffed to his chest, the best he could manage without doing further damage to her emotional state. Her mouth bored a hot circle into his back. He heard them calling outside.

"Your truck's open, Harry."

"Harry, your truck's open!"

"Hel-lo!"

He cracked the door wide enough for his head. Miss Dazzle was still stuck behind him. "I know. Thank you. I'm unloading some boxes. How was the barbecue?"

That wasn't going to stop them. Already he saw Jo and Jean angling their heads to see through the door gap. "Okay, I'll be there in a minute," he called, a futile attempt to forestall them. They had already said something to Beth, who was bounding over.

"She's coming," Harry pleaded. Even now he couldn't find the nerve to shove her away.

Miss Dazzle broke off and turned to her desk.

"Hello, Beth," Harry said.

Beth pushed through him and entered the office. "Why is Miss Dazzle crying?" she asked.

"She's not crying. She's going through her papers on the desk. Did you have a good barbecue?"

"Yes thank you. Why is she crying?"

"She has a lot of paperwork."

"Because Harry's such a gentleman," Miss Dazzle said and sniffled.

You can go now, Harry wanted to say but he couldn't say that either. "I'll be over to the room in a few minutes," he told her.

"Okay," Beth said and stood there.

"Could you tell your mom I'll be over there in a few minutes?" He waved good-bye.

"Okay," Beth said.

Harry waved good-bye again and reluctantly she departed.

"I wish you hadn't said that," Harry told Miss Dazzle.

"Why? Do you think she understands?"

"Do you think she might repeat it?"

Harry figured he'd get it over with, so after changing shirt and pants he headed to the motel room and knocked on their door. The mother answered, squinted as if to place him, and said, "I *thought* I heard a gentleman knocking."

"Does Charlie want to help me with an experiment?" Harry asked.

"Where have you been?"

"I had something I had to look into," he said. To contain the smile he felt creeping proudly across his mouth he added, "Do you want to help me, too, Beth? You can."

"No thank you," Beth said and left.

The smile Harry couldn't hold back found a proper excuse in the form of this cute little girl high-tailing it to Miss Dazzle's office (hadn't that been his niece just months earlier?—when had she become a beauty contestant?). "You don't even know what it is he's got," Jo called after Beth. "At least ask."

He said, "I think I can honestly say that I have the most exciting thing Charlie has ever seen."

"He went on a helicopter ride yesterday," Jean said.

"Oh," Harry said.

"Mr. Flaherty took us," Jo said. "Do you know him?"

"Sure."

"He was a gentleman, too. Though he didn't make us cry."

"That's good to hear."

"It's nice being surrounded by gentlemen," Jean said.

"Really nice," Jo said.

"Okay," Harry said. "I get it."

"What was going on in there between you and Miss Dazzle?"

"Nothing," Harry said.

"Harry knows nothing, sees nothing," Jo said.

"What's between Mr. Flaherty and Jimmy?" Jean asked. "Can you answer that?"

"It's the usual stuff that goes on around here. Everybody knows about it."

"We don't."

"Jimmy's still burned up over some withdrawn land the government changed its mind about and released. He thinks Flaherty claim-jumped him and he makes sure to let everyone know."

"Did he?"

"It was legal, if that's what you mean. But Jimmy's still burning over it."

"So were you claim-jumping Miss Dazzle in there?" "No, but it was legal." The two women were doubled over as Harry turned his back on them.

Charlie caught up to Harry at the truck. The evening had brought with it a dry breeze. The sleeves of Charlie's T-shirt flapped like flags. "What country's this and what country's that?" he joked to Charlie, lifting each sleeve.

Charlie shrugged.

"Did you enjoy that helicopter ride?"

"Yeah," Charlie said.

"I bet that was something, huh?"

"Yeah."

Harry pulled out his mineral bag from the truck. He took one of the samples that had fluoresced in the cave and chipped off a candy-sized piece with his pick, then pounded it into powder with the hammer side. Charlie watched. He always watched before he asked questions.

"You want to see a piece of equipment that'll run you about a thousand dollars?" Harry brought out the Mineralight. He would rather stay outside and do the test on his tailgate but the breeze would make it difficult. Plus it wasn't dark yet, and it had to be dark.

Charlie was a good kid. He regarded the Mineralight with a twelve-year-old's lust but kept a proper distance. Harry knew how bad Charlie wanted to get his hands all over it. Even after Harry had it set up on the writing table in the motel room, Charlie didn't dare touch it. He did help Harry set up the Bunsen burner on the toilet seat since it was just a Bunsen burner. Harry directed him to set the ground-up mineral sample next to it. Then Charlie heated up a loop of wire dipped in some sodium fluoride they had found in the chemistry set Miss Dazzle had lent him. Charlie kept dipping and heating until a molten bead formed. Then he touched the bead to the ground-up sample and picked up a speck, brought that back over the flame and melted the speck into the bead.

"Look at that, perfect timing. It's getting dark out. By the time the bead cools, it'll be just right. We need it nice and dark for the ultraviolet to work. Right, Charlie?" Harry made an announcement that he thought would please the boy: "Charlie can explain to any of you others what we're doing in case you're interested and don't understand." But Charlie looked increasingly, terribly unhappy. "And guess what? I just had an idea. I'm going to get the Geiger counter. We'll test it with that, too." A bonus, the idea had occurred to Harry in the middle of the bead test, but Charlie didn't manage even the barest of smiles at what Harry thought was an inspired suggestion. "I thought you'd go for that," Harry said. The smothering in his chest must be his heart breaking. He thought he'd had something for Charlie. Plus he was going to tell him all about the troll's cave, the fairy-tale adventure that sprang out of a copper mine of old. Instead he had made Charlie miserable. "Sorry," Harry said. "Thought it was something you'd find interesting."

Jean steered him out the door. "Go get your Geiger counter," she said with a push.

Harry walked ahead so Jean couldn't see his face. He thought he might start to cry.

"That's Charlie. He looks that way when he's happy." Harry turned toward the voice. Jo was following him.

"He doesn't look happy to me," Harry said.

"He is happy. That's how he looks when he's happy."

"But he doesn't look happy."

"Harry, are you listening to me?"

He felt a scolding tug on his elbow when he didn't respond.

"Charlie, he's just so happy he can't contain himself right now. I know it's hard to understand."

"I understand," Harry rushed in to say. "I'm not an ogre. Do you think I'm an ogre who can't understand?"

"Harry, what an awful thing to say. Harry . . ."

"Thank you for explaining it to me."

In this bare rush of seconds, darkness had arrived. Harry hoped the dark would shield them. If only he had parked his truck the other way, the back end would be situated so that neither the office window nor the windows of the motel room could look upon him. He felt desperate enough that he almost didn't care.

He pulled out the Prospectometer, the Detectron DG-7, the Uranium Scout de luxe (the pre–"de luxe" Scout was junk), the Lucky Strike (junk), and the Model DG-2 (also junk) and lined them up, even though he knew he wanted to use the Babbel-400. His mind gave them their full official names. Even in his thoughts he felt the urge to show off when Jo was around. *How do you know which one to use? How do I know? Well, I'm an expert for starters.*

"In fact, I was using this one today," Harry told her, picking up the Babbel.

"That's where you were," Jo said.

"Where?" Harry said.

"I don't know. Where were you?"

"I thought you knew. You said that's where you were. I thought you knew."

Jo didn't say anything.

Harry held out the Babbel's earphones for Jo and she fitted them on her head. He liked how she didn't care what small disarray it might bring to her hair. Her hair that she'd tied back with a snapped shoelace. He turned on the Babbel.

"My goodness!" she said. Her eyes lit up with victory.

"No, no, calm down," Harry told her. He reached out with his hand and touched her forearm. "It always crackles. You have to learn to tell the crackles apart. Of course when you really get something hot, there's no guessing. Like today," he said. "That happened to me today."

Jo smiled reassuringly at him but didn't ask him to go on. His hand was still on her forearm, it was still okay for it to be there, but in a few more seconds they would both be obliged to notice it. All Jo had to say now was, What happened today? and he would have his opening. Given such an opportunity, he could explain it to her; the words he always botched would be corrected by his fingertips dictating the real message on her arm, the old copper mine he was betting would yield uranium— this mine he was going to work for her. But she didn't ask, and in two ticks the time was past when he could keep hold of her forearm. He'd have to force it upon her now, but that was a disastrous option. Even in the very best red-carpeted situation he'd still have trouble getting it out right. You could give him an opportunity that was like a stunningly adorned ro mantically set table (with wine glasses!) and his personality was the thing that pulled out the linen tablecloth and toppled it all.

He swiveled with the microphone probe to buy himself time. "Any-thing different happening?" He touched the probe here and there. She nodded yes, yes, listened, squinted, shrugged, she was getting something but it remained a foreign language. "How about here?" He touched the probe to her forehead.

"Ooh, now it's going wild!" she laughed.

"Did you know that Joseph Smith's phrenology chart indicated ac-quisitiveness, alimentiveness, marvelousness, and amativeness?"

"And I thought you claimed to be such a gentleman."

Harry withdrew the probe. "So you think Charlie's liking it?"

"He's loving it. It's wonderful of you to do it. He loves that kind of stuff, you know that."

"He's a good kid. Charlie proves there's nothing to make fun of about being a gentleman."

"Of course not."

"So you know what amativeness is?"

"Yes, Harry, I do," Jo said softly.

Harry was now left with his next move staring him in the face. He could reach out and gently remove the earphones from her head, which would leave his hands cupping her neck. That was romantic. He could grab both her hands as she removed the earphones herself, and if she were anything like Miss Dazzle that would be enough to encourage her and she would do the rest for him. That was romantic, too.

He disguised a glance at her. If Leonard Dawson could see her now, he'd say that she had let herself go. He'd spew out some word meant to illustrate how she had disgraced herself. She was wearing a tattered men's dress shirt she'd taken from Jean. The dresses she always wore were replaced by those short pants ladies like Jane Russell were wearing. Her ankles and calves were banged up; the darkness couldn't block the landscape of scrapes and dirt that lured him to her skin like glittering jewelry.

"Your husband's going to be pretty mad when he finds out what you've been doing."

Miss Dazzle had said, *I'm not married, not really, you don't need to worry about that,* and he waited for Jo to say it, too.

She didn't remove the earphones. He didn't remove them for her. Instead he tapped his forehead against the truck, coming close, very close, to simply giving up. His shoulders were drooping. He could feel himself losing strength. Jo's hand came into his sideview as she set the earphones beside the Babbel. He gauged the angle of kissing her and saw there could be nothing romantic about it: he was too tall.

Give it up.

He suddenly straightened and blurted: "I don't think your husband is good enough for you."

"I know that, Harry."

"But I don't think a traveling salesman is good enough for you either."

Jo didn't answer.

"But I've got a mine I'm looking into and if it pays out . . ." He turned to tap his forehead again, took a deep breath, tap, deep breath, tap—he turned again. "Do you know what I'm talking about?"

He relived stooping into the troll's squat little cave. He got himself down low—quickly! It was an act of faith and discomfort. He bent over and blindly pulled out the tablecloth and waited for everything to topple. When it didn't, when she didn't slap him, he bent low and kissed her again. He stood up. He was out of breath.

Harry didn't know if Beth had seen them, but when he looked over she was standing in front of the office.

"Beth," Jo called.

"Hi."

"Come here. Come here."

"Where's Miss Dazzle?"

"She fell asleep on the sofa."

"Well, come on inside. Harry's got something exciting to show us."

Beth was wearing Jo's pink sweater with the pulled-out knobs. Harry couldn't stop a hot rush of embarrassment. He picked up the Geiger counter and shuffled back to the motel room. Charlie hadn't moved. He was staring at the tiny head. Harry kept a flashlight on while they turned off the other lights and pulled the curtains. When he clicked off the flashlight, they were thrown into a strangely dense inkiness, the other bodies lost to them except by some traveling force of gravity. They were there but only blindly, apparently, there.

"Anytime now, Harry," a voice in the darkness said.

When the black light came on, their bodies stayed hidden among the luminescence of white shoes, white shirt, white socks—a contagious white emitting whiteness. Harry was lost in it. A dancing luna moth became the white bandage on the mother's head.

Charlie pointed out a tingling prick of light, different in color and tonality, that began to glow upon the writing table. "It's got uranium," Charlie announced.

"It does."

"Look at that."

Harry switched on the room lights and blinked away his disorientation. He picked up the Babbel and let Charlie hold it. "Now we'll check it out on a Geiger counter but it's not going to give you much." He fitted the earphones on Charlie. "We have to get what we call a background count, Charlie, so you have something to compare it with. Stand over here."

"I took one," Jo told everyone. "I was outside taking a background count."

"What'd you find?"

"My brain is worth a fortune." When the mother started laughing, Jo laughed harder and harder at her own joke, delighted to be appreciated. She wasn't used to an approving audience, Harry could see. Well, that would change with him around.

"Charlie," Harry said, thinking of something that might be fun, "pull the light switch. Let's do this in the dark."

When they were thrown into blackness again, Harry turned on the Babbel. He had ranged it at its highest sensitivity since the sample was so small, but the lights flashed like an ambulance. "Wow!" Charlie cried out, his hand to the earphone.

Harry promptly lowered the dial. The lights, however, grew more urgent. Harry tried to back Charlie away from the sample, but everyone had stumbled together and Harry had to fight though a heap of bodies. The scrunch of bodies was disorienting him and he couldn't find the light switch.

Charlie, dowsing-style, led the Geiger counter around the room, his heap of followers holding on. From the bathroom to the bed to the window to the nightstand. To the other bed to the pillow to the other pillow to the floor on the other side. The small radioactive bead causing all this trouble was by now in an opposite corner, yet the lights flashed ever faster.

When Harry found the light switch, Charlie was standing over Beth's rucksack. Beth opened the rucksack and pulled out the piece of petrified wood and touched it to the Geiger counter's probe.

"Good lord, this thing's hot as a firecracker!" Harry said. "Turn it off, Charlie, we might blow the tube."

"That piece of wood is doing that?" Jean said.

"Here I thought it was your brain," Jo laughed.

"This is no joking matter," Harry said.

"Nobody's joking," Jean said.

"I really thought it was her brain," Jo said. "Or mine."

"Stop," Harry said. "Pay attention. This is serious. Where'd you find this?" Harry asked Beth. "Stop," he said to the two doubled-over giggling women.

"Beth found it," Charlie said.

"You found it?"

Beth nodded.

"There's more like it?"

"I didn't have a Geiger counter with me."

"No, I mean there's more petrified wood?"

"I don't know."

Harry looked at her. "Think," he said.

"I was in a hurry a little bit."

"Where was it?"

"In this, it's hard to explain."

"Try."

"I went through a crack and into a cave except it wasn't a cave be-cause it went all the way up after I got inside."

"What do you mean?"

"I could see the sky. And then I found a pool and some plants."

"Okay," Harry said.

"I mean I had to squeeze to get in."

"That's all right," Harry said. "So inside something like a mountain?"

"It was like a pyramid."

"Okay."

"I went swimming in the pool."

"You're probably radioactive now," Charlie said. "You've been dipped."

"Is that good what I did, Harry?"

"Really good."

"I was exploring," Beth said. "I like to explore."

"Could you take me there?"

"No," their mother answered.

"Could you find it again?"

"No, she can't."

Beth said, "Charlie used his compass and drew it on his map."

"Is that so, Charlie?"

"Yeah."

"You used your compass?"

Charlie glared at him.

"Of course I know you used your compass, it didn't come out right what I said. You always use your compass, I know that. What I meant was, did you mark it on your map, too?"

Charlie nodded.

"I told you that, Harry," Beth said. "I saw him do it. And I know it's right because Navajo Joe checked it out."

"Navajo Joe? You mean Joe Istaqa?"

"No. Navajo Joe."

"All right, Navajo Joe. Navajo Joe was there with you?"

"No. Earlier."

"Earlier at this cave?" Harry asked.

"Earlier at the campsite. He was bringing us water."

"Let's back up," Harry said.

"Okay," Jean said. "This interesting conversation is now coming to an end."

"Charlie, you are an amazing kid," Harry said.

"Stop right there," Jean said.

"Mom. You stop."

"Do you have the map here, Charlie?" Harry asked.

"No, Harry," Jean said. "And no we're not getting it, Harry."

Beth said, "That was pretty good of me, wasn't it? I like to explore."

"You're a fantastic explorer, Beth."

"No, Harry."

"Yes, Mom."

"Yes, Mom. Mom. Yes. We'll take you there, Harry," Charlie said. "We'll use my map."

"All right. Stop right there."

"You stop."

"We're all stopping."

"No."

"Yes."

"No."

"Yes. Yes, yes, yes."

"No."

Uranium

ONE

The next day saw a crowd of folks at Miss Dazzle's place and Beth wondered what everybody knew about the petrified wood and all the ticking and flashing lights it caused, and instantly felt guilty. She backtracked through everything she'd said and couldn't remember letting the cat out of the bag. But that didn't mean she hadn't. She was ashamed to look Miss Dazzle in the eyes after last night, and Miss Dazzle seemed a little embarrassed to look at her although she had no trouble laughing it up with Jimmy Splendid and Vincent Flaherty and egging them on in their little ongoing spat. Unlike Jimmy Splendid, Vincent Flaherty seemed altogether content to be here, sleepily content like he was lying in the sand on the beach, and he kept asking where Charlie was and when was this Mr. Einstein finally going to make his appearance.

Jimmy Splendid, on the other hand, was the type who had to keep moving. He paced around the pool, and if a cocktail party had been going on he would have been part of every conversation.

The two men scared off the three old ladies. One by one they went on their errands across the parking lot, casting long glances at the gathering. The way they casually strolled and spied at the same time—now, that was her grandmother right there. And by the way, her mother was up here at the pool, too, eating like a pig, but that was good. She hadn't been eating at all. Jimmy Splendid seemed distracted by her eating. Her mother's head was down and she was just shoveling it in. And speaking of Beth's grandmother, if she had been there to see it—the manners! In between talking and laughing and then getting a little bit mad at Mr. Flaherty and then taking a lap around the pool and going back and talking normally again with chuckling nods, Jimmy Splendid kept shooting glances at her mother, who didn't seem to notice him at all.

Well, Beth had some scabs to pick on her legs and so she did that.

Miss Dazzle passed out lemonade. "I think it's the hottest day yet," she said. Beth said thank you and Miss Dazzle said you're welcome so maybe everything was back to normal and maybe Miss Dazzle didn't even remember last night in her office. Maybe all she remembered was waking up on the sofa. She didn't say anything more to Beth than *you're welcome* so Beth couldn't tell.

"*Il fait très chaud,*" Vincent Flaherty agreed.

"Okay," Jimmy Splendid sighed, "here we go."

"Are you doing all right, Vince?" Miss Dazzle asked.

"Hot as Hades is how I'm doing," Vincent Flaherty said. "About to expire is the price tag hanging from my neck."

After another glance at Beth's mother, Jimmy Splendid said, "For God's sake, Vince, get that jacket off you and get the noose off your neck or you will expire."

"That's right, Mr. Flaherty," Jo chimed in. "Please take it off."

"I don't want to be rude," Vincent Flaherty said, "but as requested I shall remove my jacket and tie."

Jimmy Splendid sighed again. "I'm halfway sorry I mentioned it."

"Give me a hand here," Vincent Flaherty said. "I see my man is arriving." He was pulled to his feet by Jimmy Splendid—that expanding stomach of Vincent Flaherty's must have had an oven inside it set to 350 degrees. Vincent Flaherty slipped off his jacket and was loosening his tie when the man he was talking about squealed a Jeep into the parking lot and fell out onto the blacktop. Fortunately for the three old ladies, one of them was right there in the parking lot in the middle of an errand

and the man collapsed at her feet. "My God!" she screamed. "Are you all right?"

"Yes, ma'am," the man replied.

"You're not dying?"

"No, ma'am." The man got to his knees and stayed there, holding his sides. "Steering wheel," he gasped. "Hit ribs."

"You just rest there a minute," she said.

With the pipe railing pulled out of its roots, getting down from the pool required Vincent Flaherty to take three cautious steps sideways. Beth was embarrassed by his feebleness and looked away.

The three old ladies had quickly surrounded the man on all fours. He didn't wait to get on his feet before talking about a crash. Soon enough Beth realized that it was *the* crash he was talking about, and she thought, This is really bad manners telling such a bloody tale to old ladies, and then it got to the gory part, *the wing dipped and a downdraft caught him,* and by then Miss Dazzle was there crossing her arms sternly like that's enough now but at the exact same moment the old ladies cried, "Then what!"

"I don't think we need to know then what," Miss Dazzle said.

The man got to his feet, the old ladies fussing over him. In this town there were many men who looked like scavenger birds had picked them over. The man hardly stood out in that regard. And yet he stood out.

By now everyone had gathered around him, even her mother. Beth looked at the happy-injected old ladies and realized they were looking especially nice in their dresses and high heels, so no wonder she thought of her grandmother—her grandmother always wore high heels and she stepped lightly like a dancer in them. Gazing at the old ladies, Beth was jarred by a bolt of longing, for what she didn't exactly know—it went beyond just her grandmother and the ladies looking nice. She remembered now that the old ladies were going on that sightseeing trip to the A-bomb testing site, that was why they were decked out so nicely. It turned out that the sightseeing trip was a double overnighter with shopping involved, which was one reason Beth had decided not to go. The other reason was that her mom had taken her for a delectable barbecue at the Atomic Café and afterward the trip didn't sound as interesting as before.

The man was introducing himself. "Name's Timothy Carle, ma'am," he said to each old lady and shook her hand. "Name's Timothy Carle, ma'am," he said to Beth's mother.

"How do you do," Miss Dazzle said, cutting him off.

"We met once before, ma'am. I came to stay at your motel but you wouldn't let me in."

"Miss Dazzle!" the old ladies scolded.

Vincent Flaherty, mopping his face with his tie, had a good cackle at that one.

"What reason could I possibly have had for that?" Miss Dazzle said.

"Point taken, ma'am." Timothy, it was true, was pretty ugly and very dirty and, Beth now saw, also bloody, and also, as she took in more of him, he wore flapping boots tied together, and also he had tobacco juice sliding down his chin, and also he was even bloodier than she had noticed at first. For a crazy moment Beth thought he was playing a pirate, wearing a single gaudy earring in the shape of a clothespin. The three old ladies drew close to his wounds and lightly poked with an ooh, aah, mm-hmm, I bet that hurts. Timothy lifted his shirt and showed them his bruised ribs. They even touched his ear and the bloody wad covering it. Beth did have a question about the clothespin, but the old ladies looked it over like a man would a car and said, *Seems to work*. Timothy showed them how he wedged the clothespin with a tobacco plug so it wouldn't pinch the bandage too tight.

By the time Harry and Charlie pulled in, Timothy had visited each of the ladies' motel rooms and carried out their luggage. Each had one round suitcase. The ladies looked very pleased with themselves, standing in a row in the parking lot, waiting for the bus. With their round suitcases in festive colors of blue, red, and yellow, they looked to be going to a party for spare tires.

Beth was watching Harry and Charlie. She knew they were up to something. She didn't believe a single thing they'd said this morning. She noticed that Miss Dazzle wasn't looking at Harry either, in the exact same way Miss Dazzle wasn't looking at her.

Vincent Flaherty meantime wanted to know where Charlie had been sequestering himself and was there a Nobel Prize involved. Harry looked nervous.

"Timothy's here so you can get going," Jimmy Splendid said.

"What?" Harry asked.

"Remember? Our agreement."

"No," Harry said.

"You remember, don't you, Timothy?" Jimmy Splendid said. "You agreed to do a job for me."

"Yes, sir, that's why I'm here."

"Hold on a minute," Vincent Flaherty called. He had strayed from their group to rest on the bumper of his Cadillac. He pushed himself off.

"I didn't agree," Harry said.

"You're supposed to be somewhere else today," Vincent Flaherty said.

"Been there and back, sir," Timothy said.

Vincent Flaherty played a beat on his stomach. No one knew what this meant. Everyone stopped talking and waited.

"Sir?"

"I find that hard to believe, Mr. Carle. An oil change takes Joshua the better part of an afternoon and there's no traveling involved. You're telling me you've been out to the headlands and back and meantime fixed a pickup?"

"He was just out of gas, sir. Had some canisters you provided him with right there in the back. I showed him how to fill it up."

Jo's expression remained stony as Vincent Flaherty reared back and howled. Harry told Jimmy Splendid that he was taking everyone, meaning Beth and the others, back to their campsite today so he couldn't go with Timothy after all and Jimmy Splendid said, "Oh, so you do remember, Harry, you're being cagey," and then Beth's mom said, "That's all right, Harry. We don't need to get back today."

"Yes, you do," Harry said.

"Dawson's up and running is he?" Vincent Flaherty cackled.

Timothy had advanced on Jo and was saying to her, "Ma'am? Name's Timothy Carle, ma'am. I've just been informed that you're the wife of the party. Mr. Dawson would like me to deliver a message that he's coming back today and he'll be looking forward to seeing you."

"He better not be coming back," Vincent Flaherty said.

"He was a little forceful the way he said it is what I'm trying to say," Timothy told Jo.

"Thank you," Jo said.

"In fact, we'll all go along with you on your errand today," Beth's mother told Harry.

"It's too far," Harry said.

"Good," her mother said.

In the middle of all this Beth looked over at Charlie and saw him holding one of the cardboard panels for Harry's shirts. He caught her gaze and tipped the cardboard enough so that Beth glimpsed the other side and the still not-colored-in doodles of Charlie's latest map. "You had it with you after all," Beth whispered.

"Uh-huh," Charlie said.

For a while it appeared that Miss Dazzle was also going with them. She even got behind the wheel of the DeSoto and turned it on. At the last minute she got out and handed the keys to Jo. She said she had too much work to do and today would be a good day to do it with everybody gone. But Beth thought that was Miss Dazzle's problem in the first place, everybody being gone. She was lonely—in case anybody cared to hear Beth's analysis of the situation. Beth tried to force herself to wave good-bye to Miss Dazzle. She liked Miss Dazzle a lot; nevertheless, she couldn't get herself to turn her head in Miss Dazzle's direction, not until she heard the screen door slam. Then she waved at the empty office doorway, in case everyone was looking and wondering what was wrong, which she was sure they were.

"What's going on here?" Vincent Flaherty asked.

"Just jump in the car and find out, Vince. You're good at jumping in," Jimmy Splendid said.

"Wouldn't think of intruding. *Vaya con Dios,* my friends," Vincent Flaherty said.

Beth and Charlie watched Timothy unload a piece of equipment from his Jeep and clamp it onto the passenger window. He walked over to the DeSoto, dipped his head in the driver's side, and said, "You'll probably want to stay here, ma'am, at the motel. Your husband will be here soon."

"Thank you," Jo said.

"Go," her mother said. Jo hit the gas and the DeSoto peeled out. Beth and Charlie were left stranded. They got in the Jeep with Harry and Timothy. Beth had wanted to ride with Timothy, anyway.

The three old ladies stood in a row. All of them waved good-bye the same way with childlike hand flaps and all of them in time with each other. The three round suitcases were positioned at their feet like sitting dogs. "Have a good trip!" Beth called out. The one with the whitest hair cupped her ear and leaned forward. "Have a good trip!" Beth saw her rear back and nod yes. Her hair was so white it disappeared in the sun. And the sun sitting atop her head was the last thing Beth saw as they pulled away.

Two

If asked in her later years about *Beth Waterman, Uranium Girl*, Beth would use these words to describe herself: resilient, exploratory, and radioactive.

Also brave and wise, life of the party, tall, pretty, funny, thoughtful, fleet-footed, and reading level: *high*. Curious. Stubborn. Well liked. Sharp-eyed. The word that means none of this could have happened without her.

They were riding toward the foothills in Timothy's Jeep. Jo and Beth's mother had taken off in the wrong direction and Harry had gunned down the road to catch them and turn them around. Harry was driving since Timothy's ribs were still hurting. Beth had already learned from Timothy that he had been part of the rimflyer's crash, meaning he had panicked so much witnessing it that he had crashed his Jeep.

"Where do them ladies think they're going?" Timothy asked.

"Good question," Harry said.

Beth was *resilient* because when one dream was dashed she moved on to the next dream and wasn't defeated. For two days she had lingered near Miss Dazzle, trailing her, waiting for her to get up in the morning, waiting on the sofa in the office, waiting at the pool. She'd pored over the *True Romances*. More than the lurid content, which she loved, she would take away the smell: the smell of cheap printed pages that started to turn musty almost right away. She doubted she could ever again sit on a sofa with a magazine in her hand without thinking back to these two days and the moment when she realized Miss Dazzle wasn't going to heal Charlie. It was a moment pretty easy to pinpoint since Miss Dazzle had just cried herself to sleep. Miss Dazzle had started talking to her as if Beth were the adult, and that was when Beth knew. Adults coming to a kid for advice probably weren't in any position to save someone else. Miss Dazzle had patted a spot on the sofa and said *Come*—that was when Beth thought it would happen, the big news Miss Dazzle had been saving up to spring on her. Beth had prepared herself for this moment and had practiced faking surprise. She faked surprise when Miss Dazzle said *Come* in a sultan's-tent kind of voice, she faked surprise when Miss Dazzle handed her a grape soda and a bowl of potato chips (big news, like movies, needed food), she not-so-much faked surprise when Miss Dazzle started to relieve not Beth's heavy burden but her own, and she completely didn't fake surprise when Miss Dazzle wept herself to a sudden drop-off. Before she entirely realized what was happening, Miss Dazzle was gone, deeply gone. Snoring.

Beth was loyal, even if the loyalty was mostly to her own cockamamie ideas, and she sat a little longer—just in case. Even with Miss Dazzle asleep she sat without reading. Much as she needed the escape offered by the top-of-the-pile cover picture of a woman pressed against a tree and blown half naked by the wind, it seemed disrespectful to search in that pile for the January issue with Part II. She'd read Part I that morning, about Buster, the hottest thing in Rome since the chariot races. Despite Miss Dazzle's tearful warning never to fall in love, she really really wanted to read Part II. The album with "Once I Had a Secret Love" had just finished playing but the phonograph scratched onward and when Beth closed her eyes someone was in the room comforting her, going ssh, ssh in a grainy voice. And when she opened her eyes it was dark and time to leave. Harry and Jo were outside as if they knew and were waiting for her. What happened next with the uranium discovery in the motel room was destined to become a classic moment in *Beth Waterman, Uranium Girl.*

Timothy fiddled with the bar he had attached to the passenger window, then checked the meter sitting on his lap.

"I see you have the Prospectoscope," Harry said. "You prospect from your car?"

"Only way to travel," Timothy said. He said he and Vernon Rutledge had a system worked out whereby he would drive along and Vernon would fly along and they'd signal each other if they got into a hot zone.

"That sounds like a good idea," Harry said.

"Sir, it sounded like a good idea but it didn't work out like a good idea." Timothy turned to make sure the kids were okay. "You kids okay?" Every minute he'd swivel in his seat and ask the same question until Beth started thinking he had a disease that made him do it. Even Harry must have been bothered by it because he said, "Charlie and Beth are okay. Don't worry about them. Keep a lookout for me, why don't you. We don't want to miss it."

"It's still a ways, sir." Timothy told a story about how as a kid he had made that thing that flies around when you hang it and the story didn't get started for several moments while they guessed flying object, no, paper airplane, no, piñata, no, mobile—MOBILE! He'd made himself a mobile out of balsa-wood airplanes and hung it from a tree branch and he used to lie under it and watch the airplanes go 'round. When he came to the next part Harry supplied the word without hesitation so Beth knew he had heard the story before. Timothy said it was like DÉJÀ VU, he was lying in the sand remembering his MOBILE as Rutledge flew in circles above him. That mobile was spinning around in his mind when the airplane flew into the rocks. Vernon Rutledge was a darn good flyer, he told Beth and Charlie. He flew in the war.

Well! Harry cleared the air with a big well! and said who would like to hear about *his* day yesterday and how he visited an old abandoned copper mine that was right out of the Wild West and would anyone like to hear about that? She saw Harry shoot a glance at Charlie in the rearview mirror and she could see his face fall a little because Charlie didn't answer, but that was just Charlie's way because of course he wanted to hear. Harry started in about having to drive his truck up a gargantuan boulder blocking the road like a giant and then not knowing what to do once he got to the top. Timothy turned in his seat—you kids okay? Charlie immediately got to laughing. Harry glanced in the rearview mirror, then turned around to make sure the mirror wasn't lying. Harry said he just gunned the engine and flew out over the boulder and somehow landed in one piece on the road he was right about believing was there. Timothy gave a knowing chuckle like he did that kind of stuff all the time. Charlie was laughing harder. Maybe Harry was getting a little carried away because he had Charlie in such a fit and he kept pivoting his head to check on Charlie as if he couldn't believe his good luck. The way Harry talked about this giant boulder guarding the road made Beth think that by the time he got to the mine itself it was going to be guarded by a giant three-headed dog boulder and that snake-haired lady boulder who turned you into another boulder if you looked at her, which explained all the rocks everywhere in front of the entrance.

Correction. She was wrong. A troll guarded the entrance.

Beth was *exploratory* because she went new places alone and climbed up heights that were dangerous just so her brother could have his measurements. She let her legs be tied off with rope, also so her brother could have measurements. She was personally responsible for a new measurement known throughout the world as the bethometer. As a member of a small expedition, she had taken part in discovering a cave artifact named by the scientific community as Rawhide Joe. Most importantly, on a treacherous solo journey, her explorations had led her to the discovery of uranium.

"You know, sir, I feel like I might have caused that crash." Timothy looked back at them—you kids okay?—then stared intently over at Harry. "It was spinning around in my mind when Vernon flew into the rocks.

That airplane thing . . ." He turned to Beth for help, twirled his finger. *Mobile.* "That mobile, thank you. I could see it plain as day. Like I knew it was going to happen."

Charlie folded over in convulsions.

"Well, maybe because I knew beforehand, then maybe I caused it by thinking on it. If I had changed the subject of my thinking . . . you see what I'm saying? What do you think?"

Harry searched for Charlie's doubled-over figure in the rearview mirror. "I think you probably caused it," Harry said. Timothy took Charlie's hysterics in stride, and his face floated with a bland contentment. He checked his meter and adjusted the probe. "I'm getting a little reading here. Let's stop."

"No," Harry said. "We should keep going."

"Might be something."

"I'm sure others have scoured this road a million times."

"Ain't but nobody going on this road except the Mormons. You're a Mormon, ain't you, Harry?"

"Yes," Harry said.

"Figured."

"How'd you figure?"

"'Cause you're the one came into the church and got me and not Mr. Splendid."

"You're observant."

"Yeah I am. Lots of mothers and that deal?"

"No," Harry said.

"Just one mother then?"

"Two," Harry said after a bit.

"Two." Timothy shrugged. "Two's not many. Vernon, he was living with them and he liked them."

"What do you mean, he was living with them? Where was he living? You're not talking about the Mormon camp, are you? Is that where we're heading?"

"Yes, sir."

"Lord!"

"I thought you liked Mormons, Harry, being one of them."

Beth had never seen Harry so flustered. "It's just—" Harry threw up his hands and they slammed back against the steering wheel. "It's just—never mind."

"No. Continue, sir."

"If you'd told me a Mormon camp at the very start, I could have—well, I would have . . ."

"I see your drift." Timothy turned around and smiled at her and Charlie—you kids all right? Every time he turned, the seat nicked the clothespin hanging from his ear. The bandage was starting to leak blood. He gazed back at Harry. "I had a butcher once who used to throw up his hands just like how you did. Any kind of meat you ordered—anything—he'd throw his hands up like you were asking for something crazy like a . . . pound of moonbeam." Charlie's new fit of howling didn't alter Timothy's contented expression. The blood from his ear was starting to seep down his neck. Beth couldn't help but imagine Timothy as the principal of her school, looking up from his desk with a benign glow at the chaos and book throwing and playground fights, and even at the name-calling directed at him.

The dirt road suddenly bulged up in concrete-like shells. The Jeep jumped in the air. Her and Charlie's bodies knocked together.

"Mudslide territory." Timothy was grinning at them again. "They're all living in a mudslide."

"Well, we're here," Harry said.

Beth was *radioactive* because she'd been dipped in a pool that was hidden deep within the earth and fed by uranium fuel, and now inside her was a secret, powerful and growing, and nobody knew what that secret would be, but she had a guess. One day medicine would find out that radioactive mist tents cured the visitor, but by then she and Charlie would already know.

And those other things she was, brave and wise, life of the party, and so on: they were self-evident and needed no explanation. She was brave because she was brave, wise because she was wise, life of the party because she just was. Her reading level was high because she was a high-level reader. She was well liked because everybody liked her. She was sharp-eyed because she could look upon this squalid camp of dirty trailers and dirty inhabitants and dirty sand and see the humanity within, all the people who lived there working hard, with sores on their hands and fingers from picking rocks that contained uranium.

"This is the place, sir. You are correct." Timothy was still grinning at them. "You kids all right?"

Three

The Mormon camp sat in a scrabble basin ringed by craggy foothills. The basin served as a courseway and was prone to flooding and mudslides. Already one disaster had happened, which was how Vernon Rutledge had come to settle here, a stranger among followers of celestial marriage. The water had poured in without warning from a storm so distant no one saw it coming, and most of the trailers were washed away. Rain here traveled like lava from a faraway eruption.

No one in their right mind would continue to dwell here in a courseway, but these people did. Because they were chosen. They were chosen and lost. The husbands went out for weeks at a time to prospect and, far from encouraging their wives and children to experience the sanity (and safety) a town might provide, they kept them in an isolation that itself furthered a crazed obedience to the very thing causing the crazed obedience in the first place. Oh, Harry knew about that all right, all the knots tighter and tighter inside his mother until she had once begged him to untie them with his own promise never to get involved. The obedience was something that drove Harry a different kind of crazy, and he wanted to speak up and say so whenever he saw these wives during one of their trips to town. He could spot them right away. They were poor and looked poor, and too young and looked too young. And they were also naive and looked naive, and they were so shy. They needed each other and the group they formed, a coalition for barely eclipsed children who were now mothers, to get them through everyday grown-up events, the buying of necessities, the counting out of money, and especially the speaking to shopkeepers for special orders. Whenever they had to speak up, they seemed more like foreigners with only one among them knowing English. There were group huddles to get everything straight, huddles for every negotiation.

Harry hated to enter the camp. He knew what kind of shipwreck he would find, and it would embarrass him and he'd feel ashamed, even in front of a man who deferred to him as *sir*. Somehow he saw their squalor as tied to their religion. When his kind sank low, they did so in a biblical clump. None of those wives was going to rise up alone and claim victory (like Jo would, he was sure). On the other hand, none of them would be defeated any more or any less than any one else in the group. If it was time to smile, they would all smile. If it was time to hang up clothes, they would all hang up clothes. If they were all forlorn, they would all forlornly hang up clothes.

The non-Mormons, at least, carved out their downfalls along uniquely spiraling paths. Each fell in his own individual way, like Timothy, like Dr. Randolph, like so many in the town, Miss Dazzle's wayward husband, Joshua Backson's nephew—like Vernon Rutledge the rimflyer, whose trailer Harry believed he had now spotted. It sat on the far side of the basin away from the Mormon camp situated at the higher end. No big trailers anymore to be seen up there. All the dwellings were small campers, for faster escape. Escape they could make quickly if the weather changed. Harry didn't understand it. Well, he did understand. They were the chosen lost ones.

The mudslide had washed the big trailers down the lower basin and crashed them against the rocks. One of the trailers had happened to land upright and offered, to anyone who wanted to take the chance, a free place to live. This was Vernon Rutledge's trailer. It was jammed against the rock wall and cemented in the mud that had crested up and grabbed it. Nearby, two destroyed trailers were parked on their sides. The three trailers together made the very picture, in a uranium fever dream, of a happy-homemaker two-car family.

Around his trailer Rutledge had built a picket fence of tumbleweeds by staking a line of poles on which he impaled balls of the stuff like shish kebab. The poles climbed high, higher than the trailer. Harry passed through the tumbleweed gate. Timothy handed him the trailer keys, shook his head, and scuffed away. Harry went in with Jean instead. Vernon Rutledge had gone to the trouble of designing and building a fence but hadn't bothered to throw down a couple of concrete blocks for steps. Harry had to rely on a mushroom-shaped rock off to the side. It got you to the door the same way a lily pad got you to another lily pad. Harry held out his arm and swung Jean aboard.

Inside the trailer were hung oil paintings of Western scenes, a reproduction of Michelangelo's Moses, and a Japanese print of Mount Fuji. An old photograph and ticket stub were stuck in one of the frames and Harry removed them and for some reason tucked them in his shirt pocket.

The side of the trailer that had crash-landed against the rocks was dented and in one spot pierced. Rutledge had covered the hole with a Navajo rug. Harry began checking behind the pictures to see what other punctures they might be hiding. He found $210 behind a Western painting and wondered what to do with it. "Look," he said to Jean. She glanced at the money, raised her eyebrows, and shrugged without an answer. Harry stuck his head out the door and called to Timothy. Had Rutledge's family been notified?

"You mean the wife and kids?" Timothy asked. "That type of deal?"

"Yes."

"Sir, there ain't such a thing. The parents are dead, I happen to know, but they saw him home from the war and that's how they left him. Good thing, too. He was a good flyer. He served his country. That's all they knew."

"Who's the next of kin then?"

"It's like this, sir. Next next next." Timothy rolled his hand from one next to the other. "Until you get here and there is no next."

"So nobody's been notified."

"That's right, sir."

"Because there is nobody to be notified."

"Correct."

Harry shut the door. "It's yours then, I guess," Jean said. She was going through the kitchenware. The dishes had been washed and put away. She shuffled through the plates. Brown cracks streamed through all of them, and through the fragile teacups, too. She restacked the plates in the cupboard. Both of them stopped to gaze out the kitchen window; they had noticed it at the same time. The kitchen window opened to brown cliff wall a forearm's length away. One day Vernon Rutledge had reached out the window and painted a cheerful yellow sun on the rock, with a child's version of rays spoking out. It was impossible not to have a reaction to this, the painted sun shining through the kitchen window, yet neither of them said a thing. Jean had never met Rutledge, but Harry had. Harry could see Rutledge's mouth smack in satisfaction as he withdrew his arm and studied his bright yellow orb and the new imaginary light it cast in his trailer. Rutledge was a man who could fill himself with a lot of deceptions—well, darn, he was a rimflyer, of course he could fill himself with a lot of deceptions. Every day he had deceived himself that his job wasn't dangerous enough to kill him.

Being in his trailer, Harry felt he knew Vernon Rutledge a little better and liked him a little more. Suddenly he wanted to sit down. He was tired. There was a sofa but it was dusty and already burdened with a ceramic green Buddha taking a sprawling nap on it. Harry chose a metal stool. It was too short for him and his knees came up comically to his chest. But it was something to sit on. He pulled out the photograph and ticket stub he had taken from one of the picture frames. Neither one was special; they barely made it to ordinary. In the photograph a younger

Rutledge was paused on a busy street while people rushed behind and around him. That was all. The ticket stub was to see the Jan Garber orchestra, 1948.

"So," Jean said. "Found what you're looking for?" She looked down at the photograph. "That's interesting," she said.

"I was thinking the exact opposite."

When she reached out for it, Harry let her have it. He glanced over at the rifle Rutledge had propped by the flimsy door. "I'm betting on that," Harry said, nodding toward the rifle case. Somehow he knew the maps would be in there. He was inside Vernon's head and didn't especially like being there. He didn't have the energy to move. He wanted to get back to town and start off to the campsite, to have Beth show him the spot where she'd found the petrified wood. He was nervous about what lay out there; it was not beyond reasonable hope that a prime Chinle or Morrison formation lay within that mountain. He could walk inside with Beth and there would be the stone walls leaking pitch, black patches of vanadium. And then he'd know. Wouldn't even need a scintillator to confirm it. He was nervous about all the plans involved, nervous about telling Jo the good news, nervous about setting up the operation. He was glad to be alone with Jean for a few minutes. Though tired, he felt calmer with her here. She had forbidden the kids to go back out there where Beth had found the petrified wood, but that was the one thing he wasn't nervous about. He was sure that ban wouldn't last. She'd give in sooner rather than later. When she found out he and Charlie had already secretly registered the claim at the assessor's office, she'd start to feel the excitement. They'd all be out there together, a family, and when Jean saw what was there, she'd be more thrilled than anyone.

Outside Jo and Beth and Charlie were kicking around at the smashed trailers. Timothy was rolling a cigarette, and then he stood with his hands locked in his pockets while he smoked. Harry kept the anomaly maps in the rifle case to protect them. He held out the rifle to Timothy. The cigarette rolled around like a toothpick while Timothy studied the rifle.

Didn't touch, just looked, hands still locked in his pockets. "That's yours," Harry said. That ticket stub bothered him. The Jan Garber orchestra, 1948. An orchestra, seven years ago. My God, was the last time Vernon Rutledge had fun seven years ago?

Timothy's cigarette twitched up toward the other campground. A group had gathered and they stared down. Children and women. No wonder Rutledge had made himself a tumbleweed fence; they were situated higher and could see into his place and were probably always spying. Harry didn't like the way they all stood, hands hanging down, just hanging.

"These are that kind, aren't they?"

"I don't know," Harry said.

"It sure looks like a harem up there."

Their trailers formed a pattern of upside-down U's scribbled along the rim of the basin. They were all the same, shaped like metal igloos, and linked together. Harry recognized the brand of camper, the Trotwood trailer, probably '48s, too. Behind them the rocks rose into an empty darkness that stretched toward the purple steel of mountains. Nowhere for children to play, but Harry was certain they did anyway.

"They're doing plenty of multiplying, too."

"This is yours, too," Harry said, handing him the bills he had found behind the Western painting.

Timothy pulled out his hands. "What's this?'

"It was in there. Since he didn't have any kin."

Timothy counted the money. Somehow the total came out to $225 when he did it. "That's a lot of money, sir."

"I'm sure you can use it."

"Seeing that I might have caused his death and all, it might be bad luck if I took it."

"You're bleeding again," Harry told him.

Timothy pulled some more of the Temple underwear from a shirt pocket. His packet of tobacco fell out with it. He unpinned his ear, let the bloody swatch drop, and was wadding clean material to his ear when

Harry recognized crotch seams and grabbed the material away. From the pieces in Timothy's hand he picked out another swatch and covered his ear for him, then tucked the underwear and tobacco packet in Timothy's shirt.

"Thank you, sir."

"I sold Rutledge that Prospectoscope about a year ago," Harry said. "The one you have on your Jeep." Harry knew it belonged to Rutledge. He had checked the case and found his identifying mark: what looked like two tiny cursive *l*s. It was really *hl.*

"Do you need it back, sir?"

Harry had to admit that he was taking a liking to Timothy. He was thinking about approaching him with the copper mine idea. Timothy wasn't the mealworm he at first appeared to be. He would work hard. He was honest. Harry could run the show and grubstake him. Meanwhile, he'd have another operation going to mine the uranium ore Beth had found. Pretty soon he'd have a huge business up and running. He stared over at Jo while he thought. Figuring all of this out . . . stop being so nervous, he told himself. Getting Dawson out of the picture, getting himself in it—he couldn't help but worry. It would take some time, he had to expect that, but once he got the business going, the mine working, once he had a respectable self to present to Jo, things would work out. Hey, but that Charlie was some kid. His map had pinpointed the spot exactly and it matched the assessor's map. Turned out the map had been in Charlie's rucksack all along, and Charlie had come to his truck later in the night to tell him. They'd gone ahead and sneaked over to the assessor's in the morning and registered the claim. Nobody needed to know they hadn't actually staked it yet.

"I'll pack that 'Scope in your truck when we get back," Timothy said.

"No, I sold it to him. What I mean is, he gave you his stuff. You're the closest there is to being his next of kin."

Timothy dropped his cigarette on the bloody wad in the dirt and watched it smolder.

"What's wrong?" Harry said.

"That thought about next of kin kind of scares me, sir. When I apply it to myself, I mean."

"I think we should leave," Harry said. The people from the campsite were making their way down. Harry had a wild fear that if they saw the sacrilegious nature of the bandage Timothy was wearing, they'd be upon them. There was no telling about their kind. They'd sunk low, yet still thought highly of themselves. That was a dangerous combination. Harry didn't know if Timothy had ever been respectable, but he knew these people had been. Once, they had been. Now they were something from the Middle Ages, feudal creatures. Uranium fever had gotten them. And now it had gotten Harry.

Four

Harry scrambled off so quickly Jean was afraid he'd leave them. The children were still exploring the last of the stuff tossed from the insides of the trailers. Mud-painted cushions were littered about like fake Hollywood rocks. All the catapulted books had somehow landed on their spines and popped open to a chapter. Any clothes on the ground had been twisted into tattered scarves.

Things a child might want were gone—taken, presumably, by the lineup that stared down at them. Jean had heard about polygamist camps, but it was hard to believe. The eerie blankness on the children's faces, however, convinced her that something was not right. Time to leave this place.

Harry's truck had made it all the way to the campground, but Miss Dazzle's DeSoto was parked farther down the road. When they reached it, Timothy was already there, clamping his Prospectoscope to the back window.

"Didn't you already do that?" Jean asked.

"Other side of the road, ma'am."

"Does this mean you're riding with us?"

"Yes, ma'am."

"Why?"

"Orders."

"Doesn't that machine work out of Harry's truck?"

"Orders, ma'am." Timothy propped his rifle in the backseat, then climbed in after it.

Jo shifted into gear after Harry passed them. A very specific yet unidentifiable nervousness was starting to crawl through Jean. She actually closed her eyes and took deep rhythmic breaths. Was she having a panic attack? Hard to believe. She left that kind of stuff up to her mother. The letters from her mother were back in the motel room, each one no doubt warning her about this very thing, the panic that will shut you down and then you'll understand something else about motherhood. Each one saying when it happens you'll be trapped with no way out and then you'll sympathize with how I'm feeling sitting in Springfield, Ohio, with no way of knowing if my daughter and two grandchildren are safe.

"Was it interesting in there?" Jo asked.

"Yes, it was interesting," Jean said. She opened her eyes. Was she feeling calmer? No. "Cleaner than you'd expect for a bachelor." Absurdly she waved the photo of Vernon Rutledge as proof. Here was a photo of a man she didn't know, and a bad photo at that, but she wanted it.

"Did you get what you were looking for?" Jo asked Timothy.

"Yes, ma'am. Thanks to Harry." Timothy sat in the middle of the backseat. His presence was disconcerting. He had positioned himself directly behind the frontseat divide so that he almost seemed to be sitting with them in the front. Jean kept hearing rifle noises coming from the backseat. Clicks and bolts. She heard but didn't want to turn and look.

It was driving her crazy. She twisted around with a warning scowl. "That's not loaded, is it?"

"No. But don't worry, ma'am, I can load it quick enough." Timothy leaned way back so he could get his hands into the coin pocket of his pants. He pulled out a rifle bullet. "It's enough to get us out of trouble. I'll get more in town."

"So you only have one bullet?" Jean asked.

"Yes, ma'am."

"Save yourself first, all right?"

"No, ma'am."

"Orders," Jo said.

Jean directed her smile out the window, then turned to Timothy and showed him the photograph. "Is this a picture of your friend?"

"Which friend would that be, ma'am?"

She tried not to exchange a glance with Jo, and she could feel Jo trying not to exchange a glance with her. "Your friend we just visited."

Timothy didn't answer.

"The dead one," Jo explained.

Timothy leaned forward into the frontseat gap and stared at the picture. His clothespin grazed Jo's shoulder and she flinched and grimaced over at him and the car swerved just a little bit.

"I don't recognize him," Timothy said.

"It would be when he was a lot younger," Jean said.

"In that case, perhaps so." Timothy leaned back and adjusted the rifle over his lap. "I believe you're right, ma'am. That is a picture of him."

Jean wanted to whisper *and you're wondering why we got him for the ride home?* She held the photo to the steering wheel so Jo could take a peek. "But that's nothing," Jo said. "It's of nothing and you can barely see him."

"It was the only photo in there. Doesn't that tell you something?"

"It's sad, isn't it?"

"Did you find his medals in there?" Timothy asked.

"No. I didn't see any medals."

"He flew in the war. He was a good flyer. He served his country well."

Jean didn't like hearing that rifle click again. She glanced back to check. "Everything all right?" she asked.

"Fine, ma'am."

"Where's that bullet?"

Timothy patted his pocket.

"The war took its toll," Jo commented.

"Not on him."

Jo shrugged in bewilderment and her palms left the steering wheel and surrendered.

The photo sat on Jean's lap. This photo—of nothing—intrigued her. Mr. Rutledge was on a street where many people were walking. That was it. That was the extent of the description she could give because that was all there was to it. Some of the people in the crowd behind him were actually in clearer focus than he was. A passerby had turned his head toward the camera at the exact moment it had snapped. You could make yourself believe the photo was of him instead of Vernon Rutledge. If Jean carried it around with her long enough, maybe she'd run into that passerby and he would recognize himself and ask could he have the picture.

Something like that had happened to her once, when she located herself in somebody else's photo album, playing the bit part of a passing stranger. It happened at a dinner party. The host and hostess were older by a decade than Jean and seemed glamorous. They paired their good looks into an overpowering event, leaving the guests helpless. Everyone seemed drunkenly delighted when they were served, instead of dessert, a photo album thick as a funeral registry. Every step of the couple's journey to California had been documented, from the glamorous hostess standing in front of the car in the driveway, to the glamorous hostess standing in line at the airport, to the glamorous hostess standing on the steps to the airplane where the friendly stewardess and tolerant passengers also waved to the camera—*prisoners like us,* her sober husband had whispered to her. In the next shot the hostess swam into the lens at a disorienting angle. If the pictures before hadn't given context, she would have been viewed as ugly. But context kept her beautiful, and context immediately identified a blurry patch of navy blue shoulder as the stewardess. The stewardess's smile that dwelled outside the photo was nonetheless experienced, and her guiding helpful hand as well.

And then this, in the insignificant corner of the photo: the back of a passenger disappearing into the plane. And there she was. Barely half of

herself was presented—half of her disappearing back—and beyond that
she sported a hairstyle shorter and curled and unrecognizable against her
current style, yet Jean's recognition of herself was instant and positive.
You could not see her body's shape under the coat but you could see in
the half-hidden, hurried posture her own molecular striving. It was unnerving to see protoplasm involved in such a trivial tilt of her head—a
giveaway tilt. My goodness, didn't everybody there at the dinner party
see it! When would the shout go up! She could feel her forehead burst
into dampness as the hosts droned on about each picture, not turning the
page, not turning the page, not turning the page.

What happened to dessert? her husband asked that night when they got
home. They were young, twenty-two, playing adult; she was pregnant,
playing mother-to-be. She was married, playing happy. Brushing her
teeth, she studied her body's positions in the mirror. Everything already
taken care of. Nothing left up to her. In bed all she could envision was
the molecular force driving her unhappiness, the corpuscles delivering
unhappy oxygen to her fingers, toes, and brain, and she knew she could
no more fix it than fix the angle of her elbow when she brushed her teeth.
She was married; she wasn't unhappily married, but she was married and
it wasn't in her distorted elemental form to enjoy this state. She was pregnant and she didn't want to be pregnant. How different from saying she
was pregnant with Charlie and didn't want to be pregnant with Charlie!
for that sentence could never be truly written or spoken. The words
themselves would fly from each other like opposing magnets. But at that
time it was simply this: she was pregnant and didn't want to be pregnant
and she'd fed the pregnancy with the molecules of her unhappiness. It
was her, not her husband's genetic nightmare, not his aneurysm. It was
her. She had done it. She was the cause of what had happened to Charlie.

She reached over and grabbed Jo's arm. "Jo!"

"All right, but I'm driving," Jo said.

"When we get home, you need to pound him right away."

"Charlie's fine," Jo said.

"I'll do it then."

"Calm down. I'll do it. Is your head okay?"

"It's fine. My mistake not to let Harry take us back to the campsite today."

"No it wasn't," Jo said. "Charlie's having the time of his life. Did you see those two going off this morning?"

"You're right," Jean said. She chuckled and leaned back. Then the tears came pouring from her eyes.

"Where'd that come from, now?" Jo said.

Jean buried her face in her hands. "It's okay. It's nothing."

Jo reached over and rubbed her shoulder.

"I'm fine," Jean said.

"I can do that for you." Timothy leaned in and touched her neck.

"You're not hearing any of this," Jean told him.

"Yes, ma'am."

"No, I said you're not hearing it."

"Ma'am, I'm agreeing to that I didn't hear anything. Do you want me to rub your back for you while you finish crying?" Jean buried her face once more and her shoulders began to shake. "It's okay," Jo said, starting to reach over again, but then Jo's shoulders started to shake as well and she turned away. Jean shook harder.

"That's right, you just let it out, ma'am," Timothy encouraged, rubbing big circles on her back. He scooted farther forward but the rifle across his lap blocked him so he straightened it and laid it in the gap between the seats. The rifle misbalanced on the dash and toppled, the barrel at Jean's feet and the butt nearly clocking Jo on the temple before falling over the brake and accelerator and clutch. Timothy squeezed through the seat gap and crawled on the floor to retrieve it. He lost his clothespin and when he surfaced with the rifle his ear was naked and freshly bleeding. He dove back down and felt around at their feet. They were looking down at him and at the bloody swatch that had somehow found its way onto his back between his shoulder blades, and Jo said, "Is that underwear?"

It burst out of both women and Jo had to stop the car and they sat there shaking.

When Jean got control of herself and lifted her head, she found Harry standing by her window. "Is everything okay?"

Timothy's head bobbed up from the clutch. "Found it," he said He held up the clothespin, gathered his rifle, and plopped back in his seat.

"What's going on?"

"I didn't hear a thing, sir. I don't know anything about it."

Jean lowered her face to her hands. "You come with me," Harry told Timothy.

"Mom, are you all right?" It was Beth, standing beside Harry.

"She's fine, honey," Jo said. "Are you having fun riding in the Jeep?"

"Mom?"

"I'm fine, darling." Jean wiped her eyes and looked up.

"Mom, are we going to have another barbecue before we leave?" Beth asked.

"If you want to."

"Do you want to?" Beth asked.

"A barbecue sounds nice," Timothy said.

"Come on, out," Harry said to Timothy.

"Sure, let's have another barbecue before we leave," Jean told her daughter.

"Okay," Beth said.

"Out."

But Jo took off before Harry could say another word. She laid on the horn, sending out loud toots for the kids. Jean heard Beth's squeal of laughter. Beth found a pure joy over little things, she could worry over little things, jump up and down over little things, and giggle hysterically over little things. Her panic over little things melted Jean's heart. As long as Beth could panic over trifles, it meant she didn't have big things to worry about. That Randolph fellow, she wouldn't say doctor, he scolded Beth for being selfish enough to ask about a barbecue instead of her mother's head injury. It was the one thing Jean thought she had done right as a parent: letting her child stay selfish.

"That barbecue sounds nice, ma'am," Timothy said.

FIVE

Timothy took such delight in the idea of a barbecue that they stopped at the Atomic Café. Jean felt reckless with her money. The mood that shot through her was charged with a heightened purpose. Where this feeling came from she had no idea; it had visited before although always during times identifiably consequential. After eating they drove out of town to find a spot and Harry parked the car but kept the radio on ("Your battery, Harry!" she warned), and all the songs that came on were happy songs, "Shake Rattle and Roll," "I Get a Kick Out of You," "Hey There," that nevertheless detoured her happy emotions toward tears. Everyone screamed in delight (well, Beth and Jo) when "Once I Had a Secret Love" came on not just once but as a double play (they must have nothing to do out here in the desert, Jean said, finding her own remark hysterically funny). But that wasn't exactly true since the disc jockeys were from far away, not in Utah, and Harry said looky here and to prove his point dialed in to the Opry show with Old Judge Hay and Minnie Pearl. "That's the desert for you," he said. Jo took Charlie off to clap him, and if Timothy heard he made no note of it and Harry found countless ways to busy himself and play dumb. Timothy rolled cigarettes and gave them to her and Harry as presents.

When they pulled into the Stagecoach Oasis, she saw Miss Dazzle,

Jimmy, and Mr. Flaherty gathered poolside. Evening getting on toward night, and they were still here.

"Find those anomaly maps?" Mr. Flaherty burst out laughing at his own unfunny remark, much as she had done listening to Harry's radio.

On the poolside table were the scraps of their meal, chicken bones and mashed potatoes and melted ice cream with chocolate syrup on top. Looked like even the men had poured on syrup. The three of them were working on their drinks. The sky was clear and now with sundown the air was getting chilly.

"Does it ever rain here?" Jean asked.

"No."

"Nope."

Miss Dazzle said, "It floods but it doesn't rain, not normal rain anyway. A nice normal shower, for example. Nothing happens here unless it can come as a catastrophe." She got up and cleared the plates.

"Find those anomaly maps?" Mr. Flaherty asked again.

"That's right," Jimmy said. "Jump into my business. You're good at jumping in."

"The only anomaly you're going to find went down in a plane crash."

"He was a good flyer, sir," Timothy told Mr. Flaherty. "He flew in the war."

"You don't go rimflying if you ain't got a wide bowl to swim around in," Mr. Flaherty said.

"He was a decorated war hero, sir."

"Used to tight spots, I guess," said Mr. Flaherty.

"You kids want ice cream?" Miss Dazzle asked.

"Yes please," Beth said.

None of these people would ever discover themselves in another person's photograph, Jean thought. Everything was empty as the desert, maybe because this was the desert, but regardless, a photo out here would include him, her, it, and the mountain range behind. No crowds, no karmic passersby, no strangers who would serendipitously surface as

friends in a season or two. There were no secrets of fate you could ponder in such photographs, just the literal captured fact of what you were
doing or who you were posing with. The only thing that could happen
was that if you saved the photograph long enough, the person you were
then might arrive as a stranger years later to visit the person you had become—but if you got old enough, it happened to everyone. The three
old ladies, for example, and those three little girls in the newspaper
photo. It wouldn't bother Jean so much to see her young self when she
was old, but it would kill her to see a young Charlie.

She left the pool for her room.

Jo came in as she lay on the bed. "Everything all right?" Jo asked.

"Just tired," she said.

"I think they've been drinking all day."

"Even Mr. Flaherty?"

"Well, not him, I don't think."

"I would hope not," Jean said. "He looks like he's going to keel over
any second."

Harry came into the room. "Everything all right?" he asked.

"Just lying down," she said.

Harry sat on the other bed. Jean hadn't realized how soft the mat-
tresses were until Harry's knees flew to his chin. He fell backward, then
got himself steadied. "Well," he said, "the whole world seems to know
about it."

"About what?"

"That's my suspicion anyway," Harry said.

"About what?"

"The petrified wood."

"That little piece?"

"It's hot," Harry said.

"So?"

"Never mind," Harry said. "But your children seem to understand
what's at stake."

"Good for them."

"Maybe you should let her rest," Jo said.

"No, I'm getting up." Jean went to the bathroom and she didn't bother to shut the door because she knew it would drive Harry out and it did.

Jo came in and stood over the sink and looked in the mirror. She fingered her hair with obvious dissatisfaction. "Is this your lipstick?" Jo picked up a tube on the sink, twisted it open and frowned at the color.

"No. Isn't it yours?"

"Where'd it come from?" Jean asked.

"Maybe Miss Dazzle is throwing us a hint." Jean flushed the toilet and budged Jo aside so she could wash her face and hands. It felt good to wash her face. When she came out, Vincent Flaherty awaited her, sitting on the desk chair.

She tried to stammer something. Gave up.

"My wife died in my arms, my dear, not pleasantly either. Nothing in regard to our corporeal selves has fazed me since."

"What can I do for you, Mr. Flaherty?"

Mr. Flaherty said, "You know, my dear, when a Geiger counter starts ticking, it sends out a Morse code loud and clear to every person in the state of Utah and then some."

"It didn't tick *that* loudly."

Mr. Flaherty reared back and ho-ho'd—Santa's reaction to an outlandish request. "I needed to meet you a lot earlier in my life, you know that?"

"Your wife was alive a lot earlier, remember that?"

"You planning to register those claims?" he asked.

"I have no idea."

"Because you'll need somebody like me involved."

"We have Harry, and I'll appreciate it if you don't laugh when I say that."

"Harry's a good man," Mr. Flaherty said. "But he's not a businessman and I am. I know what to do and how to do it. You might want to sell stocks in that mine, for example."

"What mine?"

"And my transportation services can't be beat. Do you really want to suffer a roller-coaster truck ride back and forth? See? Makes you motionsick just thinking about it."

Jean said, "I was about to take a nap. Maybe that's why I'm a little confused. It was one piece of petrified wood."

"Just talked to Harry, my dear. He thinks there's a Chinle formation in there."

"And that would hold a lot of meaning for me, wouldn't it?"

"I'm only here to help you, my dear, secondarily of course. Primarily I would like to help myself."

"Mr. Flaherty, I'm sure you're hoping for me to be completely disarmed by your honesty."

"Oh, my dear, this is why I needed to meet you earlier in my life. What a woman you are. As was my wife, I quickly add."

"Who died in your arms."

"Tragically so."

"How can I say no to a man whose wife died in his arms? What would she think of you using her like that to get sympathy?"

"Her motto was 'Whatever it takes.'"

"I doubt that."

"Kept her alive two years longer than the doctors gave us. Two years. Seven hundred and fifty-some days. Whatever it takes. I've since adopted her motto as my own."

Jean nodded.

"The only thing I ask," Mr. Flaherty said, "is that we keep this among ourselves. No need to involve Jimmy with it."

"Why is that?"

"Jimmy and I don't get along."

"Maybe that would be good for us. Checks and balances. For our sake."

"No. I don't think so."

"I'll have to think about that, Mr. Flaherty."

"It would be a wise decision not to involve him." He pushed up from his chair, patted her knee, and lumbered out.

Miss Dazzle was having a good laugh, tipping back a glass, when Jean walked into the office to settle the bill. Jimmy was bent over the maps he had spread across the counter. Miss Dazzle was posed shoulder blades to counter, chest thrust out, elbow to opposite elbow with Jimmy.

In less than the time it took her vision to fill in the edges of this scene Jean decided not to involve Jimmy.

Miss Dazzle let her laugh die into a sleepy chuckle that was close enough to a romantic moan to redden Jean's face.

"Hello," Jimmy said, spinning around with a big smile. He began to roll up his maps.

"Anything good?" Jean asked.

"It'll take a while to tell. Let me put these in the truck. I'll be right back. I've been looking for you."

"Looking for her?" Miss Dazzle asked suggestively. "Oh, Harry's got her heart, didn't you know?"

"That worries me." Jimmy laughed. "Be right back."

"Don't forget to lock those maps up tight," Miss Dazzle called giddily.

"You shouldn't make such fun of Harry," Jean said once they were alone.

"I'm not making fun of Harry."

Jean shrugged. "I'm here to square the bill."

"So it's true. Big plans, huh."

"I don't have any big plans," Jean said.

"You're leaving. There's rumors why."

"My," Jean said.

"With the ladies gone I'll be all by myself." Miss Dazzle squinted in her glass and tinkled the ice cubes, then sucked out another swallow.

"Maybe you should let some other people stay here. You're the only motel not filled up."

"I'm fussy. But I like you. And I like those kids."

"They've had a fabulous time," Jean said. She opened up her checkbook.

"You're not coming back?"

"Of course we're coming back. We have to get the car checked out, get a few things. We'll be back."

"Pay then," Miss Dazzle said. Jittery, she marched in circles around the office. "No, I insist," she said when she looked up and saw Jean writing. "That way I know I'll see you again."

"All right." Jean closed her checkbook.

"Why do you think I make fun of Harry? I can't think of anyone who's nicer to Harry than I am. Do you think you treat him nicer?"

Jean didn't answer. Finally: "I guess that's why it surprised me to hear you say anything. You're always the one to stand up for him."

"Stand up for him? My God, he's a man. I'm a woman. He's a man. Since when does a woman stand up for a man? He's a man!" Her redhead's skin flamed at the throat.

"I think you're very nice to Harry," Jean said.

"Well, a man. Since when does a man . . ." Miss Dazzle collapsed on the sofa and buried her head in her hands.

After one moment of shock and another moment when she considered dashing from the office, Jean made a slow reluctant advance to the sofa, folded down beside Miss Dazzle and laid her hand on the thick mane of hair, pulling it back from Miss Dazzle's abruptly blotched face. "What's wrong?"

"Oh, I couldn't tell you, honey," Miss Dazzle sobbed. "You have much bigger problems of your own. And I'm very sorry. I'm certainly very sorry about all of that. I'm sure you'll let me know how selfish I'm being. I guess that's why he left me. Why they all leave me. Because I'm so selfish."

It had been a long time since Jean had sat down with somebody and tried to offer sympathy. It was definitely a skill and like all skills needed practice. People had practiced plenty on her, but not the other way around.

"What is this all about again?" she asked.

Miss Dazzle wept into her hands, and certainly, Jean thought, the drinks were involved in these tears, but they were real enough tears notwithstanding.

"Is it about you being selfish?"

Miss Dazzle nodded into her hands.

"That's what you're upset about?" Jean rubbed Miss Dazzle's shoulder. She said, "Do you realize how much we love staying here with you? We would never stay anywhere else. Remember how you washed our clothes when we first came? That's not being selfish. You're one of the most giving people I know. Look how you wait on everyone. Those ladies worship you. They have a happy life because of you. They get to swim, which they love, they get to spy on all your interesting customers and gossip about what they see. . . ."

Miss Dazzle tearfully laughed.

"Remember those sandwiches you made for them with the secret ingredient?"

"And their whiskey sours," Miss Dazzle sniffled. "I'm the only one who can make them the way they like."

"That's right." For being so out of practice, Jean thought she was doing a credible job. "And what about those bathing suits you loaned Charlie and Beth? They adore you."

"Don't tell me about your son," Miss Dazzle wept. "I don't want to hear how I've brought a bit of sunshine into his last days. Please don't do that. That's not fair."

"What are you saying? I wasn't going to do that," Jean said. "These aren't his last days. Who told you that?"

"Told you what?" asked Jimmy, striding into the office. The air in the office shifted and the spaces between all their bodies shifted. Jimmy asked, "Why are you crying?" then drew eerily close to Miss Dazzle while still maintaining his distance. The air space between the two of them took on a shape—the two bodies of Jimmy's and Miss Dazzle's were curved into each other like dancers torn apart—and the intimacy Jean had instantly surmised then instantly dismissed upon Jimmy's radiant smile at her entrance was now reconfirmed. "Why? Why are you crying?" Jimmy repeated, and finally Miss Dazzle started to cough out something about Charlie, and Jean hushed her.

"Charlie?" Jimmy seemed surprised. "I'll go get him."

"No. No, don't do that," Jean said.

"Don't do that, I didn't mean it that way," Miss Dazzle entreated.

But Jimmy was already out the door.

When Miss Dazzle's wet gulps started up again, Jean had had enough. "Maybe you should stop," Jean said. The hand she kept on Miss Dazzle's shoulder chilled to ice. She didn't want to give sympathy to someone else about Charlie.

In the end she didn't care about Miss Dazzle. She didn't care about any of them. The way they decided to cast the truth was their own business. If they wanted to dream, let them. But Charlie was her business—and only her business. The truth of his dream had to be made to last. All dreams ended, but all these people would wake up to was no uranium. If that was the only nightmare they feared, she would trade places with them any day.

Six

Already there was something unreal about it. The campsite was just as Harry remembered, but it had been turned into a ghost town. The tent with its sagging sides. The Rambler. The lonely piñon. Everything was the same and in its place, yet something cold swept through him and he had to remind himself that nothing was wrong. The silver Airstream was there, too, and if Jo weren't here with him, he might have been tempted to go inside and hunt for his shirt button. A different man had done that. He felt changed and distant from himself.

"This is a nice place," Timothy said.

Harry opened up the back of the Harvester and studied the equipment and got it straight in his mind what they would be needing.

"I'll help you," Jo said

"No. There's not much."

"Let me."

Harry looked at Jo. That night he'd kissed her she'd been wearing a frayed man's shirt and her unkempt hair had been an afterthought, tied back with a shoelace. Today a different person had showed up. Jo had bedecked herself in a white blouse and orange pedal pushers. A yellow paisley bandana was tied at her throat in the crisp knot of a Boy Scout's neckerchief. And her sneakers were clean; they even looked new. Their bright pretty yellow grabbed your attention. But they were that cheap kind of sneaker without any arch and just two measly eyelets on each side. You would barely be able to get them tied up correctly, which didn't really matter since footwear that cheap wouldn't be around for long. Likely she'd been to the bargain bin at the grocery store. He'd seen the group of young Mormon mothers there buying those sneakers by the bushel. And that stiff bandana was new, too. What he liked about the grubby version of Jo was that it made him believe something more important had taken over. Something beyond herself had made her forget herself, and Harry could think part of that something had to do with him. Love? Love did that to people. If you were a person careless about your appearance, love made you spruce up. But, maybe, if you were someone like Jo, already beautiful, love did the opposite, it made you forget all the finishing-touch paraphernalia. Maybe beautiful people had to put love to the test by stripping the beauty from themselves as much as possible. Harry had certainly passed that test. He loved her dirty, slovenly, hair unwashed, in the ugliest housedress possible or swimming in that lived-in man's shirt. Not that she didn't look nice bedecked this way. Timothy had told her so out loud and Harry had certainly thought it. She was brilliant and beautiful in her yellow colors. She shone as brightly as Vernon Rutledge's painted-on sun and that should have cheered him, but it didn't. It did just the opposite.

Harry said, "Let's make sure the helicopter's here first before we carry all this stuff." Jo stepped into the Airstream, so he and Timothy went off to find the helicopter. Beyond the horseshoe wall was an open area where Harry expected to see the helicopter. This was the place where the mother had found him that first night, curled over and sick. Everything, every single thing, was different from that night. It was true, his premonition, as he had settled by the piñon tree listening to a mother and two kids inside their tent: something was coming that would change his life.

Timothy scampered up an outcropping to have a look; he called down that he'd spotted the helicopter over the next set of domes. They wouldn't have to climb the domes to get there, just go through the pass, but still . . . They had equipment to load into the helicopter and now they would have to hike to do it.

Jo was waiting for them at the campsite. "Is it there?" she asked.

"It's far away there," Harry said.

They went back to the truck and Harry pulled out the detection instruments, the Geiger of course and the black light. Timothy pepped up at the sight of one thousand feet of extension cord tucked in the back of Harry's truck. "With an extension cord, sir, we can use the Detectron." The Detectron Geiger counter, Timothy explained to Jo, had a drill-hole probe that could be attached to an extension cord. Jo offered an encouraging smile to Timothy's excited explanation, but Harry could see she didn't get it.

"It's like this, ma'am. We hook the probe onto this extension cord and then we drop it into the canyon slot from above." With his rising and dipping hands, Timothy became the puppeteer to this maneuver. But even with invisible dolls acting it out, Jo's tentative smile didn't grow any more assured. "From the helicopter. You lower the probe down." Timothy mimed paying out rope. "You see? Little by little. And we got a thousand feet of lowering we can do!"

"It sounds dangerous."

"Yes, ma'am!" Timothy retightened his already loaded backpack. The backpack strained into a taut rectangle. So expertly was it packed, it looked to be compressed into one thing, something military and leaden, a munitions case perhaps, but Harry had watched Timothy pack most of it in town, and in there was food and a stove, and a frying pan and bean pot and extra water and rolled blankets. It looked impossible even to lift off the ground, but Timothy swung it up and Harry guided it over his other shoulder. Timothy twisted into it, then settled comfortably, legs apart.

Jo had packed a rucksack of stuff from the Airstream. She swung it over her shoulders and indicated her two free hands. "Let me help," she said.

Timothy tossed an ore pick and geologist's hammer into a bucket and handed that along with a shovel to her.

Harry carefully packed up the Detectron. He left the Mineralight for the second trip. Ax and spare batteries and tube and more cooking fuel. And now somehow this orphaned bottle of Jim Beam that Jimmy Splendid had sampled. There it was rolling around in the truck. Harry stuffed that in, too. On second thought he dropped it into Jo's bucket. Wouldn't matter if it broke.

"I can take the ax, too," Jo said.

"No, ma'am, too heavy. Right here, boss," Timothy said, swerving his backpack toward Harry. Harry tied the ax to the top of Timothy's pack. Timothy set down the rifle to help Harry shoulder his pack. Harry's heart was pounding. He wondered if he looked as intrepid as he felt, a savage jungle guide unfazed by piranhas or charging rhino.

They hiked out over to the knobs with the first load. For Harry it was a storybook hike through an enchanted desert. He couldn't stop smiling no matter how hard he tried. They found Flaherty sitting in his helicopter, reading a book and eating an orange.

"Hello, fellas."

"Quite a hike," Harry said though he had told himself he wasn't going to mention it. Actually he'd enjoyed the hike, but it might have been too much for Jo. Carrying a heavy bucket in your hands was harder than shouldering a pack. As soon as the helicopter was in sight, she took a break to shake out her arms and asked them to go on ahead. "Was there a problem?" Harry asked Flaherty.

"Everything went like a peach." Flaherty threw out the orange peels. The bright peels blended into the sand more easily than Harry would have expected, just two or three shades beyond the color of the ground and probably by tomorrow the same shade. Harry glimpsed Charlie's map on the passenger seat. Not just a panel of it. The complete edition.

He picked it up and unfolded the squares of cardboard collected from Mel's Cleaners and he and Timothy studied it and got out their compasses and the map made pretty good sense. The sand and gradations of outcroppings and the single snake of river were painstakingly colored with the inks Harry had bought Charlie at the hardware store.

Flaherty handed them the single loose panel of Charlie's map. Harry recognized it as the one they had used for registering the claims. Charlie had colored it in yesterday after coming back from the assessor's. "Map's accurate," Flaherty said. "Not that it matters. Been there with the troops and back." Flaherty held out the palm of his hand and stroked it—"The only map you're going to need, fellas, is right here now. Hello there, my fair maiden!"

Jo set down her bucket and waved.

"Have an orange!" Flaherty shouted gleefully.

"Thank you, sir."

Flaherty laughed at that one. "Yes, you, too," he said to Timothy.

"Lovely," Jo said.

"No thanks," Harry said. "We got another load. We'll be back."

"I'll come," Jo said.

"Stay here and enjoy your orange," Vincent Flaherty told her. "Enjoy two oranges."

"That's a good idea," Harry said. "You stay here. We only have half a load left—unless we need to bring the generator, too?"

"Did I say I was going to supply the generator?" Flaherty asked.

"Yes," Harry said.

"Then it has been supplied."

Harry and Timothy hiked back to the campsite and they were at the truck trying to figure out how they could possibly carry a thousand feet of extension cord so they would be able to enact Timothy's grand idea when Harry heard it, another engine. He knew who it was. He could guess now why Flaherty might have landed where he had and he felt stupid for voicing something that must have sounded like a complaint. He heard the box of bullets they'd bought at the hardware store rattling around in Timothy's shirt pocket, and that sound was the sound of trouble. He wished Timothy hadn't left his rifle at the helicopter.

"Hello there!" Timothy greeted Leonard Dawson. "How's that pickup treating you?"

Leonard Dawson nodded but didn't say anything. He was dirty and scruffed up, not that Timothy looked any better.

"I told it to treat you nice," Timothy said. "All you gotta do is keep that gasoline in it. She'll stay happy."

"Yeah," Leonard Dawson said.

"Yeah, you just keep that little girl filled with gasoline and you'll be all right. Keeps the engine going. Well," Timothy said, looking at the extension cord, "there's a couple things we can do." He pulled out his packet of rifle bullets and shook out a bullet and tucked it in the corner of his mouth while he thought.

"Is she here?" Dawson demanded.

"I haven't seen her," Harry found himself saying. He was nervous, but he thought his voice sounded pretty normal.

Dawson eyed them suspiciously. "What are you doing?"

"Did you have any luck out there?" Timothy asked.

"What have you found? Where are you going?"

"We got a problem here," Timothy said, more to himself than to Leonard Dawson. He took the bullet from his mouth, exhaled, then tucked it back in. "How we gonna portage it?"

"You're up to something, aren't you? You two." When they didn't answer, Dawson demanded, "Where is she?"

Timothy kept working at the extension cord. He looped it into a spiraling pile as tall as his shoulders. Way too high. He undid the pile, then tried again. While he watched Timothy work, Harry ate one of the sandwiches Jo had made.

He was glad to be with Timothy, who didn't seem upset by any of Dawson's antics, and he wasn't playacting either. He was busy relooping the extension cord. Now the pile flung out in a wide, much flatter lariat. Timothy strapped it in two places and they tested it as something they could drag. "It's possible," Timothy said. "We need something underneath, to protect it from getting chewed up." Timothy turned to Leonard Dawson. "You got anything in your truck we might could borrow?"

To Harry's surprise Leonard Dawson said, "Take a look."

"Something to slide it on would be nice. A sheet of metal."

"How about some wood?" Harry asked.

"That'd be all right depending."

Harry left Timothy in the camp, and hiked out to the toilet and pulled off one of the planks covering the hole. He started to drag it, then backtracked for some toilet paper.

Timothy said he thought they could work with that plank of wood yes sir. He sawed it in half, then set the extension cord on the two runners and roped it. Harry bolted up the Harvester. He shouldered the rucksack with the Mineralight, and he and Timothy each slung an end of rope over their shoulders and pulled the extension cord through the camp, past the steps of the Airstream, where Leonard Dawson sat glaring at them. "You'll be leaving footprints, you know," Dawson said.

Harry and Timothy stopped to readjust, positioning the planks like skis.

"I'll be looking for my wife," Dawson warned them as they left.

"Good luck finding her, sir," Timothy said.

They rounded the horseshoe wall, pulling through dirt and tough cheat grass. They mushed the extension cord to the open area. In the deeper sand they pulled up for a break. When Harry turned around, Dawson was following them. So it was going to be like that. Nothing he could do about it.

"How's my luck now?" Dawson taunted.

Timothy swigged from his canteen. His tongue pushed around the bullet in his mouth. He never turned his head to notice Dawson's presence. "You help us pull this," he said, directing his remarks to the canteen, and Leonard Dawson did.

Not surprisingly, Dawson threw a fit when he spotted Jo sitting inside the helicopter with Flaherty. The more he ranted, the more calmly Flaherty peeled his next orange. Dawson threatened to kill them all if they tried to take his wife away and Flaherty said nobody was taking his wife. Dawson yelled that he wanted to kill them all right here and now. And what the hell were they doing if they weren't taking his wife? And Jo said, "Lenny, please, there's no reason to use such rude language." Dawson yelled that he would teach them the meaning of rude once he killed them all right here and now.

Timothy spat out the bullet and began wiping it with a bloody bandana he pulled from his pocket. He slid the bullet into his rifle. There was a sudden lull in the exchange.

"Let's all have a nice conversation now," Flaherty said.

Dawson fell silent.

No one spoke.

"Dadadadada for which we are about to receive," mumbled Vincent Flaherty. "Amen. Everybody ready now for a nice conversation?"

Nobody answered.

"Mr. Dawson, your wife and I and several other colleagues are off to an undisclosed business location."

"Then I'm coming too."

"And we would be most happy to welcome you, but as you can see you'll have to arrange for your own transportation. We're already too full. You sure you need all this wire here?"

"Yes, sir."

"What is it?"

"Extension cord."

"Hmm. Therefore . . ." Flaherty said.

"Therefore you're leaving me here to rot," Dawson said. "You think I don't know when somebody's trying to cheat me?"

"Mr. Dawson, you didn't let me finish. Therefore, what I'm going to do for you is to disclose to you the exact coordinates of our top-secret business location. Hey—hey! No kicking the helicopter. Here's a map to our location. As you can see, it's not far."

"This is not a map," Dawson said, sneering down at the panel of cardboard Flaherty had placed in his hands.

"This is one of the finest maps you'll ever see."

"This is a kid's goddamn scribble."

"Lenny! My goodness, stop," Jo cried.

"A scribble complete with compass points and topography and a pretty good go at distance. And it's not that far. If the distance is off by a mile or two, it's not going to hurt you."

"Not in a helicopter it wouldn't," Dawson muttered.

"You can't give him that!" Harry said. "That's Charlie's map! You can't give him that."

"It will be returned to us upon Mr. Dawson's arrival. Do I have your word on that?"

"This is something you'd put on your goddamn refrigerator!"

"Lenny!"

"Do I have your word on its safe return?"

"Sir, does he have your word?"

"This is not a kindergarten out here, this is a goddamn desert. Yes, he has my word!"

"Lenny, please!" Jo wept.

Timothy sidled up beside Dawson with his rifle.

"Here's where we are." Vincent Flaherty let his finger drift in the air at a spot outside the map panel. "And here's where we're going." His finger hovered over the cardboard and plopped down on a fringe of brown triangles.

"What's this?"

"This is a rendering of coxcomb cliffs. Dark brown, see that? Because they're higher. Kid does topography, too. You got a nice set of coxcomb cliffs to lead you in, with an eastern gate of pinnacles. Right here. See that? Simple as pie, my man. Been there and back already."

"Come back and get me," Dawson said.

"Would love to. Fuel considerations prevent it."

"You expect me to walk!"

"The health benefits of walking are widely known, my good man. Bring some extra food when you come!" Flaherty shouted as he started up the engine. "No drinking either. We're running a dry camp. Stand back, now."

Dawson, big shoulders huddling, drew back angrily from the slicing rotors. His threatening stance went from larger than life to smaller. Arms tensed in a boxer's boast, fist against fist with barely the air to beat, his mighty pyramid of a stance yielded nothing more than the point of his head as they rose above him. All of him ceased to exist in another few seconds.

Flaherty's body erupted in gleeful convulsions. "No worries, my dear," he shouted joyfully, squeezing Jo's neck. "That man couldn't find his way in a two-aisle grocery store!"

SEVEN

When Beth climbed her first outcropping, the world was quiet. It seemed almost not to exist and yet it was there, a hovering force watching her. The whole silent world was watching, eager, on the edge of its seat. She scrambled faster, on all fours, racing to the top. She had found a place in the universe, she alone had discovered this spot where she now stood, where the noisiest thing in the world was a rock.

She picked up a tiny pebble that probably no one in the world had picked up before and with this she marked a place in history. This was a hard thing to explain to people. But now that she had discovered uranium as well, she wouldn't have to do much explaining. People would appreciate her abilities on this level they could grasp.

She could tell Harry was excited about the uranium. Together they retraced her route, sidestepping through the tight passage to the wider shaft. Harry had checked out the shaft, and then they had tunneled past the hooved rock to the inner courtyard and the pool of radioactive water she had dipped herself into. Harry's wide eyes drank in the cave garden. Almost reluctantly he turned on his Geiger counter. Beth could see him, a little boy. He was wearing his one dress shirt that didn't fit right; the sleeves were too short and his hands bulged overgrown at the ends of his arms. He said it was a good reading, pretty good, though lots of things could explain it. But she could see he was excited.

"But is it pretty good, Harry?"

"Yeah, it's pretty good," he said.

"So what do you think?"

"Well, I think it's pretty good."

"I mean, about me finding it."

"How did you ever find it?" Harry asked.

"I was just exploring."

"You're a great explorer, Beth. An amazing explorer."

"Thank you."

Their camp followed a shallow but long strip of shade from one end of an overhang to the other. Vincent Flaherty had set up a portable chair and was leaning back as if enjoying his summer vacation. The belt across his stomach became unreal: as he stretched, it tightened into something painted on.

Timothy stood before Vincent Flaherty, recounting some kind of story that required him to pound his hands on an imaginary piano above his head. By the time Beth got near enough Timothy had stopped talking and his hands had dropped to his sides and Vincent Flaherty was calling Charlie Einstein over to listen to this. The big grin across his face meant that Vincent Flaherty was taking Timothy's story, whatever it was, as a joke and he simply wanted to share the joke with Charlie. He said to Charlie, "Give her a hand there, boy," and Charlie pulled with all his strength, but tugging on Vincent Flaherty was like tugging an ocean liner. Harry came and he and Timothy joined in. They pulled, then pulled harder, then pulled harder still. Vincent Flaherty went from mired to midair and they had to catch him by his belt as he flew past them.

Vincent Flaherty came with his own set of built-in entertainments. He was like one of those slapstick comedians in the movies who zipped around like a popped cork and never got hurt.

Vincent Flaherty said, "Come on, Charlie, we're going up in the helicopter." In order not to be rude, he turned to Beth: "You, too, little girl?" but she shook her head. If he'd really wanted her, he would have said come on! come on, now! but he didn't. He was already on his way. She didn't care. She liked adventures but they didn't necessarily have to come in helicopters. She had some thinking to do anyway.

Beth walked with Charlie to the helicopter. Charlie looked increasingly miserable, which meant he was getting more and more excited, so Beth was happy for him. The helicopter was parked on the other side of the inward-leaning cliffs Vincent Flaherty described as a coxcomb, an impossible chore to climb. Luckily a narrow passageway sliced a shortcut right through the middle.

Between them Harry and Timothy carried a generator. Once in the narrows, the path was too skinny in some places to walk side by side and they had to carry it single file, as if the generator were a dead deer tied to a pole. Beth didn't like the hemmed-in feeling the narrows gave her. She asked why they needed a generator, and Harry said for a plug. The cliff walls spun back their words in bell-toned echoes. Beth asked Harry what was going on and he said an experiment. *An experiment an experiment,* the cliffs repeated. Beth got sidetracked for a minute, trying to think who it was in mythology that got dipped in a magical pool. They reached the end of the narrows and the desert rushed open in a scape of reds and browns and tans. It was beautiful. There sat the helicopter in the wide expanse.

Timothy and Harry lifted the generator inside. Harry pointed out the black coils stuffed in the back of the helicopter and said, "There's your plug, Beth." And then Harry said, "Your other end goes to a Geiger counter," but by then it was too much information. She did, however, like the way Charlie, Timothy, and Vincent Flaherty stood together like best friends.

The helicopter was up in the air flying around before her mother caught on and came dashing through the narrows. Harry lied to her and said Charlie was with Jo. Harry wasn't a good liar but he covered his lie by hiding his face behind field glasses.

Charlie's head was visible next to Vincent Flaherty's but her mother left without noticing him. Harry whispered, "They're crazy."

"Who?" Beth asked.

"Your mother wouldn't like Charlie being up there with those two."

"Don't you think it'll work?" Beth asked.

"It's crazy."

"It's not going to work, Harry?"

"It's so crazy," he said. "But it'll work. You've got the right two crazy people for the job. Wouldn't work if a normal person tried it."

"But it'll work with them?"

"Yep."

Achilles! That was it. That was the mythology guy. He was dipped in a radioactive pool and then he was immortal, except for his heel.

"You just watch 'em," Harry added.

Timothy sat on the skids of the helicopter. Beth could see a rope around his chest. Behind him the extension cord trailed like a misbehaving kite string. It wasn't hanging down; it was being blown back. Vincent Flaherty circled around the pyramid of rock, drawing the helicopter's circles tighter until it rocked in one place. The extension cord settled into limpness. Hand over hand, Timothy fed it to the opening at the top of the pyramid, then leaned out as far as he could with the extension cord.

Harry said, "Aim's a little off, but they got the system worked out."

Vincent Flaherty took off again, circling around. As he flew, Timothy hauled in the cord, then drew his feet under his rear end so that he was now squatting on the skids rather than sitting on them. When the helicopter rocked in place again, Timothy stood up and slanted so far out Beth shuddered at the midair dive he was launching into. An arm poked out of the helicopter and grabbed the rope around Timothy's chest. The extension cord snaked down and it kept going, which meant Timothy must have found the opening. He calmly fished in midair (she thought calmly even though she couldn't see his face, but something about him, he just seemed so casual up there; his hand even went up to check on his ear).

Jo and Beth's mother appeared beside them. "Well, here's Jo," her mother said.

"Okay," Harry said.

"You lied to me."

"About what?"

"You said Charlie was with Jo."

Harry took his eyes from the field glasses and glanced at Jo. "Where were you?"

"Not with Charlie," Jo said.

Timothy was slowly folding into a squat on the skids. As he pulled up the extension cord, it disappeared into the helicopter, so Beth guessed Charlie was in charge of reeling it in. Timothy's arm wrapped around something inside. Once he was braced, the helicopter beelined away. Beth looked at her mother. She was hooking and rehooking loose strands of hair behind her ears.

Beth darted from the landing area as the helicopter began to descend. The wind whipped at her back. Jimmy Splendid's hat flew off her head, caught a thermal, and glided into the narrows. Beth ran in to get it. Her hat floated against a sheer wall, hanging as if by static cling. She went on tiptoes to grab it. *Get out*, somebody whispered behind her. She was too afraid to turn around. She snatched the hat and dashed out.

With the blades still chopping the air, Vincent Flaherty maneuvered himself out of the helicopter. He planted himself boldly on the scrabble, hands on hips, the dangerous rotors swinging axes toward his head. Charlie and Timothy stayed put in the helicopter.

Beth and Harry and Jo and Beth's mother drew closer to Vincent Flaherty, but not too close. The blades danced in head-chopping dips that barely kept missing. Vincent Flaherty stayed directly underneath them. Never looked up, never acted like the blades were even there. It was funny how Beth found herself creeping toward him so cautiously, as if she were approaching a dangerous animal.

Vincent Flaherty added a scowl to his pose. He stared at Beth's group a long time. "We got ourselves a reading, boys and girls," he said. He announced this as a tragedy. Beth had seen that tactic before in the movies, too, somebody acting very sad before they sprang the good news on you. Except that her mother seemed to be treating Vincent Flaherty's tragic delivery as genuine. She hooked her loose strands and her expression remained expressionless. All the hospital visits, all the face-to-face whispering with doctors and nurses—Beth had been around enough to know that her mother went expressionless when things turned bad.

"Now what?" Jo asked.

Charlie got out of the helicopter and her mother said come here. Charlie slouched over to her. He kept coming until he bumped blindly into her chest as if by accident, and she was forced to put her arms around him. It was a hug they could pass off as something else, a prison sentence. As part of their punishment they had to hug each other. That was Charlie. Beth herself liked being hugged and she didn't mind if the whole world knew about it.

When Timothy got out of the helicopter and stood up straight, the rope around his chest dropped down to the ground in a stiff loop. Timothy stepped out of it and handed it to Vincent Flaherty and Beth saw that the rope was actually Vincent Flaherty's belt.

"What now?" Jo asked.

"What now!" Vincent Flaherty repeated the question like it was the silliest question on earth. Why, of course it was the silliest question on earth because the answer was so obvious. What now! Beth waited to hear the obvious answer to this silliest of questions, but Vincent Flaherty didn't say anything else. His fists still dug into his hips.

"I would, my friends . . ." Vincent Flaherty finally began, haltingly, his mournful tone a theatrical clue to Beth that the greatest of news lay in the second half of the sentence, ". . . like to propose a toast." With an important sniff he hiked up his pants. "To our new band of uraniumaires." Immediately his hands flew out to stem the applause. "Congratulations, my friends"—again that gloomy voice. And then this boisterous holler: "May you spend your millions most unwisely!"

EIGHT

Her mother had been there that evening when it had all begun to unravel for Jean. A neighbor tapped on their screen door. Mr. Van Gundy (Jean wouldn't give in to his pleas to call him Jack) was alarmed, he said, by the "worrisome noises escaping your house." She wondered how long it had taken him to come up with this descriptive phrase. She'd heard from other neighbors that he often went to bars. She pictured him there, convinced of his own cleverness. She didn't think he was alarmed by Charlie's situation one bit. She thought he wanted a date, despite the fact that he was married. It was summer and the windows were thrown open. The ventilation fan, loud enough to be heard outside, assured the claim of worrisome noises. He could affect an innocence that he no doubt believed increased his appeal. Worrisome noises made a good excuse to get himself inside the house.

"They say your boy has bronchitis," he began.

"They? Are you referring to the doctors?"

"No, I'm referring to the neighbors."

"What do you think?"

"I'm just very troubled by what I'm hearing."

"From others?"

"By what I hear myself. Coming out of your house."

She didn't say anything.

"When I'm strolling by in the evening," he explained. "I keep hoping you'll be sitting out enjoying a drink."

She wanted to say something that would make him wither. She hated this place. She hated everyone here.

"I hope it's only bronchitis," he said. "What do the doctors say?"

"You'd have to ask them."

"So there is more than one. A team of doctors? It must be serious."

"I'm not following you, I'm afraid." Suddenly her heartbeat was on alert.

"Is there anything I can do?"

"No," she said.

"Are you sure?"

"Yes," she said.

"I'd like to help," he said.

"My mother's here, and she's helping."

"When she leaves then."

She latched the screen door on his boyish confident smile, but it burned right through the mesh. She made herself stand there until he backed off the porch; then she closed the front door and the breeze tunneling through immediately died. The air was dreadful and stale and hot and it was spoiled with the smells of illness. She was shaking. In the middle of the night she awoke to a ghostly riot: a mob was gathering down the street, gathering to come and get her. She found her mother at the kitchen table with a static-bursting radio, her elegance lost, frantic and inept as she tried to dial through to a clear station.

The same sort of crackling traveled to her now, but it came from the bonfire up on the ridge. It was a happy noise. Jean watched her children leaping about the flames like warriors in battle. The rock wall behind them enlarged their shadows to monstrous size.

She slipped on her old shirt for warmth, buttoned the top button and rolled down the sleeves. In the shirt's breast pocket was the latest letter from her mother. Harry—oh, Harry!—had found it necessary to stop at the post office again. How many letters would arrive, she wondered, during the several days it would take them to drive home? Who would claim them, who would read them? Tomorrow maybe they would start out. She didn't want to wake Charlie from his adventure, but she would have to.

The letter remained unopened of course. The gauzy arc of the Milky Way splashed light across the envelope and there was no escaping her mother's handwriting, the address, the return address, the insistent **AIRMAIL!!** in capital letters. On the back a quick note was jotted across the seal: *Ralph says hi—that's all.*

"Ma'am?" Timothy came over with his rifle and sat down beside her.

"Catch any bad guys?"

"No, ma'am."

There came war whoops and other disturbing sounds.

"It was nice of you to build the children a fire."

"They did it themselves, ma'am."

"You mean they think they did it themselves. They're not too high up?"

"No, ma'am."

"They won't fall off?"

Timothy chuckled. "It's real nice and safe up there."

They sat for a while. Jean heard Harry and Jo talking. She couldn't locate where they were. They might have been nearby, tucked into an overhang, or they might have climbed farther up on some slickrock.

"Ma'am, I hope you don't think I'm horning in on your action," Timothy said.

"No, of course not. I enjoy the company."

"I don't mean that."

Harry's voice was above them, echoing down: Of course I've had a drink before. I had a drink right before this one.

And right before that one, too. Jo's voice.

"What do you mean then?" she asked Timothy.

"I know everyone's celebrating the uranium, but I want you to know.

That is to say, ma'am, if I could use that money to buy back my friend's life, then maybe you'd have to look out for me. Since that is not the case, you don't have to worry about me horning in."

"Timothy, I don't know whether to hug you or kiss you."

"Well, neither, I suppose," Timothy said.

Harry's voice: Now that we're going to be rich, I guess we'll be working together.

We'll have to. Jo's voice.

Harry's voice: Did I tell you about the old copper mine I'm going to start working? I'm the owner now, or soon will be.

Are you? Jo's voice, dreamy.

Harry voice, emboldened: It'd be nice if we were partners in that, too.

Crazier things have happened. Jo's voice, slurred.

You think maybe it'll happen? Harry's voice, excited.

I think maybe it might, Harry. Jo's voice, dreamy, slurred, half asleep.

"You better go get that bottle from those two," Jean told Timothy. "I think they've had enough."

She guessed she felt bad about not telling Jimmy Splendid their plans. It was his own fault. He'd brought it on himself. She didn't like the way she felt about Jimmy, that is, she didn't like the fact that she liked the way she felt. She didn't even know what it was she liked about the man. All she could enumerate to herself were the ways in which she didn't like him.

She heard a sound and twisted toward it. She knew the footsteps would belong to Timothy. She imagined Jimmy stepping into the moonlight and wondered what that would be like.

Timothy swept a blanket around her shoulders. "I'm stealing your blanket," she whispered.

"It's yours now, ma'am," he said. He sat down beside her. From his pocket he pulled out what looked to be a pillbox, accordioned it into a cup, shook out the sand, and poured himself a drink.

"Did they leave you any?"

"Yes, ma'am. Can I get you one?"

"No, thank you. Wouldn't mind a cigarette though."

Timothy took a swig, then set down his cup. "Those kids are having fun, aren't they?" He pulled out his pouch. His packet of rolling papers was empty.

"Use this," she said, handing him the letter. "It's airmail. That means onionskin stationery. And I'm guessing it's blue. How's blue onionskin for cigarettes?"

"Would roll up nice, ma'am. Go good with a drink, too."

"Maybe I will have a drink."

Timothy handed her the cup. "You take this." He tipped back the bottle for a gulp. "I'm fine with this here."

"You hear all that whispering?" she asked.

"They've been whispering all night."

"I don't mean them. Harry and Jo. Or the children."

"I know, ma'am. The other whispering."

"You hear it?"

"Oh yes, ma'am."

"So I'm not going crazy?"

"No, ma'am. People used to live out here."

"What does that mean?"

"Means they're letting you know they used to live out here."

Jean's grip around the letter tightened. *Ralph says hi—that's all—* scribbled on the back. Ralph was her mother's favorite teller at the bank. Oh, her mother was on to her. She knew Jean wasn't opening the letters. So now she was giving her a code, *Ralph says hi,* meaning: money inside, don't be afraid, money for you and the kids. *That's all,* meaning: truce.

And now Jean, having accomplished nothing, would presently be heading back to her. Whatever, *whatever,* gave you such an idea? Her mother's last words to her. They were backing out of the driveway, running late to the Greyhound station because Mr. Jackson had misplaced his eyeglasses. In the passenger seat her mother sat erect, lavender vanity case on lap, unperturbed of course by the prospect of missing her bus (Mr. Jackson's absurd search in the trash cans halfway convinced her he and her mother were in secret alliance). The arm Mr. Jackson rested upon her roof continued to stay put even as she shifted into reverse to warn him. *Be nice, Jean. After all, he loaded your station wagon for you,* her mother undertoned. But Jean couldn't wait. She eased out the clutch, swiveled around to see out the back, glimpsed Beth's encouraging but tentative smile, and eyed the Rambler's reversal out the drive. When her gaze came forward, Mr. Jackson's arm had been pulled along and now stretched toward her in a dancer's entreaty. "Whatever, *whatever,* gave you such an idea?" her mother loudly blurted, then was too upset to say anything more. Even to the children she could not muster a good-bye. She kept her face averted as she trotted, daintily knock-kneed, to the driver waving her to hurry. Finally, climbing the steps to the bus, she turned with her usual mastery of expression. One hand, forming an exaggerated clothespin over her nose, let them know the driver smelled. The other hand, tipping an imaginary cup, let them know the cause. Suddenly her face contorted into a sob; she waved and slipped inside. Seeing her collapse, Jean was now ashamed to say she had felt herself grow cold. Something literally like ice had slid down her throat and chest and into her heart. It was the same sensation she'd had with Miss Dazzle when Miss Dazzle wept over Charlie. Giving sympathy about Charlie was the one place she couldn't go. She wasn't trying to lay perverse claim to her territory; she simply couldn't do it. Maybe that was the problem between her and her mother. Neither could yet give the other sympathy, but each of them needed it from the other.

Perhaps inside this envelope were the first words of their new truce. They would need a truce to get through this with Charlie.

She handed the envelope to Timothy. He opened it for her, pulled out two sheets of paper and smiled.

"Onionskin. We're in luck, ma'am."

A twenty-dollar bill fell out between the two sheets. "Even more luck," she said.

Timothy tore a square out of the letter and sprinkled tobacco over the words. *Hope you are doing fine.* Jean held the rest of the letter while Timothy rolled the cigarette and lit it. Words being burned when he inhaled, more words waiting on the page in her lap. Words, that was all, only words. Just words.

"What should I do?" she asked Timothy.

"I always say hello."

"Really?"

"Did as soon as I got here, ma'am. I always do. Here. Take a sip first."

She took a good swallow. "Hello!" she called out. "Hello!"

"Feel better?"

"Yes, I do."

NINE

Because of the dust, Harry kept his equipment tightly wrapped. In the morning he went off by himself and unpacked everything and lined up the items on burlap shrouds, as neatly as if they decorated the mantel of a fireplace. He couldn't help his smiles as he admired one piece after the other. He picked up a log book, bound and sealed in metal. On sale for two years now, the price stair-stepping downward every few months. No one had ever come close to buying it—still too expensive; also big and heavy. The prospectors liked their pocket-sized notebooks and didn't listen to Harry when he explained how easily lost or destroyed such a flimsy tidbit could find itself. History, Harry said, slapping the metal binding. Brain cooked by the sun, a prospector was not likely to understand the lofty notion of history, a record of something beyond today and tomorrow. They were as a group pretty foggy about concepts. Protection, Harry said, slapping it hard. Protection against all forms of destruction. His final argument. But neither did they believe they'd need something indestructible. It was like buying fire insurance on your house. Who was going to believe your own house up in flames?

So now the log book was his. He checked around for a pen to write his name inside. Voices called him to breakfast. "Harry!" "Harry!" Every voice took a turn, each one a different note. There was that song again, the one Harry could never finish. He dawdled, just so the voices would call again and clarify the tune. He began to tremble, admiring his lineup of supplies and listening to the singing. He was trembling, he realized, with joy. Soon he would be a partner with Jo in this operation, and soon he and Timothy would be working the old copper mine. He'd be sole owner of that but who knew, perhaps Jo would decide to come aboard. If they got married, she'd be a partner by default.

"Harry." It was Jean, standing beside him.

"Oh," he said.

"What's wrong?" she asked. "Didn't you hear us calling?"

"I was just . . . listening."

"Listening to us call you over and over again." Jean made the question into a statement that called Harry himself into question. "We're having breakfast."

"I know."

"Don't not eat," she said. "Don't even think about it. Don't make me worry about you because I don't want to have to worry about you."

"I'm eating," Harry said. "And don't worry about me. I'm eating a lot." In fact, Harry had awakened with the sensation that beset other folks on a daily basis. He was hungry, exceptionally hungry. Starving for any burned morsel that Timothy might tong out of the fire.

"Come on, Harry."

"Coming." He wrapped the Mineralight in its satchel, left the other stuff out. He gave Jean a comradely hug as they walked back. The hug surprised even him. Jean pulled back and tugged his forearms until she got his proper attention. She stared up at him. She didn't say anything. "What?" he asked.

"Are you going to make me say it?"

"What?" he asked.

"Oh God, it hurts my neck to look at you. Harry . . ."

Her eyes were that turquoise, a color that craved more blue or craved more green, and not getting either shone all the brighter. He would never forget those eyes. And why had he suddenly thought that? They were going to be working together, after all. He'd be seeing those eyes again and again.

"What?" he asked. "What's wrong?" Some kind of menace pricked at his neck and his hairs stood on end.

"Harry, you know we can't stay."

"But we've found it."

"And that's nice. But we have to go back, the children and me."

"For how long?" Harry asked.

"At least for the summer."

"Well, okay. That's all right. The kids need a break. And then you can come back."

"And then there's school, Harry."

Harry fought against the strange foreboding. "You can still . . . You'll still be a part of it. You can come back and check up on things. I'll keep things going. I will. I'll keep it going. And Jo and I will let you know and then maybe Charlie can come back out now and again."

"Okay, Harry, keep it going for us." Her tone was dismal, but her eyes were lit up, that irradiated color in search of a base. Harry didn't believe a word she said. They'd stay. This was just the doomsday style she tried on each morning. By afternoon she'd change her mind. In the last couple of days she had looked better than ever, younger and more eager. And if she did take a break, the desert would send her home a person renewed, and it wouldn't be long before she realized she needed to be back here. Harry loved the desert, how its harsh challenges stripped you down to the essential decisions. He never wanted to leave it, and now he wouldn't have to. She'd find out; it would just take her longer, being from Ohio.

For breakfast Timothy served black toast topped with canned meat and bubbling slices of cheese. Harry beheld the black and crusty and fatty gob in his hands and began to rethink this hunger business, but his gushing good cheer needed to be filled with something so it might as well be food. Aside from this, his new responsibility toward the others would have forced any meal, defective or not, down his throat. Although Flaherty came across as their leader, Harry knew that in a crisis it would come down to him. He looked at Flaherty sitting in his camp chair. The legs that poked out of him were the type of sticks that wouldn't ever take on any bark. Everything had gone to his stomach and whatever was happening in there was pumping more redness and sweat into his already flushed, perspiring face. If he died today, it would be a tragedy but not a surprise.

Over coffee, Vincent Flaherty pulled out a pillbox and passed it around. "Salt tablets. Do you a world of good."

"Thank you, sir," Timothy said.

Harry was squatted down on his tiptoes. He couldn't squat the way the kids could. Down low on flat feet, rear ends not an inch from the ground, Charlie and Beth were both balanced sturdy as plywood boxes. Harry dipped a tea bag into a cup he held between his knees. The cup handle was so hot he had to hold it with a bandana. Normally he'd be sneaking glances at Jo, thinking up ways for them to be thrown together. Now he was content to keep his distance, knowing they were partners. Freed from the pressure to force each moment into a headline-grabbing event featuring another of Harry's Superior Merits! he could relax and let time rally to his aid, the slow crescent of days, his virtues and dependable disposition incrementally revealed. Harry wasn't a *wow* person. It took more than one second to get to know him. That wasn't a bad thing.

"Who's that?" Beth asked.

Squatting on his tiptoes, Harry swiveled and lost his balance. His arm shot out, the cup of tea held up like a toast.

"Celebrating my arrival, I see." He strolled right into their camp circle. Just as Harry was thanking the slow tick of the hour hand, here came Jimmy Splendid, a *wow* person if there ever was one, and in one second he had taken command.

"Creeping up on us like a mountain lion," Flaherty said.

Trailing behind Jimmy was Leonard Dawson.

"I don't get a hello?" Jimmy asked.

The stunned women were silent.

"I'll have some more coffee," Flaherty said to Timothy. "And then, Jimmy, you can explain to us poor dumb folks here what in the world you're doing in our camp. Uninvited. You know the rules, Jimmy."

"And you don't. Reason I'm here."

Leonard Dawson scraped forward. "Hello, Jo." He reached to fluff her hair, but she turned away.

"Hey! Whoa whoa whoa." Flaherty shot up his hand. "You talk to her later. Let's not get into the niceties without a little information first about the not-so-niceties. Not so nice of you to pull an ambush on us."

"How are you?" Dawson asked Jo.

"Hey! Did you hear me?" Flaherty made an attempt to get out of his chair by himself, then plopped back.

"I'm talking to my wife."

"Shut up," Jimmy told Dawson.

"I can talk to my wife!"

"You're married to her. You can talk to her the rest of your life."

"Explain yourself, Jimmy," Vince said.

Jimmy said, "Vince, everyone knows what's going on. Belinda told me, of course, but I knew. I'm not meaning to ambush you. Just the opposite. Thought I could help is all. Came up to the ladies' campsite and this man here, Mrs. Dawson's husband, he showed me the map and we followed it." He tipped his hat to Jean. "Hello."

In Dawson's hand was Charlie's map panel. "Here," Dawson said, handing it to Jo. Jo didn't look up. He tapped her head with it, then tapped again.

"It's not mine," Jo said to the dirt. But Leonard Dawson rapped her again with the map.

"It's Charlie's, you know it's Charlie's!" Harry grabbed the cardboard panel from Dawson. He held the map behind his back so no one would notice his shaking hands. The blood in his shoulders and arms was writhing insanely and his throat thickened with a heavy fullness. He wondered if he was having a heart attack. He couldn't sense his heartbeat at all, yet everything in his chest was filling up.

Flaherty said, "You're getting real close to doing something you shouldn't be doing, Jimmy."

"And who would know better about that?"

"You didn't hear me about the coffee?" Flaherty demanded of Timothy.

"Making more, sir," Timothy answered. "On the way."

Jimmy said, "You've got servants now, Vince. That's nice."

"Turns out Timothy here's a regular Epicurean of the potables and edibles."

"I'll have some coffee, too, thank you," Jimmy said. He took a seat on a rock.

"Oh, please don't feel the need to make yourself at home. The uninvited among us are now invited to be on their way."

"Vince, nobody invited you to jump my claim, yet I've broken bread with you on more than one occasion since. I'll have the coffee," he said to Timothy, who was hesitating. Jimmy grabbed a cup and shook it out. "Pour."

Jean said, "Mr. Flaherty, there's no reason Jimmy can't have a cup of coffee with us."

"I usually don't provide coffee to someone who's arrived in the very manner of a claim jumper yet refers to me as the claim jumper. My dear, in your part of the country that might not mean much, those words. But here you don't throw those words around. People have been shot for less."

"I don't think he meant it," Jean said.

"Epithet retracted, coffee proffered."

"That's right, keep the distractions coming with all the word games."

"Simple English language, Jimmy."

"And so predictable, too," Jimmy said. "Hot!" Halfway through getting his coffee poured, Jimmy whipped out his bandana for use as an oven mitt. "I come out here and I see it starting: it's all going according to how I thought it would. Vince comes on board and completely takes over and every single one of you lets him. Do you know what's next? This has happened before, folks, and it's not a pretty sight. When Vince gets involved . . . Harry, I'm surprised at you. You know his record. I thought you'd at least look out for these ladies. It's a good thing I showed up."

"I'm looking out for them," Harry said.

Jean jumped in. "Jimmy, that's not kind of you. There's really no call to talk to Mr. Flaherty like that."

"Let him release his venom, my dear," Vincent Flaherty said. "It's the only way to calm him down. Then he'll go back to contentedly sunning himself for a while."

"That all your equipment back there, Harry?" Jimmy asked.

"Yes," Harry said.

"Figured," Jimmy said. "Looks like salesman stuff. Won't get you too far."

"It's gotten me pretty far."

"You know, Vince," Jimmy said, shifting away from Harry, "I just knew I'd walk into camp and find you sitting like the king of Sheba, *on a chair*, no less—your throne, Vince?—while everyone else scampers around you. Did you all know that's how it works before you signed up with this man?"

"Jimmy, let's not have a fight," Jean said. "After all, Mr. Flaherty got us here in his helicopter."

"He's good at doing that."

"Well, yes he was," Jean agreed. "I don't know how we could have done it without him."

"You could have done it with me, that's how," Jimmy said.

"You were too busy with Belinda," Jean said.

"Ahh—"

"Why exactly are you here?" Harry heard himself speak and hoped he sounded firm.

"Harry, is that you, Harry? Did you say something?"

"Sir, he asked you why you were here." Timothy was still on his knees, fiddling with coffee-making. His voice was unperturbed.

Jimmy didn't answer, but he couldn't ignore Timothy either. All the things that were dirty and scruffed up about Timothy served to repulse women but somehow earned a man's respect. Jimmy's silence to Timothy's question was a thrown spear, landing at their feet.

Flaherty picked up his cigar pouch and took his time looking for a cigar and lighting it up. He didn't do it with his usual flair, however.

"Why am I here?" Jimmy asked. But his delay had sent more warning prickles swarming over Harry's body. "I'm here to save you, literally and financially. Don't laugh, Vince."

"No laughs here," Flaherty said.

"Because he likes to laugh and tell jokes to get you distracted."

"No laughing, no jokes," Flaherty said, taking a puff of his cigar.

Dawson was the only one not paying attention to Jimmy. He was looking straight at Jo, straight at her profile as she tried not to acknowledge him.

Jimmy reached for Jean's elbow. He drew her toward him until she acknowledged his gaze. "Did you bother to ask him his record before you decided to throw in with him? You didn't ask, did you? Because it had nothing to do with him. I wish you would have talked to me. That wasn't really fair, was it?"

"Maybe not," Jean said, not pulling away from his grip.

"So to spite me for some reason I'm not clear on, you made a deal with the devil."

Jean sputtered a false start.

"Say what you want," Flaherty said. "A devil? I'm flattered. Just don't call me a claim jumper."

Jimmy pulled Jean aside so he could face Flaherty straight on. "That's what you are."

"Little help, Timothy," Flaherty commanded, reaching out from his chair. With a single yank Timothy blasted Flaherty into the air and he was propelled against Jimmy's chest. Coffee surged from both cups as they bumped apart. The coffee took flight as a brown pair of wings. "What did you say? Come again, Jimmy?"

"I said, and I'm saying, you jumped my claims."

"You staked on withdrawn lands," Flaherty said.

"And you jumped the claims I'd already made."

"That's okay," Jean said. "We don't need to argue about this. Ancient history." Her hands gripped Flaherty's shoulders and pulled him away.

"On withdrawn lands," Flaherty said, stumbling back. "I staked after the withdrawn status was cancelled by the government of the United States of America. Those are the laws I happen to obey, not the laws made by the United States of Jimmy Splendid."

"And you jumped my claims."

"The government canceled the withdrawn status and then I staked my claims. As I had a legal right to."

"You staked your claims over my claims."

"You had no claims. For God's sake, Jimmy, get it through that wooden noggin. You had no claims!"

"It was unethical."

"It was entirely perfectly legal."

"It was entirely perfectly immoral," Jimmy said. "You jumped my claims."

"I didn't jump anybody's claims!" Flaherty took his cigar and stepped forward and stabbed it into Jimmy's shoulder. Jimmy slapped the cigar away. Flaherty fell back against Jean and they both plunged to the ground.

Jimmy showed no reaction, either to his smoldering vest or to Flaherty on the ground. Jean quickly pulled her dress down over her thighs and stood up and waved Harry away. "I'm fine," she said, brushing herself decent. He and Timothy rolled Flaherty over to his side and wedged him up that way.

Settled in his chair, Flaherty was silent. Jean handed him a glass of water and he sat with it on his lap. Harry began to get worried, not for what Flaherty said but for what he wasn't saying at all. His face, almost always an apple in shape and color, had lost all tone, and the bursting plumpness divulged a slight but discernible hollowing in the cheeks. Most alarming, he did not address Jean with concern for her own well-being or with a grand *merci* for the water.

"Where do you keep your nitroglycerin pills?" Harry asked.

Flaherty gulped in a clenched inhale. His hand dropped to the cigar pouch by his chair. In the cloth pouch, the cigars were shoved in loose, some of them crumbling. Buried in the crumbs of tobacco were tiny white pills. When Harry picked out a pill, a pinch of tobacco came with it. Flaherty deposited the wad under his tongue.

"Mr. Flaherty," Jean said.

Flaherty held up a finger.

"Are you in pain?" Jean asked.

Tears of sweat ran down Flaherty's cheeks and dropped off his chin.

"Let me explain the situation to the ladies," Jimmy continued.

"Not now, Jimmy," Jean said. "No more fighting. No one meant to cheat anyone before. No one's cheating anyone now. There's enough uranium for everyone."

"So you've determined that?"

"I believe with all my heart that Mr. Flaherty did not mean to cheat you."

"All right," Jimmy said. "I'll accept that. You say there's enough uranium for everyone?"

"There's plenty," Jean said with disgust.

"Do you personally know that?"

"Yes, we do," Jo piped up.

Jimmy said, "I guess convincing yourselves is about the only thing left to do in the desert."

No one answered.

"What makes you so sure?"

"We took some readings," Jo said, sounding very professional.

"Okay," Jimmy said.

"We ran a probe right down through that there pinnacle," Timothy said.

"Dare I ask how you did that?"

"Helicopter."

"Criminy," Jimmy whistled. "Well, what are you going to do now?"

"We'll proceed," Harry said.

Jimmy said, "Next step's core samples, it seems to me. Right, Vince?"

Flaherty didn't answer.

Jimmy continued: "Vince doesn't have a mining camp, see? Doesn't have one. The equipment you're going to need for core samples? Where's he going to get it? Right down the road, all the equipment you're ever going to need. From me." He paused to let it sink in. "Jean. Why didn't you just ask?"

"I told you. You were so busy with Miss Dazzle I didn't have a chance."

"Okay." Jimmy stretched back and worked his jaw muscles. "All right. I thought it might be something like that."

"Let's not have this conversation now." Jean went back to Flaherty, her fingers stroking his temple.

"Later then."

Flaherty prodded at his face with a bandana. He covered his eyes and blew out a whispered ten count.

"Right, Vince? You don't have the equipment for core samples, right?"

"Jimmy, wait! Better?" Jean asked, kneeling beside Flaherty.

Flaherty counted up to twenty before huffing out a "Thank you, my dear."

"Right, Vince?"

"Ssh. Enough, Jimmy," Jean said. "We all get it. You have the equipment and we don't."

"I can get the equipment here tomorrow or the next day."

"Fine!" Jean said.

"Did you hear that!" Dawson whispered to Jo, pulling her into him.

Jimmy said, "Unless I hear no from you, Vince, I'm going to assume everyone agrees. Vince?"

"Mr. Flaherty?" Jean took the bandana from him and wiped at the rivers of sweat. "How are you feeling?"

In a clenched voice Flaherty said, "Once I get up to two hundred and fifty, I'm okay." He ground out his breaths in rhythmic pants.

"Where are you now?" Jimmy asked.

"Hunru." Pant. "Thir-sev."

"He'll never make it," Jimmy said.

Harry and Charlie showed Jimmy where the petrified wood was found. "Holy moly," Jimmy said. Jimmy's body was jammed into the entrance and at this point it was one and the same to go forward or retreat. "I think I'm stuck."

Harry hadn't considered this possibility as he slipped inside. He was taller than Jimmy, but that didn't mean bigger. The entrance crevice, spacious for legs and hips and head, bowed outward in line with Jimmy's barrel chest. The rock's smooth surface had ushered Jimmy into a vice grip. "Just two more steps," Harry encouraged.

"Don't lie to me, Harry." Jimmy's voice held a little concern. He sucked in his breath, grunted. He panted, expelled his breath, then grunted again.

"It widens out here," Harry assured him. He waited for a glimpse of a wedged body part.

"It's pitch black, Harry. I can't see a thing. Shine your flashlight in here."

"You've got the flashlight," Harry said. "Just one more step. Then you'll be able to see perfectly."

Harry stood in the shaft. It was good-sized, and it opened to the sky way above them. A ladder of sunlight shot down so hard that Harry could almost believe its sharp outline was climbable.

Jimmy's arm freed itself and lashed blindly in the air. Harry grabbed on and pulled in rhythm with Jimmy's convulsive exhales. Jimmy disgorged into the shaft with a volcanic wheeze. "Criminy," he whispered, wiping himself off.

Next came Charlie, quick as a lizard.

A couple of culprits hadn't helped matters any, Jimmy told them, slipping off his vest. From one chest pocket he tugged out a cigarette lighter and case; from the other pocket a small but thick log book. Made his big chest just that much bigger. A bullet hole from Flaherty's cigar had singed through the vest. Harry checked Jimmy's shirt and there was a hole through there as well. Though he had showed no reaction, Jimmy must have gotten burned.

Jimmy aimed his flashlight into the high recesses of rock. The walls were just as in Harry's daydream, streaked with such a rich black they might have been leaking pitch. It threw Harry back in time. This was how you used to search. Nowadays all the new equipment did your searching for you, probing through stuff your naked eye would otherwise walk away from. Things had gotten so modernized since the uranium rush started, you forgot canyon walls like this still existed.

"We're not looking at carnotite," Harry said.

"No, we're not."

"You're running a carnotite mine over yonder, aren't you?"

Jimmy didn't answer.

"I'd say we're looking at pitchblende or vanadium."

Jimmy said, not kindly, "How would you know, Harry?" He kicked through the shaft to its false end.

"There's a hanging garden behind that."

Jimmy stared up at the fissured shelf of rock. "Do I see petrified wood?"

"That's where Beth got it from."

"Who's Beth?"

"Charlie's sister."

"Right." Jimmy glanced down at Charlie.

"And there's more behind this," Harry said.

"I've squeezed through enough for one day. We'll have to blast an opening in here just to get ore samples. What do you think of that, Charlie?"

"Yeah, okay," Charlie said.

"You mind if we blow up this place a little bit?"

Harry didn't treat Charlie like that, asking dumb questions, paying
him this phony kind of respect. "That all right with you if we do some
blasting?" Jimmy repeated. Charlie shrugged and moved away, straight
into the ladder of sunlight and Harry had that sensation again that someone, Charlie this time, could grab hold of the light and climb up.

"There's a little hanging garden getup behind that rock at the end,"
Harry said.

"You told me already, Harry. I'll take a look after I blast a bigger
doorway. As it stands now, I'm wondering if I'm gonna be able to get out
of here." Charlie took Jimmy's vest for him and slithered back outside.
Jimmy prepared himself with several exhales, deflating his chest as much
as possible, then sidestepped into the crack as Harry guided him into the
best position. Jimmy fled into the blackness—as if speed could boost
him out of there. Harry heard him run out of breath and start gulping.

"All right?" Harry asked.

No answer. Several moments later, "Okay, Harry, come on through."

Jimmy seemed satisfied enough with what he had seen to start staking claims with Harry and Timothy. Charlie tagged along. Each time
Jimmy spoke to Charlie, saying something like *When my men get here,
Charlie, you're going to have to set them straight,* Harry hoarded another
misreading of this boy Harry prided himself on never underestimating.

Every so often Jimmy lifted his head and barked out, "Dawson!"

A cloud of gnats seemed to be sparking about Harry, poking him with a strange anxiety. The hairs on his neck were erect. Harry swiveled in a circle. Every direction was the same direction with the same landscape and the same simple choices: *yes, no, go, come.* That was all the desert demanded of a person; that was all it had ever demanded. Nothing had changed. There was nothing wrong. He squinted at the sun— that had changed, however. He was surprised by its stain of pink. The noon sun typically beat with a fierce invisibility, but now it was soaked in the beginnings of color, as if sunset were approaching.

"Dawson!" Then to them: "Is there dinner or anything like that?" Jimmy had grown increasingly irritated.

"Seems kind of early for that," Timothy said.

"Not when you've been working. Dawson!"

Harry picked up his metal log book and logged in another claim, then scribbled out a claim notice and stuck it in one of Timothy's empty tobacco tins.

"Harry!"

"What?"

"Who's the cook here?" Jimmy asked. He looked from Harry to Timothy, perusing each of them like an item on a store shelf. And what did that look mean, Harry wondered: that if Jimmy did you the honor of selecting you, you'd jump off the shelf and go cook for him? Why did you start feeling you had to do Jimmy's bidding? As soon as he showed up, anywhere, in a room or out in the desert, he stood there as the *wow* man in charge.

"Dawson!"

"Yeah, what," Dawson said, finally appearing.

"A little help staking claims here!"

"I need to be with my wife," Dawson said.

"Since when?" Jimmy said.

Dawson ignored him. His neck and ears were filthy, and his hair had been sweated into bare threads. Despite something beaten in his huge slumped shoulders, Dawson exuded a strong scent of pride. Harry had not noticed before that Dawson had no eyelashes. He could see how it was when Dawson had met Jo, scrubbed up clean for a first date (he would hope so!), hair shampooed into thickness, and then those naked eyes calling out with a newborn's plea for love and protection. Jo: too soft to resist.

"You can still work," Jimmy ordered.

Dawson turned his back on Jimmy and left.

"Is that man as lazy as he seems?" Jimmy spat out the dust in his mouth and drank from his canteen.

Jean climbed up to them. Still hadn't bought herself a pair of boots. She was wearing dress shoes but lower-heeled than the cocktail-party ones Harry had found her in.

"Lunch is here." Jimmy sighed and straightened up expectantly.

Harry squinted at the sun again and saw that it was taking on a deeper blush. He scratched at his neck. Jean told Charlie it was time to get back. Jimmy pulled off his hat and swiped the bandana from this back pocket and cleaned his face. Jimmy didn't have any idea what Jean was really meaning. Harry hoarded this secret, too.

As Jean turned and headed back, Jimmy said, "Excuse me, Jean, I thought you were calling us for lunch."

"Lunch? We brought stuff to make sandwiches," she said. "Do you like peanut butter and jelly? Didn't you tell him we had stuff, Harry?"

"Didn't know you did," Harry said.

"Do you have anything else on the menu?" Jimmy asked.

"Cheese," Jean said. "Spam. Mustard."

"Anything hot?"

Jean looked stumped. Timothy said, "I can make you coffee, ma'am."

"Coffee," she said to Jimmy.

Jimmy smiled. He had an infectious smile whenever he decided to try it out. Harry supposed he was the type women found irresistible although the block shape of Jimmy's face and body reminded Harry of a totem pole painted with a white man's face. Jimmy was smiling now with his white teeth, his eyes fastened on Jean, who was clearly sidetracked by Charlie. Harry thought, looking at the perplexed mother, Well, you're the only person on earth to get a smile from Jimmy Splendid upon not delivering the goods he demands. He'd like to see Jimmy give anyone else that smile when they said no to him.

He and Timothy continued with the staking after Jimmy left them. Timothy, who had been silent with Jimmy around, started up talking again, about Vincent Flaherty's nautical abilities, about Vernon Rutledge's nautical abilities, about how nice Mrs. Dawson looked, about how it seemed to him though he was no expert on the matter, that she was dressing up especially for Harry. Timothy was likely the only other person who had not experienced the mysterious tides between a man and a woman, how they can hate each other and hate each other and hate each other and crash and hate each other and choke and drown and come up for more. Harry's fitting company in ignorance about love was someone who thought ships and planes were interchangeable, who still had a clothespin dangling from his ear, even though at this point it was an entirely optional part of his wardrobe, and who ate the stubs of his rolled cigarettes rather than pollute the ground.

"Where's that coffee!" came a distant shout.

"Looks like I better get water boiling," Timothy said and left.

Harry lay down on the slickrock. It was cool in the right places and warm in the right places, and lumpy and concave just where his sore muscles needed it. He was in two kinds of pain, his back and his heart. The slickrock helped his back. It did nothing for his heart.

He found he could keep his eyes open. The sun's color had dulled it to viewable. He stared at it without seeming to know what it was: the sky's heart, beating red. The sky was leaking blood and the throbbing sun sucked it up. He could detect the sun swelling, then contracting. He sat up. Something quickened his blood.

Rock surrounded him. In the distance were the cliff alcoves with their ancient granaries of ancient people. At every compass point was a battleground of turrets and domes and geological disasters now resting as boulders. The same landscape. The same landscape as always. The desert's simple message: *Make your choice, Harry, yes, no, go, stay.*

Except this time. A menaced buzzing brushed near him. The message was different.

It said: *Leave.*

He bolted up and found himself twirling like an idiot, feverishly glancing about for a presence.

Some water from a canteen, a bite from the jerky he now kept in his pocket. The electricity shivering down his spine lessened.

Time to rejoin the others.

The red sun was lurid as a sunset as he climbed down. His mother had always said that sunset was the best time to think. It was the time of day that encouraged reflection: about this particular day that was ending, or this particular evening that was coming on, or about all your days in general. And then she'd add, wiping her hands on her apron and sitting with him for a moment on the back porch, but I'm too tired to have any thoughts. What about you, Harry, what are you thinking? And Harry was forever afraid to tell her because all his thoughts were about escaping.

In the nearly six years that he had been trundling from one mining camp to another, Harry had sold every kind of instrument and machine piece dedicated to finding an ingredient coveted by the United States government without much conviction about where it all would lead. He knew he was doing something his country encouraged, and that gave him a vague sense of himself as a patriot. Vague because he himself was vague and he had to stop being that.

The sun's red ball was beautiful. Naturally it was beautiful. There was nothing out here that wasn't gorgeous. And now what were his thoughts as he sat on the desert's back porch? What was he thinking? His mother was the only one who had asked that question of him. She had never lied to him, not intentionally, but the covetous, ravenous interest of a parent was itself the lie. She was once one of those too-young mothers he had seen at the Mormon camp, and she had turned to Harry, a son, to make her life right. And what had he done? Nothing. He hadn't entered into a celestial marriage. He hadn't entered into any marriage at all. He had sold supplies.

TEN

Beth had watched them fight, Jimmy Splendid and Vincent Flaherty, and although a little frightening, the confrontation was mostly exciting with comical overtones. She pondered how to insert a firsthand witness account into her next book report. Just use quotation marks?

But then her mother decided to get involved and next glance Vincent Flaherty was going after Jimmy Splendid with a knife—only the knife was a cigar but Beth didn't know it was a cigar. She couldn't see because of her mother. All she could see was Vincent Flaherty's raised hand, poised to strike—Beth instantly toppled with panic. That raised hand was how you stabbed somebody.

As her mother fell to the ground, Beth jumped to her feet. Certain that her mother who had already been shot had now been knifed, she did nothing but stand there and sway back and forth. She didn't run to help or call out to her mother. She froze. Jimmy Splendid's vest sent up ringlets of smoke as he stood over them. Now she knew this about herself and she was not too happy to know it: in a crisis she was a girl who jumped to her feet *to get a better view.*

So that was her rather violent morning. Things didn't look much better for the afternoon, mainly because Leonard Dawson was back and that was enough to ruin everything. It was no exaggeration to say Beth hated him as much as ever although she was no longer afraid of him the way she had been before. Violence was something she been able to make a close study of, coming as it did right toward the end of her Lois Lenski supply, and every day she had applied herself to learning more about it. She was probably an expert in violence by now and could doubtless write her own book about it although unfortunately violence was not a suitable topic for girls—although maybe if she got Mr. Jackson for fifth grade he would like to hear what she had to say. After explaining to him, via her latest report, who Leonard Dawson was, ugly, buffalo-hump shoulders, blah blah blah, she would go on to observe that violence in Leonard Dawson was like a big heavy knapsack he carried around, swaying him with its awkward weight. It made him seem a little bit silly no matter how scary or angry he became. Violence in Jimmy Splendid, however, oozed like the haircream in his hair (or like the elegant wisp of smoke slinking from his vest); you might not ever notice it unless things stopped working for him the way he wanted them to work. Until then he could be smooth.

Then there was Vincent Flaherty. How to explain Vincent Flaherty so that a fifth grade teacher could understand? He was not normal. Well, a lot of people weren't. But Vincent Flaherty was not normal in a continually spellbinding way. And so sometimes you thought everything about him was a joke. Even Beth Waterman, a girl usually so astutely perceptive, had been deceived. Fact was, Vincent Flaherty came with his own brand of not-normal violence. Cigar weaponry, case in point. She had witnessed firsthand that a dark capacity lay as bosom buddy with Vincent Flaherty's outgoing chumminess. A jolly bear hug, his beach-ball belly bouncing into you with promises of fun . . . Of the three men it was Leonard Dawson who scared her moment to moment and Vincent Flaherty who scared her to death. And Beth had seen the two of them together and knew it would always be Vincent Flaherty flying the helicopter and Leonard Dawson sniffing the ground.

Timothy helped her feel safe. Now, Mr. Jackson, when it comes to Timothy, think of Bazooka Joe and that turtleneck that goes up over his chin. That was Timothy's jawline. And he had none of Leonard Dawson's muscles, or bulging shoulders and back. And none of Vincent Flaherty's unusual sort of intelligence that kept people cowed and guessing. But do you believe it—Timothy made her feel safer than anyone, and the men didn't mess with him. And when Leonard Dawson arrived this morning, she was able to astutely perceive right away that he was scared of Timothy. This didn't surprise her at all.

Timothy didn't mind if you stared at him while he cooked. He liked to ask if you were all right a bunch of times, but other than that he let you be. Beth thought the lunch he made was one of the best meals she had ever eaten. Lemon-lime Flavor Aid. Oatmeal. Butter and jelly on toast. Timothy had stored the butter in the jar of grape jelly so he wouldn't have a melted stick on his hands. He grilled the bread slices over the fire until they were stiff and on the black side. The butter, all liquidy, spilled over the toast. The jelly stayed put, a quivering mountain. Timothy checked on the coffee pot and boiling water, lifting their lids; he poured in some oatmeal, cleaned the eating utensils on his shirttail and knee, and then he turned back to the crisp black sheet of bread and spooned out another buttery lake and grape mountain. Beth watched, fascinated. Almost everything Timothy did fascinated her and yesterday he had popped out the splinter the doctor had refused to believe was lodged in her knee since the day of her mother's accident. And some pus got on him and he didn't mind; in fact, he admired the fact that it was a good splinter. And then at night he had climbed up to a bench with a rock amphitheater behind it and built them a big bonfire that cast their giant dancing shapes across the desert, and he made them flat cakes. He scooped his hand in flour, shook cinnamon and sugar in his palm and kneaded it with a little water—you kids all right? he asked—and with a smile dropped the flat cakes directly into the fire. Delicious. There was only one way to describe them. Delicious, delicious. She and Charlie slept up there alone and in the morning Beth looked down at all the sleeping forms till she spotted the caterpillar her mother had become.

After Timothy's delectable lunch, which Jimmy Splendid nonetheless groused about, she and Charlie went into the garden cave and Charlie swam in the radioactive pool while Beth hunted along the walls for some sign Rawhide Joe might have stayed there. Charlie didn't have a towel so he used his T-shirt and when they got outside he laid the T-shirt in the sun. They sat on a rock and watched it dry. Then Charlie said that was silly, a wet T-shirt would help him stay cool.

Vincent Flaherty was lolling back in his summer vacation chair over by his tent. Everyone stood around him and Beth was sure he was dead. Perhaps a nicer girl would not have thought, *Hmm, interesting development.* Then she saw his hands drumming the ever bigger drum of his stomach. She waited for him to explode into pieces. Vincent Flaherty's head lifted and he called out, "We're starting without you."

"If you're talking to me, sir, I'll catch up to you," came Timothy's reply, broadcast over the desert air. The cliff tops loudly played the clanging of his cleanup.

"We're not going anywhere," Vincent Flaherty called back. "We're having a meeting."

Beth still couldn't get over the phone system out here in the desert. Timothy was nowhere to be seen, but the desert cupped his voice into a receiver by your ear. "Stand in the sun, Charlie," she carefully whispered. Charlie was starting to shiver. His hair had come out of the cave pool in a hairstyle. Usually it hung down to his brow in a seahorse, a straight thatch twisted by a cowlick. Now his wet hair was swept back off his forehead in a darker brown. A tendril had sprung loose and tick-tocked across his forehead as his gaze turned from person to person. Even that hanging strand was perfect. All the movie stars Beth liked had exactly that hairstyle.

"I propose," Vincent Flaherty began, "that we reach some kind of agreement."

"What does that mean?" Jimmy Splendid asked.

"An official consensus of opinion."

"What's that?" Jo asked.

"You're looking lovely today, my dear," Vincent Flaherty told her.

"You keep your foul tongue to yourself," Leonard Dawson growled.

"In that case, tell your wife that it's a binding legal agreement by signatories."

"That sounds interesting," Jo said. She sent a shrug to Beth's mother. Leonard Dawson moved next to her and grasped her hand—actually her fist, since she didn't grasp back.

"Now . . ." Vincent Flaherty's upraised palm awaited whatever it was he expected to be laid there. Everyone turned to everyone else. "With a slip of paper and a pen we could outline our agreement. Jimmy here has to leave soon and I have a postprandial nap with my name on it."

"You're leaving?" Jo asked.

"In a few minutes," Jimmy said.

"Why?" Beth's mother asked.

Jimmy smiled at her. "I'll be back. I have to get back to the mining camp and arrange to get some equipment."

"Obviously the women have not been paying close attention to the activities going on around here," Vincent Flaherty said.

"Well," Beth's mother said.

"And I'm not criticizing you for it, my dear. You had nursing duties for which I'm very grateful. Let me bring you up to speed."

"How long is this going to take?" her mother asked.

"Just a few minutes," Vincent Flaherty said.

"No, I don't mean that."

"Are you going with him, Lenny?" Jo asked.

"I'm staying here with you," Leonard Dawson said, setting her captured fist against his thigh.

"Very well, my friends," Vincent Flaherty said. "If no one is interested in drawing up an agreement, I'm glad to become sole owner of the operation."

Jimmy Splendid cut him off. "What's the agreement, Vince? Make it plain and simple and let's get it over with."

"Mr. Einstein, our friend is getting agitated. Paper and pen, please."

"Don't forget my name on that thing," Leonard Dawson said.

"What?" Harry said. "Since when is he part of this group?"

"Harry!" Vincent Flaherty ordered. "Discussion is tabled until after the contract."

"It's a contract now, is it?" Jimmy Splendid said.

"Here, Charlie." Beth's mother gave him an envelope from her apron and Charlie handed it to Vincent Flaherty.

"Or do you think I'm being all wet, Charlie?" Vincent Flaherty let out a tired chuckle.

"And pen," Jimmy said, forcibly opening Vincent Flaherty's hand and smacking it with a pen. Timothy arrived just in time to steady Vincent Flaherty in his chair.

"All right then," Vincent Flaherty sighed. He examined the envelope, read the address, and turned it over. "'Ralph says hi—that's all.' Can I scratch that out or do you want it as part of the agreement?"

"You can scratch it out," her mother said.

"'Ralph says hi.' Sorry, Ralph. Looks like you're spoken for back home, my dear." Vincent Flaherty began writing with thick short fingers that could have been his own chewed-off cigars. Behind him a dusky pillar of sandstone rose high in the air in the shape of an oil derrick. Beth followed it to its point where she imagined the oil to be spurting, and yes indeed a black splash seemed to be there. "Writing something of such august importance on the back of an envelope puts me in mind of the Gettysburg Address." Vincent Flaherty lifted his head and merrily announced this tidbit. As usual, he turned to Charlie for private approval.

"Let's see what you got," Jimmy Splendid said.

"I'm just getting started," Vincent Flaherty said. "But I think we're off to a fine beginning."

He handed the envelope to Jimmy Splendid, who grimaced at the handwriting and began to read it for everyone.

Be it hereby agreed that the undersigned have jointly endeavored to stake and register the claim known to the parties as The Place the Little Girl Found.

Jimmy Splendid broke off. "That's what you're going to call it, 'the place the little girl found'? My God, Vince."

"Sounds kinda Indian, don't you think?"

"I like it," Beth's mother said.

"And she likes it."

Said claim is located in the State of Utah and its precise coordinates and description are attached hereto as Appendix A.

"There's already an appendix?"

"Thinking ahead, Jimmy. More envelopes, anyone?"

"Plenty," her mother said.

"I believe you might be thinking a little too far ahead. You're not aiming to cheat us out of anything, are you?" Jimmy Splendid poked a finger through the hole in his vest.

"I was just getting to the one-fifth interest part."

Jimmy Splendid did a head count. "There's six adults here, Vince."

"Seven," Leonard Dawson said.

"You're not included, obviously," Harry told him.

"What the hell!"

"Lenny, please!" Jo cried, jerking her fist away.

"You can't listen to this polyg," Dawson said.

Vincent Flaherty said, "We'll get to you in a second, Dawson. I counted Harry and Timothy as one. Harry, I thought Timothy worked for you."

"That's correct, sir," Timothy said.

"That's not really fair for Timothy," Harry said.

"I don't mind, sir. It's how I'd rather have it. All the money in the world isn't going to bring back my friend."

"A philosopher," Jimmy Splendid said.

"Jimmy," her mother scolded.

"What friend is this we're talking about?" Vincent Flaherty asked.

"Vernon Rutledge."

"Ah yes, the rimflyer. Sadly, correct. Money will not bring him back."

"Put Timothy's name down, please," Harry said.

"No, sir," Timothy said.

"As you wish, Mr. Timothy. I will abide by your request. I think it's up to him, Harry."

"And it's up to me that I want to have my name down there," Leonard Dawson interrupted.

"Your wife's name, yes. Your name, no."

"It should be in my name."

"What's hers is yours, so pipe down."

"But I'm the man!"

"And I'm the judge and jury." As he wrote, Vincent Flaherty said aloud: "Josephine Dawson."

"And you can just start over and put my name down," Leonard Dawson shouted. "You're letting a polyg tell you what to do?"

"I will, sir, ask you to leave if you don't shut up," Timothy said.

Leonard Dawson pawed the earth but said nothing more.

"So we're talking about five signatories of interest all of sound mind. 'Be it therefore witnessed . . .'" Vincent Flaherty mumbled to himself as he wrote.

"How many envelopes is this going to take?"

"For your sake, Jimmy, I'll try to keep it down to a bare minimum of Anglo-Saxon syllables."

"Much appreciated."

"Can I say 'the undersigned,' Jimmy, or do I need to spell it out?"

"Finish it up, Vince. Steamroll it over us and make it legally binding too before we know what hit us."

"There's that word again, not spoken but implied. Nobody's cheating anybody," Vincent Flaherty said.

"We'll see."

Beth's fourth grade teacher had told the class, *The cheater you are today is the cheater you'll be tomorrow,* and the warning which had a nice ring to it made no difference at all to the cheaters who went right on cheating. Beth believed she could help the teacher by writing her a note explaining that she should instead devote her teacherly energies toward setting clever traps to catch the cheaters. Beth signed the note *anonymous* but the teacher knew who it was and Beth received a lecture about the note writer she was today being the note writer she would be tomorrow, not in those exact words but that was the point. Beth sort of liked it out here in the desert where there were more important things to worry about than whether she was going to grow up to be a note writer. Rawhide Joe was smiling in his cave not worrying about any of it, outlasting cheaters and claim jumpers and rimflyers, and even, depressingly enough, note writers. She supposed she could come back here when she was an old lady and nothing would have changed, at least on his end.

After finishing the contract, Vincent Flaherty handed envelope and pen to Jo, who searched for something to write on other than Vincent Flaherty's thigh. Jimmy Splendid stood up. "Here. Use this." Jo pressed the envelope over a flat spot on Jimmy Splendid's rock. She asked to see the first envelope which began the contract. She stared at it as if she were deep in study. She sent another shrug to Beth's mother, then leaned over and signed. Beth's mother didn't bother to pretend; she dashed off her signature without a glance to its contents. Harry and Jimmy Splendid both took their time, but in the end they signed it, too.

"I guess you're staying with your wife?" Jimmy Splendid said to a pouting Leonard Dawson, who refused to answer. Jimmy Splendid finished up his coffee, then turned to make his way out of camp.

"You're leaving already?" Jo called.

"Good-bye!"

Jo lowered her voice. "He's fast."

"When are you coming back?" Beth's mother shouted after him.

Jimmy Splendid pivoted and waved his hat to her. "Tomorrow. Or the next day. Wait for me." He tapped on his hat; his hands smoothed the brim. "I didn't hear your answer."

"I said all right." Beth saw her mother start to smile, then bite her lower lip when she caught Beth watching her.

Beth could feel something bothersome in the air. Her forearms were raised in gooseflesh, and her ears were tingling as if from frequencies too high to decipher. It got worse just as Jimmy Splendid was abandoning them to Vincent Flaherty and Leonard Dawson. She told herself to stick close to Timothy.

Vincent Flaherty laid himself out on the sand. He lifted his head toward her mother. "You like that man, don't you?"

"No," her mother said.

"Yes, you do."

Her mother shrugged.

"Bad choice." Then he was asleep. His stomach was so big his chest couldn't rise or fall. So many people out here slept away the afternoons. It was an easy thing to be tempted into: in the burning sunlight you could hardly think straight so why not sleep instead? Even at Miss Dazzle's motel the shimmering heat cascaded over the buildings and blacktop and gathered the town in a dreamscape. People didn't do things, the everyday things, like they did in normal places. It was too easy to nap away the stifling afternoons, dreams piling up like dirty dishes, awaking groggy and happy about tomorrow's million dollars.

Her mother stared ahead stonily, cross-legged in the sand. Her eyes were alert, darting but not focusing on anything. She was doing it again, checking off a list. She wouldn't show how she was feeling. Maybe she could fake indifference about Jimmy Splendid, but she wouldn't be able to hold back when Beth told her the news of Charlie's dip in the cave pool. Then her mother would show a bit of excitement. One of the immediate effects of his dip was the new hairstyle. Charlie would hate it if he knew he had a hairdo atop his head, but at least it was a sign that things were already working.

Beth thought of something. The instructions to Charlie's chemistry set said,

You live in an **EXCITING** *world.*

The instructions also said,

Never eat any chemical or the product of an experiment.

Jo pushed herself up from the sand. "I might take a nap, too," she said and trudged off lifelessly. Leonard Dawson followed her.

"Why does he have to go with her?" Harry asked.

"I suppose because he's her husband."

Harry didn't answer.

"Harry?"

"What?"

"You understand that, right?"

"It doesn't always work that way," Harry said.

Beth scooted close to her mother and held on.

"It's time we went back," her mother said.

"Right now? That's crazy. This is the hottest part of the afternoon," Harry said. "You don't want to walk during the hottest part of the day. Wait till tomorrow. Maybe Flaherty'll give you a ride. Or I'll go with you."

Her mother said, "He's had a hard day."

The sun was moving fast. Feet to head, the shade over Vincent Flaherty's body was section by section unblanketed. His face jerked as the sunshine bit into him. Another jerk, and Vincent Flaherty snorted awake.

"Mr. Einstein, how long have I been asleep? You got something in your experiment bag for narcolepsy?" Vincent Flaherty blinked around. "Ah, Timothy. How do you do. And the lovebirds? Off?"

"Oh now," her mother said.

It was clear they had nothing to do before Jimmy Splendid came back, and that was going to be a long while. Timothy stirred up some more Flavor Aid, tangerine this time. He made it in a coffee pot. Beth liked the way the pretty orange poured from the spout. The spout looked like somebody's perfect nose.

Leonard Dawson returned and held out his hand for a cup. Jo stood beside him.

"An announcement," Vincent Flaherty said. "Can tell by the way you're standing."

"Lenny has something to tell everyone," Jo said.

"I read people," Vincent Flaherty said with a shrug.

Jo bowed her head and nodded at the ground. "Go ahead, Lenny."

"Out with it, man," Vincent Flaherty said.

"Lenny didn't exactly come from our campsite," Jo said. "He and Mr. Splendid spent the night somewhere else. Tell him where, Lenny."

"That powder outfit over there," Lenny mumbled. His chin signaled toward a vague direction.

"Get your hands out of your pockets and point," Vincent Flaherty said.

"I know who he means," Beth's mother said. "Paul Morrison. I met him."

"You spent the night at Paul Morrison's?" Vincent Flaherty asked.

"I guess that was the name."

"Got a weirdo sidekick?"

"Yeah."

"And what happened at Paul Morrison's?"

"Nothing. Him and Splendid went off alone."

"Paul Morrison!" Vincent Flaherty shouted gleefully. Then he was silent.

"Wait! Hold on a minute." Harry took off up the slickrock. Timothy ran after him.

"Yeah, check it out," Vincent Flaherty called after them. "We're on the same wavelength, that man and me. Never would have thought it."

"Is that good or bad about Paul Morrison?" her mother asked.

"You met him," Vincent Flaherty said. "What was your impression?"

"A nice man."

"But?" Vincent Flaherty prompted.

"He set up a water supply for us."

"But?" Vincent Flaherty said.

"He had a couple of laughs at our expense—I felt. But maybe he needed a laugh."

"Who doesn't?" Vincent Flaherty said nothing more.

"You know him, too?" her mother prompted.

"Paul Morrison? Oh yeah. He's a man who specializes in running nuisance claims."

"Is that good or bad? " her mother asked. "I mean, I assume it's bad."

Vincent Flaherty nodded and turned to Jo. "Looks like your husband's been trying to pull a fast one on us."

"Not me!" Leonard Dawson cried. "I didn't have nothing to do with it. It was that Splendid guy, not me. I was just minding my own business and he shows up and he's gonna steal my map only I made sure I went with him. That guy used me."

"And to think you work for me," Vincent Flaherty said.

"I don't work for you. I ain't partnered up with you yet. Now no reason to. My wife did all the work for you. Fat man, you can stay off my back. I'm trying to help you out."

Harry rushed back breathless. "Gone," he said.

Vincent Flaherty chuckled.

"What?"

"All the claim notices we staked," Harry told her mother. "He took them all."

"Jimmy did that?" Beth's mother said.

"Doesn't matter," Vincent Flaherty said. A beat. Then: "Does it, Harry? Confirm my conviction."

"'Course not. I logged them in my book."

Vincent Flaherty said, "So what's the deal here, Mr. Dawson? What have they got planned?"

"They didn't include me. I told you."

Jo said, "Lenny did the right thing, telling us. You did the right thing, Lenny."

"A lot of thanks I get," Leonard Dawson muttered.

"Doesn't matter. I know exactly what they're planning."

"But we've got the contract," Beth's mother said.

"Who's got the contract?" It was with an inexplicable delight that Vincent Flaherty asked this question. "That contract is riding in a truck right about now, and on about the third or fourth wash, which we call traffic signals out here, when our Mr. Splendid gets out to take a short break, he'll leave behind a nice handful of confetti on top of a juniper log."

"What?" Jo asked.

"He took the contract with him, ma'am," Timothy said.

"Don't bother looking," Vincent Flaherty said as Beth's mother searched. With a satisfied sniff he folded his hands atop his stomach. "They're going to claim jump us, you see."

"I had letters in those envelopes," her mother said. She opened up his cigar pouch.

"They're not in there, honey."

"Those are my letters. Those are my private letters. They belong to me." She thrust her head into her hands.

"Ma'am, if it'll help, I got this letter still." Timothy pulled out a blue sheet of paper.

"Roll me a cigarette," she told him. "Damn him!" From Vincent Flaherty's cigar pouch she produced a small pill and pinch of tobacco. "You might want this."

"No thank you, my dear," Vincent Flaherty said. "I'm actually quite enjoying this. The exquisite irony of the situation. Delightful."

"Don't you think we'd better go get him?" Jo said.

"Just for another minute more I'd like to enjoy myself. A man so irate over my purported claim jumping that he takes up battle was all along planning to claim-jump us. I take my hat off to you, Jimmy Splendid."

"You don't seem very upset, Mr. Flaherty," Jo said.

"I have a helicopter, my dear. Fast as Jimmy can go in his truck, I can go much faster."

"But he's had a big head start," Jo persisted.

"My goodness," Vincent Flaherty said, "the woman is actually worried I may not be able to carry out this mission."

"Don't call her 'the woman,'" Leonard Dawson snarled.

"Lenny, please," Jo said.

"You got a regular name," Leonard Dawson said.

Beth watched everyone ignore him. She liked the way Leonard Dawson seemed to be shrinking, especially if she squinted her eyes just right. Nobody was saying anything now and Vincent Flaherty was sitting in his chair, looking sleepily content.

After a stretch her mother said, "What if he does get there before us? Then what?"

"It doesn't matter, Mom," Charlie said.

Her mother said, "Oh, Charlie," in a way that didn't follow the flow of conversation. Beth felt a shiver in her bones. Her mother twitched, as if taken aback herself. She righted her voice and quickly said, in a normal way, "What do you mean, honey?"

"Maybe I shouldn't say."

"No, go ahead, Charlie," Harry said. He pushed his hands into his pocket and his shoulders and head caught a bouncy rhythm, and a smile crossed his face.

"We registered the claim already," Charlie said.

"What's that you say, Einstein?"

"Harry and I, we went to the assessor's office."

"Oh, Charlie," Jo said. Beth thought she sounded just like a love-struck movie actress.

"Everyone's pulling a fast one on ol' Vince," Vincent Flaherty said.

"It wasn't a fast one," Harry said.

"It wasn't like that, sir, at all," Timothy said.

"You were there? You knew about it, too?"

"No, sir."

Vincent Flaherty threw up his hands.

Harry said, drawing Charlie against him, "Charlie and I—we just. Well, we just needed to do it. It was between us, and I'm not going to apologize for it. I thought it would be nice for Charlie to register a claim. We used his map. It wasn't quite, maybe it wasn't altogether legal since we hadn't staked anything. But now we have staked it. All we have to do is fix the coordinates. Hey, the assessor was pretty darn impressed with Charlie's map."

"What'd he say?" her mother asked.

"He said how impressed he was."

"What were his exact words?"

"Mom."

"Charlie, I just want to know."

"He doesn't talk much," Harry said. "But he did this." Harry let out a whistle, whipped off his hat as if from a sudden boil, and mopped his brow.

"Really?" Her mother sat back grinning. "Charlie," she said, "did you know you were going to save the day? You realize what you've done?"

"Mom," Charlie warned.

"All right. But he did."

"Yes he did," Vincent Flaherty said.

Timothy picked up his rifle and came over to offer a hand to Vincent Flaherty. Vincent Flaherty studied the hand while he continued drumming on his stomach.

"You'll want to get going, sir," Timothy said.

"I suppose," Vincent Flaherty said. "Mr. Einstein, I salute you, but duty prevails on me to administer the final blow." He stumbled inside his tent. He emerged on all fours with a satchel. Timothy and Harry helped him up. Vincent Flaherty sighed, then said, "Well, looks like Jimmy and Mr. Paul Morrison and that Quasimodo sidekick of his will have a surprise waiting for them at the assessor's office. Think Miss Dazzle will mind if we land a helicopter in her parking lot?"

They were jolly sentences but they were not spoken in a particularly jolly way.

"Who's going where? Nobody's going anywhere without me." Leonard Dawson pounced forward as if the boxing bell had rung. Everyone ignored him as they filed out of their shelter. The cool rock of the overhang had almost made Beth chilly. Now she met the sun. The extremes left her light-headed.

As a group they walked in silence toward the helicopter.

"You're tired, Mr. Flaherty." Her mother broke the still air. "Will you be all right flying?" They were beyond their campsite and the flatscape of sand. They were moving into the narrows. Beth wasn't sure what the exact plan of action was. She knew only that, whatever the plan, she didn't want to part from Timothy. He would keep her safe.

The narrows was both mossy and hot. The shaded base rock of the cliffs sent out breaths of cold. At the same time the sun laid a precise fiery ribbon down the middle. Inside the tight passageway it was starting. It was inside Beth's head and getting worse. The narrows had begun its song. *Leave.*

"Oh, I'll be fine, my lovely lady," Vincent Flaherty said. "A nice steak, a good night's sleep in a bed. In fact, my friends, steaks for everybody!"

"We can't all fit in your helicopter," her mother said.

"Quite true." Vincent Flaherty fell quiet and he stayed that way.

Leave.

The back of Beth's neck rose in menacing prickles. Her mind, idly at first and then with a kind of panic, began to search for an escape route, but they were imprisoned by high sandstone. The crags and cliff walls soared above them, moving ever inward to block the sun. That only made the light squeeze harder, and Beth felt every part of her heat up and begin to boil, and her neck was now surging with electrical sparks. On the sand, the sun's tight focus had drawn a sharp silhouette of her nose and elbow. She watched herself as marionette, a keen jerking shadow. Yet she could still feel it, the coolness from the rocks.

Leave.

The overhead caverns and alcoves hummed with unhappiness. She made the mistake of looking up there. Honeycombs of human-made bricks nestled inside them. If she looked long enough, things would begin to move. Everywhere a blur of sandstone, moving closer. Everywhere a warning. The brightness threw everything off, sharpening her shadow until it fooled her into believing she was her own dream. The humming from the honeycombs intensified.

She dared not look up again for the people she might see standing in the alcoves.

Their alarmed calls chased down her neck.

She threw herself at her mother and they staggered out of the narrows. Her mother held her tightly as Leonard Dawson turned upon them with fists beating the air. "I'm not about to get cheated a second time!" he screamed wildly.

From his crushed silence in the narrows to this. Leonard Dawson seemed crazy. He had been hearing it, too.

"Stop," Vincent Flaherty ordered, pushing him away. "Hold up. Stop now."

Leonard Dawson charged toward the helicopter and swung himself into the front seat. "You're not cheating me again, fat man!"

"I haven't had the pleasure of cheating you the first time!" Vincent Flaherty yelled back at him. "Give me that," he ordered Harry, jerking Charlie's map out of his hands. "Pen!" he yelled. His breath was rapid, his face shuddering forth new rivers of sweat, and when he started to say something else, the words he couldn't find left him choking. Vincent Flaherty was coming unglued. Beth had seen him angry, she'd seen him violent, but she had never seen him unable to make a mockery of reality with a lightly plucked sentence at his disposal.

You shouldn't be here: the lofted honeycombs hummed their message.

On the back of Charlie's map Vincent Flaherty rapidly scribbled. "There," he said. "Good enough. 'The undersigned agree to a partnership to claims staked in mapped area on obverse side.' Sign!" he barked. Leonard Dawson hopped out of the plane.

Harry leaned over and signed. Vincent Flaherty kept a tight hold on Charlie's map. Leonard Dawson shoved Harry aside and pulled the pen from his grip.

"Get back in that helicopter," Vincent Flaherty said.

"I'm signing."

"Get back in the helicopter and I don't want to hear one more word or I swear I'll crash the damn thing just to be rid of you."

"I'm signing."

"You're doing nothing of the sort."

"You go to hell." Leonard Dawson dove toward the map panel, but Vincent Flaherty merely swished it away like a matador's cape and Leonard Dawson landed on the ground. From his crab-walk position he booted the earth at Vincent Flaherty, but the hardpack yielded only flaky clods that skittered sideways. When Timothy strode over with his rifle,

Leonard Dawson scrambled to his feet and kicked a furious path to the helicopter. Timothy followed and inclined his head close to Leonard Dawson. Beth heard his quiet whispers.

"You're coming along, right, Harry?" Vincent Flaherty said.

"Of course," Harry said. "But Timothy needs to stay."

Beth almost cried to hear this good news.

Vincent Flaherty held out the cardboard panel to Jo and passed her the pen and she signed "Room for one more in the helicopter," he told her. "Make your choice."

"I don't know," Jo said.

"Make it, honey. We're leaving."

"Come on!" Leonard Dawson called. "Get in!"

"One more thing," Beth's mother said, accepting the pen. "Charlie hasn't signed."

"The cartographer hasn't signed? Sign," Vincent Flaherty said. "The cartographer must sign off. Don't look so unhappy, boy. Sign. Quickly now."

"Go ahead, Charlie," her mother said, dashing off her signature. "Here. Put it here, under my name."

"It's your map, Charlie," Harry said. "You have to sign it."

Charlie hesitated. "All right. I guess." He took the pen and dipped forward, but Vincent Flaherty yanked the map from under him and lunged away. Charlie, pen poised, was left to autograph the air.

Vincent Flaherty was moving quickly, despite the lumbering waddle. "Good Lord," he said.

Beth stayed hugged to her mother.

"Good Lord, come look at this," Vincent Flaherty said.

They followed the line of Vincent Flaherty's raised arm and stared at the desert's vista of brown everything and brown nothing.

"Over here. Over here. A tester," Vincent Flaherty said quietly. Then he was his old boisterous self. "Boys and girls, we've got ourselves a tester!"

They faced the horizon where Vincent Flaherty pointed. Beth saw nothing. She heard nothing—nothing outside herself, that is. But the sounds inside her were squalling to a breaking point. Then: as mysteriously as they had arrived, they left. The pressure released itself to the sky.

It began to happen after that. Everybody saw; huddled close, they watched. The light snapped and a pillar pushed out of the horizon's red soil, uncurling from the earth like a flower's stem. The pillar climbed and climbed. Beth couldn't decide whether it was moving fast or slow. It seemed so slow.

At long last the pillar stopped climbing and trembled over in full blossom, and a dam of atomic power unfolded in silence. The mushroom posed before them, a distant portrait handsome and serene, and something else: secretly painted on the sky was this message for Beth to behold. *You see what I'm trying to tell you?* A new story had begun, Beth saw this much. Where it would lead she didn't know, but in time she would learn this story.

"Now, that's a pretty sight!" cried Vincent Flaherty. With a whoop he took off. His difficult amazing waddle fired ahead like a go-cart. Whatever miracle had propelled him now propelled Beth and Charlie. They took off running, too. They blew past Vincent Flaherty and kept on going. Through the scrabble. Through the sand. Her imagination had craved this sight, and here it was, the mushroom cloud alive before her. She raced toward it, eclipsing the thrumming honeycombs and mute sandstone, into the bedazzling ions. She lived in an exciting world. On she sped, racing past the canyons and the rising derricks of rock, on toward the dreamy scroll of desert, on toward the bomb.

FIC   Zafris, Nancy.
Zafris
             Lucky strike.

$23.95

DATE			

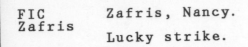
e kept
ly
ewed

BAKER & TAYLOR